Resources for Teaching

THE STORY
AND ITS WRITER

An Introduction to Short Fiction

Third Edition

PREPARED BY

Ann Charters
William E. Sheidley

Bedford Books *of* **St. Martin's Press**

BOSTON

For information, write: St. Martin's Press, Inc.
175 Fifth Avenue, New York, NY 10010

Editorial Offices: Bedford Books *of* St. Martin's Press
29 Winchester Street, Boston, MA 02116

0–312–03469–5

Cover Art: *Room in Brooklyn*, 1932, Edward Hopper. Oil on Canvas, 29 x 34 inches. The Hayden Collection. Courtesy, Museum of Fine Arts, Boston.

PREFACE

The entries in this manual include commentaries on each story in the anthology, along with questions for discussion, writing assignments, and suggested readings. The commentaries offer brief critical analyses of the stories and suggest ways to approach them in class. Like the questions that follow, the commentaries aim to promote a lively exchange of responses and perceptions without insisting on any particular interpretation or critical methodology.

Three kinds of Topics for Writing are offered, but not all three are proposed for each story. The topics for Critical Essays are usually phrased as sentence fragments in order to point in directions that may prove fruitful without predicating the conclusions a writer might reach. The Exercises for Reading are founded on the premise that putting words on paper can serve as a powerful aid in understanding what one reads; the Related Subjects map our nontraditional writing projects, including experiments in fiction. Instructors using these resources will readily see ways to rephrase, restructure, and reapply these assignments to suit their own purposes and the needs of their students. Some writing topics may serve equally well as discussion questions, and vice versa.

The reading lists that conclude most entries are neither exhaustive nor highly selective; they simply cite interesting and, when possible, readily available criticism that proved useful in preparing the manual or that contains information and approaches to the stories that could not be incorporated in the commentaries. Thanks are due to the authors mentioned, to whose insights and scholarship these resources are generally indebted.

At the end of these resources is a chronological listing of authors and titles, a thematic index of stories, a list of films from some of the stories in *The Story and Its Writer*, and a list of film distributors and their addresses.

CONTENTS

Contents

PART ONE

THE STORIES

Chinua Achebe

Dead Men's Path (p. 10)

At first glance this story appears to be a straightforward anecdote about the inability of a young, progressive schoolteacher to change the ways of the superstitious residents of an African village. After all, the story begins with a description of the school in the past: "it had always been an unprogressive school, so the Mission authorities decided to send a young and energetic man to run it." Students should be encouraged, however, to read this story more carefully. Its opening sentence is not meant to be taken literally. If read ironically, it is a clue to Achebe's intent.

The young headmaster's arrogance is masked by Achebe's account of his abilities in the rest of the opening paragraph, but careful readers will note the casual hint that the teacher's slavish wife has been "completely infected" by his passion for the "modern methods" of his profession. Her lack of sophistication is further underscored by her imitation of the trite dialogue in a women's magazine fiction when she talks to her husband. Thus the reader is prepared for the naive young couple's head-on collision with the superstitious villagers in the second half of the story.

The meeting between the headmaster and the village priest is the story's climax. Achebe is consistent in delineating the narrowly "progressive" views of the headmaster. Ironically, the more experienced priest is willing to compromise: "What I always say is: let the hawk perch and let the eagle perch." The story's denouement is inevitable, and with great economy Achebe writes the final comment as part of the state supervisor's unfavorable report on "the misguided zeal of the new headmaster."

Questions for Discussion

1. Is this a fully developed short story or just an anecdote? What qualities in the narrative—characterization, setting, plot—lead you to your answer?
2. What is the point to the wife's imitating the language of women's magazines when she talks to her husband?
3. How many levels of racial conflict can you find in the story?

Topics for Writing

1. Achebe once wrote that the fundamental theme for all African writers must be "that African people did not hear of culture for the first time from

Europeans; that [tribal societies] had a philosophy of great depth and value and beauty, that they had poetry and, above all, dignity." How does this story illustrate Achebe's theme?

2. Donald Barthelme's story "The School" is also about a schoolteacher. Compare and contrast this story with "Dead Men's Path."

Related Commentaries from Part Two

Chinua Achebe, An Image of Africa: Conrad's "Heart of Darkness," p. 1379
Chinua Achebe, Work and Play in Tutuola's *The Palm-Wine Drinkard,* p. 1385.

Suggested Readings

African Stories. Ed. Chinua Achebe and C. L. B. Innes. London: Heinemann, 1985.
Chargois, J. A. *Two Views of Black Alienation: A Comparative Study of Chinua Achebe and Ralph Ellison.* Bloomington: Indiana UP, 1973.
Wren, R. W. *Achebe's World.* Washington, DC: Three Continents, 1980.

ALICE ADAMS

The Oasis (p. 13)

One key to this story is the author's use of parenthetical expressions. "Parenthesis" is defined as "an additional word or phrase inserted in a passage that is grammatically complete without it, and usually marked off by dashes or commas or parentheses." Adams inserts her first parenthetical phrase in the second sentence of her opening paragraph, and it sets the tone for the remainder of the story.

This initial parenthesis introduces an element of questioning or uncertainty (or self-consciousness) into the protagonist's thinking processes. The second sentence of "The Oasis" reads, "Perhaps they are embarrassed at finding themselves among so much opulence (indeed, why are they there at all? why not somewhere else?), among such soaring, thick-trunked palms, such gleamingly white, palatial hotels."

This questioning of the presence of "the poor" (who are always with us) in Palm Springs by Clara Gibson, the upper-middle-class woman whose story this is, is at the heart of "The Oasis." But this story's heart is displaced, faltering, "not in service." The title itself is given an ironic cast when we learn that Clara has mistakenly come to Palm Springs two days early. She is without money and finds no comfort in her unexpected "holiday" from her husband. Instead the bag lady provokes a guilty conscience in Clara, who gives the poor woman most of her cash.

Clara still has her credit cards, and her marriage to a successful surgeon, and her well-educated, financially successful daughter. Her spontaneous act of charity is like a parenthesis in her life, changing nothing in her social or moral situation. Yet she resolves to eat dinner in "a big, flashy delicatessen" in an effort to continue her adventurous contact with the city's poor. She hopes that the deli will furnish her a second chance to meet the bag lady.

As Clara walks away from the bar of the expensive hotel, she tells a social lie, the way most of us do if caught in such a situation. She says to the wealthy couple who befriended her, "Well, I've certainly enjoyed talking to you." We are told that Clara "very much hopes" this "will be her last lie for quite some time, even if that will take a certain rearrangement of her life."

Questions for Discussion

1. Is Clara's hope of rearranging her life at the end of the story any more profound (less parenthetical) than her spontaneous sympathy for the bag lady? Explain why or why not.
2. Presumably neither the author nor the protagonist regards the meeting with the bag lady as a parenthetical experience, but how deep is Clara's social conscience? She has felt its first stirrings, but do you think it is sufficient for her to rearrange her life?
3. Could Clara be taken as a representative of her class and her nation — the affluent American? Can the story thus be read as an allegory?
4. Do we trust Clara? Why or why not? Does Adams mean her to be a sympathetic or an unsympathetic character?

Topics for Writing

1. Analyze Clara's relationships with her husband and daughter. Does Adams give you enough information to judge them yourself, or are you dependent on Clara's evaluation of them?
2. Compare and contrast Adams's use of parenthetical expressions with John Barth's parenthetical expressions in "Lost in the Funhouse." What are the similarities between the protagonists of these two stories? What are the differences? How have the differences enabled Barth to explore his protagonist's situation as a metafiction? (A "metafiction" is a fictional work that comments on the art of telling stories.)
3. Rewrite "The Oasis" in the form of Margaret Atwood's story "Happy Endings," giving different endings to the encounters between Clara and the other characters.

Related Commentary from Part Two

Alice Adams, Why I Write, p. 1388.

Suggested Readings

Holt, P. "Publisher's Weekly Interviews: Alice Adams." *Publisher's Weekly* 16 Jan. 1978: 8–9
"On Turning 50." *Vogue* 173 (1983): 230.

Woody Allen

The Kugelmass Episode (p. 20)

Like most works of fiction based on impossible or unlikely suppositions, "The Kugelmass Episode" entertains us with the device on which it is grounded. Rather than developing the intellectual puzzles of science fiction, however, Allen mainly offers gently satiric jokes made possible by the incongruities arising from his donnée. When her class notices that on page 100 "a bald Jew is kissing Madame Bovary," the teacher in South Dakota, without consulting her desk copy, blames the problem on a mass-media stereotype, drug-crazed students; a professor at Stanford sees in the incredible instability of the text a confirmation of a mindless academic cliché: "Well, I guess the mark of a classic is that you can reread it a thousand times and always find something new." Thus we transform what is unfamiliar into bricks for the wall of presupposition that barricades us from the truth. Meanwhile, Allen delights in collapsing the distance between "good literature" and everyday banality. Emma admires Kugelmass's leisure suit; he thrills her with black panties and designer slacks; and, like every other good-looking girl who goes to New York, she dreams of a career on the stage.

But the fantasy on which Allen bases his tale has deeper roots. Like Faust, Kugelmass dreams of transcending human limitations, of living for a while free from the constraints of time and ordinary causation. He abandons human science and philosophy, here represented by his shrink, and turns to magic. Although Persky resembles an auto mechanic more than Mephistopheles, he offers an equally dangerous and meaningful temptation to Kugelmass. If the professor lacks the poetry and grandeur of his Faustian predecessors, he is motivated by parallel desires. Bored with his life and unable to love the people he shares it with (who can blame him?), he bargains for something he expects will be better. Appropriately, given the diminished scale of modern heroism, he signs away not his soul but merely a "double sawbuck." As happens especially with Marlowe's Dr. Faustus, for his reward Kugelmass gets only what he is capable of imagining. Emma Bovary as he experiences her talks and acts like any woman he could have picked up at Elaine's — exactly what he wanted, and what he turns her into by bringing her out of the novel and into the Plaza Hotel.

After the near-disaster of his affair with Emma, Kugelmass swears off philandering, but of course he has not learned his lesson. When he asks Persky to use the wondrous machine to send him for a date with "The Monkey" of *Portnoy's Complaint*, Kugelmass reveals the utter emptiness of spirit that hides behind his glib pop-culture romanticism, and it is fitting that he ends up scrambling through a desert inhabited by predatory words without meaning.

The intellectual and moral universe that Kugelmass inhabits even before his final translation is no less devoid of meaning. Allen's fantasy shows how the sophistication of modern life can drain the spirit out of human language, desires, and relationships. Kugelmass claims to have "soul," but his needs are quoted from advertisements in *The New Yorker*. The language of commercial psychology debases even his dreams, whose imagery is thirdhand and probably phony: "I was skipping through a meadow holding a picnic basket and the basket was marked 'Options.' " Kugelmass picks his mistress as from a menu; he decides to plunge into the supernatural (but for exceedingly *natural* reasons) more easily than he chooses between red and white wine (as if those were the only possibilities); significantly, he is most comfortable minimizing the importance of what he is doing: "'Sex and romance,' Kugelmass said from inside the box. 'What we go through for a pretty face.'"

Through the fantastic device of Persky's box, Allen achieves the small dislocation necessary to reveal that remark of Kugelmass's as a pitifully inadequate cliché. The story is full of such instances, and the technique embodies its larger vision. We choose the things we say to describe our lives to ourselves because they have been purged of discomforting truths. Allen shows that these statements are illusions. Kugelmass regards his life as a novel that has turned out badly. Rather than seeking to understand why he has come to a second marital dead end burdened with financial obligations and bored with his family, he tries to escape from the present and reenact the past. He wants only to enter *Madame Bovary* before page 120, and he dreams of starting life over in Europe, selling the (long defunct) *International Herald Tribune* "like those young girls used to."

The story leaves us with an implicit question: What redemption is possible for Kugelmass and the culture — our culture — that he represents? Is there an alternative to the Hobson's choice between desperation and meaninglessness?

Questions for Discussion

1. Comment on the situation of Kugelmass as described in the first two paragraphs. Do you think his circumstances are unusual? Where should we lay blame for his predicament?
2. Kugelmass "had soul." What does that term seem to mean in this context?
3. Interpret Kugelmass's dream. Is it profoundly symbolic?
4. How effective is Dr. Mandel? Why does Kugelmass need a magician?
5. Discuss Persky. What might be Allen's basis for this character? How important is Persky to the story?
6. What factors enter into Kugelmass's choice of a mistress? What does this event suggest about his attitude toward literature? toward women?
7. Explore the implications of this quip: "She spoke in the same fine English translation as the paperback."
8. Review the first conversation between Kugelmass and Emma. Has Kugelmass really been transported into *Madame Bovary*? Does it resemble the novel as you read it or as you imagine it to be?
9. What does Allen achieve by noting the effect of the sudden appearance of the Kugelmass episode in the novel on various readers?
10. "By showing up during the correct chapters, I've got the situation knocked," Kugelmass says. Consider the implications of that idea. Would you like to live only certain chapters of your life?
11. Why does Emma want to come to New York? Why does Kugelmass want to take her there? Are the ensuing problems entirely the result of her being a character in a novel?
12. As Persky struggles to repair his box and Emma consumes "Dom Pérignon and black eggs," Kugelmass becomes more and more agitated. Finally, he contemplates suicide ("Too bad this is a low floor") or running away to Europe to sell the *International Herald Tribune*. How serious is he? Explain why those ideas accord with his character.

13. Why does it take Kugelmass only three weeks to break his resolution, "I'll never cheat again"?
14. *Portnoy's Complaint* examines, among other things, masturbation and adolescent sexual fantasies. What does it imply about Kugelmass that he chooses that book for his next adventure?
15. Do you think the ending of the story is appropriate? Why should Allen choose a remedial Spanish grammar for Kugelmass's hell rather than, say, a book in which adulterers are punished or in which none of the characters is a good-looking young woman?

Topics for Writing

CRITICAL ESSAYS

1. Crossing the border between life and art: "The Kugelmass Episode" and Allen's film *The Purple Rose of Cairo*.
2. The theme of meaningless language in "The Kugelmass Episode."
3. Responses to marvels in Allen's "The Kugelmass Episode" and García Márquez's "A Very Old Man with Enormous Wings."
4. Kugelmass as an anti-Faust.

EXERCISE FOR READING

1. Study the use of language in Allen's story. List familiar phrases. What are their sources? Examine the conversations between characters. How much communication is taking place?

RELATED SUBJECT

1. People often wish aloud for something they know to be impossible or speak of what they would do *if only*: "If only I had her looks and his money." "If only I were in charge." Imagine a character — yourself or someone you know, perhaps — whose impossible wish comes true. Then what? Follow Allen's lead by using the device to express the real truth in a surprising new way.

Suggested Readings

Gianetti, L. "Ciao, Woody." *Western Humanities Review* 35 (1981): 157–61.

Jacobs, Diane. *Magic of Woody Allen*. London: Robson, 1982.

Reisch, M. S. "Woody Allen: American Prose Humorist." *Journal of Popular Culture* 17 (1983): 68–74.

Rose, L. "Humor and Nothingness." *Atlantic* 255 (1985): 94–96.

Shechner, Mark. "Woody Allen: The Failure of the Therapeutic." *From Hester Street to Hollywood*. Ed. Sarah B. Cohen. Bloomington: Indiana UP, 1983. 231–44.

"Woody Allen on the American Character." *Commentary* 76 (1983): 61–65.

SHERWOOD ANDERSON

Death in the Woods (P. 31)

"Death in the Woods" presents a religious image of the earth mother, the principle of connectedness by which life is fostered and sustained. Anderson's depiction of the woman whose job it is to feed animal life, "in cows, in chickens, in pigs, in horses, in dogs, in men," congeals in the visionary revelation of her death scene. To the men and boys who stand around her, the moonlit glimpse of her naked breast — effectively foreshadowed in the incident in which, as a girl, she had her dress ripped open by the German farmer she was bound to — conveys a sense of wonder: They look upon a marble statue of a beautiful young woman in the snow. Near her, or perhaps around her, lies the oval track left by the dogs, at once a prayer ring and a symbol of the interdependence and endless continuity of the life she has served.

It is appropriate that the basis of Mrs. Grimes's scant economy is eggs, whose various connotations are obvious enough. As the nurse of living things, Mrs. Grimes establishes bonds and fosters community. The world with which she must deal, however, corrodes those bonds. When we first see her she is struggling alone: "People drive right down a road and never notice an old woman like that." The men she feeds are rapacious and cruel — to her and, as in the fight between Jake and the German farmer, to each other. The town treats them all with cold suspicion. Even the butcher who loads her grain bag out of pity would deny the food to Mrs. Grimes's husband or son: "He'd see him starve first." Not Mrs. Grimes, who tacitly reaffirms her theme: "Starve, eh? Well things had to be fed. . . . Horses, cows, pigs, dogs, men." When she dies the forces for harmony and union that she embodies achieve a momentary victory, as the townspeople fall into a ragged communal procession to witness her death — a ceremony as instinctive as the ring running of the dogs, if somewhat less orderly and beautiful.

Anderson's story progresses from an apprehension of drab poverty and ugliness to a discovery of wonder and beauty. The agency that distills religious and aesthetic emotion out of the profane world of the story is the inquiring imagination of the narrator, who muses over his recollections, reconstructs his story from fragments, and in doing so explains the process of synthesis that takes place as he writes. In its progress from the ordinary to the mystical, from ugliness and privation to a soul-nourishing beauty, the story records a triumph of the creative imagination, which penetrates the surfaces of things to find within them their inherent mythic truth.

What makes that triumph possible is the narrator's subtly expressed identification with Mrs. Grimes. The fascination that causes him to cling to his recollections and finally to work them through may arise, as William J. Scheick argues, from the shock of his initiation into an awareness "of the relation between feeding, sex, and death" that blocks his sexual development; or it may arise from a sense of the hitherto unexpressed mythic implications of the scene in the woods. In either case, the narrator recognizes that the death of Mrs. Grimes has meaning for him — as one who has worked for a German farmer, who has himself watched dogs run in a ring, and who has kept silent; as one who is fed by women; and as one who must die. The story's circular structure, like the ring of dogs and the ring of men around the corpse, transforms compulsion into worship, just as Anderson's art transforms the report of a frightening death into a celebration of life and of the power of the sympathetic imagination to render its beauty.

Questions for Discussion

1. Discuss the style of the opening paragraph. What qualities of the old woman's life are reflected in the syntax and rhythms of the prose?
2. How does Anderson modulate from generalization through recollection to specific narration? What change in narrative mode takes place in section II with the paragraph that begins "One day in Winter"? Does the story ever return to its original mode? Where?
3. "Her name was Grimes" — appropriately?
4. What does the narrator mean when he calls the Grimes men "a tough lot"? Are they alone in this in the story?
5. Describe the woman's life with the German farmer. How important to the story is the farmer's having torn "her dress open clear down the front"?
6. How big a part does love play in the relations between people in this story? What other factors are prominent — exploitation? mistrust? violence?
7. Does the butcher's generosity seem a welcome change? How does the butcher compare with Mrs. Grimes as a nurturer of life?
8. How does Anderson prepare us to accept it as probable that Mrs. Grimes would sit down under a tree and freeze to death?
9. Describe the behavior of the dogs. How does Anderson explain it? How does the narrator know it took place?
10. Comment on the tonal effect of the passage "It had been a big haul for the old woman. It was a big haul for the dogs now."
11. What does the corpse look like in the moonlight? Why does Anderson give a concise description of the corpse near the beginning of section IV rather than saving the whole revelation until the men and boys arrive on the scene at the end of that section?
12. Comment on the implications of this line: "Either mother or our older sister would have to warm our supper."
13. Explain the possible meanings of the word "everything" in the first sentence of section V.
14. Discuss the narrator's remarks about why he has told the story. What is "the real story I am now trying to tell"? To what extent is it a story about the narrator himself? About stories and storytelling?

Topics for Writing

CRITICAL ESSAYS

1. Circles — image and structure in "Death in the Woods."
2. The narrator's struggle "to tell the simple story over again."
3. The role of the community in "Death in the Woods."
4. Mrs. Grimes and the mythic roles of woman.

EXERCISE FOR READING

1. On a second reading, make notes about the narrator. Rearrange his activities, experiences, and concerns into chronological order. What is the narrator's story? What is his conflict? What does he achieve? What does he learn?

RELATED SUBJECT
1. Read several myths from Ovid's *Metamorphoses*. Rewrite the story of Mrs. Grimes as an Ovidian myth. What changes of tone are necessary? What important themes have you had to abandon? What have you had to invent?

Related Commentary from Part Two

Sherwood Anderson, Form, Not Plot, in the Short Story, p. 1393.

Suggested Readings

Burbank, Rex. *Sherwood Anderson.* Twayne's United States Authors Series 65. New York: Twayne, 1964. 125–29.
Joselyn, Sister Mary. "Some Artistic Dimensions of Sherwood Anderson's 'Death in the Woods.' " *Studies in Short Fiction* 4 (1967): 252–59
Scheick, William J. "Compulsion toward Repetition: Sherwood Anderson's 'Death in the Woods.' " *Studies in Short Fiction* 11 (1974): 141–46.

SHERWOOD ANDERSON

Hands (p. 40)

Anderson's story "Hands" might be called a portrait. Like a formal painted portrait, it depicts Wing Biddlebaum not only as he exists at a given moment but also in conjunction with certain props in the background that reveal who he is by recalling his past and defining his circumstances. The focal image of the portrait is Wing's hands, around which the other elements of the picture are organized and to which they lend meaning. Further, the story depends for a portion of its effect upon a series of painterly tableaux, from the sunset landscape with berry pickers with which it begins to the silhouette of Wing as a holy hermit, saying over and over the rosary of his lonely years of penance for a sin he did not commit.

In keeping with this achronological narration (which William L. Phillips has shown may in part result from Anderson's thinking his way through the story as he wrote it), neither Wing nor George Willard experiences any clear revelation or makes any climactic decision. Wing never understands why he was driven out of Pennsylvania, and George is afraid to ask the questions that might lead them both to a liberating understanding of Wing's experience.

The reader, however, is not permitted to remain in the dark. With the clear understanding of how the crudity and narrow-minded suspicion of his neighbors have perverted Wing's selfless, "diffused" love for his students into a source of fear and shame comes a poignant sorrow for what is being wasted. Wing's hands may be the pride of Winesburg for their agility at picking strawberries, but the nurturing love that they betoken is feared by everyone, including George, including even Wing himself, whose loneliness is as great as his capacity to love — from which, by a cruel irony, it arises.

9

Questions for Discussion

1. Define Wing Biddlebaum's relationship to his community as it is implied in the first paragraph. To what extent is the impression created here borne out?
2. Why does Wing hope George Willard will come to visit? Does George ever arrive?
3. Wing's name, which refers to his hands, was given to him by "some obscure poet of the town," and telling the full story of those hands "is a job for a poet." What connotations of "wings" are appropriate? Why is "Wing" a better name for Biddlebaum than, say, "Claw," or "Hook," or "Picker"?
4. Could Wing himself have been a poet? Why does he tell his dreams only to George?
5. Why did the people of the town in Pennsylvania nearly lynch Adolph Myers? Why was he unable to defend himself?
6. Are the people in Ohio any different from those in Pennsylvania? Explain. What about George Willard? Evaluate his decision not to ask Wing about his hands.
7. What other hands do we see in the story? Compare them with Wing's.
8. Explain the implications of our last view of Wing. What is the pun in the last line?

Topics for Writing

CRITICAL ESSAYS

1. The crucifixion of Wing Biddlebaum.
2. Anderson's Wing and Flaubert's Félicité.
3. Anderson's comments in "Form, Not Plot, in the Short Story" (included in Part Two, p. 1393) as a key to his art in "Hands."

EXERCISE FOR READING

1. After reading the story once, jot down your response, including your feelings about Wing, George, the townspeople, and the narrator. Also write, in one or two sentences, a summation of the story's theme as you understand it. Then reread the paragraphs in the order they would have followed had Anderson told the story in chronological order. Would your responses differ? Would the story have an identical theme? Explain.

RELATED SUBJECT

1. Anderson claimed to have written this story at a sitting and to have published it without rearrangements or major additions or deletions of material. Imitating his process, write a vignette about a person unknown to you whom you see in a photograph. Start with the scene in the photo and end with the same, interpolating previous incidents and background information as they occur to you.

Related Commentary from Part Two

Sherwood Anderson, Form, Not Plot, in the Short Story, p. 1393.

Suggested Readings

Burbank, Rex. *Sherwood Anderson.* Twayne's United States Authors Series 65. New
York: Twayne, 1964. 64–66.
Phillips, William L. "How Sherwood Anderson Wrote Winesburg, Ohio." *The
Achievement of Sherwood Anderson.* Ed. Ray Lewis White. Chapel Hill: U
of North Carolina P, 1966. 62–84, esp. 74–78. Originally published in
American Literature 23 (1951): 7–30.

Margaret Atwood

Happy Endings (p. 47)

Atwood's story can be read profitably in conjunction with Grace Paley's
"A Conversation with My Father." In both, the authors use humor to suggest
a certain impatience with the traditional short-story form. Both stories can be
read as "metafictions," fictions that comment on the art of telling stories. Atwood's
piece is harsher than Paley's in its insistence that happy endings are impossible
in stories; Atwood tells us clearly that death is "the only authentic ending" to
everyone's story. Paley, in contrast, clearly values both her relationship with her
dying father and her own imagination, allowing (even half-jokingly) her fictional
heroine the possibility of rehabilitation after her drug addiction and a valued
place in society as a counselor in a center for young addicts.

The first time students read "Happy Endings," they may miss the way
Atwood connects the stories from "A" to "F." "B" is the first unhappy ending
(as Atwood warns us in the third sentence), with the "worst possible scenario"
worked out in John and Mary's love affair. Atwood's vocabulary here is deliberately
harsh and unromantic, unlike the sentimental clichés of the "A" scenario.

As Atwood continues her permutations of the couples' possible relationships,
her stories get shorter and more perfunctory. Her language becomes more
elemental, preparing the reader for her summary dismissal of all plots, since
they all end in death. In the final three paragraphs, Atwood drops all pretense
that she is telling stories and directly addresses her readers, revealing that her
true subject is not the emotional life she is creating for her characters but her
awareness of the elements of fiction. She defines plot as "what" or "just one thing
after another." Then, like the instructor's manual of a short-story anthology, she
leaves the rest up to her reader: "Now try How [character] and Why [theme]."

Questions for Discussion

1. Atwood's authorial presence is the strongest element in "Happy Endings" — does this make the text closer to an essay than a short story? Explain.
2. How does Atwood elicit your curiosity, so that you continue to read this short story? Would you say that she has proven that plot is the most essential element in a story? Is there also an underlying, coherent theme to "Happy Endings"?
3. Would the story still be effective if Atwood omitted her direct address to the reader ("If you want a happy ending, try A.")? Explain.

Topics for Writing

1. Rewrite the story inventing additional outcomes for John and Mary's relationship.
2. In "Reading Blind," (p. 1395), Atwood gives her criteria for judging whether a story is "good." Using these criteria, how would you rate "Happy Endings"?
3. Ray Bradbury, in his book *Zen in the Art of Writing: Essays on Creativity* (Capra, 1990) writes, "The writer must let his fingers run out the story of his characters, who, being only human and full of strange dreams and obsessions, are only too glad to run. . . . Remember: *Plot* is no more than footprints left in the snow after your characters have run by on their way to incredible destinations. *Plot* is observed after the fact rather than before. It cannot precede action. It is the chart that remains when an action is through." Apply Bradbury's analysis to "Happy Endings."

ISAAC BABEL

My First Goose (p. 51)

The narrator in this story is an outsider, a lonely and hungry intellectual who wins a meal and the acceptance of the Cossacks by killing the old peasant woman's goose. He does it roughly, demonstrating that he will "get on all right" at the front. The act is portrayed partly as a rape, partly as a crucifixion. The quartermaster tells him, "you go and mess up a lady, and a good lady too, and you'll have the boys patting you on the back," and that is what he does, trampling her goose under his boot and plunging his sword into it while she repeats, "I want to go and hang myself," and he says, "Christ!" But the narrator recoils from his self-debasement: The night that enfolds him resembles a prostitute; the moon decorates it "like a cheap earring." Lenin says there is a shortage of everything, and though Surovkov believes that Lenin strikes straight at the truth "like a hen pecking at a grain," the narrator uses the spectacles of his learning to discern "the secret curve of Lenin's straight line," the hidden purpose of the speech. The narrator, too, has taken an apparently bold and forthright step in killing the goose, but the secret curve of his straight line has been to gain acceptance by the Cossacks and a share of *their* dinner, which reminds him of his home. As he sleeps with his new friends he dreams of women, just as he saw female beauty in the long legs of Savitsky. But in taking his first goose he has messed up a good lady and stained his heart with bloodshed, and his conscience is not at peace.

Questions for Discussion

1. Describe Savitsky. What is the narrator's attitude toward him? Why does Babel begin the story with this character, who never reappears?
2. What advice does the quartermaster give? Does the narrator follow it?
3. Why are the narrator's "specs" an object of derision? Who else in the story wears glasses?
4. Why does the Cossack throw the narrator's trunk out at the gate?
5. When the narrator first tries to read Lenin's speech, he cannot concentrate. Why?
6. How does the narrator win the respect of the Cossacks?
7. Discuss the difference between Surovkov's understanding of Lenin's speech and the narrator's.
8. Explain the last sentence. What is the narrator's feeling about himself? about the situation he is in?
9. "Lenin writes that there's a shortage of everything." Of what is there a particular shortage in the story?

Topics for Writing

CRITICAL ESSAYS

1. The function of sexual imagery in "My First Goose."
2. Why the narrator stains himself in "My First Goose."
3. The effect of Babel's extreme brevity in "My First Goose," and the way it is achieved.

EXERCISE FOR READING

1. Before beginning to read "My First Goose," write your prediction of what its subject might be on the basis of its title alone. Write a second guess as well. After reading the story, review your predictions. To what extent were the expectations aroused by the title—even if they were not confirmed — relevant to an understanding of Babel's narrative?

Suggested Readings

Carden, Patricia. *The Art of Isaac Babel.* Ithaca: Cornell UP, 1972. 97, 100, 110, 130–31.

Falen, James E. *Isaac Babel: Russian Master of the Short Story.* Knoxville: U of Tennessee P, 1974. 142–45.

JAMES BALDWIN

Sonny's Blues *(p. 55)*

The marvel of this story is the way the narrator — Sonny's older brother — narrows the physical and emotional distance between himself and Sonny until Sonny's plight is revealed and illuminated in a remarkable moment of empathy and insight. This story of drug addiction in the inner city's black ghetto is as valid today as it was when it was written. By juxtaposing the two brothers — a straight high school math teacher and a heroin addict blues pianist — Baldwin makes it possible for readers to enter the world of the story regardless of their racial background or their opinions about drugs. The author doesn't judge Sonny's plight. Instead, through the brother, he helps us understand it, sympathize with it, and transcend it in a brief shared experience of Sonny's inspired musical improvisation.

This is a long story, and its plot consists mostly of flashbacks, more "told" than "shown" in the reminiscences of Sonny's older brother. Yet the power of Baldwin's sympathy for his characters and his eloquent style move the reader along. Baldwin captures the African-American culture of strong family allegiances in the face of American racism. Both Sonny and his brother are trying to survive, and we respect them for their courage.

One of the ways to discuss the story is through an analysis of the narrator's growing sympathy for Sonny. Baldwin tells us that the narrator thinks, after the death of his little daughter Grace from polio, "My trouble makes his real." This realization motivates the first scene with the two brothers in which Baldwin begins to build the bridge between them. Separately they watch three sisters and a brother hold a revival meeting on the sidewalk opposite the narrator's apartment, and after they hear the gospel music, the silence between Sonny and his brother begins to give way to shared sound. The scene leads directly to the two brothers going to the bar where Sonny plays and creates an opportunity for the narrator (and the reader) to enter Sonny's world and satisfy his anguished need to share his music with someone who will listen to it and understand.

Questions for Discussion

1. Analyze the following speech, in which Sonny explains to his brother how he has survived (however tenuously) the experience of racism in America:

   "It's terrible sometimes, inside," he said, "that's what's the trouble. You walk these streets, black and funky and cold, and there's not really a living ass to talk to, and there's nothing shaking, and there's no way of getting it out — that storm inside. You can't talk it and you can't make love with it, and when you finally try to get with it and play it, you realize nobody's listening. So you've got to listen. You got to find a way to listen."

   How does this explanation make Sonny a sympathetic character?

2. Discuss Baldwin's comment on the blues Sonny plays with Creole and the two other musicians at the end of the story:

> Creole began to tell us what the blues were all about. They were not about anything very new. He and his boys up there were keeping it new, at the risk of ruin, destruction, madness, and death, in order to find new ways to make us listen. For, while the tale of how we suffer, and how we are delighted, and how we may triumph is never new, it always must be heard. There isn't any other tale to tell, it's the only light we've got in all this darkness.

Baldwin's subject is the music, of course, but he is also talking about other forms of creation. What might they be?

Topics for Writing

1. Chinua Achebe describes Baldwin as having brought "a new sharpness of vision, a new energy of passion, a new perfection of language to battle the incubus of race" in his eulogy titled "Postscript: James Baldwin (1924–1987)" (*Hopes and Impediments*, 1990). How does "Sonny's Blues" embody these qualities?
2. Baldwin's "Autobiographical Notes" (p. 1399) states that he found it difficult to be a writer because he was forced to become a spokesman for his race: "I have not written about being a Negro at such length because I expect that to be my only subject, but only because it was the gate I had to unlock before I could hope to write about anything else." Yet Baldwin's depiction of the life lived by African-Americans is unique and very different from Richard Wright's or Ralph Ellison's, Toni Cade Bambara's or Alice Walker's accounts. Compare and contrast "Sonny's Blues" with a story by one or more of these writers to describe how each finds his or her own way to dramatize what Baldwin calls "the ambiguity and irony of Negro life." Could "Sonny's Blues" be set in an Italian-American or Jewish-American family?
3. Compare and contrast "Sonny's Blues" with Willa Cather's "Paul's Case."

Related Commentary from Part Two

James Baldwin, Autobiographical Notes, p. 1399.

Suggested Readings

Kinnamon, Kenneth, ed. *James Baldwin*. Englewood Cliffs, NJ: Prentice, 1974.

Pratt, Louis H. *James Baldwin*. Twayne's United States Author Series 290. Boston: Hall, 1978.

Standley, F. L. ed. *Conversations with James Baldwin*. Jackson: U of Mississippi P, 1989.

Toni Cade Bambara

The Hammer Man (p. 82)

Bambara's story dramatizes several of her central ideas about social injustice. Its narrator is a black adolescent living in a ghetto neighborhood. She is a feisty, independent spirit, quick to take offense at people who pigeonhole her into stereotypical categories, such as being a poor black and being a girl. But she goes one step further: She is also quick to make independent moral judgments as to what is right and what is wrong. She has decided it's okay for her to bait a boy named Manny who "was supposed to be crazy," even though he was "officially not to be messed with." After she calls him some choice names and insults his mother, his face goes through "some piercing changes," and she decides it's time to withdraw. The story opens with her getting the news that Manny has fallen off the roof, and she's glad to hear it. Now she can come out of hiding.

Readers might well be confused at this point. Bambara's language isn't hard to follow (it's reminiscent of J. D. Salinger's adolescent talk in *The Catcher in the Rye*), but her heroine's tough-girl exterior doesn't seem to have much human decency behind it. We look to her language for a clue to her feelings. When she sees Manny, "he had his head all wound up like a mummy and his arm in a sling and his leg in a cast." Not much to go on there, but Bambara tries to make her sympathetic. The girl listens to her mother, dresses in skirts, and joins a youth group at the center to try to learn how to act more ladylike. She's a female Huck Finn, skeptical of civilizing influences. She gets thrown out of the center for playing pool with the boys when she was supposed to be sewing.

Bambara veers between the two extremes of hit-and-run terrorist in training and I'll-try-to-be-good little miss in her narrator's behavior. Perhaps she thinks that such fluctuations are normal in the behavior of young teenage girls; then so is the phenomenon of peer loyalty. While the narrator is watching Manny take his practice shots at the basketball hoop in the park one night some time later, she stands up for Manny when a cop starts yelling at him.

Finally the story focuses on Bambara's real point, exposing the racial prejudice that poisons the life of the ghetto blacks. The girl thinks, "None of my teachers, from kindergarten right on up, none of them knew what they were talking about. I'll be damned if I ever knew one of them rosy-cheeked cops that smiled and helped you get to school without neither you or your little raggedy dog getting hit by a truck that had a smile on its face, too. Not that I ever believed it. I knew Dick and Jane was full of crap from the get-go, especially them cops." Her schizoid behavior toward Manny and the corruption in her dealings with other kids ("I should've settled for hitting off the little girls in the school yard") are revealed as a mirror image of the schizophrenia and immorality in the society that has formed her.

Questions for Discussion

1. What is the point of view of the story? Describe the narrator in terms of age, sex, race, socioeconomic background.
2. What is the narrator's view of Manny? Why is Manny out to get the narrator?
3. Describe how the conflict between Manny and the narrator grows to include the entire neighborhood. Who becomes involved? How do they demonstrate their anger? What happens to end the conflict?
4. What do you feel Bambara's purpose is in presenting an overview of the neighborhood?
5. Why is Manny called "Hammer Head"? Based on her actions, is the narrator as "crazy" in her own way as Manny pretends to be?
6. What change does the opening of the center cause in the life of the narrator? How do the rules and regulations of the center contrast with those of the neighborhood?
7. What judgment has the personnel of the center made about the narrator and her family? What is Bambara's purpose in presenting this information?
8. As we follow the narrator from the streets to the center, what types of behavior does she exhibit? Do these various roles appear to cause any conflict within the girl? How would you describe Bambara's presentation of this character?
9. When does the narrator's relationship to Manny change? Who and what causes the change? How does this conflict differ from that which occurred in the neighborhood?
10. What is the theme of the story? How does the narrator's statement about her teachers and the cops reinforce Bambara's theme?

Topics for Writing

CRITICAL ESSAYS

1. The experience of adolescents in Bambara's "The Hammer Man," Wright's "The Man Who Was Almost a Man," and Ellison's "Battle Royal."
2. The effects of racial prejudice in Bambara's "The Hammer Man" and Gordimer's "Town and Country Lovers."
3. Adolescent points of view in "The Hammer Man" and Updike's "A & P."

Suggested Readings

Bell, Roseann P., Bettye J. Parker, and Beverly Guy-Sheftall, eds. *Sturdy Black Bridges: Visions of Black Women in Literature.* New York: Anchor, 1979.

Evans, Mari, ed. *Black Women Writers (1950–1980): A Critical Evaluation.* New York: Anchor, 1984. 41–71.

Giddings, P. "Call to Wholeness from a Gifted Storyteller." *Encore* 9 (1980): 48–49.

Tate, Claudia, ed. *Black Women Writers at Work.* New York: Continuum, 1983. 12–38.

JOHN BARTH

Lost in the Funhouse (p. 89)

In a brief comment written for the collection *Writer's Choice*, edited by Rust Hills (New York: McKay, 1974), Barth describes this story as occupying a medial position in a development from conventional to less conventional techniques and from youthful and presumably more personal versions of Ambrose in the earlier stories in the volume *Lost in the Funhouse* to later "more mythic avatars of the narrator." He goes on to repudiate "merely cerebral inventions, merely formalistic tours de force," and to declare his hope that the story is "accessible, entertaining, perhaps moving." Just as Ambrose is portrayed "at that awkward age," so the narrator who portrays him (a being hard to distinguish from Ambrose on the one hand and Barth on the other) appears in a transitional stage, the adolescence of his art. Quoting to himself the supposedly infallible principles of composition that he seems to have learned in a creative writing course, he struggles forward self-consciously, complaining that what is supposed to be happening as he writes does not seem to be taking place. Just as for Ambrose in the toolshed or at his baptism, observation of the proper forms does not necessarily bring the expected results. Yet, just as Ambrose is capable of experiencing unusual transports at inopportune moments, so the story, in spite of or apart from the conventions, renders a poignant account of the time and place in which it is set, of its protagonist's initiation into the mysteries of life and art, and of the narrator's unexpected triumph over the difficulties he confronts.

Readers may compare their experience of the story to the difficult progress through a funhouse, with its sudden surprises, its maddening reflections, its obvious contrivances, and the heavy atmosphere of sexuality. We enter perhaps violently yawning in the nervous anticipation that shocks are in store, but surely few readers are prepared for the upending of expectation that takes place even in the first paragraph. We stagger forward with the narrator, bumping into the pasteboard screens of his contrivance, glimpsing the pulleys and levers by which the story is operated but nonetheless responding to the images thrust before us. When the narrator complains, "We haven't even reached Ocean City yet: we will never get out of the funhouse," the reader knows he is referring to the story itself as well as to the boardwalk attraction.

Fiction is traditionally supposed to be an imitation of life, made the more credible, as the narrator remarks, by the artifice of illusion. By extension, then, the funhouse can be called an imitation of life, and of that part of life called art (the commentator wanders in these mazes too). While the funhouse may be fun for lovers, for Ambrose and the narrator it begins as *"a place of fear and confusion,"* mastered only by the fantasy of control with which the story concludes. Life, too, which resembles the funhouse in having seduction, coupling, and propagation as its central purpose, appears to the sensitive adolescent a frightening labyrinth that he must enter. The realities of war, death, and suffering — masked by the diversions of the funhouse or glimpsed behind them — lie in wait, and perhaps the Operator of the whole show is dozing at the controls. Although Ambrose has theoretical access in Magda to the "fun" life has to offer, he recoils with nausea from his visions of the universal copulation, can bear only the lightest contact with her body, and recalls their precocious experience in the toolshed mainly by reference to the image of a muselike woman with a lyre printed on a cigar box, her lower parts peeled away. When he loses Magda in the funhouse, Ambrose feels relief, and although he finds his name, with its suggestions of enlightenment (or vision) and divinity, he loses *himself* in the multiple reflections of the mirrors.

The narrator knows that a conventionally structured story would reach its climax in Ambrose's escape from the funhouse, but what would this story become if its culminating image were the emergence of Ambrose from the funhouse in uneasy companionship with a blind, black Ariadne? Barth's self-regarding experimental narrative technique enables him to beg the question of his protagonist's escape from the literal funhouse and to leave him lost in the figurative one, blocked from enjoying the "fun" but assured of his ability to create through his art even better "funhouses for others."

The discovery of this assurance constitutes a victory for Ambrose over his initial *"fear and confusion,"* and it proclaims the narrator's triumph over the problems of his art with which he has struggled throughout the story. It is a triumph gained in large measure by means of acknowledging the struggle. Like Joyce's *A Portrait of the Artist as a Young Man*, to which Barth alludes more than once, "Lost in the Funhouse" combines a nostalgic realization of the circumstances that determine the protagonist's vocation with the assertion of a provisional theory according to which he intends to carry it out. Just as Stephen Dedalus's resolution to take wing is subject to an ironic interpretation that sees it as an expression of his emotional immaturity, so Ambrose's decision to *substitute* the detached manipulation of the funhouse for living his life might be regarded as an expression of adolescent neuroses that he will outgrow. Barth makes clear, however, that the combined sensitivity to and detachment from his experience that make Ambrose an artist do not simply result from a trauma in the toolshed; rather, as existing qualities of his personality (perhaps inherited from his father, whom he resembles as Peter resembles Uncle Karl), they have conspired to render that occasion a tangible memory for Ambrose while for Magda it remains, if it lingers at all, an aspect of her vague but condescending warmth to Peter's little brother. Barth's handling of the double *pas de trois* that evolves its intricate parallels and contrasts in the front and back seats of the La Salle and along the boardwalk at Ocean City demonstrates that the artist's way of revealing the hidden realities of life does not have to follow the repellent naturalism of Ambrose's flashlight view below the boardwalk or the oversimplifications of his fantasies about the essential activities of his ancestors and the world at large. No less than *A Portrait*, Barth's story is a tour de force whose own principles of composition criticize the conclusions reached by its protagonist.

Questions for Discussion

1. How are italics used most frequently in this story?
2. Examine the remarks about nineteenth-century realistic fiction in the second paragraph. If Barth's story seeks to convey an illusion of reality, what reality does it represent? A family's trip to Ocean City, or a writer's effort to narrate that trip? or to narrate his effort to narrate that trip?
3. Starting with the fourth sentence in the story, trace all references to American history, society, and current events, including World War II. How important are these concerns? What do you think Barth intends to accomplish by bringing them up?

4. Describe the seating arrangements in the car. What parallels do you notice between the two rows of people? Later, as they walk on the boardwalk similarly disposed, the narrator remarks, "Up front the situation was reversed." Explain. The name Peter means "rock." What objects and qualities are associated with Uncle Karl?

5. The narrator worries that "if one imagines a story called 'The Funhouse,' or 'Lost in the Funhouse,' the details of the drive . . . don't seem especially relevant." What does Barth accomplish on this drive with his characters, setting, and theme?

6. What does Barth succeed in communicating about Ambrose by tracing the chain of associations involving cigars, the banana, and Magda?

7. Immediately after chiding himself for having "nothing in the way of a theme," the narrator produces the account of Ambrose's visit to the toolshed with Magda. Explain the thematic implications of that passage. Do they account for Ambrose's moving away his hand as Magda sits down?

8. Why does Uncle Karl warn the young people to "stay out from under the boardwalk"? How are the various elements of this and the next few paragraphs related? Trace the associations in Ambrose's mind; in the narrator's.

9. Who asks, "How long is this going to take?"

10. Why does the narrator remark, "Nobody likes a pedant"? Is his attention to language part of what separates Ambrose from Magda?

11. If diving is a literary symbol, what does it symbolize? Judging from his choice of words, what is Ambrose thinking of as he talks to Magda about Peter's diving?

12. The next two paragraphs leap ahead to the funhouse and back to the toolshed, ending with another grammatical error. What does Barth achieve by thus manipulating chronology, here and elsewhere?

13. Analyze the paragraph that begins, "Let's ride the old flying horses! " Whose thoughts are transcribed there? What kinds of alternative plots are envisioned? In the next paragraph, the narrator contemplates still other ways of ending his story. What is the effect of our discovery that one of these endings may be more or less what "actually" happened?

14. Why do Ambrose's initiations — toolshed, baptism, Boy Scouts — all leave him cold?

15. Is Ambrose correct in his insight about the point of the funhouse?

16. One effect of Barth's manner of narration is to put off Ambrose's entry into the funhouse until the last possible moment. What does he gain by doing so?

17. Referring to the second diagram, a variant of "Freitag's Triangle," what event or events in the story of Ambrose should be represented by C? by CD? And what events in the story of the narrator's effort to tell the story?

Topics for Writing

CRITICAL ESSAYS

1. The realistic narration of "Lost in the Funhouse."
2. The meaning of nausea in Barth's story.

3. The funhouse technique — obvious imagery, abrupt changes, and surprising drafts from below.

EXERCISE FOR READING

1. "Lost in the Funhouse" resembles an author's journal or an early draft of a traditional story coming into existence on the page. Outline that story as it finally emerges, and outline the story of the process by which it develops. Do you believe that this is an accurate account of how stories are written?

Suggested Readings

Beinstock, Beverly Gray. "Lingering on the Autognostic Verge: John Barth's *Lost in the Funhouse.*" *Critical Essays on John Barth.* Ed. Joseph J. Waldmeir. Boston: Hall, 1980. 201–09. Esp. 206–09. (Originally published in *Modern Fiction Studies* 19 (1973): 69–78.)

Knapp, Edgar H. "Found in the Barthhouse: Novelist as Savior." *Critical Essays on John Barth.* Ed. Waldmeir, cited above. 183–89. (Originally published in *Modern Fiction Studies* 14 [1968–69] : 446–51.)

Morrell, David. *John Barth: An Introduction.* University Park: Pennsylvania State UP, 1976. 87–90.

Schulz, Max F. *Black Humor Fiction of the Sixties: A Pluralistic Definition of Man and His World.* Athens: Ohio UP, 1973. 34–36, 129–30.

Seymour, Thom. "One Small Joke and a Packed Paragraph in John Barth's 'Lost in the Funhouse.'" *Studies in Short Fiction* 16 (1979): 189–94.

Donald Barthelme

The School (p. 107)

Barthelme's stories usually dispense with the familiar kinds of plot structures that depend on causal interactions between character and event and lead toward some clearly meaningful resolution. Contemporary experience is better rendered, Barthelme believed, according to the "principle of collage," which he called "the central principle of all art in the twentieth century in all media" (quoted by Thomas M. Leitch). Most students will be familiar with visual collage, and many will have composed collages themselves out of magazine clippings or "found" materials. They should be able to transfer from the visual mode to Barthelme's verbal collage their ability to posit meanings for unexpectedly juxtaposed images.

Barthelme's stories rely on humor for their underlying effect. In "The School" the narrator is a grammar school teacher, and his account of the losses of the school year is a tale of disaster, pure and simple. Trees, snakes, herb gardens, gerbils, white mice, salamanders, tropical fish, a puppy, the Korean orphan Kim—not to mention eleven parents, assorted grandparents, even the classmates' "tragedy" of little Matthew and Tonya—are graphic illustrations of the ever-present power of death, the mysterious force that rules the classroom.

The surprising end of the story—the cathartic kiss of the two teachers that evokes the arrival of the new gerbil—underscores the situation's wackiness. Juxtaposition was everything to Barthelme, since the only meaning of the events he describes is in their happening—and their ultimate absurdity.

Questions for Discussion

1. Describe the schoolteacher's personality, as much as you can deduce it from the way he talks and the kinds of things he does and doesn't tell us. Why do the children look to him for the answers to their questions?
2. How do the three dots function in the text? Can you imagine them as part of the way the teacher interacts with his class?
3. How can the narrator be so oblivious to the chaos around him, both in and out of his classroom?

Topics for Writing

RELATED SUBJECTS

1. In *Growing Up Absurd* (1960), the cultural critic Paul Goodman castigates American society by saying, "It is hard to grow up when existing facts are treated [by American adults] as though they do not exist. For then there is no dialogue, it is impossible to be taken seriously, to be understood, to make a bridge between oneself and society." Discuss how Barthelme's story dramatizes this insight into the pernicious effects of the socialization process as it is carried out on the young pupils in "The School."

EXERCISE FOR READING

1. Some time after you have finished reading "The School" and without referring to the text, write a list of the specific things in it that you remember most vividly. Consider what they have to do with one another and with what you take to be the story's central idea. Why do you suppose you remembered these particular items?

Suggested Readings

Gordon, Lois. *Donald Barthelme*. Twayne's United States Authors Series 416. Boston: Hall, 1981.

Leitch, Thomas M. "Donald Barthelme and the End of the End." *Modern Fiction Studies* 28.1 (1982): 129–43.

O'Hara, J. D. "Art of Fiction: Donald Barthelme." *Paris Review* 80 (1981): 181–210.

Related Commentary from Part Two

John Barth, Honoring Barthelme, p. 1403.

ANN BEATTIE

The Burning House (p. 112)

Beattie's narration is so oblique that on first reading students may feel they have missed the point of this story. They will not, however, escape the numb depression that mutes the narrator's—and the reader's—response to the incidents to such a degree that the narrative seems disjointed. Of course it is not, and discovering its continuities is a gratification for attentive readers.

Not even a casual first reading can obscure the power of the last scene between Frank and Amy. Amy insists that her husband tell her if he's planning to stay or go to his mistress, and his answer is brutally explicit—as his name, "Frank," would lead us to expect. He tells her, "Your whole life you've made one mistake—you've surrounded yourself with men. . . . I'm going to tell you something about them. Men think they're Spider-Man and Buck Rogers and Superman. You know what we all feel inside that you don't feel? That we're going to the stars."

A classroom discussion could revolve around the differences between Amy and the males who live in her house. Even Sam the dog shows himself to be "man's best friend" by his devotion to Freddy. In an age of feminist fiction, Beattie's story is a subtle but unmistakable depiction of the gender battleground, and Amy's vulnerability makes her a fragile heroine in this fictional fight to the finish.

Questions for Discussion

1. How does Amy differ from the men in the story? How do the men differ from each other?
2. Does the ending come as a surprise? Explain why or why not.

Topics for Writing

1. Write an essay comparing and contrasting "The Burning House" and Katherine Mansfield's "Bliss." How are the two stories' heroines similar? dissimilar?
2. Compare and contrast the subject of weekends in the country in "The Burning House" and Fay Weldon's "Weekend." Ann Beattie has also written a story called "Weekend" that might illuminate this comparison.
3. Write a story from the point of view of a narrator who is hiding something from himself or herself about his or her spouse. Show how the unrecognized truth presents itself gradually to the narrator.
4. Susan Minot, in her story "Lust," shares some of Beattie's complaints about men as unfaithful lovers and companions. What are the similarities and the differences between "The Burning House" and "Lust"?

EXERCISE FOR READING

1. Find the order in Beattie's reflection of chaos by noticing the conjunctions and coincidences she details. Explain why the narrator thinks these particular thoughts, perceives these images, and makes these associations.

AMBROSE BIERCE

An Occurrence at Owl Creek Bridge (p. 125)

What is the reason for the enduring interest of this contrived and improbable tale? Surprise endings frequently draw groans similar to those that greet bad puns, but Bierce's final twist is more likely to elicit shock and recoil. Perhaps the story's success results more from its realization of an intimate and familiar fear than from its sharp, vivid style or its tense pacing. The idea of continued life is all that the human mind, unable to imagine mere "darkness and silence," can propose in view of impending death. By narrating a fantasy of escape so persuasively that we succumb to it, and then by revealing it with the snap of a neck to have been only a fantasy, Bierce forces us to recognize once again the reality of our mortal situation.

If, out of the desire to evade that recognition, the reader seeks to repudiate the story as a piece of literary chicanery, he or she will not succeed. A clearheaded review of section III reveals that the exciting tale of escape could not have been real. Even before Farquhar enters the nightmare forest with its strange constellations and peculiar, untraveled roadway, he has experienced a preternatural heightening of sensory awareness that happens only when one sees with the eyes of the mind, and he has undergone sensations better explained by reference to a slow-motion expansion of a hanging than to his imagined plunge into Owl Creek. The images of his dream emerge from Farquhar's instinctual desire to live, and Bierce renders them with such clarity that the reader can cherish them as well. The same intensity of sensory awareness marks Bierce's conjecture about what it must be like when the noose jerks tight. We feel the constriction, see the flash of nervous discharge, and hear the cracking vertebrae.

Our close participation in the imaginary and real sensations of dying countervails the doomed man's symbolic isolation, which is the burden of section I. While the executioners enact the formal rituals that establish distance from the victim, who is being expelled from the human community (even the sentinels are turning their backs on him), Bierce leads the reader into an empathic communion with him. The agency of this imaginative projection is the coolly exact observational style, which carries us across the plank — Farquhar's first thought to which we are privy is his approval of this device — and into the psyche of the condemned.

Before launching into Farquhar's dying fantasy, however, Bierce goes back, in section II, to narrate the events leading up to the execution. Besides establishing for Farquhar an identity with which we can sympathize, this passage presents him as active rather than acted upon, and so generates a momentum that continues into the story of his escape. The section ends with one of several stark, one-line revelations that conclude passages of uncertainty, illusion, or false conjecture in the story: "He was a Federal scout"; "What he heard was the ticking of his watch"; "Peyton Farquhar was dead." This device of style expresses Bierce's major theme: whatever we dream of, life is entrapment by death, and time is running out.

Questions for Discussion

1. In what ways does section I suggest a psychological time much slower than actual time?
2. Why is it appropriate that the execution take place on a bridge over a river?
3. What is the function of Farquhar's conjectures about escape at the end of section I?
4. In what ways does Bierce try to gain the reader's sympathy for Farquhar? Why does he need to do this?
5. Which events in section III might be read as dislocations of sensations experienced by a man in the process of being hanged?
6. Contrast the descriptive style of a passage from section III with that of a passage from section I.
7. What would be the result if Farquhar's imagined reunion with his wife took place *after* the snapping of his neck?

Topics for Writing

CRITICAL ESSAYS

1. Bierce's handling of time and chronology in "An Occurrence at Owl Creek Bridge."
2. The fiction of effect as a fiction of despair in the works of Bierce, Gogol, and Poe.

HEINRICH BÖLL

Like a Bad Dream (p. 134)

The husband who narrates this story is like one of Poe's madmen — he's living in his own dreamworld. How odd to be impressed by the social conventions of everyday reality: like his wife, Bertha's, ability to know the clothes he should wear to be suitably dressed for their dinner guests, the wealthy Mr. and Mrs. Zumpen; her ability to time the correct interval before answering the doorbell after they arrive; her ability to squeeze attractive mayonnaise garnishes on the appetizers and get dinner on the table and know when the guests have seen enough family photographs. She is much too adroit in her role as a wife to interfere when he lets the Zumpens go home without discussing the business contract for the excavation work for Housing Project Fir Tree Haven, although this contract is the ostensible reason for inviting them for dinner. Gently Bertha initiates her husband into the ways of the business world by suggesting they pay a call on the Zumpens a half hour later. Odd that the husband didn't think of it himself — after all, as he says at the start of his story, "I have married into the excavating business."

In the hands of an inexperienced or clumsy writer, the husband's simplicity would be ridiculous and strain our credibility. In Böll's hands, however, the controlled tone of the story, the perfect choice of the trivial details of the dinner party, the chilling politeness of Bertha's expert management of her husband (and her cold-blooded business instincts, raising the bid on the contract ten pfennigs beyond what Mrs. Zumpen suggests) all work together to create a pattern of manipulation and corruption that is the point of the story. The narrator is taken by the hand and led from his naive dreamworld as a docile, trusting husband in a comfortably materialistic world into another world within it that is the real bad dream.

The irony and truth of the story is that he is good at finding his way once he has been initiated. He may be a docile witness to Bertha's complicity with Mrs. Zumpen, raising his original bid and kicking back a percentage to the Zumpens, but by the time the phone rings after he's back in his study with a large cognac, he is in possession of his wits. He tells Mr. Zumpen that Bertha raised the price on the contract with his consent, and he begins to bargain down Mr. Zumpen's figure for the kickback. At this point in the narrative, the husband thinks, "It's like a bad dream," but he goes on bargaining, and he instinctively knows when to settle the price. He becomes as smooth an operator as Bertha; no wonder she took a chance and married him.

Böll understands the infinite moral distance between our ideals and the actual world we live in. We make our choices, and in turn we are made by them. As Böll sees it, honor and dishonor, fair play and foul, are as closely related in the world that humans inhabit as a loving husband and wife.

Questions for Discussion

1. How would you characterize the narrator of the story?
2. What is the narrator's view of his wife, Bertha? How does she compare and contrast with him? What type of a marriage do they share?
3. Around what issues does the story revolve? What generates the conflict?
4. Who are the Zumpens? How are they involved in the conflict?
5. What characters propel the action? What comment is Böll making on modern society through these characters?
6. "Life . . . consists of making compromises and concessions," says Bertha. Relate this statement to the central theme of the story.
7. What does the narrator find "beyond understanding"? Why? How does the narrator change over the course of the story?

Topics for Writing

CRITICAL ESSAYS

1. A young man's initiation in Böll's "Like a Bad Dream" and Hawthorne's "My Kinsman, Major Molineux."
2. Themes of materialism and corruption in Mishima's "Three Million Yen" and Böll's "Like a Bad Dream."
3. The marital relations of the couple in Böll's "Like a Bad Dream" and Gabriel and Gretta in Joyce's "The Dead."

RELATED SUBJECT

1. Rewrite the story from the point of view of the Zumpens. How do they view this young couple?

Suggested Readings

Cunliffe, W. G. "Heinrich Böll's Eccentric Rebels." *Modern Fiction Studies* 21 (1975): 473–79.
Kurz, P. K. "Heinrich Böll: Not Reconciled." *On Modern German Literature.* Trans. Mary Frances McCarthy. University of Alabama P, 1977. 4:3–36.
Wilson, A. L. "Art of Fiction: Heinrich Böll." *Paris Review* 25 (1983): 67–87.

JORGE LUIS BORGES

The Garden of Forking Paths (p. 140)

Most students will find this story very difficult to follow, because few of Borges's tangible clues as to setting or characterization are what they seem to be on first reading. The opening reference to Liddell Hart's *History of World War I*; the statement by Dr. Yu Tsun, with the missing first two pages, that describes the actual plot to follow; and the footnote about Hans Rabener, alias Viktor Runeberg, will mystify many readers. Students should be urged to read the story at least twice before attempting a discussion. In fact, some class time might profitably be given to a guided reading of the story, with students explaining their comprehension as they go along.

The two commentaries on the story in Part Two should also prove helpful. Borge's explanation of his fascination with the image of the labyrinth as "a symbol of bewilderment, a symbol of being lost in life" (p. 1412) explains the motivation behind Yu Tsun's desperate effort to complete his spy mission before he is killed by Captain Richard Madden. Knowledge of his impending death sharpens his concentration on his last action in life. His dilemma might be compared with Flannery O'Connor's dramatization of the final moments of her fictional characters' lives.

Peter Brooks's analysis of "The Garden of Forking Paths" (p.1414) reveals an interpretation that might clarify the story for some students. Brooks summarizes the plot and explains the story as a metafiction, a story whose meaning is an insight about the significance of fiction itself. In Brooks's reading, "The labyrinth is ultimately that of narrative literature, which is ever replaying time, subverting and perverting it, in order to claim that it is not simply 'time lost,' always in the knowledge that this loss is the very condition of the meanings that narrative claims to relate."

Borges's story is different things to different readers, but some highlights to examine are his skill in pacing the narrative to extract maximum suspense from the confrontation between Yu Tsun and Stephen Albert, Yu Tsun's emotional dilemma in his conflicting loyalties, and the inexorable approach of Richard Madden. Borges's description of the labyrinth, with its "high pitched, almost syllabic music" audible as Yu Tsun approaches Albert's house, is also a tour de force, not likely to be forgotten if one has read the story carefully.

Questions for Discussion

1. Why does Borges begin this story in such an indirect manner?
2. Who is Yu Tsun? Richard Madden? Stephen Albert?
3. Why is Stephen Albert's last name important?
4. Why is Yu Tsun so loyal to his German chief in Berlin?
5. How does Borges establish this as a war story? How do wartime conditions contribute to the narrative?
6. Are there racist overtones in the statement "I wanted to prove to him [the chief] that a yellow man could save his armies"?
7. Borges describes the meeting between Stephen Albert and Yu Tsun very simply: "We sat down—I on a long, low divan, he with his back to the window and a tall circular clock." Why is this description particularly appropriate?
8. Explain the "ivory labyrinth" in Albert's possession and the "chaotic manuscripts" left by Ts'ui Pen.

Topics for Writing

1. Compare Borges's description of Ts'ui Pen's manuscript with the metafictions of Margaret Atwood, John Barth, or Robert Coover in this anthology.
2. Research the Greek legends about labyrinths and relate them to Borges's story.

Related Commentaries from Part Two

Jorge Luis Borges, The Labyrinth in "The Garden of Forking Paths," p. 1412.
Peter Brooks, A Narratological Analysis of Borges's "The Garden of Forking Paths," p. 1414.

Suggested Reading

McMurray, George R. *Jorge Luis Borges.* Modern Literature Monographs. New York: Ungar, 1980.

TADEUSZ BOROWSKI

This Way for the Gas, Ladies and Gentlemen (p. 149)

Borowski's story can be taught with another Holocaust story in this anthology, Cynthia Ozick's "The Shawl." "The Shawl" is told by an omniscient narrator describing the ordeal of a woman victim of the concentration camps. "This Way for the Gas, Ladies and Gentlemen" has a more complex point of view, since the narrator is a Polish political prisoner (indeed, he is the writer), and he voluntarily helps the Nazis unload and brutalize the newly arrived Polish Jews.

The thoughtful comments of the Italian concentration camp survivor Primp Levi are helpful here. In *The Drowned and the Saved* (Summit, 1988), Levi explores the situation of the prisoners of war who, like Borowski, survived to tell their tales. According to Levi, the survivors who wrote about their experiences were often political prisoners like Borowski. The camps held three categories of prisoners—political, criminal, and Jewish—and the political prisoners had "a cultural background which allowed them to interpret the events they saw; and because precisely inasmuch as they were ex-combatants or antifascist combatants even now, they realized that testimony was an act of war against fascism."

Furthermore, according to Levi, "the network of human relationships inside the Lagers [camps] was not simple: it could not be reduced to the two blocs of victims and persecutors." The context of the "prisoner-functionary" [like Borowski] is poorly defined, "where the two camps of masters and servants both diverge and converge. This gray zone possesses an incredibly complicated internal structure and contains within itself enough to confuse our need to judge."

Levi continues,

> The arrival in the Lager was indeed a shock because of the surprise it entailed. The world into which one was precipitated was terrible, yes, but also indecipherable: it did not conform to any model; the enemy was all around but also inside. . . . One entered hoping at least for the solidarity of one's companions in misfortune, but the hoped for allies, except in special cases, were not there; there were instead a thousand sealed off monads, and between them a desperate covert and continuous struggle. This brusque revelation, which became manifest from the very first hours of imprisonment, often in the instant form of a concentric aggression on the part of those in whom one hoped to find future allies, was so harsh as to cause the immediate collapse of one's capacity to resist. For many it was lethal, indirectly or even directly; it is difficult to defend oneself against a blow for which one is not prepared.

"This Way for the Gas, Ladies and Gentlemen" is one of many stories in this anthology that is based on actual personal experience, meticulously observed, remembered, and re-created as a "story" or work of autobiographical fiction or "autofiction." Borowski, the narrator, was interned at Birkenau with Communists and Jews from France, Russia, Poland, and Greece. He survived the camp because he cooperated with his jailers in the persecution of victims less fortunate than himself. How does he present his story so that the reader is forced to sympathize with him, even while realizing that this sympathy is itself a faint mirror image of the prisoner's moral dilemma?

A highly rational structure holds together this totally irrational nightmare. The unities of place, time, and point of view are strictly observed. The passage of time is orderly, paralleling the organization of the transport of human beings from train to trucks to crematoria. The narrator is new to his job, and we learn it as he does. As train follows train through the stifling August afternoon and into the evening, we grow exhausted with him. The only variety is the ever-changing stream of prisoners who leave the train, take their brief walk on the platform, and disappear onto the trucks or are sorted out for the work camps. Occasionally an individual achieves humanity, like the young blonde who is so beautiful that she appears to descend "lightly" from the packed train, or the calm, tall, gray-haired woman who takes the bloated infants' corpses from the narrator, whispering to him, "my poor boy." For the narrator, such moments of grace are withheld: he hangs on to his self-control by concentrating on sheer physical endurance.

Questions for Discussion

1. How did the narrator become a storyteller? (The headnote might be helpful here, but students should be encouraged to talk about the cathartic process in the creation of fiction.)
2. What elements of narrative—plot, character, setting, language, theme— are most striking in this story?
3. Is it necessary to know the historic context of the Nazi atrocities in World War II to understand the story? Explain.

Topics for Writing

1. Compare Borowski's story with another example of Holocaust or prison literature you have read, Cynthia Ozick's "The Shawl," or Anne Frank's diary, or Alexander Solzhenitzyn's *One Day in the Life of Ivan Denisovich*.
2. Report on a documentary film or a book about the Holocaust, such as Primo Levi's *The Drowned and the Saved*.
3. Compare the psychology of prisoners in Borowski's story and in Frank O'Connor's "Guests of the Nation."

PAUL BOWLES

A Distant Episode (p. 163)

This story is one of the most brutal in the anthology. It is clear enough in its presentation of action and motivation, but it is less clear in theme. The plot is easy to summarize. A professor (possibly French) of linguistics, intent on studying Maghrebi dialects in North Africa, is lured into a trap outside a native town. He is robbed and beaten, then has his tongue cut out by nomad tribesmen wishing to enslave him. In the shock he temporarily loses his mind, but he regains his sense of identity a year later, after the bandits sell him to a wealthy native in town. The professor is so overwhelmed at recognizing the French letters on a calendar that he breaks out of the house where he is confined. Seeing him, a French soldier calls him "a holy maniac" and fires a potshot at his head as the professor runs into the evening darkness.

Students may protest that this plot is unlikely, and that the story's description of human brutality is as sensationalized (i.e., falsified) as the description of human passion in romance novels. But Bowles has crafted his story carefully. The professor's naiveté and gullibility are well motivated. He is presented as a passionate collector of boxes made from camel udders; he doesn't ask whether the waiter who promises to supply him with these boxes is the owner of the restaurant until after they have left town, and he doesn't return to his hotel even though he senses danger.

In short, the know-it-all professor walks into a trap, and Bowles mocks the inadequacy of his rationality and expertise with native dialects: "It occurred to him that he ought to ask himself why he was doing this irrational thing, but he was intelligent enough to know that since he was doing it, it was not so important to probe for explanations at that moment." As in many of his stories, Bowles is dramatizing here the failure of intelligence to cancel the appeal of instinct and intuition in dangerous situations. The impersonal world of nature makes its comment on the professor's fatal errors of judgment: "Only the wind was left behind, above, to wander among the trees, to blow through the dusty streets of Ain Tadouirt, into the hall of the Grand Hotel Saharien, and under the door of his little room." This wind ending the first half of the story prefigures the "lunar chills" that descend on the sun-warmed garage wall behind the French soldier who watches the demented professor's "cavorting figure" at the close.

What theme can be abstracted from this tale? The title offers a clue. "A Distant Episode" refers of course to the setting, the pitiless Sahara Desert and the merciless life of the nomads and slave traders who inhabit it. The title also refers to the professor's coming back to an awareness of his own reality, his life as a linguist during the "distant episode" of his professional identity, before his kidnapping and brutalization into the role of a buffoon. Bowles seems to be saying that our reality and our sense of identity are precarious at best. We live in treacherous times, and the veneer of civilization is thin indeed.

Questions for Discussion

1. What details in the story add credibility to the professor's assertion that he is a linguist? Why is his profession so important? Would the story's meaning be altered if he were a geologist or an engineer?
2. How does Bowles carefully build a sense of the danger facing the professor as he takes his walk with the waiter?
3. What part do the dogs play in the professor's demoralization?
4. How does Bowles convey the professor's disorientation and breakdown after he is attacked by the nomads?
5. Why does Bowles write such strange English to describe the "old man's Arabic" after the professor is sold to the man in town? How does this diction prepare the reader for the professor's response to the calendar?
6. Why does the professor's new owner kill the Reguibat? Is Bowles suggesting that justice is done to the bandits who kidnapped the professor?

Topics for Writing

1. Write an essay in which you argue that "A Distant Episode" is a fable, not a realistic story.
2. Compare the professor in "A Distant Episode" with the grandmother in Flannery O'Connor's "A Good Man Is Hard to Find."
3. Write your own version of the story as if it were a mugging in a city like New York.

Suggested Readings

Bailey, J. "Art of Fiction: Paul Bowles." *Paris Review* 23 (1981): 63–98.

Bowles, Paul. *Without Stopping: An Autobiography.* New York: Ecco, 1985.

Halpern, D. "Interview with Paul Bowles." *Triquarterly* 33 (1975): 159–77.

Patteson, R. F. *A World Outside: The Fiction of Paul Bowles.* Austin: U of Texas P, 1987.

Pounds, Wayne. *Paul Bowles: The Inner Geography.* New York: Lang, 1985.

Wolff, T. "A Forgotten Master." *Esquire* 103 (1985): 221–22.

T. Coraghessan Boyle

The Overcoat II (p. 174)

The story is probably most enjoyed after students have read and discussed the original Gogol story, "The Overcoat." Boyle's title, "The Overcoat II," is reminiscent of a film series — *The Godfather, The Godfather II,* and so forth.

Discussion about Boyle's version may be stimulated by asking the class why he wanted to retell the story. Notice that this version is permeated with references to American culture, as in his description of the old woman in the shopping line who calls out "Meat, meat!" She may evoke memories of the woman in the American television fast-food commercial who asked "Where's the beef?"

Questions for Discussion

1. Has the atmosphere or meaning of Boyle's parody changed since Mikhail Gorbachev has come to power and brought major changes to Soviet society? Explain.
2. How does Boyle get your sympathy for his "little clerk"?

Topics for Writing

1. Write your own version of "The Overcoat" using a familiar situation involving social harassment — for example, your tangles with your local post office, employment agency, or other institution.

ITALO CALVINO

The Distance of the Moon (p. 196)

The narrator (Qfwfq) is the character with whom the reader shares feelings in this preposterous, amusing story. Plot, setting, characters are all outlandish, but the narrator's unrequited love for the Captain's wife is real, and Calvino makes us feel for him. The narrator is a born storyteller, delighting in details, impressions, explanations, drama, and surprises. He is the one who remembers the details and the sense of wonder in what has happened, and he captures them for his listeners. Calvino invents a world out of science-fiction elements, but, as in all good science fiction, perennial human feelings are at play here, and the stakes in the adventure are real enough to get us involved.

In Calvino's essay "Cybernetics and Ghosts" (in *The Uses of Literature*, 1986), he imagines a situation in which stories are created by machines. One might think the result would be a story like "The Distance of the Moon." Yet the wealth of its emotional suggestions and verbal links to human psychology, mythology, history, and science are so rich that this is as far from a "mechanical story" as one could wish.

The narrator's love for the Captain's wife, Mrs. Vhd Vhd, and his discovery of the extent of his love for the Earth when he fears he has lost the chance to return to it are the emotional grounds of the plot that Calvino cultivates. First he gives us a perspective, describing a time so long ago that most of his listeners can't remember it, when the Moon was closer to the Earth. The parties foraging for Moon-milk, the delicate maneuvers climbing the ladder to the Moon, the acrobatic tumbles and wooing of the gravitational field involved in the return to Earth are all artfully described.

Gradually Qfwfq introduces the characters, beginning with his deaf cousin, then going on to the curvaceous Captain's wife, with her silvery arms and piercing harp. The minor adventure of little Xlthlx and the recovery of her magnetized body suggest the peril involved in these nocturnal adventures, but the main drama of unrequited love begins shortly after. Then Qfwfq sweeps us away in his description of his pursuit of Mrs. Vhd Vhd, overshadowed by the menace of the inexorably enlarging elliptical drift of the Moon.

Questions for Discussion

1. Who is Qfwfq? Mrs. Vhd Vhd? the Captain?
2. What is the purpose of the unusual names — all symmetrical — of the major characters in this story?
3. The situation of Calvino's story is fantastic, but, as with Franz Kafka's "The Metamorphosis," once the reader accepts the opening premise, the story develops logically and consistently. What does this fact suggest about the appeal of narrative for the reader?
4. Qfwfq seems to sense the characters' unspoken thoughts. For instance, he intuits Mrs. Vhd Vhd's plan to hide on the Moon for a month with the Deaf One. What elements in the story condition us to accept Qfwfq's omniscience as narrator?

Topics for Writing

1. Analyze the importance of setting in "The Distance of the Moon."
2. Rewrite the story from the point of view of one of the other characters.

ANGELA CARTER

The Werewolf (p. 206)

"Adult Tales," the subtitle of Carter's collection *The Bloody Chamber* (from which "The Werewolf" is taken) indicates that some of the stories are based on traditional folktales, such as "Puss in Boots" and "Beauty and the Beast," which are retold as erotic fantasies. "The Werewolf" is a retelling of "Little Red Riding Hood," but instead of the child-victim, we have the child-slaughterer, fearless and bold, as adept as Douglas Fairbanks with her father's hunting knife.

There is a hint of the dismemberment to come in the description of "the leg of a pig hung up to cure" in the second paragraph. The morbid tone is introduced in the next paragraph with the description of the devil worship in this remote forest settlement. Carter is mocking but respectful in her reference to the superstitions of these people: "At midnight, especially on Walpurgisnacht, the Devil holds picnics in the graveyards and invites the witches; then they dig up fresh corpses, and eat them. Anyone will tell you that."

This tone of bemused participation continues in the description of the struggle between wolf and child: "It went for her throat, as wolves do, but she made a great swipe at it with her father's knife and slashed off its right forepaw."

The magic transformation occurs inside the grandmother's house, when the severed paw falls out of the basket and is revealed to have changed into "a hand, chopped off at the wrist, a hand toughened with work and freckled with old age. . . . By the wart, she knew it for her grandmother's hand."

Proof that her grandmother is a witch is too much for the child. She cries out for the neighbors, who drive the sick woman from her bed and stone her to death. The effect on the child of this violent reaction is not commented on. As in all good fairy tales, she lives happily ever after by inheriting her grandmother's house and prospering. We know she is much too good with a hunting knife to turn her hand to witchcraft.

Questions for Discussion

1. How many elements of the traditional "Little Red Riding Hood" folktale can you find in Carter's story?
2. What is the effect of the wildly imagined details in this story, such as the wart being described as a "witch's nipple"?

Topic for Writing

1. Compare and contrast this story with Robert Coover's "The Gingerbread House" and Shirley Jackson's "The Lottery."

RAYMOND CARVER

What We Talk about When We Talk about Love (p. 210)

The scarcely veiled animosity between Dr. Mel McGinnis and his wife, Terri, gives tension to this story of three married couples. Through Mel's thoughts and experiences, Carver is investigating the nature of married love. Like the naive boy in Sherwood Anderson's classic short story "I Want to Know Why," Mel insists on asking an impossible question: What is the nature of love? What is the meaning of sharing?

The three pairs of lovers represent different stages of marriage. At one end of a spectrum are Laura and Nick (the narrator), married only a year and a half, still infatuated, glowing with the power of their attraction for each other.

At the other end of the spectrum are the old married pair in the hospital whom Mel and the other doctors have patched up after a catastrophic highway accident. Glad to learn his wife has survived, the old man — as Mel tells the story — is depressed, not because of their physical suffering but because he can't see his wife through the eye holes in his bandages. As Mel says, "Can you imagine? I'm telling you, the man's heart was breaking because he couldn't turn his goddamn head and *see* his goddamn wife."

Between the two extremes of perfect love, Mel and Terri are veterans (four years married to each other), who are past the bliss of their first attraction and not yet two halves of a whole because they've survived the long haul together. Each has been married before, and each is obsessed with the earlier partner. First Terri talks too much about her sadistic ex-husband Ed; then Mel reveals that he hates his first wife because she kept their kids and "she's bankrupting us." The talk appears to ramble, but Carver keeps it under control by sticking to his subject — specific examples of the different varieties of love — and organizing the four friends' conversation by chronicling the stages of their drunkenness as they go through two bottles of gin in the afternoon.

The passing of time is brilliantly described, paralleling the waxing and waning of the stages of love. When the story opens, sunlight fills the New Mexico kitchen where the four friends with their gin and tonics are talking around the table. Midway, when the narrator is beginning to feel the drinks, he describes the sun like the warmth and lift of the gin in his body. "The afternoon sun was like a presence in this room, the spacious light of ease and generosity." As the conversation wears on and Mel tells Terri to shut up after she's interrupted one too many times, the light shifts again, the sunshine getting thinner. The narrator is a shade drunker, and his gaze fixes on the pattern of leaves on the windowpanes and on the Formica kitchen counter, as if he's staying alert by focusing deliberately on the edges of the objects around him. "They weren't the same patterns, of course." Finally, mysteriously, the light drains out of the room, "going back through the window where it had come from." The alcoholic elation has evaporated. At the end of the story, the couples sit in darkness on their kitchen chairs, not moving. The only sound the narrator hears is everyone's heart beating, separately.

The person we know least about is the narrator, Nick. Perhaps Carver deliberately echoes the name of Nick Adams, Hemingway's autobiographical narrator in his stories of initiation; or Nick Carraway, the narrator of Fitzgerald's *The Great Gatsby*. The role of Carver's Nick in the story is also like that of Marlow in Conrad's "Heart of Darkness," as Nick voyages through the conversation of Mel and Terri into uncharted, deep waters of the heart. But this Nick is also a participant, through the gin and the sunlight, in the feelings of his troubled, overworked doctor friend.

Questions for Discussion

1. As the story opens, what is the setting in time, place, and situation?
2. How would you describe Terri? What type of person is Mel?
3. What was Terri's experience with her first husband, Ed? In what way was Mel involved in this experience? How does Terri's view of Ed contrast with Mel's view of him? What does this contrast reveal about the character of Mel and Terri's relationship?
4. In the discussion about Ed, what do we discover about the couple with whom Mel and Terri are socializing? What is their relationship both to each other and to Mel and Terri? Compare and contrast their marriage with Terri and Mel's.
5. What is the point of view in this story? Who is the narrator? How reliable is he?

6. Does Mel view his first wife in the same way he does Terri? What are we told about his first wife?
7. What are some of the questions about love that Carver raises through his characters? Does he offer any answers to these questions?
8. A third couple is introduced in the story. What astonishes Mel about their relationship?
9. What changes in the setting, if any, can you identify over the course of the story? In what way does the setting mirror Carver's message about the stages of love?
10. What does each of the couples represent? What is the significance of the last paragraph?

Topics for Writing

CRITICAL ESSAYS

1. Theme and characterization in "What We Talk about When We Talk about Love."
2. The question posed by the title of this story: What does Carver (and the reader) talk about when he (and we) talks about love?
3. The types of love in Carver's story and Joyce's "The Dead."

RELATED SUBJECT

1. Think about married couples you know and discuss what their views on love might be as well as the quality of their relationships.

Related Commentary from Part Two

Raymond Carver, Creative Writing 101, p. 1417.

Suggested Readings

Simpson, M. "Art of Fiction: Raymond Carver." *Paris Review* 25 (1983)193–221.
Stull, W. L. "Beyond Hopelessville: Another Side of Raymond Carver." *Philological Quarterly* 64 (1985): 1–15.

WILLA CATHER

Paul's Case (p. 221)

Students may feel repelled by this story and reject its ending as heavy-handed. The structure of the plot, which pits a sensitive adolescent against an ugly and confining bourgeois society, invites us to admire Paul's rebellion and to glamorize his suicide, but Cather takes great pains to make Paul as unattractive in his way as the family, school, and neighborhood he hates. Quite apart from his supercilious mannerisms, which his teachers feel some inclination to forgive, Paul's quest for brightness and beauty in the world of art and imagination is subjected to Cather's devastating criticism, so readers who were ready to make a stock tragic response to his demise may find it difficult to care.

Try meeting this objection directly by examining the implications of the story's concluding passage. The vision presented here comes close to formulaic naturalism. Paul is not only caught in a universal machine, he is himself a machine. The imagination that has sustained him against the ugliness of his surroundings is dismissed as a "picture making mechanism," now crushed. The world against which Paul rebels is plain, gray, narrow, and monotonous. Its combination of saints (Calvin, Washington) and customary homilies precludes all that is in itself beautiful, pleasant, and fulfilling in the present moment. Paul's reaction, however, is merely the obverse. His habitual lies reflect his general resort to the artificial. He may be "artistic," but not in the sense of being creative, and his romantic fantasies involve no more satisfactory relations with others than does his ordinary life. Paul's world is so intolerable to his sensitivity that he is driven to escape from it, even at the cost of sitting in the cellar with the rats watching him from the corners. His escape inevitably becomes a form of self-destruction, as manifested in his criminal act — which to him feels like confronting "the thing in the corner" — and finally in his suicide. Paul passes through the "portal of Romance" for good, into a dream from which "there would be no awakening."

If it could be termed a choice, it would clearly be a bad choice, but Cather presents it rather as a symptom of Paul's "case," a disease of life from which he suffers, has suffered perhaps since his mother died when he was an infant, and for which, at first glance, there seems to be no cure. No wonder readers may be inclined to dismiss the story as unduly negative because unduly narrow. But Cather, at the same time that she meticulously documents the inexorable progress of Paul's illness, defines by implication a condition of health whose possible existence gives meaning to Paul's demise. As Philip L. Gerber explains: "Although [Cather] extolled the imaginative, her definition of imagination is all-important; for rather than meaning an ability 'to weave pretty stories out of nothing,' imagination conveyed to her 'a response to what is going on — a sensitiveness to which outside things appeal' and was an amalgam of sympathy and observation."

Paul's refuge is the product of the first, false kind of imagination, but the reality and the power of an imagination of the second sort is evident throughout the story, in the masterful evocations of Cordelia Street, of the school and its all-too-human teachers, and not least of Paul himself. When Paul's case finally becomes extreme enough to break through the insensitivity of bourgeois Pittsburgh, the world of the street that bears the name of King Lear's faithful daughter at last begins to live up to its name, sympathizing with Paul's plight and offering to embrace him with its love. To Paul, however, whose own unregenerate imagination is still confined to making pretty pictures rather than sympathetic observations, the advances of Cordelia Street seem like tepid waters of boredom in which he is called upon to submerge himself. The potential for growth and change that is reflected in his father's abandoning his usual frugality to pay back the money Paul has stolen and in his coming down from the top of the stairs into Paul's world to reach out to him, escape Paul's notice — but not that of the reader.

Questions for Discussion

1. Describe Paul's personality as Cather sets it forth in the opening paragraph of the story. Is this someone we like and admire?
2. Why do Paul's teachers have so much difficulty dealing with him? What does the knowledge that Cather was a teacher in Pittsburgh at the time she wrote this story suggest about her perspective on Paul's case?
3. What techniques does Cather use to establish the reader's sympathy for Paul? What limits that sympathy?
4. Contrast the three worlds — school, Carnegie Hall, and Cordelia Street — in which Paul moves. Why does Cather introduce them in that order?
5. What is the effect of Cather's capitalizing the word "Romance"?
6. Discuss the three decorations that hang above Paul's bed. What aspects of American culture do they refer to? What do they leave out?
7. Explore the allusion embodied in the name "Cordelia Street." Why does Paul feel he is drowning there?
8. Discuss Paul's fear of rats. Why does he feel that he has "thrown down the gauntlet to the thing in the corner" when he steals the money and leaves for New York?
9. Explicate the paragraph that begins "Perhaps it was because, in Paul's world, the natural always wore the guise of ugliness." To what extent does this paragraph offer a key to the story's structure and theme?
10. Describe the effect of the leap forward in time that occurs in the white space before we find Paul on the train to New York. Why does Cather withhold for so long her account of what has taken place?
11. What is admirable about Paul's entry into and sojourn in New York? What is missing from his new life?
12. Why does Paul wink at himself in the mirror after reading the newspaper account of his deeds?
13. On the morning of his suicide, Paul recognizes that "money was everything." Why does he think so? Does the story bear him out?
14. What is the effect of Paul's burying his carnation in the snow? of his last thoughts?
15. Compare Cather's account of Paul's death with accounts of dying in other stories, such as Tolstoy's "The Death of Ivan Ilych" and Bierce's "An Occurrence at Owl Creek Bridge."

Topics for Writing

CRITICAL ESSAYS

1. "Paul's Case" as an attack on American society.
2. Cather's commentary on Mansfield (printed in Part Two, p. 1421) as a basis for criticism of "Paul's Case."

EXERCISE FOR READING

1. Cather's story is punctuated by several recurrent images and turns of phrase. Locate as many as you can and take note of their contexts. What does this network of internal connections reveal?

Related Commentary from Part Two

Willa Cather, The Stories of Katherine Mansfield, p. 1421.

Suggested Readings

Daiches, David. *Willa Cather: A Critical Introduction.* Ithaca: Cornell UP, 1951. 144–47.

Gerber, Philip L. *Willa Cather.* Twayne's United States Authors Series 258. Boston: Hall, 1975. 72–73, 101, 141, 163.

JOHN CHEEVER

The Swimmer (p. 238)

One way to reconstruct a naturalistic time scheme for the story, so Neddy's "misfortunes," the awareness of which he seems to have repressed, can be dated with regard to the other events in the narrative, is to imagine a gap in time covered by the line "He stayed in the Levys' gazebo until the storm had passed." The authoritative point of view in the opening paragraphs seems to preclude placing the misfortunes before Neddy begins his swim, while the gathering clouds and circling de Haviland trainer assert the continuity of the first phase of his journey. After the storm, however, signs of change appear, and it is possible to reconcile Neddy's subsequent encounters with the proposition that he is continuing his swim on another day or days under quite different circumstances. Before the storm, he visits the Grahams and the Bunkers, who greet him as the prosperous and popular Neddy Merrill described at the beginning of the story, but after the storm Neddy visits only the empty houses of the Lindleys and the Welchers; the public pool where any derelict may swim; the peculiar Hallorans, who mention his troubles; the Sachses, who have problems of their own and refuse him a drink; the socially inferior Biswangers, who snub him; and his old mistress Shirley, who implies that this call is not the first he has paid in this condition.

But Cheever is not interested in a realistic time scheme. If he were, he would not have burned the 250-page novelistic version of the story (mentioned in the headnote) that presumably filled in the blanks. Instead, he has constructed the story so Neddy's recognition of his loss strikes the reader with the same impact it has on Neddy. By telescoping time, Cheever thrusts us forward into a state of affairs that exists only as a dim cloud on the horizon on the day the story begins and at first seems to be entirely taking place.

What accounts for the reversal in Neddy's life? Surely it is possible to tax Neddy for irresponsibility and childishness in turning his back on his friends and family and so casually setting off on an odyssey from which he returns far too late. Neddy's own view of his adventure is considerably more attractive. The only member of his society who seems free from a hangover on this midsummer Sunday, Neddy simply wishes to savor the pleasures of his fortunate life: "The day was beautiful and it seemed to him that a long swim might enlarge and celebrate its beauty." Although he has been (or will be) unfaithful to his wife with Shirley Adams, and although he kisses close to a dozen other women on his journey, Neddy does not construe his departure as infidelity to Lucinda. Rather, to swim the string of pools across the suburban county is to travel along "the Lucinda River." As "a pilgrim, an explorer, a man with a destiny," Neddy plunges into this river of life aware of the gathering storm on the horizon but regarding it with pleasurable anticipation. When it finally breaks over the Levys' gazebo, he savors the exciting release of tension that accompanies the arrival of a thunder shower, but with the explosion of thunder and the smell of gunpowder that ensues, Neddy finds his happy illusions, his world of "youth, sport, and clement weather," lashed by a more unpleasant reality, just as the "rain lashed the Japanese lanterns that Mrs. Levy had bought in Kyoto the year before last, or was it the year before that?"

What Neddy now confronts, though he tries gamely to ignore it, are the twin recognitions that his youth is not eternal and that the pleasant society of the "bonny and lush . . . banks of the Lucinda River" is unstable, exclusive, and cruel. Grass grows in the Lindleys' riding ring, the Welchers have moved away, and the sky is now overcast. Crossing Route 424 in his swimming suit, Neddy is subjected to the ridicule of the public, and at the Recreation Center he finds that swimming does not convey the same sense of elegance, pleasure, and freedom that it does in the pools of his affluent friends. The validity of the society Neddy has previously enjoyed is called further into question by the very existence of the self-contradictory Hallorans, whose personal eccentricity is matched by their political hypocrisy. Neddy's visits to the Biswangers and to Shirley Adams complete the destruction of his illusions, but it is Eric Sachs, disfigured by surgery and (with the loss of his navel) symbolically cut off from the human community, who embodies the most troubling reflection of Neddy's condition. "I'm not alone," Shirley proclaims, but Neddy is, and as this man who "might have been compared to a summer's day" recognizes that his summer is over, it is not surprising that for "the first time in his adult life" he begins to cry. While the reader may relish Cheever's indictment of a society whose values have so betrayed Neddy, it is hard not to feel some admiration for a man who, by executing his plan to swim the county through the now icy autumn waters, has indeed become a legendary figure, an epic hero of a sort.

Questions for Discussion

1. Who is referred to by the word "everyone" in the opening sentence? Who is not?
2. How does Neddy Merrill relate to the world in which he moves? Why does he decide to swim home?
3. Why does Neddy name his route "the Lucinda River"? The Levys live on "Alewives Lane." Alewives are a kind of fish that swim up rivers to spawn. Is there a sexual component to Neddy's journey?
4. Is the storm that breaks a surprise? How does Neddy feel about the beginning of the rain?
5. What differences can be noticed between what Neddy experiences before and after the storm? How might they be explained?
6. What new elements enter the story when Neddy crosses Route 424? Why do the drivers jeer at him?

7. Before he dives into the unappealing public swimming pool, Neddy tells himself "that this was merely a stagnant bend in the Lucinda River." How characteristic is this effort to assuage his own doubts and discontents?
8. Based on what the Hallorans, the Sachses, the Biswangers, and Shirley Adams say to Neddy, what is the truth about himself and his life of which he is unaware?
9. Cheever has his hero discover the season by observing the stars. What effect does that choice among various possibilities have on our attitude toward Neddy?
10. It is not difficult to say what Neddy has lost. What has he gained?

Topics for Writing

CRITICAL ESSAYS

1. Why Neddy Merrill talks only with women.
2. Rusty Towers, Eric Sachs, and Neddy Merrill.
3. Neddy Merrill's voyage of exploration and discovery.
4. Cheever's attitude toward the swimmer.

Related Commentary from Part Two

John Cheever, Why I Write Short Stories, p. 1426.

Suggested Readings

Coale, Samuel. *John Cheever*. New York: Ungar, 1977. 43–47.
Waldeland, Lynne. *John Cheever*. Twayne's United States Authors Series 335. Boston: Hall, 1979. 94–95.

ANTON CHEKHOV

The Darling *(p. 248)*

One of the liveliest discussions about a short story in this anthology could be started by a class debate based on the contradictory interpretations of "The Darling" by Leo Tolstoy and Eudora Welty included in Part Two (pp. 1520 and 1534). Tolstoy was convinced that Chekhov was misguided in satirizing women's tendency to depend on men for meaning and direction in their lives. In Tolstoy's view, Chekhov had allowed himself to become a women's rights advocate under the pernicious influence of his "liberated" wife, the actress Olga Knipper. Welty, in contrast, reveals the subtle emotional tyranny of the protagonist, Olenka. In Welty's interpretation, the schoolboy shows us at the end of the story that men want their "space" too. Students could be assigned Tolstoy's or Welty's interpretation and asked to support or refute it. Certainly neither interpretation is unassailable.

Other critical perspectives can also be applied to this provocative story. A feminist reader could argue that Olenka has been handicapped by the environment around her: uneducated for a profession, she can have no ideas or life of her own. A psychological interpretation could concentrate on the darling's early, possibly traumatic fixation on her father and his long mortal illness just as she reaches manageable age. A formalist approach might look closely at the words the schoolboy uses as he cries out in his sleep: "I'll give it you! Get away! Shut up!" Welty assumes that the boy is dreaming of Olenka. He could just as well be dreaming of his teacher at school, other students fighting with him in the schoolyard, or his own mother, who appears to have abandoned him. He could even be repeating the cruel words his mother might have said to drive him away from her before she left him with Olenka.

The English short-story writer H. E. Bates interpreted the story yet another way. Comparing Chekhov's technique with Maupassant's, Bates writes, "Both like to portray a certain type of weak, stupid, thoughtless woman, a sort of yes-woman who can unwittingly impose tragedy or happiness on others. Maupassant had no patience with the type; but in Olenka, in the 'The Darling,' it is precisely a quality of tender patience, the judgment of the heart and not the head, that gives Chekhov's story its effect of uncommon understanding and radiance."

Bates saw Chekhov as subtle: His

> receptivity, his capacity for compassion, are both enormous. Of his characters he seems to say, "I know what they are doing is their own responsibility. But how did they come to this, how did it happen? There may be some trivial thing that will explain." That triviality, discovered, held for a moment in the light, is the key to Chekhov's emotional solution. In Maupassant's case the importance of that key would have been inexorably driven home; but as we turn to ask of Chekhov if we have caught his meaning aright, it is to discover that we must answer that question for ourselves—for Chekhov has gone.
> . . . Both [Maupassant and Chekhov] knew to perfection when they had said enough; an acute instinct continually reminded them of the fatal tedium of explanation, of going on a second too long. In Chekhov this sense of impatience, almost a fear, caused him frequently to stop speaking, as it were, in mid-air. It was this which gave his stories an air of remaining unfinished, of leaving the reader to his own explanations, of imposing on each story's end a note of suspense so abrupt and yet refined that it produced on the reader an effect of delayed shock.

Questions for Discussion

1. How does Chekhov characterize Olenka at the beginning of the story?
2. Why does he have the "lady visitors" be the first ones to call her a "darling"?
3. Olenka "mothers" each of her husbands. Could she have been both a good wife and a good mother if she had had children of her own? Why or why not?

Topics for Writing

1. Interpret Sasha's words at the end of "The Darling." Identify the person he is talking to, and find details in the story that justify your interpretation.
2. Continue "The Darling," supposing that the "loud knock at the gate" is a message from Sasha's mother, who wants him to join her in Harkov.

Related Commentaries from Part Two

Anton Chekhov, Technique in Writing the Short Story, p. 1428.
Leo Tolstoy, Chekhov's Intent in "The Darling," p. 1520.
Eudora Welty, Plot and Character in Chekhov's "The Darling," p. 1534.

ANTON CHEKHOV

The Lady with the Pet Dog (p. 258)

Anna Sergeyevna comes to Yalta because she wants "to live, to live!" Gurov begins his affair with her because he is bored and enjoys the freedom and ease of a casual liaison. At the outset both are undistinguished, almost clichés — a philandering bank employee escaping from a wife he cannot measure up to, a lady with a dog and a "flunkey" for a husband. By the end of the story, however, after having been captured and tormented by a love that refuses to be filed away in memory, the two gain dignity and stature by recognizing that life is neither exciting nor easy; and, by taking up the burden of the life they have discovered in their mutual compassion, they validate their love.

Chekhov develops the nature of this true love, so ennobling and so tragic, by testing it against a series of stereotypes that it transcends and by showing a series of stock expectations that it violates. Anna Sergeyevna reacts differently from any of the several types of women Gurov has previously made love to, and Gurov finds himself unable to handle his own feelings in the way he is accustomed to. Anna Sergeyevna proves neither a slice of watermelon nor a pleasant focus of nostalgia. Most important, as the conclusion implies, she will not remain the secret core of his life, bought at the price of falsehood and suspicion of others.

In observing the evolution of the lovers, the reader is led through a series of potential misconceptions. We may want to despise Gurov as a careless breaker of hearts, but it is clear that he has one of his own when he sees Anna Sergeyevna as a Magdalene. Later, when Gurov is tormented by his longings for Anna Sergeyevna, we are tempted to laugh the superior realist's laugh at a romantic fool: Surely when Gurov arrives at S——, disillusionment will await him.

And in a sense it does. Just as there was dust in the streets at Yalta, the best room in the hotel at S—— is coated with dust; reality is an ugly fence; and even the theater (where *The Geisha* is playing) is full of reminders of how unromantic life really is. But Anna Sergeyevna has not, as Gurov supposes at one point, taken another lover, nor has she been able to forget Gurov.

The antiromantic tone is but another oversimplification, and the story comes to rest, somewhat like Milton's *Paradise Lost*, at a moment of beginning. The lovers' disillusionment about the nature of the struggle they face creates in them a deep compassion for each other, which finds its echo in readers' final attitude toward them as fellow human beings whose lives are like our own and who deserve a full measure of our sympathy. Or perhaps they draw our pity; surely their fate, which Chekhov so skillfully depicts as probable and true, inspires tragic fear. Gurov and Anna Sergeyevna have met the god of love, and Chekhov awes us by making him seem real.

Questions for Discussion

1. Why does Gurov call women "the inferior race"?
2. At the end of section I, Gurov thinks that there is "something pathetic" about Anna Sergeyevna. Is there? What is it?
3. Why is Anna Sergeyevna so distracted as she watches the steamer putting in?
4. How does Anna Sergeyevna differ from other women Gurov has known, as they are described in the paragraph that ends "the lace on their lingerie seemed to him to resemble scales"? Compare this passage with the paragraph that begins "His hair was already beginning to turn gray."
5. In view of what follows, is it appropriate that Gurov should see Anna Sergeyevna as a Magdalene?
6. What is the function of the paragraph that begins "At Oreanda they sat on a bench not far from the church"?
7. What "complete change" does Gurov undergo during his affair with Anna Sergeyevna at Yalta? Is it permanent?
8. Explain Gurov's remark at the end of section II: "High time!"
9. Why is Gurov enraged at his companion's remark about the sturgeon?
10. Discuss the possible meanings of the objects Gurov encounters in S—: the broken figurine, the long gray fence, the cheap blanket, and so on.
11. Seeing Anna Sergeyevna enter the theater, Gurov "understood clearly that in the whole world there was no human being so near, so precious, and so important to him." What is Chekhov's tone in this statement?
12. Explain Anna Sergeyevna's reaction to Gurov's arrival. Why does she volunteer to come to Moscow?
13. Discuss the implications of Gurov's "two lives" as Chekhov explains them in section IV. Do you agree with the generalizations about the desire for privacy with which the paragraph ends? Relate these ideas to the story's ending.
14. What will life be like for Gurov and Anna Sergeyevna? Anna has previously said, "I have never been happy; I am unhappy now, and I never, never shall be happy, never!" Is she right?

Topics for Writing

CRITICAL ESSAYS

1. Chekhov's characterization of the wronged spouse in "The Lady with the Pet Dog."

2. The meaning of the three geographical locales in "The Lady with the Pet Dog."
3. Geography and adultery in Chekhov's "The Lady with the Pet Dog" and Bessie Head's "Life."

EXERCISE FOR READING

1. On your first reading of the story, stop at the end of each section and write down your judgment of Gurov and Anna Sergeyevna and your prediction of what will happen next. When you have finished reading, compare what you wrote with what turned out to be the case and with your final estimate of the protagonists. To the extent that your initial impressions were borne out, what points in the text helped to guide you? To the extent that you were surprised, explain what led you astray. What might Chekhov have wanted to accomplish by making such misconceptions possible?

Related Commentaries from Part Two

Anton Chekhov, Technique in Writing the Short Story, p. 1428.
Vladimir Nabokov, A Reading of Chekhov's "The Lady with the Little Dog," p. 1487.

Suggested Readings

Kramer, Karl D. *The Chameleon and the Dream: The Image of Reality in Chekhov's Stories*. The Hague: Mouton, 1970. 171.
Rayfield, Donald. *Chekhov: The Evolution of His Art*. New York: Barnes, 1975. 197–200.
Smith, Virginia Llewellyn. "The Lady with the Dog." Anton Chekhov's Short Stories: Texts of the Stories, Backgrounds, Criticism. Ed. Ralph E. Matlaw. New York: Norton, 1979. Excerpted from Smith, *Anton Chekhov and the Lady with the Dog* (New York: Oxford UP, 1973). 96–97, 212–18.

Kate Chopin

Regret (p. 273)

"Regret," considered in conjunction with Jewett's "A White Heron" and James's "The Beast in the Jungle," can open the door to an interesting discussion on a highly topical question: Must a woman who rejects the traditional female roles of marriage and motherhood thereby consign herself to isolation and loneliness? Chopin's quiet sympathy for Mamzelle Aurélie, whose peculiarities characterize her without making her in the least grotesque, differs from both the impassioned concern of Jewett and the tantalizing restraint exhibited by May Bartram in James's story. The result is a treatment of the woman's dilemma that is perhaps more insightful and balanced. Chopin faces squarely all that her heroine has lost and the regret she feels as a result of becoming aware of it, but she never implies that Mamzelle Aurélie was a fool to have lived as she has.

A consideration of the substantive issues raised by the story should not, however, divert attention from matters of style and structure. Chopin's comment on Maupassant (included in Part Two, p. 1430) describes the virtues of her own work even better than it does those of her master. Like Maupassant's, her "direct and simple" observations are precisely aimed toward her artistic purpose. With a few deft observations about her figure, clothing, and activities, Chopin establishes Mamzelle Aurélie's masculine, even military bearing, and then traces the rapid stages by which looking after the children awakens not only her maternal feelings but also her power to relate to others as individuals. At the start, Mamzelle Aurélie deals in categories — chickens, Negroes, children — and pursues her "line of duty" toward them. But when she finds it impossible to put the children to bed the way she would shoo the chickens to the henhouse, she begins to listen — to the children and to Aunt Ruby — and she begins to learn new ways. Her adaptation to the children (efficiently set forth in the paragraph beginning "Ti Nomme's sticky fingers . . .") and their adaptation to their temporary home (reflected in their whereabouts at the moment of Odile's return) are narrated without a trace of emotional excess. Simply, "Mamzelle Aurélie had grown quite used to these things." Even after the children are taken away, when she feels her loneliness for the first time, Mamzelle Aurélie's identity does not dissolve; she cries, but "like a man." (Would Maupassant have had her commit suicide with her fowling piece?)

Chopin's artistry marks her handling of other elements of this remarkably compact story as well. That Odile departs in a rush to the bedside of her sick mother, and that she returns, joyous that her mother is not dying, to delighted screams of welcome from her own daughter cannot be without meaning for Mamzelle Aurélie, the only character in the tale who is no one's mother or child. Although she leads an active life managing her farm, in her relations with other people Mamzelle Aurélie remains as Chopin symbolically portrays her, standing on her gallery (porch), "looking and listening."

Questions for Discussion

1. What does Chopin's choice of words in the first descriptive phrase that she offers about Mamzelle Aurélie — "a good strong figure" — imply about her attitude toward her heroine?
2. How does Chopin arouse and control the reader's anticipation of the epiphany or revelation toward which the story builds?
3. Discuss Odile and Aunt Ruby as foils for Mamzelle Aurélie. In what ways is she superior to them?
4. How does Chopin avoid saccharine sentiment in portraying the four children, while still making it credible to the reader that Mamzelle Aurélie should come to love them?
5. Note Chopin's use of sense imagery other than the visual. What do such images contribute to the story's impact on the reader?
6. How important is Chopin's use of Cajun dialect and local color? What would the story lack without them?

Topics for Writing

CRITICAL ESSAYS

1. Chopin's Mamzelle Aurélie and Jewett's Sylvia.
2. The stages of Mamzelle Aurélie's awakening.

RELATED SUBJECT

1. Write a review and evaluation of "Regret" from a feminist point of view.

Related Commentary from Part Two

Kate Chopin, How I Stumbled upon Maupassant, p. 1430.

Suggested Reading

Seyersted, Per. *Kate Chopin: A Critical Biography.* Baton Rouge: Louisiana State UP, 1969. 125–30.

KATE CHOPIN

The Story of an Hour (p. 276)

Does the O. Henryesque trick ending of this story merely surprise us, or does Chopin arrange to have Louise Mallard expire at the sight of her unexpectedly still living husband in order to make a thematic point? Students inclined to groan when Brently Mallard returns "composedly carrying his gripsack and umbrella" may come to think better of the ending if you ask them to evaluate the doctors' conclusions about the cause of Mrs. Mallard's death. Although Richards and Josephine take "great care . . . to break to her as gently as possible the news of her husband's death," what actually kills Mrs. Mallard is the news that he is still alive. The experience of regeneration and freedom that she undergoes in the armchair looking out upon a springtime vista involves an almost sexual surrender of conventional repressions and restraints. As she *abandons herself* to the realization of her freedom that *approaches to possess her*, Mrs. Mallard enjoys a hitherto forbidden physical and spiritual excitement. The presumption that she would be devastated by the death of her husband, like the presumption that she needs to be protected by watchful, "tender" friends, reduces Mrs. Mallard to a dependency from which she is joyful at last to escape. Chopin best images this oppressive, debilitating concern in what Mrs. Mallard thinks she will weep again to see: "the kind, tender hands folded in death; the face that had never looked save with love upon her, fixed and gray and dead." Although had she lived Mrs. Mallard might have felt guilty for, as it were, taking her selfhood like a lover and pridefully stepping forth "like a goddess of Victory," Chopin effectively suggests that the guilt belongs instead to the caretakers, the "travel-stained" Brently, the discomfited Josephine, and Richards, whose "quick motion" to conceal his error comes "too late."

Questions for Discussion

1. In view of Mrs. Mallard's eventual reactions, evaluate the efforts of Josephine and Richards to break the news of her husband's death gently.
2. What purpose might Chopin have in stressing that Mrs. Mallard does not block out the realization that her husband has died?
3. What might be the cause or causes of the "physical exhaustion that haunted her body and seemed to reach into her soul" that Mrs. Mallard feels as she sinks into the armchair?
4. Describe your reaction to the view out the window the first time you read the story. Did it change on a second reading?
5. Mrs. Mallard's face bespeaks repression. What has she been repressing?
6. Discuss the imagery Chopin uses to describe Mrs. Mallard's recognition of her new freedom.
7. What kind of man is Brently Mallard, as Mrs. Mallard remembers him? In what ways does he resemble Josephine and Richards?
8. Describe your feelings about Mrs. Mallard as she emerges from her room. Is the saying "Pride goeth before a fall" relevant here?
9. In what way is the doctors' pronouncement on the cause of Mrs. Mallard's death ironic? In what sense is it nonetheless correct?

Topics for Writing

CRITICAL ESSAYS

1. The imagery of life and the imagery of death in "The Story of an Hour."
2. "The Story of an Hour" as a thwarted awakening.
3. Tragic irony in "The Story of an Hour."

EXERCISE FOR READING

1. On a second reading of "The Story of an Hour," try to recall how you responded to each paragraph or significant passage when you read it the first time. Write short explanations of any significant changes in your reactions. To what extent are those changes the result of knowing the story's ending? What other factors are at work?

RELATED SUBJECTS

1. Can falsehood be the key to truth? Narrate a personal experience in which your own or someone else's reaction to misinformation revealed something meaningful and true.
2. How long is a turning point? Tell a story covering a brief span of time — a few minutes or an hour — in which the central character's life is permanently changed. Study Chopin's techniques for summarizing and condensing information.

Related Commentary from Part Two

Kate Chopin, How I Stumbled upon Maupassant, p. 1430.

Suggested Readings

Bender, B. "Kate Chopin's Lyrical Short Stories." *Studies in Short Fiction* 11 (1974): 257–66.

Fluck, Winifred. "Tentative Transgressions: Kate Chopin's Fiction as a Mode of Symbolic Action." *Studies in American Fiction* 10 (1982): 151–71.

Miner, Madonne M. "Veiled Hints: An Affected Stylist's Reading of Kate Chopin's 'Story of an Hour.' " *Markham Review* 11 (1982): 29–32.

Seyersted, Per. *Kate Chopin: A Critical Biography*. Baton Rouge: Louisiana State UP, 1969. 57–59.

COLETTE

The Hollow Nut (p. 280)

Colette named her daughter Bel-Gazou, a name that Colette's biographer Margaret Crosland explains was adapted from an expression meaning "fine speech." (The daughter was baptized Colette de Jouvenel.) In this story, the character Bel-Gazou is based on Colette's imagination of her eight-year-old daughter's behavior on a holiday. The little girl is at the age her mother enjoyed best. Colette was never what she called a "besotted mother" when her daughter was a baby. She said she preferred the next stage of development, "when intelligible speech blossomed on those ravishing lips, when recognition, malice, and even tenderness turned a run-of-the-mill baby into a little girl, and a little girl into my daughter."

The critic Robert Phelps has recognized that Colette was essentially "a lyric poet, and her basic subject matter was not the world she described but the drama of her personal relation to the world. Her injunction to those around her was always 'Look!' and her own capacity to behold was acute and untiring. But when she is writing at her best, it is not what she describes so much as her own presence, the dramatic act of herself watching, say, a butterfly, which becomes so absorbing, morally exemplary, and memorable."

In "The Hollow Nut," Colette's Bel-Gazou is persona, an imaginary character who responds to the seashore as a wild bird or a butterfly might. There is no pretense that Bel-Gazou actually thinks in the words on the page describing the landscape surrounding her or inventories the contents of her pocket with the vocabulary used in the story: "Three shells like flower petals, white, nacreous, and transparent." What eight-year-old would use the word "nacreous" to describe a shell? Not even Colette's daughter! Yet the evanescence of the childhood experience, the girl's sensitivity to the natural world around her, and her instinctive moral placement of it above the self-absorbed world of the adults on the beach are captured perfectly in Colette's words. The sketch is a tour de force, communicating a radiant sense of the child's ability to "taste a scent, feel a color, and see . . . the cadence of an imaginary song."

Questions for Discussion

1. This sketch is "an imaginary song," in which Colette envisions her daughter's sensuous response to the summer afternoon at the beach. What details make you see, hear, and taste the seacoast?
2. How does Colette convey the innocence of Bel-Gazou?
3. How does Colette arouse your interest in what she is writing?

Topic for Writing

1. Write a sketch by imaging the response of someone you know well—one of your parents, a brother, sister, or roommate—to a strikingly beautiful natural landscape.

Suggested Readings

Crosland, Margaret. *Colette: The Difficulty of Loving.* London: Owen, 1973.
Phelps, Robert. Introduction to *The Collected Stories of Colette.* New York: Farrar, 1983.
Richardson, Joanna. *Colette.* London: Methuen, 1983.

Joseph Conrad

Heart of Darkness (p. 283)

At the center of the concentric layers out of which Conrad constructs this story lies a case of atavism and the collapse of civilized morality. Kurtz casts aside all restraint and becomes as wild as his surroundings; or rather, the darkness around him calls out the darkness within his innermost being. Kurtz is a man of heroic abilities and exemplary ideals, yet at the end of the story, he explodes, unable to control his own strength.

Conrad does not provide an intimate inside view of Kurtz. To do so would destroy the aura of mystery and special significance that marks the story's theme as a profound revelation, the "culminating point of [Marlow's] experience," gained at "the farthest point of navigation." Instead, Conrad positions Kurtz in the midst of an impenetrable jungle, at "the very heart of darkness," as far from home and as remote from familiar frames of reference as possible. Then he causes the reader to approach Kurtz through a series of identifications that make the revelation of his debasement a statement not just about Kurtz, but about us all.

Conrad creates this effect mainly through his use of Marlow as narrator, and no discussion of the story can avoid exploring his function. He is on the one hand a kind of prophet — his pose resembles that of an idol or Buddha — whose wisdom arises from his having looked beyond the veil that screens the truth from common view ("the inner truth is hidden — luckily, luckily"), and on the other hand an adventurer like the heroes of epic poems, descending into Hades and emerging shaken with his dark illumination. But Marlow's vision is neither of heaven nor of hell. His journey up the Congo River is in fact a descent into the inner reaches of the human soul. Forced by a combination of circumstances and preconceptions into a special association with Kurtz, Marlow recognizes in that "shadow" the intrinsic darkness of human nature, in which he shares. When he plunges into the jungle to redeem Kurtz, who has crawled away on all fours to rejoin the "unspeakable rites" of his worshipers, Marlow embraces what Kurtz has become no less than what he once was or might have been, acknowledging his own kinship with the deepest depravity. Kurtz dies crying, "The horror! The horror!" — apparently having regained from his rescuer enough of his moral bearings to recoil from his own behavior. Marlow, who judges the truth "too dark — too dark altogether," preserves the innocence of Kurtz's "Intended," leaving her "great and saving illusion" intact.

Conrad may be suggesting that only by a conscious lie or by willful blindness can we avoid sinking into the savagery that surrounds us, that dwells under externally maintained restraint within us, and that animates our civilization in various guises, such as the "flabby, pretending, weak-eyed devil of a rapacious and pitiless folly." The conquest of the earth, which is what the civilized society portrayed in the story is engaged in, "is not a pretty thing when you look into it too much," Marlow says. "What redeems it is the idea only . . . an unselfish belief in the idea — something you can set up, and bow down before, and offer sacrifice to." But such idolatry of our own idea is not far from its horrible perversion into the worship of himself that the would-be civilizer Kurtz sets up. It leads to a civilization aptly portrayed in Kurtz's symbolic painting of a blindfolded woman carrying a torch through darkness. If Conrad offers a glimmer of light in the dark world he envisions, it is in the sympathetic understanding that enables Marlow to befriend Kurtz and to lie for Kurtz and his Intended, even at the cost of having to taste the "flavor of mortality" he finds in lies, which he detests like the death it suggests to him.

Questions for Discussion

1. What does Conrad gain by having his story told by Marlow to a group of important Londoners on a yacht in the Thames estuary? What is implied by the association of the Thames with the Congo? by Marlow's assertion, "And this also . . . has been one of the dark places on the earth"?

2. Marlow enters on his adventure through a city he associates with "a whited sepulcher"; he passes old women knitting who remind him of the Fates; the Company office is "as still as a house in a city of the dead." Locate other indications that Marlow's journey is like a trip into the underworld. What do they suggest about the story's meaning?

3. In what ways is the French warship "shelling the bush" an apt image of the European conquest of Africa? What does this historical theme contribute to our understanding of Marlow and Kurtz?

4. Discuss the Company's chief accountant. Why is it appropriate that Marlow first hears of Kurtz from him?

5. Marlow calls the men waiting for a post in the interior "pilgrims." Explain the irony in his use of the term.

6. Marlow is associated with Kurtz as a member of "the gang of virtue." Explain the resonance of that phrase.
7. Describe the journey up the Congo as Marlow reports it in the pages that follow his remark, "Going up that river was like traveling back to the earliest beginnings of the world." In what ways does Conrad make it a symbolic journey as well as an actual one?
8. Discuss Marlow's attitudes toward the natives. What do they mean to him?
9. As the boat draws near Kurtz's station, people cry out "with unrestrained grief" from the jungle. Why?
10. After the attack of the natives is repulsed and the narrative seems at the point of reaching the climax toward which so much suspense has been built—the meeting with Kurtz—Conrad throws it away by having Marlow stop to light his pipe and speak offhandedly and abstractly about what he learned. Why? Does this passage actually destroy the suspense? Is the story rendered anticlimactic? Or is the climax changed? What is the true climax of the story?
11. Why do you think the heads on stakes are facing Kurtz's house?
12. Discuss the Russian and his attitude toward Kurtz. Why does Conrad trouble to add this European to Kurtz's train of cultists?
13. Marlow is astonished that the Manager calls Kurtz's methods "unsound." Why? What does this passage reveal about each of them?
14. Explain what happens to Marlow when he goes into the bush after Kurtz. Explain what happens to Kurtz. Why does Marlow call Kurtz "that shadow"?
15. Marlow claims to have "struggled with a soul"; he tells Kurtz that if he does not come back he will be "utterly lost." Is Marlow a savior for Kurtz? Is Kurtz saved?
16. Why does Marlow lie to Kurtz's "Intended"?
17. Contrast the last paragraph of the story with the opening.
18. Comment on the title of Kurtz's pamphlet, about the "Suppression of Savage Customs," and on the significance of its scrawled postscript, "Exterminate all the brutes."

Topics for Writing

CRITICAL ESSAYS

1. Conrad's use of foreshadowlng.
2. Traditional symbolism and literary allusion as ways of universalizing the theme of "Heart of Darkness."
3. The function of the frame in this novella.
4. Journey into madness: conrad's "Heart of Darkness" and Gilman's "The Yellow Wallpaper."

EXERCISE FOR READING

1. Marlow frequently concludes a segment of his narrative with a generalization that sums it up and takes on a quality of special significance, such as, "I felt as though, instead of going to the center of a continent, I were about to set off for the center of the earth"; or, "It was like a weary pilgrimage among hints for nightmares." Locate as many such passages as you can. What do they reveal about the mind of the narrator?

RELATED SUBJECT

1. Conrad frequently uses an impressionist technique that Ian Watt has called "delayed decoding." When the steamboat is attacked, for example, Marlow first sees "little sticks" flying about, and only later recognizes them as arrows. Find other instances of delayed decoding in the story, and then write a narrative of your own using a similar method.

Related Commentaries from Part Two

Chinua Achebe, An Image of Africa: Conrad's "Heart of Darkness," p. 1379.
Lionel Trilling, The Greatness of Conrad's "Heart of Darkness," p. 1524.

Suggested Readings

Berthoud, Jacques. *Joseph Conrad: The Major Phase.* New York: Cambridge UP, 1978. 41–63.
Conrad, Joseph. *Heart of Darkness: An Authoritative Text, Backgrounds and Sources, Criticism.* Ed. Robert Kimbrough. Rev. ed. New York: Norton, 1971.
Gekoski, R. A. *Conrad: The Moral World of the Novelist.* New York: Barnes, 1978. 72–90.

ROBERT COOVER

The Gingerbread House (p. 351)

This story is included in Coover's collection *Pricksongs & Descants*. The book begins with the story "The Door: A Prologue of Sorts," in which Coover retells the tale of Jack and the Beanstalk and describes Jack chopping down the beanstalk and thinking of himself as a storyteller: "He'd given her her view of the world, in fragments of course, not really thinking it all out, she listening, he telling." Coover, like his giant killer, Jack, is furious at the corruption of heaven, "enraged at life that it should so resist" his efforts to make it reasonable. As John Updike once wrote about John Barth, Coover also "hit the floor of nihilism hard and returns to us covered with coal dust."

Tone is one key to "The Gingerbread House." It is flat but not numb, as in a story by Ann Beattie. The flatness furnishes the real conflict in Coover's story by its contrast with his unmistakable pleasure in inventing for his reader the wondrous physical details of the life he is imagining—the luminous sunlight in the dark evergreen forest; the rough texture of the grandfather's worn jacket; the gay, hand-sewn stitches in the bright orange of Gretel's apron; Hansel's plump fingers kneading his pellets of bread. Like Barth taking irrepressible pleasure in playing with language and literary conventions in "Lost in the Funhouse," Coover says one thing in his fiction (nihilism) and upholds another (literature).

So the tone of "Gingerbread House," along with its parceling out into forty-two segments or "pellets," is Coover's originality in this version of the folktale.

Stories about abandoned children and the suffering of families fallen victim to poverty and starvation abound in folk literature. The witch in black robes holding the throbbing heart of the innocent dove symbolizes involuntary sacrifice, evoking images of poor crops, corrupt state government, lack of birth control—whatever has contributed to the triumph of Evil over Good in our imperfect world.

Questions for Discussion

1. Folktales tend to be episodic, told by a storyteller in a series of scenes taking place in different settings. How has Coover modified this narrative strategy in "The Gingerbread House"?
2. Why is the story titled "The Gingerbread House" instead of "Hansel and Gretel"? Why doesn't Coover ever give names to the brother and sister?
3. The evil stepmother plays an important role in the Grimm version of this folktale, insisting that the children's father abandon them in the forest so the rest of the family can survive on the little food available. Does the absence of the stepmother weaken Coover's story? How has he compensated for her absence?
4. By telling the story in forty-two sections, does Coover eliminate the need for a closed ending? How do you think "The Gingerbread House" will end?

Topics for Writing

1. Choose a folktale or fairy tale that you like and retell it in unconnected episodes as Coover has done in "The Gingerbread House."
2. Write a book report on Coover's collection *Pricksongs & Descants*, describing his treatment of other folktales in that volume or his experiments with segmented narration in stories such as "Quenby and Ola, Swede and Carl" or "The Babysitter."

JULIO CORTÁZAR

Blow-Up (p. 362)

In the mid-1950s this story had a strong influence on young American writers who later developed as metafictionists—John Barth, Donald Barthelme, and Robert Coover, to mention three in this anthology. Cortázar's story showed them a way to disrupt conventional narrative so as to introduce an element of self-reflexive estrangement in an otherwise realistic context.

Cortázar prepares us for the unusual with his opening paragraph, the narrator's commentary on the difficulty of forcing himself to sit at his typewriter to get his story down on paper. Clouds outside his window distract him, and they will continue (through parenthetical expressions) to be not always unwelcome intruders in his consciousness. Thirty years later, Alice Adams used a similar means in "The Oasis" to suggest her heroine's disorientation. In the 1950s Cortázar's technique was startlingly innovative, borrowed from Surrealist poets and painters to enrich the texture of fiction. Now readers are more accustomed to it, and we are perhaps in a better position to appreciate Cortázar's skill as a storyteller.

The fits-and-starts description of the protagonist/narrator's wandering around Paris with his camera on a sunny Sunday morning (or the wanderings of Cortázar's imaginary persona, "Roberta Michel, French-Chilean, translator, and in his spare time an amateur photographer") soon bring him to the square where he sees the adolescent boy and the older blond woman. The narrator is immediately attracted to the boy, whom he sympathetically imagines wandering the city without money, hungry, like all boys his age, for french fries or pornographic magazines. The narrator is just as instinctively turned off by the woman, who evokes images of predators ("two eagles") or disintegrating matter ("two puffs of green slime").

The magic of Cortázar's story occurs after he has broken up what he imagines as the blonde's potential seduction of the young boy by taking a photograph of the scene. The narrator/translator returns home, develops his film, and blows up the image of what he thinks he has witnessed in the square. Obsessed by the poster-sized photograph, which he has pinned on the wall in front of him, he hallucinates its coming to life, beginning with "the almost furtive trembling of the leaves on the tree."

This time he interprets what he sees differently: the woman was not trying to seduce the boy for herself; she was acting on the orders of the man in the car, and the boy—wanting money—was tempted to fall, to allow himself to be brought to the man, like "the prisoners manacled with flowers" (an image reminiscent of Jean Genet's autofiction, *Our Lady of the Flowers*, a book popular in France at the time). The narrator feels powerless to intercede, yet he believes he must rescue the boy. He is trapped in the prison of the photograph, moving inexorably toward a violent confrontation with the depraved couple, until something (a large bird?), "outsided the focus" of the photograph, frees him from his obsession, and he finds himself once again alone in his room, watching the boy escape by running back to the city.

Questions for Discussion

1. Explain why you think the narrator feels such enormous sympathy for the boy in "Blow-Up."
2. What part does Roberto Michel play in the story? What are his similarities to Julio Cortázar?
3. Which of the two scenarios explaining the three people in the square is more likely the correct one?
4. How does Cortázar prepare the reader for the introduction of a surrealistic element in the narrative, when the enlarged photograph "comes to life" in his room?

Topics for Writing

1. Cortázar's observations on photography in "Blow-Up" are insightful. List the statements about photography in the story; then explain what you think Cortázar meant by them.

2. Imagine a third scenario explaining the relationship of the trio in the photograph.
3. Cortázar said, "In my stories the fantastic takes off from the 'real' or is inserted into it and . . . this abrupt and usually unexpected disruption of a reasonable and satisfying perspective with an invasion by the extraordinary is what makes them effective as literary works." Analyze this explanation as it applies to "Blow-Up."

Suggested Readings

Alazraki, Jaime, and Ivar Ivask, eds. *The Final Island: The Fiction of Julio Cortázar.* Norman: U. of Oklahoma P., 1978.
Cortázar, Julio. *Around the Day in Eighty Worlds.* Tr. Thomas Christensen. San Francisco: North Point Press, 1986. Esp. 17–23, 158–67.

STEPHEN CRANE

The Open Boat (p. 374)

Crane's story fictionalizes an actual experience. A correspondent himself, Crane happened to be aboard the *Commodore* when it went down, and he included in his newspaper report of the event this passage (as quoted by E. R. Hagemann):

> The history of life in an open boat for thirty hours would no doubt be instructive for the young, but none is to be told here now. For my part I would prefer to tell the story at once, because from it would shine the splendid manhood of Captain Edward Murphy and of William Higgins, the oiler, but let it suffice at this time to say that when we were swamped in the surf and making the best of our way toward the shore the captain gave orders amid the wildness of the breakers as clearly as if he had been on the quarter deck of a battleship.

It is good that Crane did not write "at once" but let his experience take shape as a work of art which, instead of celebrating the "splendid manhood" of two or four individuals, recognizes a profound truth about human life in general — about the puniness of humankind in the face of an indifferent nature and about the consequent value of the solidarity and compassion that arise from an awareness of our common fate. Crane's meditation on his experience "after the fact" enables him to become not simply a reporter but, as he puts it in the last line of the story, an *interpreter* of the message spoken to us by the world we confront.

Crane portrays the exertions of the four men in the boat without glamorizing them. His extended and intimate account of their hard work and weariness wrings out any false emotion from the reader's view of the situation. By varying the narrative point of view from a coolly detached objective observer to a plural account of all four men's shared feelings and perceptions to the correspondent's rueful, self-mocking cogitations, Crane defeats our impulse to choose a hero for adulation, at the same time driving home the point that the condition of the men in the dinghy — their longing, their fear, and their powerlessness before nature and destiny —reflects our own. By the end, what has been revealed is so horrible that there can be no triumph in survival. The good fortune of a rescue brings only a reprieve, not an escape from what awaits us. Billie the oiler drowns, but there is no reason it should have been he, or only he. His death could be anybody's death.

Crane's narration builds suspense through rhythmic repetition, foreshadowing, and irony. We hear the surf periodically: Our hopes for rescue are repeatedly raised and dashed; night follows day, wave follows wave, and the endless struggle goes on. The correspondent's complaint against the cruelty of fate recurs in diminuendo, with less whimsy and self-consciousness each time.

These recurrences mark the men's changes in attitude—from the egocentric viewpoint they start with, imagining that the whole world is watching them and working for their survival, to the perception of the utter indifference of nature with which the story ends. Some stages in this progression include their false sense of security when they light up the cigars; their isolation from the people on shore, epitomized by their inability to interpret the signal of the man waving his coat (whose apparent advice to try another stretch of beach they nonetheless inadvertently follow); their experience of aloneness at night; their confrontation with the hostility of nature in the shark; and, finally, their recognition that death might be a welcome release from toil and suffering. They respond by drawing together in a communion that sustains them, sharing their labor and their body heat, huddled together in their tiny, helpless dinghy. Even their strong bond of comradeship, however, cannot withstand the onslaught of the waves. When the boat is swamped, it is every man for himself: Each individual must face death alone. Because of the fellowship that has grown up among them, however, when Billie dies, each of the others feels the oiler's death as his own. The reader, whom Crane's narrative has caused to share thirty hours at sea in an open boat, may recognize the implication in what is spoken by "the sound of the great sea's voice to the men on shore."

Questions for Discussion

1. Contrast the imagery and the tone of the first paragraph with those of the second. Why does Crane continually seek to magnify nature and to belittle the men who are struggling with it? Find other instances of Crane's reductive irony, and discuss their effects.
2. How does Crane convey the men's concentration on keeping the boat afloat?
3. Explain Crane's use of the word "probably" in the first paragraph of section II.
4. Why does the seagull seem "somehow gruesome and ominous" to the men in the boat? Compare and contrast the seagull with the shark that appears later.
5. Comment on the imagery Crane uses to describe changing seats in the dinghy (stealing eggs, Sèvres).
6. What is it that the correspondent "knew even at the time was the best experience of his life"? Why is it the best?

7. What is the purpose of Crane's understatement in the line "neither the oiler nor the correspondent was fond of rowing at this time"?
8. What is the effect on the reader of the men's lighting up cigars?
9. Discuss the meaning of the correspondent's question "Was I brought here merely to have my nose dragged away as I was about to nibble the sacred cheese of life?"
10. What do you think the man waving a coat means? Why is it impossible for him to communicate with the men in the boat?
11. "A night on the sea in an open boat is a long night," says Crane. How does he make the reader feel the truth of that assertion?
12. At one point the correspondent thinks that he is "the one man afloat on all the oceans." Explain that sensation. Why does the wind he hears sound "sadder than the end"? Why does he later wish he had known the captain was awake when the shark came by?
13. Why does the correspondent have a different attitude toward the poem about the dying soldier in Algiers from the one he had as a boy?
14. Examine the third paragraph of section VII. How important are the thoughts of the correspondent to our understanding of the story? What would the story lose if they were omitted? What would the effect of this passage have been if Crane had narrated the story in the first person? If he had made these comments in the voice of an omniscient third-person narrator?
15. Define the correspondent's physical, mental, and emotional condition during his final moments on the boat and during his swim to the beach.
16. Characterize and explain the tone of Crane's description of the man who pulls the castaways from the sea.
17. Why does Crane make fun of the women who bring coffee to the survivors?

Topics for Writing

CRITICAL ESSAYS

1. Crane's handling of point of view in "The Open Boat."
2. The importance of repetition in Crane's narrative.
3. Imagery as a key to tone in "The Open Boat."

EXERCISE FOR READING

1. After reading the story once rapidly, read it again with a pencil in hand, marking every simile and metaphor. Then sort them into categories. What realms of experience does Crane bring into view through these devices that are not actually part of the simple boat-sea-sky-beach world in which the story is set? Why?

RELATED SUBJECT

1. Write an eyewitness account of some experience you have undergone that would be suitable for newspaper publication. Then note the changes you would make to turn it into a fictional narrative with broader or more profound implications — or write that story.

Related Commentary from Part Two

Stephen Crane, The Sinking of the *Commodore*, p. 1431.

Suggested Readings

Adams, Richard P. "Naturalistic Fiction: 'The Open Boat.' " *Stephen Crane's Career: Perspectives and Evaluations.* Ed. Thomas A. Gullason. New York: New York UP, 1972. 421–29. Originally published in *Tulane Studies in English* 4 (1954): 137–46.

Cady, Edwin H. *Stephen Crane.* Twayne's United States Authors Series 23. Rev. ed. Boston: Hall, 1980. 150–54.

Hagemann, E. R. " 'Sadder than the End': Another Look at 'The Open Boat.' " *Stephen Crane in Transition: Centenary Essays.* Ed. Joseph Katz. DeKalb: Northern Illinois UP, 1972. 66–85.

Kissane, Leedice. "Interpretation through Language: A Study of the Metaphors in Stephen Crane's 'The Open Boat.' " Gullason, cited above. 410–16. Originally published in *Rendezvous* (Idaho State U) 1 (1966): 18–22.

ISAK DINESEN

The Blue Jar (p. 394)

"The Blue Jar" is an enigmatic story that illustrates Dinesen's use of fiction as an "anecdote of destiny." The narrative doesn't define the life of Lady Helena, yet after reading it we have an intuitive sense of who she is.

Lady Helena's "mind had suffered from her trials," so we cannot look too closely for rational patterns and explanations of her quest for "the right blue" jar or bowl. Perhaps she is seeking the impossible union of body and spirit, or perhaps the integration of her own soul. "Surely there must be some of it [the perfect color blue] left from the time when all the world was blue."

The image that Lady Helena describes of a parallel ship on the other hemisphere, a perfect reflection of herself, in harmony with the moon and the tides, may suggest to some students the idea of a lover (the young sailor who shared the lifeboat with her after the shipwreck?) or the more abstract projection of her "destiny" in life. This short story is rich in ambiguity and leaves a bittersweet impression of Dinesen's craft as a writer.

Questions for Discussion

1. We know that fairy tales enchant children, and we know, from works such as Bruno Bettelheim's *The Uses of Enchantment*, what strong psychological demands lie behind that enthrallment. Would you expect a fairy tale for adults to differ from those you read as a child? What expectations does the fairy-tale form of "The Blue Jar" set up for you?

2. What is the function of Lady Helena's father in this story? What plot elements of her life does he control? Why does she mimic his search for "ancient blue china"?

3. Her life now devoted to searching for the right color, Lady Helena cries, "Surely there must be some of it left from the time when all the world was blue." Can we know exactly what blue symbolizes for Lady Helena? Does this story give us enough information to be able to say that it suggests a nostalgia for paradise? What might paradise be made of? When she discovers the right blue, she says, "Oh, how light it makes one. Oh, it is as fresh as a breeze, as deep as a deep secret, as full as I say not what." What is common to these four categories? What does the common element suggest about paradise?

4. After the shipwreck, Lady Helena is compelled to do two things: search and sail. What do you make of her saying "We two are like the reflection of one another, in the deep sea, and the ship of which I speak is always exactly beneath my own ship, upon the opposite side of the globe"? Yet Lady Helena seems to see herself as the prime mover in this duality: "I draw it to and fro wherever I go, as the moon draws the tides, all through the bulk of the earth." Analyze the sexual references in this sentence.

5. Lady Helena can die after the successful completion of her task: she has found the right blue. When, after her death, her heart is cut out and laid in the jar, "everything will be as it was then." Again, Lady Helena refers to something in the past. But immediately the following sentence directs our attention to a particular time: "My heart will be innocent and free, and will beat gently, like a wake that sings, like the drops that fall from an oar blade." Why does Lady Helena compare her heartbeat to a wake, to a drop from an oar blade?

6. "The Blue Jar" is an example of what Dinesen called an "anecdote of destiny." Is destiny the implicit subject of the penultimate sentence: "Is it not a sweet thing to think that, if only you have patience, all that has ever been, will come back to you?" In what moments in this story do you see the suggestion of Lady Helena's destiny?

Topics for Writing

CRITICAL ESSAYS

1. Physiological vision compared with psychological vision in "The Blue Jar."
2. "Innocence" as defined and explored in "The Blue Jar."

Suggested Readings

Hannah, Donald. "In Memoriam Karen Blixen: Some Aspects of Her Attitude to Life." *Sewanee Review* 71 (1963): 585–604.

Landry, M. "Anecdote as Destiny: Isak Dinesen and the Story-Teller." *Massachusetts Review* 19 (1978): 389–406.

Isak Dinesen

The Blue Stones *(p. 396)*

"The Blue Stones" is told in the form of a fairy tale. It begins with the classic formula "There was once [upon a time]. . . ." This sets the story in some indefinite time, presumably far away. The place is Dinesen's native Denmark (Elsinore), but the setting is deliberately vague and almost unessential to the action.

The characters are not flesh-and-blood creatures, but instantly recognizable sexual stereotypes. They are the classic mismatched married couple of fairy tale and legend: the voyaging, trusting husband and the stay-at-home, unhappy wife. She is jealous of her husband's ship, which she rightly understands to be his idealized vision of herself — adventurous, obedient, and forever young — all qualities denied to her by her society, her personality, and life itself.

The plot is simple. The wife asks something impossible from her husband: "You had better give me the stones for a pair of earrings." He refuses to be dominated by her, replying cryptically that he can't give her the stones, and "you would not ask me to if you understood." She takes them anyway, with tragic consequences for both husband and wife.

The moral of this sad tale is an ironic reversal of the adage "Love is blind." The jealous wife is punished for her greed by actual blindness; the idealistic husband is destroyed along with his ship in a bizarre wreck. But perhaps the wreck isn't so bizarre after all. The story contains real magic. The precious blue stones have special properties; they see what they want to see.

The wife should have been content with a metaphorical blindness to her husband's attachment to his ship. Now he is joined forever with it in the wreck below the waves, while she at home has become truly blind. All this wreckage in broad daylight — but, as we know, the world of fantasy in the classic fairy tales projects its magical images from the darker regions of our psyche.

Questions for Discussion

1. What does the fairy-tale format of "The Blue Stones" lead you to expect in setting, plot, and characterization?
2. How would you describe the roles of the wife and the husband in "The Blue Stones"? Are they stereotypical or individualistic?
3. What is the husband's view of his ship? Does his wife share this view? What is her perception of the vessel?
4. What is the significance of the blue stones? Why can they be said to have magical properties?
5. What is the moral of "The Blue Stones"?
6. Comment on the jealousy and greed of the wife and the irony of her punishment.

Topics for Writing

CRITICAL ESSAYS

1. Physiological vision compared with psychological vision in "The Blue Jar" and "The Blue Stones."
2. The rewards of selfishness versus selflessness as revealed in "The Blue Stones."

RELATED SUBJECT

1. Compare and contrast the effectiveness of the fairy-tale elements in Dinesen's "The Blue Jar" and "The Blue Stones" with similar elements in Lawrence's "The Rocking-Horse Winner."

Suggested Readings

Hannah, Donald. "In Memoriam Karen Blixen: Some Aspects of Her Attitude to Life." *Sewanee Review* 71 (1963): 585–604.
Landry, M. "Anecdote as Destiny: Isak Dinesen and the Story-Teller." *Massachusetts Review* 19 (1978): 389–406.

ANDRE DUBUS

The Curse (p. 398)

The character of Mitchell Hayes is at the center of "The Curse," although he plays a very small role in the action of the story. In fact, his inaction is the origin of his feeling that he has been cursed by the girl whose rape he was powerless to stop. Thus, Hayes's guilt is the motivation for the story, even though he is innocent of any crime. Dubus details carefully at the beginning Hayes's physical age, weight, and size, but the age, weight, and size of his soul—his perception of himself—are more tangible for the reader than his body. The reader is told very briefly of his attempt to telephone for help when the five hoods begin getting rough with the girl, but we learn very little else of what occurs as he recalls the rape progressing. Hayes's point of view is kept exclusively; what he doesn't look at, we don't see.

What Hayes does notice is the behavior of the hoods on drugs he suspects but cannot name, the sobriety of the girl when she enters the bar late at night to buy cigarettes, and what the girl looks like. His description of her is precise, unerotic. The reader can guess that she is attractive ("She was young . . . deeply tanned") and totally unprepared for the assault.

As Hayes continues to relive the event in this flashback, the brutality he has witnessed begins to show in his language. The two paragraphs describing the girl on the floor and the arrival of the police cruiser and the ambulance that took her away are written in elemental English, a series of run-on sentences that suggest Hayes's hopelessness and lack of control over the events. The story winds back on itself to continue as the description of present action; the sentence structure becomes more complex, more reflective, but this is a character in shock. Not even his wife's sympathy and physical comfort or the emotional support offered by his two stepchildren the next morning lighten his depression.

The final scene brings Hayes back to the bar. Again, his friends and the regular customers are supportive, it's a night like any other, he serves as always, but the comfort extended when he's told and retold what happened the previous night leaves him "ashamed. He felt tired and old, making drinks and change, moving and talking up and down the bar." He is still in shock, emotionally closed to everyone. Then, pressing the bills from a tip into a mug by the cash register, his automatic gesture brings the memory of the rape flooding back: "From the floor behind him, far across the room, he felt her pain and terror and grief, then her curse upon him." The reader—and he—is finally allowed to enter into Hayes's feelings, and the experience is overwhelming: "The curse moved into his back and spread down and up his spine, into his stomach and legs and arms and shoulders until he quivered with it. He wished he were alone so he could kneel to receive it."

Questions for Discussion

1. Dubus has said that "The Curse" was the first story he completed after a serious accident. He wrote it in bed and "even physically it was difficult to write. I'd had eleven operations [Dubus's left leg was amputated when he was hit by a car after he'd stopped to help a woman in an accident] and my right leg was in a cast. . . . When I wrote the last word I began to weep. [My four-year-old daughter] looked at me. I told her I was crying because I was happy, because I had written a story and she said: 'This is the greatest day of my life. Daddy wrote a story.'" "The Curse" imparts deep physical and emotional suffering. Discuss the details of characterization and pacing that elicit this response.
2. Is Mitchell Hayes guilty of anything? Explain.
3. What part does Reggie play in the story?

Topics for Writing

CRITICAL ESSAYS

1. Helplessness in Dubus's "The Curse" and Frank O'Connor's "Guests of the Nation."
2. Psychological and physical brutality in "The Curse."

EXERCISE FOR READING

1. Write your responses to each sentence of the final paragraph of "The Curse" as you read it. What emotional associations do you have with the words Dubus chooses? How are you made aware of a religious connotation to what he is describing?

Suggested Reading

Kennedy, Thomas E. *Andre Dubus*, Twayne's Studies in Short Fiction 1, Boston: Twayne, 1988.

RALPH ELLISON

Battle Royal (p. 404)

In the headnote to his comments on "Battle Royal" reprinted in Part Two (p. 1435), Ellison is quoted expounding on the importance of "converting experience into symbolic action" in fiction. One of the major triumphs of "Battle Royal" (and of *Invisible Man* as a whole) is Ellison's success in the realistic rendering of experiences that are in themselves so obviously significant of larger social, psychological, and moral truths that explication is unnecessary. From the small American flag tattooed on the nude dancer's belly to the "rope of bloody saliva forming a shape like an undiscovered continent" that the narrator drools on his new briefcase, Ellison's account of the festivities at the men's smoker effectively symbolizes the condition of blacks in America while remaining thoroughly persuasive in its verisimilitude. Both the broader structure of the evening and the finer details of narration and description carry the force of Ellison's theme. The young blacks are tortured first by having the most forbidden of America's riches dangled before them, then by being put through their paces in a melee in which their only victims are their fellows and the whites look on with glee, and finally by being debased into groveling for money (some of it counterfeit) on a rug whose electrification underlines their own powerlessness. In one brief passage, the nightmare of such an existence appears in a strange subaqueous vision of primitive life: "The boys groped about like blind, cautious crabs crouching to protect their mid-sections, their heads pulled in short against their shoulders, their arms stretched nervously before them, with their fists testing the smoke-filled air like the knobbed feelers of hypersensitive snails."

Because his actual experience forms itself into such revealing images, the narrator's dream of his grandfather seems all the more credible as a statement of his position. "Keep this Nigger-Boy Running," he dreams the message of his briefcase says — not far from "You've got to know your place at all times." The narrator's grandfather knew his place and played his role, but he never believed a word of it. It is this assurance of an inner being quite different from the face he turned toward the world that makes him so troubling to his descendants. In his effort to please the white folks and in so doing to get ahead, the narrator seeks alliance rather than secret enmity with his antagonists. As a result he subjects himself to the trickery and delusions the white community chooses to impose on him. Dependent for his sense of himself on his ability to guess what they want him to do, the narrator finds himself groping in a fog deeper than the swirls of cigar smoke that hang over the scene of the battle royal. When the smoke clears and the blindfold comes off, he will recognize, as he puts it at the start, that he is invisible to the whites and may therefore discover his own identity within himself.

The first episode of a long novel does not accomplish the narrator's enlightenment, but it constitutes his initiation into the realities of the world he must eventually come to understand. Ellison says (in the Commentary in Part Two, p. 1435) that the battle royal "is a ritual in preservation of caste lines, a keeping of taboo to appease the gods and ward off bad luck," and that "it is also the initiation ritual to which all greenhorns are subjected." This rite of initiation bears a revealing relation to the primitive initiation ceremonies known to anthropologists. The battle royal, for example, separates the boys from their families, challenges them to prove their valor, and subjects them to instruction by the tribal elders in a sort of men's house. The boys are stripped and introduced to sexual mysteries. But the hazing of women that is a frequent feature of such initiations is not carried on here by the boys but by the gross elders, whose savagery is barely under control; the ritual ends not with the entry of the initiates into the larger community but with their pointed exclusion; and the sacred lore embodied in the narrator's recital of his graduation speech makes explicit the contradictions inherent in the society it describes. To cast down his bucket where he is forces him to swallow his own blood. The narrator is delighted with the scholarship to "the state college for Negroes" that he wins by toeing the line and knowing his place, and he does not object that the "gold" coins he groveled for are fraudulent. His education in the meaning of his grandfather's troubling injunctions will continue, but the reader has already seen enough to recognize their validity.

Questions for Discussion

1. In the opening paragraph the narrator says, "I was naïve." In what ways is his naiveté revealed in the story that follows?
2. Why does the narrator feel guilty when praised?
3. What is the message to the narrator behind the suggestion "that since I was to be there anyway I might as well take part in the battle royal"? Explain his hesitation. What is the most important part of the evening for the whites?
4. Who is present at the smoker? Discuss the role of the school superintendent.
5. What techniques does Ellison use to convey to the reader the impact that seeing the stripper has on the boys?
6. What does the stripper have in common with the boys? Why are both a stripper and a battle royal part of the evening's entertainment?
7. During the chaos of the battle, the narrator worries about how his speech will be received. Is that absurd or understandable?
8. Does the deathbed advice of the narrator's grandfather offer a way to handle the battle royal?
9. Why does Tatlock refuse to take a dive?
10. Explain the narrator's first reaction to seeing the "small square rug." In what sense is his instinct correct?
11. What is the meaning of the electric rug to the whites? What do they wish it to demonstrate to the blacks?
12. Explain Mr. Colcord's reaction when the narrator tries to topple him onto the rug.
13. Analyze the narrator's speech. What is the implication of his having to deliver it while swallowing his own blood?

14. Why is the school superintendent confident that the narrator will "lead his people in the proper paths"?
15. Why does the narrator stand in front of his grandfather's picture holding his briefcase? Who gets the better of this confrontation?

Topics for Writing

CRITICAL ESSAYS

1. Seeing and understanding in "Battle Royal."
2. Sex, violence, and power in Ellison's "Battle Royal" and Dubus's "The Curse."
3. The battle royal and black experience in America.
4. The "permanent interest" of "Battle Royal." (See Ellison's Commentary in Part Two, p. 1435).
5. The blonde, the gold coins, and the calfskin briefcase in "Battle Royal."

EXERCISE FOR READING

1. Select a passage of twenty lines or less from this story for detailed explication. Relate as many of its images as possible to others in the story and to the general ideas that the story develops. To what extent does the passage you chose reflect the meaning of the story as a whole?

RELATED SUBJECTS

1. Recall an experience in which you were humiliated or embarrassed. What motives of your own and of those before whom you were embarrassed put you in such a position? Narrate the incident so these underlying purposes become evident to the reader.
2. Write a description of a game or ceremony with which you are familiar. What set of principles or relationships (not necessarily malign) does it express?

Related Commentary from Part Two

Ralph Ellison, The Influence of Folklore on "Battle Royal," p. 1435.

Suggested Readings

Blake, Susan L. "Ritual and Rationalization: Black Folklore in the Works of Ralph Ellison." *PMLA* 94 (1979): 121–26. esp. 122–23.

Horowitz, Ellin. "The Rebirth of the Artist." *Twentieth-Century Interpretations of "Invisible Man."* Ed. John M. Reilly. Englewood Cliffs, NJ: Prentice, 1970. 80–88, esp. 81. (Originally published in 1964.)

O'Meally, Robert G. *The Craft of Ralph Ellison.* Cambridge: Harvard UP, 1980. 12–14.

Vogler, Thomas A. *"Invisible Man:* Somebody's Protest Novel." *Ralph Ellison: A Collection of Critical Essays.* Ed. John Hersey. Englewood Cliffs, NJ: Prentice, 1974. 127–50, esp. 143–44.

LOUISE ERDRICH

The Red Convertible (p. 417)

The story takes place in 1974, when Henry Junior comes back to the Chippewa Indian reservation after more than three years as a soldier in Vietnam. He is mentally disturbed by his experiences in the war, and, as his brother Lyman (who narrates the story) says laconically, "the change was no good."

Erdrich has structured her story in a traditional manner. It is narrated in the first person by Lyman, who uses the past tense to describe the finality of what happened to his brother and the red Oldsmobile convertible they once shared. The plot moves conventionally, after a lengthy introduction giving the background of the two brothers and their pleasure in the car. They are Indians who work hard for what they earn, but they also enjoy their money. As Lyman says, "We went places in that car, me and Henry." An atmosphere of innocence pervades this part of the story. They enjoy sightseeing along the western highways, going when and where they please, spending an entire summer in Alaska after they drive a female hitchhiker with long, beautiful hair home.

The story moves forward chronologically (although it is told as a flashback after the opening frame of four paragraphs), organized in sections usually several paragraphs long. Its structure is as loose and comfortable as the brothers' relationship. Then, midway, the story darkens when Henry goes off to Vietnam. For three sections, Lyman describes Henry's disorientation after the war. Then Henry fixes the convertible, the boys get back behind the wheel, and it seems briefly as if the good times are again starting to roll. But Henry feels internal turmoil similar to that of the flooded river they park alongside. The story reaches its climax when Henry suddenly goes wild after drinking several beers, deteriorating into what he calls a "crazy Indian." Lyman stares after him as he jumps into the river, shouting, "Got to cool me off!" His last words are quieter, "My boots are filling," and then he is gone.

The last paragraph of the story is its final section, Lyman describing how he drove the car into the river after he couldn't rescue Henry. It has gotten dark, and he is left alone with the sound of the rush of the water "going and running and running." This brings the story full circle, back to the beginning, where Lyman told us that now he "walks everywhere he goes." His grief for his brother is as understated as the rest of his personality. Erdrich has invented a natural storyteller in Lyman. We feel his emotional loss as if it were our own.

Questions for Discussion

1. In the opening paragraph, Lyman says that he and Henry owned the red convertible "together until his boots filled with water on a windy night and he bought out my share." When does the meaning of this sentence become clear to you? What is the effect of putting this sentence in the first paragraph?

2. Also in the opening paragraph, Erdrich writes: "his youngest brother Lyman (that's myself), Lyman walks everywhere he goes." If Lyman is narrating this story, why does he name himself? Does speaking of himself in the third person create any particular effect?

3. What is the function of the third section of the story? Why does the narrator tell us about their wandering, about meeting Susy? What associations does the red convertible carry?

4. Watching Henry watching television, Lyman says, "He sat in his chair gripping the armrests with all his might, as if the chair itself was moving at a high speed and if he let go at all he would rocket forward and maybe crash right through the set." How would you describe the diction in this sentence? What effect does the sentence's length — and its syntax — create? What is the tone? What does this line, and the paragraphs around it, tell you about Lyman's reaction to Henry's change?

5. Where do Lyman and Henry speak directly to each other in this story? Where do they speak indirectly? How do they communicate without speech? Describe how Erdrich presents the moments of emotion in this story.

6. Why is Lyman upset by the picture of himself and his brother? When does the picture begin to bother him? Do we know if it's before or after Henry's death? Does it make a difference to our interpretation of the story? What burden of memory does this picture carry?

7. Consider the tone of the final paragraph, in which Lyman is describing how he felt when he gave his car to his dead brother. Look at the diction surrounding the red convertible here: It plows into the water; the headlights "reach in . . . go down, searching"; they are "still lighted. . . ." What attribute does the diction give the car? How is the car different now from the way it's been in the rest of the story? Does this transformation of the car invoke a sense of closure in the story?

8. The closing sentence says "And then there is only the water, the sound of it going and running and going and running and running." How does this statement comment on the relationship between the two brothers?

Topics for Writing

CRITICAL ESSAYS

1. Brotherhood in "The Red Convertible."
2. Lyman's initiation into maturity and that of Julian in O'Connor's "Everything That Rises Must Converge."
3. Erdrich's use of setting to determine tone.

RELATED SUBJECT

1. Rewrite the story from the third person point of view.

Suggested Readings

Erdrich, Louise. "Excellence Has Always Made Me Fill with Fright When It Is Demanded by Other People, but Fills Me with Pleasure When I Am Left to Practice It Alone." *Ms.* 13 (1985): 84.

——"Where I Ought to Be: A Writer's Sense of Place." *New York Times Book Review* 28 July 1985: 1+.

Howard, J. "Louise Erdrich." *Life* 8 (1985): 27+.

WILLIAM FAULKNER

A Rose for Emily (p. 426)

Few stories, surely, differ more on a second reading than does "A Rose for Emily," which yields to the initiate some detail or circumstance anticipating the ending in nearly every paragraph. But Faulkner sets the pieces of his puzzle in place so coolly that the first-time reader hardly suspects them to fit together into a picture at all, until the curtain is finally swept aside and the shocking secret of Miss Emily's upstairs room is revealed. Faulkner makes it easy to write off the episodes of the smell, Miss Emily's denial of her father's death, the arsenic, and the aborted wedding (note the shuffled chronology) as the simple eccentricities of a pathetic old maid, to be pitied and indulged. The impact of the final scene drives home the realization that the passions of a former generation and its experience of life are no less real or profound for all their being in the past — whether we view them through the haze of sentimental nostalgia, as the Confederate veterans near the end of the story do, or place them at an aesthetic distance, as the townspeople do in the romantic tableau imagined in section II.

In his interviews with students at the University of Virginia (excerpted in Part Two, p. 1439), Faulkner stressed Miss Emily's being "kept down" by her father as an important factor in driving her to violate the code of her society by taking a lover, and he expressed a deep human sympathy for her long expiation for that sin. In the narrative consciousness of the story, however — the impersonal "we" that speaks for the communal mind of Jefferson — Miss Emily Grierson is a town relic, a monument to the local past to be shown to strangers, like the graves of the men slain at the battle of Jefferson or the big houses on what long ago, before they put the sidewalks in, was the "most select street." Because all relics are to a degree symbolic, one should not hesitate to take up the challenge found in Faulkner's ambiguous claim quoted in the headnote, that "the writer is too busy . . . to have time to be conscious of all the symbolism that he may put into what he does or what people may read into it." Miss Emily, for example, may be understood to express the part of southern culture that is paralyzed in the present by its inability to let go of the past, even though that past is as dead as Homer Barron, and even though its reality differed from the treasured memory as greatly as the Yankee paving contractor — "not a marrying man" — differs from the husband of Miss Emily's desperate longings. Other details in Faulkner's economical narration fit this reading: the prominence of Miss Emily's iconic portrait of her father; her refusal to acknowledge changing laws and customs; her insistence that the privilege of paying no taxes, bestowed on her by the chivalrous Colonel Sartoris, is an inalienable right; her dependence on the labors of her Negro servant, whose patient silence renders him an accomplice in her strange crime; and, not least, her relationship of mutual exploitation with Homer, the representative of the North — a relationship that ends in a morbid and grotesque parody of marriage. In this context, the smell of death that reeks from Miss Emily's house tells how the story judges what she stands for, and the dust that falls on everything brings the welcome promise of relief.

But Faulkner will not let it lie. Seen for what she is, neither romanticized nor trivialized, Miss Emily has a forthright dignity and a singleness of purpose that contrast sharply with those representatives of propriety and progress who sneak around her foundation in the dark spreading lime or knock on her door in the ineffectual effort to collect her taxes. And as the speechless townsfolk tiptoe aghast about her bridal chamber, it is Miss Emily's iron will, speaking through the strand of iron-gray hair that lies where she has lain, that has the final word.

Questions for Discussion

1. The story begins and ends with Miss Emily's funeral. Trace the chronology of the intervening sections.
2. Emily is called "a fallen monument" and "a tradition." Explain.
3. Why does the narrator label Miss Emily's house "an eyesore among eyesores"?
4. Define the opposing forces in the confrontation that occupies most of section I. How does Miss Emily "vanquish them"?
5. Discuss the transition between sections I and II. In what ways are the two episodes parallel?
6. Apart from her black servant, Miss Emily has three men in her life. What similarities are there in her attitudes toward them?
7. Why is Homer Barron considered an inappropriate companion for Miss Emily?
8. Consider Faulkner's introduction of the rat poison into the story in section III. What is the narrator's avowed reason for bringing it up?
9. At the beginning of section IV, the townspeople think Emily will commit suicide, and they think "it would be the best thing." Why? What is the basis of their error regarding her intentions?
10. Why do you think Miss Emily gets fat and develops gray hair when she does?
11. Why does Miss Emily's servant disappear after her death?
12. Describe Miss Emily's funeral before the upstairs room is opened. In what way does that scene serve as a foil to set off what follows?
13. Discuss the role of dust in the last few paragraphs of the story.
14. Why does Faulkner end the story with "a long strand of iron-gray hair"?

Topics for Writing

CRITICAL ESSAYS

1. Various attitudes toward the past in "A Rose for Emily."
2. The meaning of time and Faulkner's handling of chronology in "A Rose for Emily."
3. Emily Grierson — criminal, lunatic, or heroine?
4. The title of "A Rose for Emily."
5. "A Rose for Emily" and the history of the South.
6. The narrator of "A Rose for Emily."

EXERCISE FOR READING

1. Were you surprised by the story's ending? On a second reading, mark all the passages that foreshadow it.

RELATED SUBJECT

1. Imitate Faulkner by telling the events that lead up to a climax out of chronological order. What new effects do you find it possible to achieve? What problems in continuity do you encounter?

Related Commentary from Part Two

William Faulkner, The Meaning of "A Rose for Emily," p. 1439.

Suggested Readings

Hall, Donald. *To Read Literature: Fiction, Poetry, Drama.* New York: Holt, 1981. 10–16.

Heller, Terry. "The Telltale Hair: A Critical Study of William Faulkner's 'A Rose for Emily.'" *Arizona Quarterly* 28 (1972): 301–18.

Howe, Irving. *William Faulkner: A Critical Study.* 2nd ed. New York: Vintage, 1962. 265.

Leary, Lewis. *William Faulkner of Yoknapatawpha County.* Twentieth-Century American Writers. New York: Crowell, 1973. 136.

WILLIAM FAULKNER

Spotted Horses (p. 433)

Eudora Welty tells us that a sense of place is the key to understanding Faulkner's humor in this story: "It is the most thorough and faithful picture of a Mississippi crossroads hamlet that you could ever hope to see. True in spirit, it is also true to everyday fact." Students unfamiliar with the dialect Faulkner uses in his narrator's account of how the spotted horses were brought from Texas to be sold in the Mississippi backwoods hamlet might find an entrance into the story by listing the physical details in the description of place or by attempting an analysis of what Welty refers to as the "social fact" that dominates the human landscape: the pecking order of the characters, beginning with the humble Mrs. Armstid and running all the way to the invincible, incorrigible opportunist Flem Snopes.

In Welty's opinion, "Faulkner had no malice, only compassion" for the folly of his fellow Mississippians. His narrator is an innocent bystander, whose voice controls the tone of the story and insists on its good-natured ignorance much as Sherwood Anderson's narrator does in "I'm a Fool." We forgive the narrator's naiveté because he's such a virtuosic storyteller, creative in his choice of details, such as his comparisons in the first paragraph of one of the wild horses let loose on the road to a billboard and a hawk.

Feminist readers might take exception to Faulkner's treatment of Mrs. Armstid. Her husband is punished for his brutality toward her by his broken leg, set by the rural practitioner Uncle Billy without the benefit of "this here chloryfoam." Her meekness in accepting the nickel bag of candy from Flem Snopes is so remarkable that she appears as a saint in her apron and tennis shoes, and we recall that according to Scripture (if not Faulkner), the meek will inherit the Earth.

Questions for Discussion

1. "A Rose for Emily" and "Spotted Horses" describe a spectrum of town and country life in Faulkner's imaginary Yoknapatawpha County. In what ways are these depictions of town and country life different? Do you see any similarities?
2. How would a feminist critic interpret Faulkner's portrayal of women in "Spotted Horses"? Are Mrs. Armstid and Mrs. Littlejohn stereotypes, or do they come alive on the page?
3. Analyze the use of hyperbole for humorous effect in the story.
4. What expressions in the narrative are dialect? Can you define the non-standard words, like "chaps" (children)?

Topic for Writing

1. Faulkner implies that the spotted horses—half-breeds—have affinities to the prolific Snopes family. Trace the similarities between the horses and the Snopeses. Analyze the implications of what Faulkner is saying about society in post-Reconstruction Mississippi.

Related Commentary from Part Two

Eudora Welty, The Sense of Place in Faulkner's "Spotted Horses," p. 1536.

F. SCOTT FITZGERALD

Babylon Revisited (p. 449)

"Babylon Revisited" develops a paradox about the past: It is irretrievably lost, but it controls the present inescapably. Charlie Wales revisits the scenes of "the big party" carried on by stock-market rich Americans in Paris during the 1920s — a party at which he was one of the chief celebrants — and shakes his head over how much things have changed. His memories of those times come into focus only gradually, and as they do his nostalgia modulates to disgust. His guilt-ridden desire to repudiate his past behavior reaches a peak *not* when his negotiations to get his daughter back remind him that he brought on his wife's pneumonia by locking her out in the snow, but only when Lorraine's *pneumatique* reminds him that for several years his life was given over to trivial foolishness. For a man trying to reestablish himself as a loving and responsible father, the memory of harming his wife in wild anger at her flirtation with "young Webb" is less embarrassing than the memory of riding a stolen tricycle all over the Étoile with another man's wife.

The problem for Charlie Wales is that his past — for the moment embodied in the pathetic relics Duncan and Lorraine — clings to him despite his efforts to repudiate it. The reader (like Marion) is inclined to fear that Charlie might return to his past ways, but Charlie is not tempted by Lorraine or by the lure of alcohol. His lesson has been learned, but that does not prevent the past from destroying his plans for the future. Or perhaps, as David Toor argues, it is Charlie who clings to the past; perhaps he ambivalently punishes himself out of a guilt he refuses to acknowledge, as when he sabotages his campaign to get Honoria from the Peterses by leaving their address for Duncan with the bartender at the Ritz. As the story ends, history is repeating itself. Just as Charlie caused Helen's sickness, the inopportune arrival of his old friends has sickened Marion. As a result he loses Honoria, at least for six months of her fast-waning and irretrievable childhood — just as he has lost Helen for good.

Questions for Discussion

1. Why does Fitzgerald begin the story with what seems to be the end of a conversation that then begins when Charlie walks into the bar in the next paragraph?
2. As Charlie rides through Paris on his way to see his daughter, he thinks, "I spoiled this city for myself." What reason might Fitzgerald have for treating this subject so mildly and in such vague terms here?
3. Characterize the Peters family. To what extent are we to approve of their attitudes?
4. What is the effect of Charlie's repeatedly taking "only one drink every afternoon"? Does the reader expect him to regress into alcohol abuse?
5. What does Charlie's brief encounter with the woman in the *brasserie* contribute to the story?
6. Why does Charlie identify the fine fall day as "football weather"?
7. Discuss the impact of the appearance of Duncan and Lorraine after Charlie's lunch with Honoria.
8. Why is Marion reluctant to release Honoria to her father? Why is Charlie able to win her consent, temporarily?
9. When Marion suggests that Charlie may have caused Helen's death, "an electric current of agony surged through him," but Lincoln says, "I never thought you were responsible for that." Was he? What does Charlie himself think? Explain his reaction.
10. Explain Charlie's reaction to Lorraine's *pneumatique*. Why does he ignore it? Why does that tactic fail?
11. Why does Fitzgerald introduce the arrival of Duncan and Lorraine precisely where he does, and in the way he does?
12. What does Paul mean when he supposes that Charlie "lost everything [he] wanted in the boom" by "selling short"? What does Charlie mean when he replies, "Something like that"?
13. Explain the irony of Charlie's present financial success, apparently unique among his old friends.
14. What does the title mean?

Topics for Writing

CRITICAL ESSAYS

1. Fitzgerald's use of recurring motifs and foreshadowing in "Babylon Revisited."
2. Charlie Wales — a study of remorse.
3. Techniques of characterization in "Babylon Revisited" — the secondary characters.
4. Charlie's daughter's name as the key to his underlying motives.

EXERCISE FOR READING

1. After reading each of the five sections of the story, write a paragraph giving your assessment of Charlie Wales and your prediction of what will happen to him. Is there consistency, or a progression, in your judgments?

Suggested Readings

Gallo, Rose Adrienne. *F. Scott Fitzgerald*. Modern Literature Monographs. New York: Ungar, 1978. 101–05.

Gross, Seymour. "Fitzgerald's 'Babylon Revisited.' " *College English* 25 (1963): 128–35.

Male, Roy R. " 'Babylon Revisited': The Story of the Exile's Return." *Studies in Short Fiction* 2 (1965): 270–77.

Toor, David. "Guilt and Retribution in 'Babylon Revisited.' " *Fitzgerald/Hemingway Annual 1973*. Ed. Matthew J. Bruccoli and C. E. Frazer Clark, Jr. Washington, DC: Microcard Eds., 1974. 155–64.

GUSTAVE FLAUBERT

A Simple Heart (p. 467)

Students may find Flaubert's long narrative boring and pointless, its central character too narrow and insignificant for such extended treatment, and its plot lacking the qualities of conflict, suspense, and climax customary in well-structured fiction. Rather than assuring them of the work's recognized perfection or quoting Ezra Pound's judgment that "A Simple Heart" embodies "all that anyone knows about writing," you might try placing the work in contexts that will make it more interesting and accessible.

That the tale is an autobiographically intimate recollection of the people and places of Flaubert's childhood, some of them revisited while it was being written, underlines the degree to which his objective narration controls strong personal feelings. Add that Félicité is run down by the mail coach at precisely the same spot on the road where Flaubert suffered the first onset of the epilepsy that led him to choose a life of retirement and dedicated labor at his art — a life in many ways comparable to Félicité's own obscure and laborious existence — and students may find themselves ready to give the story a second look.

Flaubert wrote "A Simple Heart" during the last years of his life as one of three interrelated tales, the *Trois Contes*, on religious themes. By this time Flaubert had suffered the humiliation of seeing Normandy and his own home occupied by the invading Prussians; he had lost most of his money through misguided generosity to the husband of an ungrateful niece; and he had watched his friends die off. One of them was the novelist George Sand, for whom he was writing "A Simple Heart" in response to her chiding him for insensitivity in his detached style of fiction. The *Trois Contes* each in a different way, embody Flaubert's reaction to these losses. Each subjects pride and worldliness to a devastating confrontation with humility and self-abnegation.

The genre of "A Simple Heart" is the saint's life; its deceptively simple chronological structure traces the stages by which the protagonist throws off selfishness and worldly desires and, in the process, attains the spiritual purity requisite for miracles, martyrdom, and assumption into bliss. With the loss of Théodore, Félicité leaves ordinary erotic love behind her and enters upon a lifelong devotion to selfless labor. She does this not as a self-conscious and would-be heroic rejection of the world but only because she knows of nothing else to do. The love she feels subsequently, however, is as selfless as her labor. It goes virtually unrewarded by Paul, Virginie, and Victor, but it is in a sense its own reward, for it enables Félicité to experience a vicarious life of the imagination seemingly more real than her own, as in Virginie's first communion or Victor's trip to Havana. As the world relentlessly strips her of each beloved person and finally even of the very senses by which to apprehend them, Félicité can resort to the power of her imagination, unrestrained by any conventional critical intellect. Imagination blooming into faith allows her not only to find the answer to her loneliness in a parrot but also to endow the dead, stuffed bird with spiritual life and to experience her final beatific vision of the parrotlike Holy Ghost spreading over her from heaven.

Flaubert worried that his tale would seem ironic and Félicité's confusion of the parrot Loulou with the deity absurd. On the contrary, he insisted, "it is in no way ironic, as you may suppose, but . . . very serious and very sad" (quoted by Stratton Buck, p. 105). The question of tone should lead a class discussion straight to the fundamental issues raised by the story. Félicité's utter lack of pretension, as Jonathan Culler argues, defeats the impulse toward irony because it allows nothing for irony to deflate, while Flaubert, by avoiding commentary and committing himself to the pure and precise rendering of the facts of the case, presents the reader with the necessity, in order to give meaning to Félicité's life, of imagining a sacred order in which her vision of the parrot is not a mockery but a divine blessing and a fit reward.

Questions for Discussion

1. One critic (Peter Cortland) remarks that in a way Félicité's life is "entirely covered" by Flaubert's opening sentence. How is that so? In what sense does that sentence miss everything?
2. Why does Flaubert introduce his second section by defeating any excitement or special interest the reader might feel about Félicité's affair with Théodore?
3. What is the effect of Flaubert's detailed descriptions of the Norman countryside as well as the other settings and circumstances of the story?

4. Explain the purpose of Félicité's musings about the Holy Ghost in the third section.
5. Why is Virginie's first communion more meaningful to Félicité than her own reception of the sacrament?
6. Compare the reactions of Félicité and Mme Aubain to the death of Virginie. What do the differences reveal about their characters?
7. What is the effect on the reader's attitude toward Félicité of the passage that begins when she is whipped by the coachman?
8. Why does Flaubert have Mère Simon tell herself, as she sponges the sweat from the dying Félicité's temples, "that one day she would have to go the same way"?
9. *Félicité* means happiness, good fortune, or bliss. Is the name of Flaubert's heroine ironic?

Topics for Writing

CRITICAL ESSAYS

1. The episode of Loulou's disappearance and return, and the consequences of Félicité's search for him as an epitome of the story.
2. The circumstances of Félicité's death as a key to Flaubert's theme.
3. The function of the brief, one-sentence paragraphs that punctuate the text at certain points.

EXERCISE FOR READING

1. Review the story and make a list of everything Félicité loses. Is it possible to make a corresponding list of things she gains?

RELATED SUBJECTS

1. Study Flaubert's description of Mme Aubain's house in the first section and write a similar description of a house you know.
2. Write an obituary for Félicité such as might have been published in the Pont-l'Évêque newspaper. Are you satisfied with the result?

Related Commentary from Part Two

Roland Barthes, A Structuralist View of the Sentences of Flaubert, p. 1405.

Suggested Readings

Buck, Stratton. *Gustave Flaubert*. Twayne's World Authors Series 3. New York: Twayne, 1966. Esp. 103–08.

Cortland, Peter. *A Reader's Guide to Flaubert*. New York: Helios, 1968. 127–46

Cross, Richard K. *Flaubert and Joyce: The Rite of Fiction*. Princeton: Princeton UP, 1971. 17–25.

Culler, Jonathan. *Flaubert: The Uses of Uncertainty*. Ithaca: Cornell UP, 1974. Esp. 11–19, 208–11.

MARY E. WILKINS FREEMAN

The Revolt of "Mother" (p. 494)

In "The Revolt of 'Mother,'" Freeman draws a sharp but subtle portrait of a woman character whom most students will find appealing, although she acts in a devious, underhanded way to assert her will over her husband. Freeman is careful to enlist our sympathies for the wife in the beginning of the story, yet she is presented in humorous terms at the end to minimize the implications of her domestic rebellion. A close reading of the opening paragraphs will reveal the skillful ways Freeman makes Mrs. Penn a sympathetic character in the conflict with her husband.

The story opens with an exchange of dialogue between the husband and wife. Really, though, *dialogue* is not quite the term, since Mr. Penn tries to avoid his wife's direct question: "What are them men diggin' over there in the field for?" He is silent until his wife repeats the question. Then he tells her to go back in the house and mind her own business. Implacable, she stands her ground.

The dialect used in the conversational exchange is colloquial, and Freeman takes pains to make us *hear* the characters. The husband "ran his words together, and his speech was almost as inarticulate as a growl." Freeman's language as narrator is more sophisticated than her fictional characters' speech. Reading the story, we accept her view of the situation as an informed bystander, even if we suspect that she is not an impartial one.

The characters in these opening paragraphs are defined by what they do as well as what they say and how they say it. The husband's face drops at his wife's question, and he jerks the collar roughly over his bay mare and slaps on the saddle. Mrs. Penn is less physically aggressive than her husband, but her will is at least as strong as his. Freeman takes pleasure in describing her inner strength as she waits for her husband to answer her. "Her eyes, fixed upon the old man, looked as if the meekness had been the result of her own will, never of the will of another." She is like John's sister in Gilman's "The Yellow Wallpaper," a conventional woman who is (as Gilman wrote) a "perfect and enthusiastic housekeeper, and hopes for no better profession."

"The Revolt of 'Mother'" is a realistic local-color story, but the New England landscape and lives depicted in it have symbolic overtones too. It is spring, a time of growth and renewal. Mrs. Penn's will is like the dandelions in the vivid green grass, determined to survive even if unencouraged by her husband. Mr. Penn sees his wife in symbolic terms: "She looked as immovable to him as one of the rocks in his pasture-land, bound to the earth with generations of blackberry vines." In due time, Mrs. Penn, a "perfect and enthusiastic housekeeper," will be preserving these blackberries and baking her family delicious berry pies. She is no infertile rocklike earth goddess or unconventional rebel girl. She is the living spirit of the domestic hearth, and she deserves a home larger than the "infinitesimal" one her husband has provided for her, "scarcely as commodious for people as the little boxes under the barn eaves were for doves."

Mrs. Penn's actions at the end of the story continue on the larger-than-life level introduced so carefully with the symbolism in these early paragraphs, only now Freeman shifts her tone to suggest burlesque. Mother's feat moving into the new barn "was equal in its way to Wolfe's storming of the Heights of Abraham," an allusion to the war between the English and the French in Quebec, when the British general James Wolfe led his troops to victory on the Plains of Abraham. Mrs. Penn's action has "a certain uncanny and superhuman quality" when she takes over her husband's new barn. Its threshold "might have been Plymouth Rock from her bearing." Freeman meant her readers to find this symbolism and hyperbole funny, but today's readers (even if they aren't feminists) may see the revolt of "mother" in a different light. Was Freeman too sympathetic toward her heroine in the early pages of the story or too heavy-handed in the later ones? Don't let students miss the ambivalence in the treatment of Mrs. Penn.

Questions for Discussion

1. What does the opening scene of this short story establish about the character of Sarah Penn? How does her husband, Adoniram, view her? Is this view similar to or different from the narrator's presentation of her?
2. How would you describe Adoniram Penn? Based on the opening scene of the story, what would you say is the nature of the relationship between the Penns?
3. Are the characters defined only by their conversations, or by their actions as well? Give examples.
4. Note the colloquial dialect used by Sarah and Adoniram Penn. How does this differ from that used by the narrator of the story? What devices does Freeman employ to make us "hear" the conversation of the characters?
5. What is the point of view of this story? In your opinion, can we trust the judgment of the narrator? Why or why not? How impartial do you feel the narrator is?
6. What is the setting of the story? How is it one of the main sources of conflict?
7. Note the fact that only the narrator refers to Sarah and Adoniram by name. Within the story itself, these characters are referred to, and refer to each other, only as "mother" and "father." To what extent do the characters fulfill these symbolic roles? Has Freeman given them any individuality outside these roles?
8. What is the function of Sammy and Nanny? Are they necessary to the story?
9. Toward the end of the story, Sarah Penn becomes larger than life and almost superhuman. Were does this shift of treatment take place? How does Freeman accomplish it? What problems does this ambivalent treatment of Sarah Penn create in the story?
10. Freeman's treatment of Adoniram Penn also changes. How would you describe this shift, and what does it contribute to your understanding of Adoniram as an individual?
11. What significance would you attach to Freeman's putting the word "mother" in quotation marks in the title of the story?

Topics for Writing

CRITICAL ESSAYS

1. The dilemma of individuality versus societal expectations and roles as shown in the characters of the story.

2. The relationship of children to parents and the tendency of children to emulate their parents as an element in "The Revolt of 'Mother.' "
3. The importance of setting to the conflict of the story.

EXERCISE FOR READING

1. State the themes of Freeman's story as they relate to philosophy and social criticism.

RELATED SUBJECT

1. Try to rewrite the story from the point of view of Adoniram Penn. From the point of view of Nanny or Sammy.

Suggested Readings

Gallagher, Edward J. "Freeman's 'The Revolt of "Mother." ' " *Explicator* 27 (1969): Item 48.

McElrath, J. R., Jr. "Artistry of Mary E. Wilkins Freeman's 'The Revolt.' " *Studies in Short Fiction* 17 (1980): 255–61.

Pryse, M. "An Uncloistered New England Nun." *Studies in Short Fiction* 20 (1983): 289–95.

Toth, S. A. "Defiant Light: A Positive View of Mary Wilkins Freeman." *New England Quarterly* 46 (1973): 82–93.

CARLOS FUENTES

The Doll Queen *(p. 508)*

Fuentes's introductory paragraph sets the tone and mood of this narrative, foreshadowing the inexplicable tragedy that befalls the lively, beautiful seven-year-old girl befriended by the protagonist when he is a fourteen-year-old playing hooky from school. The title of the story is a paradox, suggesting the young girl's hold on the narrator's memory as the embodiment of carefree youth in contrast with the decadent effigy lying in state that he faces years later in her parents' house. "Why?" ask the imaginary children who hear such grotesque fairy tales in the narrator's introductory paragraph, but Fuentes does not attempt an answer.

Instead, his story is a retelling of a fairy tale as psychological thriller. The child Amilamia has left a white card on which she has drawn a map to her house, writing, "Amilamia will not forget her good friend—com see me here lik I draw it." Ironically, fifteen years must elapse before the narrator uses her map, and when he sees her on her doorstep, after confronting the two dragons who guard her (her parents), he is no Prince Charming and she is no Sleeping Beauty.

There are no awakening and no triumphant "And they lived happily ever after" ending in this postmodernist tale. Instead, the heroine is in a wheelchair with a "hump on her chest." She lights a cigarette, "staining the end with orange-painted lips" before telling him, "No, Carlos. Go away. Don't come back." This confrontation contrary to the narrator's fantasy of bewitching grace and beauty in the park fifteen years before is reminiscent of the scene near the end of Vladimir Nabokov's novel *Lolita* when the narrator sees the Lolita he loved as a pubescent girl changed into a grotesque, ordinary adult woman.

Fuentes uses a dense prose style here. We are reading "The Doll Queen" in translation and cannot generalize on the effect of the original Spanish, but the paragraphs create a world of darkness and obstruction in their piling up of detail of heavy, ponderous subordinate clauses. Each one has the effect of a labyrinth, slowing the reader down, contrasting with the lightness of the movement described. For example, Fuentes tells us, "I am running as I approach the one-story house. Rain is beginning to fall in large isolated drops that bring forth from the earth with magical immediacy an odor of damp benediction that seems to stir the humus and precipitate the fermentation of everything living with its roots in the dust." The three- and four-syllable words here have a heavy movement in English, in contrast to the narrator's action. It's as though Fate had reserved something very different for him something that he couldn't anticipate, and Fate has the upper hand, putting boulders in his path. He tells us that when they played in the park, he sensed that "Amilamia's seriousness, apparently, was a gift of nature, whereas her moments of spontaneity, by contrast, seemed artificial." Their enchanted hours together encapsulate a brief interlude, before the unpredictable and serious business of life caught up with them.

Questions for Discussion

1. How does the setting of the story contribute to the mood?
2. What instances of foreshadowing occur after the opening paragraph?
3. Why does Amilamia's mother allow the narrator access to the house when she knows she is lying about Señor Valdivia?
4. Why does the narrator present the "clues" of the comic book and the lipstick in the living room?
5. As the narrator proceeds methodically from room to room in Amilamia's house, how does the suspense mount? How does the introduction of the girl's father contribute to the story?
6. What was your reaction to the scene with the "Doll Queen" lying in her coffin?
7. Is the narrator also the author? Explain.

Topics for Writing

1. Compare and contrast this story with Edgar Allan Poe's horror stories in this anthology.
2. Analyze the theme of assault on the innocence of a young person in the stories by Julio Cortázar, Carlos Fuentes, and Nathaniel Hawthorne in this anthology.

Related Commentary from Part Two

Carlos Fuentes, International Writers and Their Novels, p. 1443.

Suggested Readings

Brody, Robert, and Charles Rossman, eds. *Carlos Fuentes: A Critical View.* Austin, U of Texas P, 1982.

Faris, Wendy B. *Carlos Fuentes.* New York: Ungar, 1983.

GABRIEL GARCÍA MÁRQUEZ

A Very Old Man with Enormous Wings (p. 521)

The word "allegories" in the headnote presents a challenge to readers of this story, and the inevitable failure of any simple scheme of interpretation to grasp fully the mystery at its heart, reflects García Márquez's central theme exactly. Like the crabs, which come into the human world from an alien realm, the "flesh-and-blood angel" constitutes an intrusion of something strange and unfathomable into the comfortable world of reality as we choose to define it. Everybody, from the "wise" woman next door to the pope, takes a turn at trying to find a slot in which to file the winged visitor, but no definition seems satisfactory, and even Pelayo and Elisenda, whom the angel's presence has made wealthy, spend their money on a house "with iron bars on the windows so that angels wouldn't get in." When at last the old man flies away, Elisenda feels relief, "because then he was no longer an annoyance in her life but an imaginary dot on the horizon of the sea."

In discussing how he receives artistic inspiration, García Márquez says, "There's nothing deliberate or predictable in all this, nor do I know when it's going to happen to me. I'm at the mercy of my imagination." Without intending to limit the story's implications, one might associate the angel with this sort of unpredictable intrusion of the visionary and wonderful into everyday life. As an old man with wings, the angel recalls the mythical symbol of the artist, Daedalus, except that his wings are "so natural on that completely human organism that [the doctor] couldn't understand why other men didn't have them too." Bogged down in the mud, the angel seems less an allusion to Daedalus's son, the overreacher Icarus, than a representation of the difficulty of the artistic imagination in sustaining its flight through the unpleasant circumstances of this "sad" world. True artists are often misunderstood, ill treated, and rejected in favor of more practical concerns or of the creators of ersatz works that flatter established prejudices. Just so, nobody can understand the angel's "hermetic" language, and when he performs his aggressively unpractical miracles, no one is delighted. Exploited by his keepers, to whom he brings vast wealth, the angel receives as royalties only his quarters in the chicken coop and the flat side of the broom when underfoot. Popular for a time as a sideshow attraction, the angel is soon passed over in favor of the horrible "woman who had been changed into a spider for having disobeyed her parents," a grotesque and slapdash creation of the lowest order of imaginative synthesis, whose "human truth" gratifies both sentimentality and narrow-mindedness. But the artistic imagination lives happily on eggplant mush, possesses a supernatural patience, and though functionally blind to the bumping posts of ordinary reality, ever again takes wing. The angel has, perhaps rightly, appeared to his human observers "a cataclysm in repose";

but near the end, as he sings his sea chanteys under the stars, he definitely comes to resemble "a hero taking his ease," preparing to navigate the high seas beyond the horizon.

Questions for Discussion

1. Why are there crabs in the house? Is it for the same reason the old man with enormous wings has fallen in the courtyard? What other associations does the story make between the old man and the crabs?
2. Pelayo first thinks the old man is a nightmare. What other attempts are made to put this prodigy into a familiar category?
3. How does the old man differ from our usual conceptions of angels? What is the essential difference?
4. Explain Father Gonzaga's approach to the angel. What implications — about the angel and about the church — may be derived from his failure to communicate with him effectively?
5. Comment on the angel's career as a sideshow freak. Who receives the benefit of his success? Why does he fall? Compare what he has to offer with what the spider-woman has. What reasons might people have to prefer the latter?
6. Why do you think the angel tolerates the child patiently?
7. What are the implications of the angel's examination by the doctor?
8. How do we feel as the angel finally flaps away at the end? Does Elisenda's response adequately express the reader's?

Topics for Writing

CRITICAL ESSAYS

1. The ordinary and the enormous in "A Very Old Man with Enormous Wings." (Consider the etymological meaning of "enormous.")
2. García Márquez's fallen angel — fairy tale, myth, or allegory?
3. Recharging the sense of wonder: how García Márquez makes the reader believe in his angel.
4. "A Very Old Man with Enormous Wings" and other presentations of the supernatural. (Hawthorne's, for example.)

EXERCISE FOR READING

1. Read the story aloud to a selected spectrum of people (at least three) of various ages and educational levels. Tabulate their responses and opinions, perhaps in an interview. Combining this evidence with your own response to the story, try to define the basis of its appeal.

RELATED SUBJECT

1. Select a supernatural being from a fairy tale or other familiar source (the cartoons involving talking animals that wear clothes and drive cars might be worth considering), and imagine the being as a physical reality in your own ordinary surroundings. Write a sketch about what happens.

Suggested Readings

McMurray, George R. *Gabriel García Márquez*. New York: Ungar, 1977. 116–19.
Morello Frosch, Marta. "The Common Wonders of García Márquez's Recent
Fiction." *Books Abroad* 47 (1973): 496–501.

CHARLOTTE PERKINS GILMAN

The Yellow Wallpaper (p. 528)

Gilman wrote "The Yellow Wallpaper" between 1890 and 1894, during
what she later recalled were the hardest years of her life. She had left her first
husband and child to live alone in California after a nervous breakdown, and
she was beginning to give lectures on freedom for women and socialism while
she kept a boardinghouse, taught school, and edited newspapers. During this
time, her husband married her best friend, to whom Gilman relinquished her
child. The emotional pressures and economic uncertainties under which Gilman
lived contributed to the desperate tone of this story.

Early readers of "The Yellow Wallpaper" compared it with the horror
stories of Edgar Allan Poe (William Dean Howells said it was a story to "freeze
our . . . blood" when he reprinted it in 1920 in *Great Modern American Stories*.
Like Poe's homicidal narrators, Gilman's heroine tells her story in a state of
neurotic compulsion. But she is no homicidal maniac. Unlike Poe, Gilman suggests
that a specific social malady has driven her heroine to the brink of madness:
the bondage of conventional marriage.

Her husband is her physician and keeper, the father of her beloved but
absent child, the money earner who pays the rent on the mansion where she
is held captive for her "own good." When she begs to get away, he replies
practically, "Our lease will be up in three weeks, and I can't see how to leave
before." Insisting that he knows what is best for her, he believes that the cure
for her mysterious "weakness" is total rest. The husband is supported in his view
by the opinion of the foremost medical authority on the treatment of mental
illness, Dr. S. Weir Mitchell, a name explicitly mentioned in the story. Gilman
had spent a month in Dr. Mitchell's sanitorium five years before. In her autobiography
she later reported that she almost lost her mind there and would often "crawl
into remote closets and under beds — to hide from the grinding pressure of that
profound distress."

Gilman transferred the memory of her physical debilitation and "absolute
incapacity" for normal (read "conventional") married life into her heroine's state
in "The Yellow Wallpaper." The story dramatizes Gilman's fear while living with
her first husband that marriage and motherhood might incapacitate her (as it
apparently had Gilman's mother) for what she called "work in the world." She
felt imprisoned within her marriage, a victim of her desire to please, trapped
by her wedding ring. Gilman left her husband, but in "The Yellow Wallpaper"
her heroine is sacrificed to the emotional turmoil she experiences.

As a symbolic projection of psychological stress, "The Yellow Wallpaper"
has resemblances to Kafka's "The Metamorphosis," although it is more specific

in its focus on social injustice to women. Like Gregor Samsa, Gilman's heroine is victimized by the people she loves. The yellow wallpaper surrounding her is "like a bad dream." It furnishes the central images in the story. The reader can use it like a Rorschach test to understand the heroine's experience of entrapment, confinement, and sacrifice for other family members. Like Gregor Samsa, she regresses to subhuman behavior as a self-inflicted punishment following her psychological rebellion — the wallpaper's bad smell, its bars and grid, its fungus and toadstools, and its images of the creeping (dependent, inferior) woman. But unlike Gregor Samsa, Gilman's heroine thinks she is freed from the "bad dream" by telling her story, not to a "living soul," but to what she calls (nonjudgmentally) "dead paper."

Telling her story enables her to achieve her greatest desire — the symbolic death of her husband. The story ends, "Now why should that man have fainted? But he did, and right across my path by the wall, so that I had to creep over him every time!" The central irony of the story, however, is that by the time she realizes the twisted ambition fostered by obediently following "like a good girl" her passive role as a conventional member of the "weaker sex," she has been driven insane.

Questions for Discussion

1. Why have the narrator and her husband, John, rented the "colonial mansion"? What is its past history, and what is the reaction of the heroine to this estate? Does she feel comfortable living in the house?

2. Give a description of John. Why does the heroine say that his profession is *"perhaps . . .* one reason I do not get well faster"? How does the narrator view her husband? Does she agree with John's diagnosis and treatment? Who else supports John's diagnosis? What effect does this have on the heroine?

3. What clue does the narrator's repeated lament, "what can one do?" give us about her personality? Describe other aspects of the woman's personality that are revealed in the opening of the story. What conflicting emotions is she having toward her husband, her condition, and the mansion?

4. How would you characterize the narrator's initial reaction to, and description of, the wallpaper?

5. After the first two weeks of residence, describe the narrator's state. Has John's relationship with his wife changed at all?

6. Who is Jennie? What is her relationship to the narrator, and what is her function in the story?

7. How has the narrator changed in her description of the wallpaper? Is it fair to say that the wallpaper has become more dominant in her day-to-day routine? Explain.

8. By the Fourth of July, what does the narrator admit about the wallpaper? What clues does Gilman give us about the education of the narrator and her increasingly agitated state? Is she finding it more and more difficult to communicate? Explain.

9. As the summer continues, describe the narrator's thoughts. What is her physical condition? Is there a link between her symptoms and psychological illness?

10. How does the narrator try to reach out to her husband? What is his reaction? Is this her last contact with sanity? Do you think John really has no comprehension of the seriousness of her illness?

11. Why do you think Gilman briefly changes the point of view from first person singular to the second person as the narrator describes the pattern of the wallpaper? What effect does the narrator say light has on the wallpaper?

12. Who does the narrator see in the wallpaper? How have her perceptions of John and Jennie changed from the beginning of the story?

13. Abruptly the narrator switches mood from boredom and frustration to excitement. To what does she attribute this change? How does John react to this? What new aspects of the wallpaper does she discuss?

14. By the final section of the story, what is the narrator's relationship to her husband? to Jennie? to the wallpaper? How has the narrator's perspective changed from the start of the story? What change do we see in her actions?

15. Identify what has driven the narrator to the brink of madness. How does she try to free herself from this element? What is her greatest desire? What is the central irony of the story?

Topics for Writing

CRITICAL ESSAYS

1. The husband-wife relationship and its outcome in Gilman's "The Yellow Wallpaper" and Henrik Ibsen's play "A Doll House."

2. The monologue in Gilman's "The Yellow Wallpaper" and Poe's "The Cask of Amontillado" or "The Tell-Tale Heart."

3. The concept of marriage in Gilman's "The Yellow Wallpaper," Freeman's "The Revolt of 'Mother,'" Carver's "What We Talk About When We Talk About Love," and Walker's "Roselily."

Related Commentaries from Part Two

Sandra M. Gilbert and Susan Gubar, A Feminist Reading of Gilman's "The Yellow Wallpaper." p. 1446.
Charlotte Perkins Gilman, Undergoing the Cure for Nervous Prostration, p. 1449.

Suggested Readings

Bader, J. "The Dissolving Vision: Realism in Jewett, Freeman and Gilman." *American Realism; New Essays.* Ed. Eric J. Sundquist. Baltimore: Johns Hopkins UP, 1982. 176–98.

Delaney, Sheila. *Writing Women: Women Writers and Women in Literature, Medieval to Modern.* New York: Schocken, 1983.

Feminist Papers: From Adams to de Beauvoir. Ed. Alice S. Rossi. New York: Columbia UP, 1973.

Hanley–Peritz, J. "Monumental Feminism and Literature's Ancestral House: Another Look at 'The Yellow Wallpaper. '" *Women's Studies* 12.2 (1986): 113–28.

Hill, Mary A. "Charlotte Perkins Gilman: A Feminist's Struggle with Womanhood." *Massachusetts Review* 21 (1980): 503–26.

———. *Charlotte Perkins Gilman: The Making of a Radical Feminist, 1860–1896.* Philadelphia: Temple UP, 1980.

Lane, Ann J. "Charlotte Perkins Gilman: The Personal Is Political." *Feminist Theorists.* Ed. Dale Spender. New York: Pantheon, 1983.

Nies, Judith. *Seven Women.* New York: Viking, 1977. 127–45.

Shumaker, C. " 'Too Terribly Good to Be Printed': Charlotte Gilman's 'The Yellow Wallpaper. ' " *American Literature* 57 (1985): 588–99.

Nikolai Gogol

The Overcoat (p. 542)

"The Overcoat," like Gogol's work in general, has been the subject of widely differing critical responses, some of which will surely be replicated in class discussion. A humanitarian view that sees the story as the vindication of a downtrodden little man coordinates fairly well with an interpretation that stresses the story's satiric attack on the rigid Czarist bureaucracy. Readers who note the grim joke with which the story ends, however, find its report on the destruction of a being too paltry even for contempt to be harrowingly cynical and heartless, while those who closely attend to the shifting narrative tone praise Gogol for producing a masterpiece of that combination of comedy and horror that we designate as the grotesque.

In some ways an obverse of romantic or Laforguian irony, which expresses a self-conscious revulsion from one's own emotional enthusiasms, the grotesque vision dissolves in grim laughter the appalled revulsion from a world devoid of any positive value. Neither Akaky Akakievich Bashmachkin (whose name in Russian alludes to dung on a shoe) nor the social and physical world with which he is at odds offers anything admirable, and the narrator's continuously shifting understatements, overstatements, verbal ironies, and bathetic juxtapositions repeatedly prevent the reader from any mistaken investment of esteem. Nonetheless, the possibility that Akaky Akakievich is our brother in ways not considered by his sentimental young colleague remains the source of the story's grip on our imagination.

Before time, which ages his coat, and the chill of the St. Petersburg winter combine to impose a need on him, Akaky Akakievich lives in a static and self-contained world of meaningless alphabetic letters, which he finds fulfillment and delight in replicating. He is a "writer" of sorts, but a writer who — like Gogol himself, according to Charles C. Bernheimer — hesitates to express himself in what he writes. With his fall from this undifferentiated condition into his struggle to acquire an overcoat, he is born into temporal human existence. His isolation breaks down, and so does his innocence: He makes a friend; he participates in a creative act; he experiences stirrings of sensuality; and he eventually manages to assert himself in words. He also becomes guilty of vanity, pride, lust, and deception. Having gained an identity as a man with a new coat, he becomes vulnerable to the destruction of that identity and consequently of the self it defines, which happens in three rapid stages.

Because we have seen him emerge from a state approximating nonexistence, Akaky Akakievich's brief history as a suffering human being does not appear to be much different from the radically reduced quintessence of the fate we imagine to be our own. That the retribution carried out by the shade of Akaky Akakievich — which suggests his vindication and the exaltation of his overcoat-identity to the stature of a myth — can finally be nothing more than a fantasy or a joke only serves to underline the inescapable dilemma that the story propounds between the meaninglessness of remaining locked within the circle of the self and the danger of aspiring beyond it.

Questions for Discussion

1. Characterize the narrative mode of the opening paragraphs. Can you define a consistent tone?
2. In what sense was it "out of the question" to give Akaky Akakievich any other name?
3. Does Gogol share the feelings of "the young man" who thinks Akaky Akakievich's complaints mean "I am your brother"?
4. Describe Akaky Akakievich's life before his coat wore out.
5. Why does Gogol bother to make Petrovich such an unsavory character?
6. Describe Akaky Akakievich's feelings about his new overcoat once he decides to acquire it.
7. What possible attitudes might one take toward Akaky Akakievich's experience at the party? about his visit to the "Person of Consequence"?
8. Near the end, the narrator speaks of how "our little story unexpectedly finishes with a fantastic ending." What is the effect of this and the narrator's other implicit acknowledgments of the fictionality of his story — made as implausible assertions of its veracity — on the reader?
9. Consider Nabokov's commentary on "The Overcoat." What "gaps and black holes in the texture of Gogol's style" seem to you to "imply flaws in the texture of life itself"?

Topics for Writing

CRITICAL ESSAYS

1. Satire as a diversionary tactic in "The Overcoat."
2. The "Person of Consequence" and a person of little consequence: two sides of the same coin?
3. Gogol's Akaky Akakievich and Melville's Bartleby as versions of the artist.
4. Disappointed expectation as the goal of Gogol's style.
5. T. Coraghessan Boyle's "The Overcoat II" as a revision of Gogol's original.

RELATED SUBJECTS

1. Study the long sentence on page 545 that begins "Even at those hours . . ." and continues nearly to the end of the paragraph it opens. Write a

similar sentence about a community with which you are familiar (e.g., college students on a campus; the residents of your neighborhood). Try to follow Gogol as closely as possible: clause for clause, phrase for phrase. How would you define the tone of what you have written? Is it the same as Gogol's tone?

2. Nabokov concludes his commentary on this story (p. 1484) by suggesting that "after reading Gogol one's eyes may become gogolized and one is apt to see bits of [Gogol's irrational] world in the most unexpected places." Write a sketch in which, by manipulating style and diction, you cause your reader to glimpse a darker world beyond the surface appearances of things.

Related Commentary from Part Two

Vladimir Nabokov, Gogol's Genius in "The Overcoat," p. 1484.

Suggested Readings

Bernheimer, Charles C. "Cloaking the Self: The Literary Space of Gogol's 'Overcoat.' " *PMLA* 90 (1975): 53–61.

Erlich, Victor. *Gogol*. Yale Russian and East European Studies 8. New Haven: Yale UP, 1969. Esp. 143–56.

Karlinsky, Simon. *The Sexual Labyrinth of Nikolai Gogol*. Cambridge: Harvard UP, 1976. 135–44.

Lindstrom, Thaïs S. *Nikolay Gogol*. Twayne's World Authors Series 299. New York: Twayne, 1974. Esp. 88–96.

NADINE GORDIMER

Town and Country Lovers *(p. 567)*

This tale includes two brilliant stories about race relations in South Africa, linked by theme. Two mixed-race couples, one from town, the other from the country, become lovers and are brutally separated by social conventions. The linking of the stories, identical in their unhappy endings yet dissimilar in their circumstances, suggests the power of the attraction between all lovers — intangible, mysterious, beyond description in words. It overcomes differences of background, education, job status, and race. Yet, as Gordimer shows in these two stories, it cannot survive the virulence of unjust social conventions.

Story I

The town lovers are grown-ups. He is Dr. Franz-Josef von Leinsdorf, a German geologist with an aristocratic background, dedicated to his work. She is a light-skinned cashier in a supermarket in Johannesburg, her nature as sweet as she is pretty. She is given no name, identified merely as "the girl," as if

Gordimer wants to suggest she isn't quite human to the aristocratic Dr. von Leinsdorf, despite their intimacy. Perhaps his emotional distance from her has something to do with the gap between her teeth, which he doesn't find attractive, thinking of it as "a little yokel's or peasant's . . . gap." Their love affair is a matter of convenience for him. She seems content with the relationship, yet she is not unintelligent and dreams of one day helping him type his notes (he teaches her to type) and sitting beside him in his car "like a wife."

After some months, just before Christmas, three policemen invade the geologist's apartment, identify themselves, and search the place without benefit of a warrant. They force entry into the locked cupboard where the girl has hidden herself, and hustle the couple off to the police station. There the girl is physically examined for signs of intercourse by the district surgeon, a procedure that feels like rape to her: "[H]e [the doctor] placed her legs apart, resting in stirrups, and put into her where the other had made his way so warmly a cold hard instrument that expanded wider and wider." After a night in a cell, she is bailed out by the clerk of the lawyer engaged for her by Dr. von Leinsdorf. The "guilty" pair meet only once again, in court, where they do not greet or speak to each other.

Story II

The country lovers are children together and grow up to become lovers. He is Paulus Eysendyck, the white son of the farm owner employing the black girl's father. She is named Thebedi; she is pretty, and clever with her hands. Her affection for Paulus is returned, and their lovemaking — which he instigates — is lyrically described: "They were not afraid of one another, they had known one another always; he did with her what he had done that time in the storeroom at the wedding, and this time it was so lovely, so lovely, he was surprised . . . and she was surprised by it, too."

The outcome of this love affair is a mixed-blood colored baby with straight fine hair and Paulus's hazel eyes. When he sees his child, Paulus cries out of anger and self-pity. His life will be ruined, his family shamed (later his father says, "I will try and carry on as best I can to hold up my head in the district." Paulus murders the infant, Thebedi buries it, but the police come and dig it up. Someone has reported that it died mysteriously. Evidence in court is insufficient, so the verdict is "not guilty." The affair is over; as the black girl says to the newspaper reporter, "It was a thing of our childhood, we don't see each other anymore."

Both stories have a similar plot structure. Story I begins in the present tense, but switches to past narrative tense when Dr. von Leinsdorf first talks to the colored girl cashier at the supermarket and their story begins. Story II begins with a paragraph in the present tense, about social customs on the farm, but when Paulus and Thebedi are introduced in the next paragraph, the narrative goes into past tense. The personal stories come to an end and require the past tense. The social background continues on.

The volatile emotions potentially in any love affair are kept in careful control through Gordimer's expert handling of point of view in Story I and character in Story II. Dr. von Leinsdorf expresses his ingrained sense of social superiority verging on racial stereotyping when he sees the colored cashier outside the supermarket and notices, "She was rather small and finely-made, for one of them. The coat was skimpy but no big backside jutted." Gordimer gives the geologist's point of view without authorial comment, resulting in an emotional distancing on the part of a sensitive reader. Thus feelings are kept in check. In Story II, Thebedi marries a native boy who accepts her baby and treats it so well that the judge later commends his "honourable behaviour." By introducing this character, Gordimer keeps Thebedi from being a tragic or sentimental figure, abandoned by Paulus and left on her own. Gordimer's decency, compassion, and restraint are in marked contrast to the laws of the society she describes.

Questions for Discussion

1. What does the opening paragraph explain about Dr. Franz-Josef von Leinsdorf's character? How is this characterization achieved? Look at the diction; he's a geologist wrapped up, enfolded, swaddled in the layers and layers of his work. How do you interpret the information that "even as a handsome small boy he presented only his profile" to his mother? What does this paragraph tell you about the geologist's ability to love?

2. On page 568, the geologist describes the "colored girl." List the parts of her body that make up his description. See page 569: "She had a little yokel's, peasant's (he thought of it) gap between her two front teeth when she smiled that he didn't much like."

3. "He said, watching her sew, 'You're a good girl'; and touched her." Does the narrator give us access to the characters' minds? Does the geologist love the colored girl? Does she him? What are their motivations? Why might Gordimer keep the reader at such a psychological distance in this story?

4. How does the introductory phrase "On a summer night near Christmas" prepare the Western reader for the conclusion? Why do the policemen search the girl and the clothes and sheets "for signs of his seed"? What effect does Gordimer's graphic description of the girl's physical examination have on your understanding of the story's denouement: "He placed her legs apart, resting in stirrups, and put into her where the other had made his way so warmly a cold hard instrument that expanded wider and wider. Her thighs and knees trembled uncontrollably while the doctor looked into her and touched her deep inside with more hard instruments, carrying wafers of gauze."

5. Both part I and part II of "Town and Country Lovers" end with the protagonists in court. Why does Gordimer close both *stories* with the court scene? Why does she give, in both stories, the quotations carried by the Sunday papers? How would you compare the stories given to the public — both legal and journalistic — and the more private stories you have had access to through reading "Town and Country Lovers"?

6. After Paulus sees his baby for the first time, he says, "I feel like killing myself." Why does this make both Thebedi and Paulus sense a return of the "feeling between them that used to come when they were alone down at the river-bed"?

7. While Paulus is murdering the baby, Thebedi thinks she hears "small grunts . . . the kind of infant grunt that indicates a full stomach, a deep sleep." She tells her husband the baby is sleeping. When she first testifies, she is hysterical, and says things that we know are not true. More than a year

later she retestifies, and tells the truth. At no point does Gordimer give the reader any explicit commentary on Thebedi's feelings and actions. How do you interpret the flat description of events in these most highly charged moments in the story?

8. What themes are common to both parts of "Town and Country Lovers"? Are the protagonists in each part similar or not?

Topics for Writing

CRITICAL ESSAYS

1. In Gordimer's essay "The Flash of Fireflies" in Part Two (p. 1451), she says that "the short story is a fragmented and restless form, a matter of hit or miss, and it is perhaps for this reason that it suits modern consciousness — which seems best expressed as flashes of fearful insight alternating with near-hypnotic states of indifference." Analyze the language and structure of "Town and Country Lovers" with reference to this definition.
2. The effects of apartheid on human relationships.
3. The effects of repressive policies on human rights in "Town and Country Lovers."

RELATED SUBJECT

1. Consider other legislation that you feel violates human rights and write a short story illustrating its effects.

Related Commentary from Part Two

Nadine Gordimer, The Flash of Fireflies, p. 1451.

Suggested Readings

Cooke, J. "African Landscapes: The World of Nadine Gordimer." *World Literature Today* 52 (1978): 533–38.

Eckstein, B. "Pleasure and Joy: Political Activism in Nadine Gordimer's Short Stories." *World Literature Today* 59 (1985): 343–46.

Gray, S. "Interview with Nadine Gordimer." *Contemporary Literature* 22 (1981): 263–71.

Hurwitt, J. "Art of Fiction: Nadine Gordimer." *Paris Review* 25 (1983): 83–127.

Smyer, R. I. "Africa in the Fiction of Nadine Gordimer." *Ariel* 16 (1985): 15–29.

NATHANIEL HAWTHORNE

My Kinsman, Major Molineux (p. 583)

The critic Lewis Leary has said that "in the hand of a master, [the short story] becomes consummately an art, suggesting more than it seems at first to reveal." This statement is certainly true about "My Kinsman, Major Molineux," which has attracted a massive number of critical interpretations. In Part Two, Simon O. Lesser brings a psychological approach to his reading of this classic tale (p. 1473).

One way to approach the story in the classroom is to compare and contrast it with "Young Goodman Brown." Both describe the experience of immature, arrogant young men who seek something outside the familiar circle of their experience; both underestimate the impediments in their paths as they search for enlightenment. Hawthorne's distance from both Robin and Brown allows him to present them ambivalently, displaying simultaneous contradictory attitudes toward their quests so that both stories suggest a good deal more than they seem "at first to reveal."

Robin sets a high value on himself, yet he is woefully ignorant of the political climate of his times; self-interest is his only concern. In the beginning paragraph of "My Kinsman, Major Molineux," Hawthorne tells us more about the hardships faced by colonial governors than Robin appears to know. Thus Robin lacks political savvy in the eyes not only of the townspeople but also of the reader. Hawthorne adopted this strategy, carried on in popular fiction writing in our own time to give historical weight to his magazine tale. But few writers inject historical material this way, to tell the reader something the protagonist does not know. Thus Hawthorne ensures that the reader will also be emotionally distanced from Robin.

Why did the author make Robin such a bumpkin? The customary answer is that Hawthorne wrote tales of initiation, dramatizing male rites of passage in the New England community. A more politicized reading would suggest that in both "My Kinsman Major Molineux" and "Young Goodman Brown" Hawthorne is investigating the darker side of the American dream of self-fulfillment, putting personal ambition before community involvement. Material advancement drives Robin, spiritual ambition rules Brown; both are the products of a society whose traditions are so recent that its citizens hope to attain power just by asking for it. Hawthorne shows us that the road to hell is paved with good intentions: which way the road to heaven?

Questions for Discussion

1. What is the importance of the historical background in the opening paragraph of "My Kinsman, Major Molineux"?
2. What are Robin's good qualities? his limitations?
3. Trace Robin's search for his kinsman. What kind of picture does Hawthorne paint of pre-Revolutionary New England life?
4. What is your interpretation of the grotesque character with his face painted in two colors whom Robin meets in the inn and later sees on the street?
5. How does the description of the moonlight help to set the scene and prepare for the end of the story?
6. What is the importance of Robin's dreams of home just before he meets the "gentleman in his prime" who befriends him?
7. How do you react to the description of Major Molineux "in tar-and-feathery dignity" on the uncovered cart? Would you have reacted the way Robin did to the sight of his uncle? What does his reaction tell you about Robin?

93

8. Interpret the last words of the "gentleman in his prime" at the end of the story. Does he have good or bad intentions toward Robin?

9. Do you think Hawthorne intended "My Kinsman, Major Molineux" to be read as a realistic tale or an allegory? Explain.

Topics for Writing

1. Contrast and compare "My Kinsman, Major Molineux" and "Young Goodman Brown."

2. Rewrite the story making Robin a contemporary young man who goes to a state capital seeking political favor from a distant relative.

Related Commentaries from Part Two

Nathaniel Hawthorne, The Agonies of Inspiration, p. 1457.

Simon O. Lesser, A Psychological Reading of Hawthorne's "My Kinsman, Major Molineux, p. 1473.

NATHANIEL HAWTHORNE

Young Goodman Brown (p. 598)

Teaching "Young Goodman Brown," you should encourage students to read "The Elements of Fiction" (p. 1554) carefully, since different aspects of Hawthorne's story are analyzed throughout the discussion of the elements of short fiction. "Writing about Short Stories" (p. 1566) also has student essays developing different ideas about "Young Goodman Brown."

Students often need help recognizing stories that are not intended to be read as realistic narrative. Some readers tend to take every word in the story literally; Hawthorne, however, meant "Young Goodman Brown" to be a moral allegory, not a realistic story. While most students will be able to recognize the use of symbolism, you might have to introduce them to the idea of allegory, in which the entire story is an extended metaphor representing one thing in the guise of another.

An allegory is a story that has a dual meaning — one in the events, characters, and setting; and the other in the ideas they are intended to convey. At first, "Young Goodman Brown" holds our interest on the level of the surface narrative. But the story also has a second meaning, which must be read beneath, and concurrent with, the surface narrative. This second meaning is not to be confused with the theme of the story — all stories have themes, but not all stories are allegories. In an allegory, the characters are usually personifications of abstract qualities (faith) and the setting is representative of the relations among the abstractions (Goodman Brown takes leave of his "Faith" at the beginning of the story).

A story is an allegory only if the characters, events, and setting are presented in a logical pattern so that they represent meanings independent of the action described in the surface story. Most writers of allegorical fiction are moralists. In this moral allegory, Hawthorne is suggesting the ethical principle that should govern human life. The *unpardonable sin* for Hawthorne is a "want of love and reverence for the Human Soul" and is typified by the person who searches the depths of the heart with "a cold philosophical curiosity." The result is a separation of the intellect from the heart, which is fatal in relationships among human beings, as shown in what happens to Goodman Brown when he returns to Salem village at the end of the story.

Questions for Discussion

1. When is a careful reader first aware that Hawthorne intends this story to be read as a moral allegory?

2. One of the characters in a Hawthorne story says, "You know that I can never separate the idea from the symbol in which it manifests itself." Hawthorne's flat characters — such as Deacon Gookin, Goody Cloyse, and the minister — represent social institutions. Why does Hawthorne include them in the story?

3. On page 599, Hawthorne writes, "But the only thing about him that could be fixed upon as remarkable was his staff, which bore the likeness of a great black snake, so curiously wrought that it might almost be seen to twist and wriggle itself like a living serpent. This, of course, must have been an ocular deception, assisted by the uncertain light." What is the assertion contained in the first sentence? What effect do the words "might almost" have on that assertion? Why does Hawthorne immediately qualify the first sentence in the second? On page 605, Hawthorne writes: "Either the sudden gleams of light flashing over the obscure field bedazzled Goodman Brown, or he recognized a score of the church members of Salem village famous for their especial sanctity." Discuss the function of this sentence and find others like it throughout the story. What is their cumulative effect?

4. Why is it important that most of the action in this story takes place in the forest? Looking through Hawthorne's story, isolate the particular words that are associated with the woods. Consider the paragraph on page 603 that begins "And, maddened with despair." List the characteristics of forests that are responsible for this long literary tradition. Consider, too, whether the idea of wilderness remains static throughout history. In the late nineteenth century, with industrialization such a potent force, would people have conceived of the forest in the same way the early settlers did? Why or why not?

5. Where does this story take place (besides in the forest)? On page 599 a man addresses the protagonist saying, "You are late, Goodman Brown. . . . The clock of the Old South was striking as I came through Boston, and that is full fifteen minutes agone." What does this detail — that the traveler was in Boston fifteen minutes ago — mean to our interpretation of the story?

6. One page 606, "the dark figure" welcomes his listeners to "the communion of your race." What is usually meant by the word "communion"? How is it meant here? What does the speaker mean by the phrase in which he uses it? What kinds of powers does the "sable form" promise the crowd? Discuss the kinds of knowledge that will henceforth be accessible to his

listeners' senses. Who is speaking in this passage on pages 606–607: "Herein did the shape of evil dip his hand and prepare to lay the mark of baptism upon their foreheads, that they might be partakers of the mystery of sin, more conscious of the secret guilt of others, both in deed and thought, than they could now be of their own"? How does this sentence guide your judgment of Young Goodman Brown in the closing paragraph of the story? How does the sable figure's sermon comment on the closing paragraph?

7. How much time does this story cover? Where do the first seven paragraphs take place? How many paragraphs are set in the forest? What do the final three paragraphs address? What might be some reasons for the story to be built this way?

Topic for Writing

1. Show how a knowledge of seventeenth-century New England history and Puritan theology can enhance a reading of the story.

Related Commentaries from Part Two

Nathaniel Hawthorne, The Agonies of Inspiration, p. 1457.
Herman Melville, Blackness in Hawthorne's "Young Goodman Brown," p. 1482.

Suggested Readings

Ferguson, J. M., Jr. "Hawthorne's 'Young Goodman Brown.' " *Explicator* 28 (1969): Item 32.
Gallagher, Edward J. "The Concluding Paragraph of 'Young Goodman Brown.' " *Studies in Short Fiction* 12 (1975): 29–30.
Robinson, E. Arthur. "The Vision of Goodman Brown: A Source and Interpretation." *American Literature* 35 (1963): 218–25.
Whelan, Robert E. "Hawthorne Interprets 'Young Goodman Brown.' " *Emerson Society Quarterly* 62 (1971): 3–6.

BESSIE HEAD

Life (p. 609)

This story opens with a paragraph of explanation about its background, reminiscent of the beginning of "My Kinsman, Major Molineux." As Hawthorne tells us that the colonial governors appointed by the king of England often ran into trouble with their subjects in the New World, Head explains that the village people in Botswana rejected city habits that were harmful to them and that "the murder of Life had this complicated undertone of rejection." In their introductory paragraphs, both Head and Hawthorne eliminate a large measure of suspense in their stories by giving broad hints of both the plot and theme to come. What, then, makes the reader want to continue on?

This question is a useful one to begin a discussion about "Life." For one thing, Head's protagonist has an unusual name, and most readers will entertain the possibility that Head is writing an allegory investigating the human situation, and that the specific twenty-seven-year-old woman named Life is a literary symbol in addition to being a realistic character.

This sense of a larger dimension to the character in Head's story — as in Hawthorne's depiction of Robin's adventures searching for his uncle — is strengthened by the author's description of the setting. In a very few pages, "Life" tells us a great deal about how people live in the villages of Botswana. We read about the traditional custom of continuing to offer a home in the village to members of families who left for Johannesburg, even as long as seventeen years after a family has departed. We learn of the village women's willingness to help Life by working to make her yard and house habitable. Traditional food, references to the feasting at weddings, the villagers' matter-of-fact attitude toward sex ("that it ought to be available whenever possible like food and water"), the division of labor between men and women, the careers available to educated women, the social differences between the respectable housewives and the beer-brewing women — all these details paint a rich picture and develop our awareness of the moral structure of village customs.

The narrator's point of view is close and balanced, not distant and ironic like Hawthorne's attitude toward Robin. Head is an omniscient storyteller; she tells us that "one evening death walked quietly into the bar" when she introduces Lesego, the cattleman who becomes Life's husband. Head succinctly defines their attraction for us: "[T]hey looked at each other from their own worlds and came to fatal conclusions." The tragedy of their marriage is the second half of the story, and what happens to them focuses the moral dimension of "Life."

Questions for Discussion

1. Is suspense lacking in the story because Head tells you the ending in her first paragraph? Explain.
2. What is attractive about Life? Is her "undertone of hysteria" attractive or unattractive?
3. Why is Lesego so confident that Life will change her promiscuous ways if he marries her?
4. Explicate the paragraph of commentary beginning "She hadn't the mental equipment to analyze what hit her" after Lesego tells Life that he will kill her if she is unfaithful to him.
5. Head's description of the activity of Life's yard — the blaring transistor radio, the people reeling around "dead drunk," the prostitution — is not presented in a judgmental way. How do you know what Head thinks of such behavior?
6. Is Head more sympathetic to the village women or to Life? Explain.

Topics for Writing

1. Analyze the function of food and drink in "Life."
2. Compare and contrast "Life" with Chinua Achebe's "Dead Men's Path" or Zora Neale Hurston's "Spunk."

3. Use a feminist critical strategy to analyze the ending of "Life," Lesego's action and his punishment.
4. In the final paragraph, Head suggests that the beer-brewing women have the last word "on the whole affair." Agree or disagree with this statement and explain your response.

Suggested Reading

Wayward Girls & Wicked Women. Ed. Angela Carter. New York: Penguin, 1989.

ERNEST HEMINGWAY

Hills Like White Elephants (p.620)

Hemingway wrote this story in May 1927, while on his honeymoon in the Rhône delta with his second wife, Pauline. According to his biographer Kenneth Lynn, the story was a dramatization of a fantasy he had about his first wife, Hadley: "[I]f only the two of them had not allowed a child to enter their lives they would never have parted." Throughout his biography, Lynn interprets the fiction in terms of Hemingway's relationships. How much this approach sheds light on the fiction each reader must judge.

This story is an early example of a minimalist technique. Characterization and plot are mere suggestions, and it is possible for some young readers to finish the story for the first time with no idea that the couple are discussing an abortion. The setting Hemingway chooses for the couple's conversation is more richly developed. The symbolism of the "two lines of rails" at the station (the choice either to end the pregnancy or have the child); the fields of grain and trees along the Ebro River, which the girl sees on the other side of the station (fertility, a settled life) compared with the barren hills, long and white like white elephants (something considered unlucky, unwanted, and rejected); the bar and the station building (the temporary escape offered by alcohol, the sense of people in transit) — one can interpret these details in perfect harmony with the couple's emotional and physical dilemma.

The man's bullying of the girl drives the story. His ignorance about abortion and his insensitivity to what she is feeling or will have to endure physically ("It's not really anything. It's just to let the air in") are not presented as weakness. They are simply part of his insistence on persuading Jig to do what he wants her to do. The girl is also worthy of discussion. Her vulnerability is idealized, yet she is not stupid. Without the suggestion of her intelligence, there would be no story.

Hemingway regarded "Hills Like White Elephants" as one of his best stories, reserving a prominent place for it in his second collection, *Men Without Women*, published in the fall of 1927. Lynn states that in choosing this title for the book, Hemingway meant to suggest "that the alienation of women from men (as well as vice versa) was one of his themes."

Questions for Discussion

1. In what ways could you categorize this story as a minimalist work?
2. What do we know about the man? About the girl? Why isn't Jig called "a woman" in the story?
3. What is a "white elephant"? How does this expression suit the story?
4. What do you think will happen to this couple after the story ends?

Topic for Writing

1. Rewrite the story in a different setting to discover the importance of the railroad station and the Spanish landscape in "Hills Like White Elephants."

EXERCISE IN READING

1. Read the story aloud in class, assigning two students the roles of the man and the girl. Is the story as effective read as dialogue as it is on the page as a literary text?

Suggested Reading

Lynn, Kenneth S. *Hemingway*. New York: Simon, 1987.

AMY HEMPEL

Daylight Come (p. 625)

This minimalist story has only one line of dialogue, Ruth's saying "Here's to you, Bingo," the dog who is nursing her puppies under the table. Yet it is reminiscent of Ernest Hemingway's "Hills Like White Elephants." Impermanence, loss, regret, a relationship seemingly in peril — the feelings are evanescent but the mood seems similar, almost as if Hempel has kept the story in her mind and is re-creating it for us on her own terms. Her effort is similar to Robert Coover's way of turning the Hansel and Gretel folktale inside out in "The Gingerbread House."

Affectionate animals, a tropical island, a honeymooning couple, hibiscus blossoms filling a conch shell — we have come to Paradise. Yet a sense of impermanence haunts the narrator. A dog (not a human) is a mother; the couples are widowers or perilously joined ("the lost wedding rings are invisible"); we only meet the narrator's companion in the public posing for a snapshot, yet we learn she is anxious about him. In the limpid prose, sand and sea and flowers and flesh are bound in a community of shared experience, but the emotional bonds are fragile and evanescent.

The elements of Hempel's story seem built on shifting sands, like the dog Belle and her charmingly imagined capacity for changing color. What kind of dog is she, in fact? What is the relationship of the narrator with her significant other? Why does she appear off balance in the souvenir photo? The more one ponders the reflection of life in "Daylight Come," the more one wants to ask, what is wrong with this picture?

Questions for Discussion

1. What qualities of "Daylight Come" characterize it as a minimalist story?
2. Is this an anecdote, a sketch, or a fully developed short story? Explain.
3. What is the state of grace suggested by the title of the story? What details in the narrative support this interpretation?
4. Hempel once quoted the writer Stanley Elkin as saying that he "would never write about someone who is not at the end of his rope." She added, "That's not a bad way to go into something." Is "Daylight Come" about someone "at the end of [her] rope"? Explain.

Topics for Writing

1. Compare and contrast this story of American tourists vacationing on an island with "insiders' stories" of island life by the West Indian writers V. S. Naipaul and Jamaica Kincaid.
2. Compare Hempel's minimalist technique in "Daylight Come" with Ernest Hemingway's in "Hills Like White Elephants."

ZORA NEALE HURSTON

Spunk (p. 628)

The title of Hurston's story has a double meaning. "Spunk" refers to Spunk Banks, the giant of a man who courts the married woman Lena and who "ain't skeered of nothin' on God's green footstool — *nothin'*!" But it also refers to the quality of "spunk" (courage) shown by Lena's timid husband, Joe, the sarsaparilla-drinking "round-shouldered figure in overalls much too large," who comes back from the grave after Spunk has shot him in order to take his revenge. It took spunk for Joe to try to get Lena back from her pistol-packing lover, and Joe's courage lasts until he succeeds at what he wanted to do.

Hurston has written a ghost story based on the revenge motif in the Florida black tradition of vernacular speech and folk superstition. Joe first comes back from the dead in the figure of a "big black bob-cat" (an unearthly color for a bobcat). In this animal form he frightens Spunk so much that Spunk can't shoot his army .45 pistol, a small revenge in itself. For the ultimate revenge, something pushes Spunk in the back onto the buzz saw. Spunk believes it's Joe's ghost and vows to get him in hell. As a storyteller, Hurston pulls out of the two men's quarrel at this point. She ends the narrative with Lena, the "small pretty woman" who is the object of the two men's affections and who holds a wake for her departed lover. Hurston's interest is firmly in this world, describing the scene with a poetic economy of detail:

> The cooling board consisted of three sixteen-inch boards on saw horses, a dingy sheet was his shroud.
> The women ate heartily of the funeral baked meats and wondered who would be Lena's next. The men whispered coarse conjectures between guzzles of whiskey.

Questions for Discussion

1. Why is the main part of the story told through the conversation between Elijah Mosley and Walter Thomas? They are, after all, outsiders to the intimate action, depending on hearsay for the bulk of their information.
2. Look at the final paragraph: "The women ate heartily of the funeral baked meats and wondered who would be Lena's next. The men whispered coarse conjectures between guzzles of whiskey." How does this paragraph, one of the few scenes related by the narrator, influence your interpretation of this story? Is "Spunk" about events that happen, or is it about the stories about events that happen? What's the difference?
3. This story is split into four parts, yet it's only five pages long. What is the effect of this structure? What is the narrative burden of each section?
4. In the opening paragraph of section II, Hurston writes, "Lena wept in a frightened manner." What are some other ways of saying this? What effect does this particular way have on your estimation of Lena's character? In the next paragraph Hurston writes, " 'Well,' Spunk announced calmly, 'Joe came out there wid a meat axe an' made me kill him.' " Is this statement factually true? Where does the language Spunk uses locate the responsibility for the killing?
5. What effect does the black Florida dialect have on the setting and characterization of the story? How much physical description is present in "Spunk"? How does the dialect convey the same ideas that physical detail might?
6. Analyze the final paragraph in section II: "A clear case of self-defense, the trial was a short one, and Spunk walked out of the court house to freedom again. He could work again, ride the dangerous log-carriage that fed the singing, snarling, biting circle-saw: he could stroll the soft dark lanes with his guitar. He was free to roam the woods again; he was free to return to Lena. He did all of these things." Notice the sentence lengths: three long sentences followed by a short one. What sentence gains the emphasis in this arrangement and why? What effect does the repetition of both words and syntax create? Look at the list of adjectives that precedes "circle-saw." How would you describe the style of this paragraph? How does it relate to the kind of story Hurston is telling?
7. What do you make of the supernatural elements that are introduced into sections III and IV? What kinds of stories contain supernatural elements like this? What is a "h'ant"?
8. With whom does the narrator place her sympathies in this story: Spunk, Joe, Lena, Elijah, or Walter? Discuss the passages that support your conclusion.

Topics for Writing

CRITICAL ESSAYS

1. Country humor in "Spunk."
2. Courage in "Spunk."
3. Supernatural elements in "Spunk."
4. Folk elements in "Spunk" and Ellison's "Battle Royal."

RELATED SUBJECT

1. Rewrite the story from Lena's point of view.

Related Commentary from Part Two

Robert Bone, A Folkloric Analysis of Hurston's "Spunk," p. 1407.

Suggested Readings

Bone, R. A. "Three Versions of the Pastoral." *Down Home: A History of Afro-American Short Fiction from Its Beginnings to the End of the Harlem Renaissance.* New York: Putnam, 1975. 139–70.

Cooke, Michael. *Afro-American Literature in the Twentieth Century: The Achievement of Intimacy.* New Haven: Yale UP, 1984.

Hemenway, R. "Zora Neale Hurston and the Eatonville Anthropology." *The Harlem Renaissance Remembered.* Ed. A. W. Bontemps. New York: Dodd, 1972. 190–214.

Howard, L. P. "Marriage: Zora Neale Hurston's System of Values." *CLA Journal* 21 (1977): 256–68.

Johnson, B. "Thresholds of Difference: Structures of Address in Zora Neale Hurston." *Critical Inquiry* 12 (1985): 278–89.

Love, T. R. "Zora Neale Hurston's America." *Papers on Language and Literature* 12 (1976): 422–37.

Lupton, M. J. "Zora Neale Hurston and the Survival of the Female." *Southern Literary Journal* 15 (1982): 45–54.

Sheffey, Ruth T., ed. *Rainbow Round Her Shoulders: The Zora Neale Hurston Symposium Papers.* Baltimore. Morgan State UP, 1982.

HWANG SUN-WON

Conversation in June about Mothers *(p. 633)*

In the comfort of a classroom in today's peaceful United States it is easy to forget that in other parts of the world the violence and brutality of war are part of everyday experience. This story, with its deceptively calm title, forces us to look at this other reality, and it does so by presenting us with a series of anecdotes, ostensibly about the relationship between mothers and their children. The setting is described almost casually. A group of men are sitting on the grass, it's a hot June afternoon, and they are telling one another about mothers. The more direct background is presented at the end of the second paragraph, when the narrator says, "we didn't know at the time that the 38th parallel was soon going to be completely impassable."

The thirty-eighth parallel is now the dividing line between North and South Korea, but the period the narrator is describing is before the 1954 armistice in the Korean War, which split the country at this point. It is also clear where the narrator's sympathies lie, since he is trying to flee from the Communist North.

The first paragraph of the anecdote told by the first narrator initiates the growing pattern of horror that the author conveys through his storytellers. A woman has just given birth and is being asked to flee to the South, but since she is too weak to travel, the family is going to be separated. In the second anecdote, the mother has abandoned her son, but the boy confronts a frightening image of her when he is severely wounded in battle. In the third anecdote a mother kills her baby while trying to escape from Communist rule, then mutilates her own body.

The effectiveness of the story lies in its double levels of meaning. The title suggests that this will be a simple description of the relationship between mothers and their children, and in each of the three narratives the author presents a man telling about a different aspect of this relationship. In reality, however, these anecdotes describe the effect war has on even this most basic human relationship.

The woman in the first anecdote is asked to give up her eldest son, and at the moment of separation — which the war has forced on her — she calls him back. In the second anecdote the war is at first not part of the background against which the mother's conduct is described — the father is away on business — but the son's confrontation with his mother's memory occurs after he's been wounded in battle. In the third anecdote the mother is part of a group trying to escape to the South during the war. Each anecdote takes us further in a confrontation with the bestiality of war; the third reaches a level of horror that is as unforgettable as it is brutal.

Questions for Discussion

1. Describe the scene of the story and what you imagine the men telling the anecdotes to be like.
2. Outline the circumstances that led to the partition of Korea, and the United States' involvement in the war that followed North Korea's invasion of South Korea.
3. Do you think someone who had not experienced war could have written this story? Why or why not?
4. Do you think war could have this effect on the relationship between mothers and their children in other countries? Explain.
5. Do you recognize these storytellers? Could they be anyone you know? Explain.

Topics for Writing

1. Discuss the images of mothers in "Conversation in June about Mothers" and Cynthia Ozick's "The Shawl."
2. Compare how Hwang Sun-won in this story and Shirley Jackson in "The Lottery" build their stories to moments of unforgettable atrocity.

YUSSEF IDRISS

A House of Flesh (p. 637)

In this richly suggestive story from contemporary Egypt the author presents a situation that could have come from the medieval tales of the Arabian Nights. A poor widow and her three unattractive daughters desperately seek a man to enter their room and their lives. The one who does is blind, but his blindness makes it possible for all the women to share him, in an arrangement conducted in stifling silence.

The author makes it clear that to him this situation has an eternal nature by presenting it almost as a parable. The essence of the story is encapsulated in an elliptical introductory paragraph. The use of the present tense also creates a sense of timelessness, since the narrative present can be any time. None of the characters has a name, and the only mention of the world outside is a reference to the fact that the reciter of the Koran comes to the door from the street. The author is describing the sexual hunger that is part of being human, and this has become, symbolically, a "house of flesh."

Sabry Hafez and Catherine Cobham have also noted this symbolic quality, and they relate it to the author's method of presenting his characters and their situation:

> It is a story in which every word matters, an example of the precision and simplicity which Idriss can command when expressing layers of meaning where each layer is as dense and real as every other. It is about the dependence and powerlessness of women without men in a particular society; sexual frustration; an idea of motherhood; and deception and self-deception. On the other hand certain key words are hammered home and continually point beyond the narrative: the "silence" and "waiting" at the beginning, implying passive dependence; the "voice" which breaks the silence and to which the women come to attach so much importance; and at the end of the story the "silence" of complicity, a mutual unspoken decision not to pursue the truth. The story is symbolic partly because Idriss's work has often been subjected to direct and indirect censorship, but also, and more importantly, for artistic reasons, as the meanings of the story are illuminated and its implications unfolded through allegory or fable.

In its description of the role of women in the culture of countries like today's Egypt, the story presents the Western reader with a number of questions, but at its most basic level the story is, as Hafez and Cobham point out, about the conspiracy the women enter into: "The main theme is of collusion; each character sees, hears, or senses the truth but it is never articulated and they all eventually become willing participants in 'the game of the ring,' and equally involved in constructing 'the edifice of silence.' "

Questions for Discussion

1. What do the relative ages of the mother and her daughters tell us about marriage customs in their society?
2. What does their inability to alleviate their poverty tell us about the role of women in their society?
3. Could this story be written about the United States today? Explain.
4. Describe the style in which the story is told. What is the purpose of this style? Is it employed successfully by Idriss?
5. Is the author's description of the women in the story a positive or negative portrayal? Explain.

Topics for Writing

CRITICAL ESSAYS

1. The role of women in non-Western societies as conveyed in "A House of Flesh."
2. The use of symbolism as a narrative device in the development of "A House of Flesh."

Suggested Readings

Hafez, Sabry, and Catherine Cobham, eds. *A Reader of Modern Arabic Short Stories.* London: Sa qi, 1988.

Hamalian, Leo, and John Yohannan, eds. *New Writing from the Middle East.* New York: NAL, 1978.

SHIRLEY JACKSON

The Lottery (p. 644)

The interpretive suggestions in the headnote should guide students toward a recognition of the main themes of "The Lottery." The near universality of the ritual sacrifice of year gods and scapegoats in primitive cultures to ensure fertility, the continuation of life, and the purgation of society has been a common assumption since the publication of James G. Frazer's *The Golden Bough.* Jackson does not explore the transmutations of these old ceremonies in the accepted religious practices and psychological mechanisms of modern humanity; rather, she attempts to shock her readers into an awareness of the presence of raw, brutal, and superstitious impulses within us all. A fruitful approach for class discussion might involve exploring how the story achieves its impact. Jackson's comments (included in Part Two, p. 1458) provide incontrovertible documentation of the power of "The Lottery" to stir the dark instincts dwelling below the surface of the civilized psyche, perhaps the same regions from which the story emerged fully formed — as Jackson claims — in the mind of the writer. No wonder readers, from the author's agent on, have found "The Lottery" disturbing.

But they have also found it compelling, fascinating, and irresistible, and the reason may have partly to do with Jackson's technical skill. For the inattentive first reader, the natural suspense of any drawing, contest, or lottery provides strong motivation to hurry through to the ending, and when the realization of what is at stake comes, it strikes with redoubled force because of the reader's increased velocity. For the more careful reader, or for the reader already aware of the ending, the subtle foreshadowing — the boys are gathering stones, the box is black, Tessie Hutchinson "clean forgot what day it was" — triggers an uncomfortable double awareness that also urges haste, a haste like that which spurs Mr. Summers's final, horrible remark, "All right, folks. . . . Let's finish quickly," and the cries of "Come on" and "Hurry up" by other villagers.

For Jackson has succeeded in gaining the reader's vicarious participation in the lottery. Even the backwoods New England quaintness of the setting draws not the kind of condescending laughter that would distance the reader but the warm sentimental indulgence we reserve for the cutest Norman Rockwell illustrations. Little boys are being little boys as they pick up the stones, the villagers are walking clichés, and even Tessie Hutchinson, singled out from the rest by her tardiness, is tardy for the most housewifely of reasons. (How different the story would be if she appeared nervous and flustered, a few moments ahead of, say, a disheveled Steve Adams!) The reader is drawn to sink into this warm bath of comfortable stereotypes, illusions intact. Totally off guard against the possibility that the good hearts of these neighborly folks might beat in time with an ancient and brutal rhythm, that superstitious fears of hunger and death might easily outweigh feelings of friendliness and compassion, the reader may well recoil from any previous fascination and, in an effort to deny involvement, recoil from the story, too. Except that we do not reject it; "The Lottery" continues to exert such power over the imagination of its readers that it clearly must be providing a catharsis for instincts similar to those that move the villagers to pick up stones.

Questions For Discussion

1. What associations does the word "lottery" have for you? Are they relevant to the story?
2. Comment on the ending of the first paragraph.
3. On what other occasions might the people of the village gather in the way they do for the lottery? Mr. Summers is in charge of "civic activities." Is the lottery one of these? Explain.
4. Discuss the degree to which the tradition of the lottery has been kept. Why does no one want to make a new box? Why is the whole institution not abandoned?
5. Examine the character of Tessie Hutchinson. She claims that her fate is not *fair*. Is there any reason why she should be singled out? Is she a tragic

heroine? Consider her cry, "There's Don and Eva. . . . Make *them* take their chance!"

6. On your first reading, when did you begin to suspect what happens at the end of the story? How soon might it become evident? What are the most important hints?

7. One reason the ending can surprise a reader is that the villagers never speak directly of what they are about. Why not? Are they ashamed? afraid?

8. Comment on the conversation between the Adamses and Old Man Warner. What is the implication of Steve Adams's last appearance in the story?

9. Does the rhyme "Lottery in June, corn be heavy soon" adequately explain the institution of the lottery? What other reasons might people have for such behavior? What is the social function of a scapegoat?

10. After her family has received the black spot, Tessie complains, but Mrs. Delacroix tells her, "Be a good sport, Tessie." Comment on this choice of words.

11. Discuss the reaction of the Hutchinson family. Why does the lottery single out a family first, then a victim?

12. Old Man Warner says, "People ain't the way they used to be." Are they? What does he mean?

13. Why are the people in such a hurry to "finish"?

14. What is the implication of "someone gave little Davy Hutchinson a few pebbles"?

Topics for Writing

CRITICAL ESSAYS

1. Jackson's "The Lottery" and Le Guin's "The Ones Who Walk Away from Omelas."
2. Jackson's techniques for building suspense in "The Lottery."
3. The usefulness of stereotypes in "The Lottery."

RELATED SUBJECT

1. Examine the behavior of groups of people with which you are familiar. Can you find actual instances of formal or informal practices similar to the one described in "The Lottery" — even though they may not lead to such a brutal finale? Have you or has anyone you know been made a scapegoat? Write an essay showing how one such case reflects and confirms the implications of Jackson's story.

Related Commentary from Part Two

Shirley Jackson, The Morning of June 28, 1948, and "The Lottery," p. 1458.

Suggested Reading

Freidman, Lenemaja. *Shirley Jackson.* Twayne's United States Authors Series 253. Boston: Hall, 1975. 63–67.

HENRY JAMES

The Beast in the Jungle (p. 652)

James's commentary on "The Beast in the Jungle" (included in Part Two, p. 1461) acknowledges it as an "elaborated fantasy — which, I must add, I hold a successful thing only as its motive may seem to the reader to stand out sharp." This somewhat apologetic explanation concludes that the reader (as a "detached witness" to James's literary efforts) might not be successful at disengaging his "treated theme" from the labyrinth of sentences surrounding it. If James was so apprehensive about the obstacles to understanding his story that the leisured class of readers who bought his New York edition of *Collected Works* might encounter, teachers have good cause to proceed with care in discussing this text in the contemporary curriculum. After all, for most students James's long, complex story competes with assigned reading lists and problem sets in several other courses.

The critic Clifton Fadiman regards "The Beast in the Jungle" as the best of James's stories, "combining the utmost concentration of effect with the utmost inclusiveness of meaning." In Fadiman's explication, the story is pure myth, grounded in James's ironic treatment of the concept of the Faustian man that dominates our society: "Faust, we say, is ourselves, is Western man, the striver, the man to whom things happen, the man who makes things happen, the hero of experience." But the truth is that most people live modestly. We "live pitifully un-Faustian lives and die pitifully un-Faustian deaths." So James shows us how to present "the un-Faustian life in imaginative terms." According to Fadiman, the subject of "The Beast in the Jungle" is "not the life we have had but the life we have missed. . . . Most of us are only dimly aware that it never happens; but it is Marcher's horrifying fate to know it intensely."

Another more recent interpretation by the gender critic Eve Kosofsky Sedgwick, argues that John Marcher was a latent homosexual (see Part Two, p. 1515). Sedgwick, unlike most of the male critics who analyze "The Beast in the Jungle," considers May Bartram's desire as something more than a supplement to John Marcher's predicament. It is this kind of fresh approach to short-story classics that may show students the value of criticism, as well as the ability of great short fiction to survive its interpreters.

Questions for Discussion

1. Describe the main characters in the story and summarize their relationships.
2. What are the main events of the plot?
3. How would you characterize James's prose style?
4. How well do you think James succeeded in this story, in terms of what he said he wanted to do? (See his commentary in Part Two, p. 1461).

Exercise in Reading and Writing

1. Assign each student in the class one sentence in the opening paragraphs of the story (the number of sentences assigned will depend on the class size). Ask

students to paraphrase their sentences, using the clearest, simplest words that convey James's meaning. Collect these sentences and assemble them to correspond to the original. Distribute copies of the paraphrased text, and discuss what has been lost (or gained) in the translation.

Related Commentaries from Part Two

Henry James, The Subject of "The Beast in the Jungle," p. 1461.
Eve Kosofsky Sedgwick, The Beast in the Closet: A Gender Critic Reads James's "The Beast in the Jungle," p. 1515.

Suggested Reading

Fadiman, Clifton, ed. "A Note on 'The Beast in the Jungle.'" In *The Short Stories of Henry James*. New York: Random, 1945.

SARAH ORNE JEWETT

A White Heron (p. 687)

Jewett portrays Sylvia, whose very name associates her with the woodland, as torn between the natural world in which she is so fully at home and the first stirrings of the "great power" of love in her "woman's heart." Her project of pleasing the young hunter and winning the treasure of his gratitude, in the form of ten dollars, leads her out of her shyness and into the heroic adventure of climbing the great pine tree. As a result of her efforts, Sylvia grows within herself. The reader worries that she may be tempted into betraying the white heron and thus into surrendering something essential to her own integrity, but Sylvia, in her vision from the top of the tree and her face-to-face meeting with the heron, has gained the prospective necessary to hold firm.

Jewett's rich evocation of the landscape and the emotional intensity with which she narrates the climactic action contribute to the story's deeper resonances. If Sylvia recalls the woodland goddess Diana — and similarly guards her chastity — she also resembles those heroes and heroines of myth and folklore who must go to some symbolic world-navel or towering height in quest of wisdom, or who must suffer an initiation that involves mastering their fear of the (sometimes phallic) *other* and reintegrating their identities in order to cope with it. Sylvia rejects the destructive gun and mounts the pine tree, "a great main-mast to the voyaging earth," electing the fecund life of a natural world she is still discovering over the destructive promises of the "ornithologist," whose grounds are populated with dead, stuffed birds. While the narrator ends fretting over Sylvia's having consigned herself to loneliness and love-longing, nothing in the story suggests that she would be better off having sold herself for ten dollars and a whistle.

Students may find it easier to approach the story through its autobiographical dimensions. According to Eugene Hillhouse Pool, who builds on F. O. Matthiessen's early study, Jewett remained childlike and single all her life, treasuring the love of her father, who used to take her on long rambles through the countryside when she was a girl. "As Sylvia elects to keep her private and meaningful secret, so is she choosing for Miss Jewett too. . . . She chooses, psychologically, to remain a child, with Sylvia." But if Jewett chose to remain a child, it is a child in terms she met in reading Wordsworth, whom she admired: as one privy to the indwelling spirit of the natural world.

The imagery that surrounds Sylvia is uniformly associated with *mother* nature until she ventures up the tree and meets the heron. Her adventure enables her to reject assertively the young man and the advancing modern world of science and machinery with which he is associated. This is a step forward from her original strategies of withdrawal and concealment. The antinomy, however, is not resolved. The only perfect marriage in the story is between the nesting herons; and Jewett offers no key to a satisfactory union between the world of nature and the civilization that threatens to despoil it.

Questions for Discussion

1. Jewett is known as a local colorist. To what extent is the locale of this story its subject? To what extent does the story transcend its specific Maine setting?
2. Discuss the presentation of the cow Sylvia is driving as the story opens. What does her "loud moo by way of explanation" actually explain?
3. Comment on the men, apart from the hunter, mentioned in the story. Is the absence of men from Sylvia's world a significant factor in the story?
4. As a child in town, Sylvia has the reputation of being "afraid of folks." Is she? Does she have reason?
5. Explain Sylvia's reaction when she hears the hunter's whistle. Why does Jewett briefly switch to the present tense here? Does she do so elsewhere?
6. Comment on the omniscient-narrative point of view in this story. How is it controlled? What does the narrative voice contribute?
7. Describe the character and appurtenances of the young hunter, and contrast them with those of Sylvia. How important are his evident gentleness and good intentions?
8. How does Jewett charge the pine tree and Sylvia's climb to the top of it with special meaning? What does Sylvia see up there that she has never seen before?
9. What do Sylvia and the heron have in common?
10. Analyze the last paragraph. What has Sylvia lost? What has she preserved? What has she gained?

Topics for Writing

CRITICAL ESSAYS

1. Elements of folk and fairy tale in "A White Heron."
2. Sylvia's nighttime excursion as a journey into the self.
3. Maternal and sexual imagery in "A White Heron."
4. "A White Heron" as a rejection of modern industrial society.

Related Commentary from Part Two

Sarah Orne Jewett, Looking Back on Girlhood, p. 1465.

Suggested Readings

Brenzo, Richard. "Free Heron or Dead Sparrow: Sylvia's Choice in Sarah Orne Jewett's 'A White Heron.' " *Colby Library Quarterly* 14 (1978): 36–41.
Hovet, Theodore R. "America's 'Lonely Country Child': The Theme of Separation in Sarah Orne Jewett's 'A White Heron.'" *Colby Library Quarterly* 14 (1978): 166–71.
————." 'Once Upon a Time': Sarah Orne Jewett's 'A White Heron' as a Fairy Tale." *Studies in Short Fiction* 15 (1978): 63-68.
Pool, Eugene Hillhouse. "The Child in Sarah Orne Jewett." *Appreciation of Sarah Orne Jewett.* Ed. Richard Cary. Waterville, ME: Colby College P, 1973. 223–28, esp. 225. Originally published in *Colby Library Quarterly* 7 (1967): 503–09.

JAMES JOYCE

Araby (p. 696)

The rich texture of imagery and allusion that Joyce weaves into "Araby" may delight the sophisticated reader, but for the classroom instructor it represents a temptation comparable to the temptation that may be brought to mind by the apple tree in the "wild garden" mentioned in the second paragraph. Students should not be asked to contemplate the story's symbolism until they grasp its plot. To begin class discussion of "Araby" with the question What happens? may well be to discover that, for a novice reader, no meaningful action seems to have been completed. When the confusion arising from this sense of anticlimax is compounded by the difficulties presented by the unfamiliarity of florins, bazaars, hallstands, and other things old and Irish, "Araby" may strike students as pointless and unnecessarily obscure.

Once it is seen, however, that the narrator's disappointment at the bazaar resolves the tension built up by his attraction to Mangan's sister and his quest to fetch her a symbol of his love, the many specific contrasts between the sensuous and romantic world of the narrator's imagination and the banal and tawdry world of actual experience become meaningful keys to understanding what has happened. The opposition between fantasy and reality continues throughout: "Her image accompanied me even in places the most hostile to romance." The story's pivotal paragraph ends with the narrator cooling his forehead against the window in one of the empty upper rooms, staring out not really at Mangan's sister but at "the brown-clad figure cast by my imagination." Before this moment, his excited fancy has transformed the "decent" and somewhat dilapidated neighborhood of North Richmond Street into a fitting backdrop for such a tale as one might find in a yellow-leaved romance. Mangan's sister, kissed by lamplight, becomes in his view a work of art like a painting by Rossetti. The narrator's soul luxuriates in a dream of exotic beauty soon to be possessed by means of a journey to Araby: "I imagined that I bore

111

my chalice safely through a throng of foes." But after the protracted visit from the tedious Mrs. Mercer and the even longer delayed return of the narrator's uncle with the necessary coin, the limitations of the romantic imagination begin to emerge. The "chalice" is replaced by a florin, held "tightly in my hand"; the quest is made by "third-class carriage"; and the bazaar itself, its potential visionary qualities defeated by failing illumination, turns out to be an ordinary market populated by ordinary shop girls from no farther east than England. At Araby, what matters is not purity of heart but hard cash.

The pitiful inadequacy of the narrator's two pennies and sixpence to master "the great jars that stood like eastern guards" at the door of the bazaar stall completes his painful disillusionment, but Joyce allows his hero one last Byronic vision of himself "as a creature driven and derided by vanity." When the lights go out in Araby, its delusive magic collapses, and the bazaar becomes as "blind" as North Richmond Street. Well might the narrator's eyes burn, for they have been working hard to create out of intractable materials a much more beautiful illusion than Araby. This imaginative power cannot be entirely vain, however, since in the mind that tells the story it is capable of evoking experiences like those described in the story's third paragraph, against which even the hoped-for transports of Araby would have paled.

Questions for Discussion

1. Why does the narrator want to go to the bazaar?
2. Why does he arrive so late?
3. Why doesn't he buy anything for Mangan's sister?
4. Enumerate the activities taking place at Araby. To what extent do they sustain its "magical name"?
5. What had the narrator expected to find at Araby? What was the basis of his expectation?
6. Define the narrator's feelings for Mangan's sister. To what extent is she the cause of those feelings? What, as they say, does he *see* in her?
7. What purpose might Joyce have had in choosing not to mention the object of the narrator's affections until the middle of the third paragraph? Describe the context into which she is introduced. In what ways is she part of the world of North Richmond Street?
8. What is the role of the narrator's uncle in the story? What values and attitudes does he represent? Are they preferable to those of the narrator?

Topics for Writing

CRITICAL ESSAYS

1. Light, vision, and beauty in "Araby."
2. "Araby" and the quest for the Holy Grail.
3. The function of nonvisual sense imagery in "Araby."
4. Joyce's control of tone in "Araby."

EXERCISE FOR READING

1. On a second reading of the story, keep two lists. In the first record ideas, images, and allusions that suggest contexts remote from the immediate

situation, jotting down associations that they bring to mind. In the second list note anything mentioned in the story with which you are unfamiliar. Look some of these items up. Then write an informal paragraph or two showing to what extent tracking Joyce's mind in this fashion helped you to understand and enjoy the story.

RELATED SUBJECTS

1. Using the first three paragraphs of "Araby" as a model, write a recollection of the way you spent your evenings at some memorable period of your childhood. Use specific sensory images to evoke the locale, the activities, and the way you felt at the time.
2. Narrate an experience in which you were disappointed. First show how your erroneous expectations were generated; then describe what you actually encountered in such a way that its contrast with your expectations is clear.

Suggested Readings

Brugaletta, J. J., and M. H. Hayden. "Motivation for Anguish in Joyce's 'Araby.'" *Studies in Short Fiction* 15 (1978): 11–17.

Cronin, E. J. "James Joyce's Trilogy and Epilogue: 'The Sisters,' 'An Encounter,' 'Araby,' and 'The Dead.' " *Renascence* 31 (1979): 229–48.

Morrissey, L. J. "Joyce's Narrative Struggles in 'Araby.' " *Modern Fiction Studies* 28 (1982): 45–52.

Roberts, R. P. " 'Araby' and the Palimpsest of Criticism, or Through a Glass Eye Darkly." *Antioch Review* 26 (1966–67): 469–89.

Stone, H. " 'Araby' and the Writings of James Joyce." *Antioch Review* 25 (1965): 375–410.

JAMES JOYCE

The Dead (p. 700)

"The Dead" is an apprehension of mortality. Joyce's carefully detailed scrutiny of the party, with all its apparent vivacity, serves only to reveal the triviality, transience, and emptiness of what passes in Dublin for life. The story involves a series of supersessions. Miss Ivors's friendliness is superseded by rigid politics, and she departs. Her kind of fervor is superseded by the "hospitality" of the dinner table that Gabriel feels so good about and that he celebrates in his speech. That conviviality, however, is exposed as mostly hypocritical, as each person reveals a selfish preoccupation — including Gabriel, who uses his oration to reassure himself after his self-esteem has been wounded by Miss Ivors. The long evening, however, generates in the heart of Gabriel a strong surge of love for Gretta that supersedes his selfishness. It is edged with jealousy and self-contempt, Gabriel's habitual weaknesses; nonetheless, the reader feels for a while that out of the waste of the soiree at least this rejuvenation has been salvaged. But Gabriel is longing for something just as dead as Michael Furey, and Gretta's devastating disclosure of a dead lover's power over her mind brings the "thought-tormented" Gabriel to his final recognition of the predominance of death. Like the monks of Mount Melleray, all people in Ireland, dead or alive — from the aged Aunt Julia on down — seem to be sleeping in their coffins.

While Gabriel's vision is triggered by the revelation of a dead man's sway over the emotions of his wife and of his consequent power to thwart Gabriel's desire, it is supported by the pervasive imagery of snow, chill, and death that comes to fulfillment in the last paragraph. The snow has been falling intermittently throughout the story. Gabriel is blanketed with it when he arrives on the scene, and images of cold and dampness pervade the narration. Last year "Gretta caught a dreadful cold"; Bartell D'Arcy has one this year. The girl in the song he sings holds her death-cold infant in a soaking rain. Not only are the physical descriptions of some characters so vivid that one almost sees the skulls beneath the flesh; even the warm, lively, cheerful elements of the story contribute to the final impression of morbidity. The Misses Morkan are giving what may be their final dance. The alcoholic antics of Mr. Browne and Freddy Malins consist only of ersatz good humor. And Gabriel himself, on whom everyone depends, can barely sustain his nerve and perform his function as master of the revels, keeper of order, and sustainer of life.

In the moribund and sterile world presided over by his three spinster aunts, Gabriel is called upon to play a role not unlike that of a year god at this Christmas season. (The party probably takes place on Epiphany, January 6.) From the outset he is willing, but in three sequential encounters he fails. Each failure strikes a blow at his naiveté, his self-confidence, and his sense of superiority. His first two defeats are followed by accomplishments (handling Freddy, his performance at dinner), but their effect on him is cumulative. Gabriel's cheerful banter with the pale, pale Lily does not suit her, as one who has been hurt in love, and his Christmas gift of a coin can do little to ease her "great bitterness." Afterward, his pretensions to take care of people are subjected to merciless ridicule in the "goloshes" passage. With Miss Ivors, Gabriel is more circumspect than with Lily, but that does not prevent him from being whipsawed between her political hostility and her personal affection. This confusing interaction not only causes Miss Ivors to abandon the company and Gabriel in his speech to reject the entire younger generation of Ireland, it also sets the stage for his ultimate failure with Gretta. Gretta's favorable response to Miss Ivors's plan for a trip to Galway now seems to Gabriel a betrayal, and the association of this trip with Gretta's love for the long-dead Michael compounds the feelings of alienation and self-contempt that Miss Ivors's disapproval fosters in him.

Gabriel's failures and self-doubts should not diminish him unduly in the reader's eyes: Joyce portrays him as aesthetically sensitive, charitable, and loving. The "generous tears" he sheds out of sympathy for Gretta's sorrow may not redeem anyone in a world devoted to death, but they are the distillation of a compassion quite opposite to the self-serving hypocrisy that has passed for friendly conversation at the Misses Morkan's ball. By the end of the story Gabriel no longer feels superior to his compatriots. He recognizes that when Aunt Julia dies his speechifying will be useless. He turns his mind away from the past and toward a future in which, as he feels his old identity fade and dissolve, at least the theoretical possibility of growth and change exists. The ambiguity of Gabriel's much-debated "journey westward" reflects the uncertainty of any future, but Gabriel's readiness to embrace it represents a major step forward from his rejection of Miss Ivors's proposition in favor of recycling of the European continent.

Questions for Discussion

1. Contrast the mood of the first paragraph with that of the second. Why does Joyce move from anticipation to rigidity?
2. Why are the Misses Morkan so eager for Gabriel to arrive?
3. What is the basis of Gabriel's error with Lily?
4. Explain Gabriel's hesitation to quote Browning.
5. What does Gabriel's interest in galoshes reveal about him?
6. Comment on the men present at the dance besides Gabriel. Why does Joyce limit his cast so narrowly?
7. Discuss the reception of Mary Jane's "Academy piece."
8. What does Miss Ivors want from Gabriel? Why is he so upset by his conversation with her? Why does she leave early? Figuratively, what does she take with her when she goes?
9. Explain Gabriel's longing to be out in the snow. Is Gabriel "thought-tormented"?
10. Explain the irony of Julia singing "Arrayed for the Bridal" to Mary Jane's accompaniment. What, in this regard, is the effect of the subsequent conversation?
11. Comment on the relevance of the dinner-table conversation to the themes of the story.
12. Why is Gabriel so cheerful when carving and when proposing his toast? Is he justified? Why does he imagine people standing in the snow before he begins to speak?
13. What is the effect of Joyce's ending the tribute to the Misses Morkan with a glimpse of Freddy conducting the singers with his fork?
14. Comment on Gabriel's anecdote about "the never-to-be-forgotten Johnny." Can it be read as a summation in a minor key of the party now ending? of the life of the Morkan family? of their society?
15. Discuss the scene in which Gabriel watches Gretta listening to D'Arcy. What is Gabriel responding to? What is Gretta responding to? What do they have in common? Trace their moods as they proceed to the hotel.
16. Why is Gabriel so humiliated when he learns that Michael Furey is dead? What other effects does this revelation have on him? Explain what he realizes in the last section of the story.
17. Discuss the final paragraph. What does its poetic beauty contribute to the story? What is our final attitude toward Gabriel?

Topics for Writing

CRITICAL ESSAYS

1. Gabriel Conroy and women.
2. Why "The Dead" is a Christmas story.
3. Gabriel Conroy's death wish.
4. Gabriel Conroy — failed redeemer.
5. Habit and hypocrisy in "The Dead."

EXERCISE FOR READING

1. After your first reading of the story, scan it again, marking the following: all
    references to cold, dampness, and snow; all references to death, illness, or
    people dead at the time of the story; all references to warmth, light, fire, and
    the like; all references to youth, young people, children, and the like. Catalog
    your findings and write a paragraph on the importance of these elements in
    the story.

RELATED SUBJECT

1. For a specific occasion, plan and compose an after-dinner speech with several
    headings like Gabriel's. Then analyze your speech, explaining what you were
    trying to accomplish for your audience — and for yourself. Compare your
    intentions with Gabriel's.

Related Commentaries from Part Two

Richard Ellmann, A Biographical Perspective on Joyce's "The Dead," p. 1437.
Frank O'Connor, Style and Form in Joyce's "The Dead," p. 1500.

Suggested Readings

Beck, Warren. *Joyce's "Dubliners": Substance, Vision, and Art.* Durham, NC: Duke UP,
    1969. 303–60.
Bernstock, Bernard. "The Dead." *James Joyce's "Dubliners": Critical Essays.* Ed.
    Clive Hart. New York: Viking, 1969. 153–69, 177–79.
Loomis, C. C., Jr. "Structure and Sympathy in 'The Dead.'" *Twentieth Century
    Interpretations of "Dubliners."* Ed. Peter K. Garrett. Englewood Cliffs, NJ:
    Prentice, 1968. 110–14. Originally published in *PMLA* 75 (1960): 149–51.
San Juan, Epifanio, Jr. *James Joyce and the Craft of Fiction: An Interpretation of
    "Dubliners."* Rutherford, NJ: Fairleigh Dickinson UP, 1972. 209–23.

FRANZ KAFKA

A Hunger Artist (p. 734)

This "brief but striking parable of alienation" (to quote Kafka's biographer
Ernst Pawel) was probably written in February 1922, shortly before Kafka began *The
Castle.* He had just returned to Prague after a four-week winter vacation prescribed
by his doctor as a sort of "shock treatment" to arrest his advancing tuberculosis and
deepening depression. Back at his desk, in his room in his parents' apartment, Kafka
described his activities in a letter to a friend: "In order to save myself from what is
commonly referred to as 'nerves,' I have lately begun to write a little. From about
seven at night I sit at my desk, but it doesn't amount to much. It is like trying to dig
a foxhole with one's fingernails in the midst of battle."

"A Hunger Artist" was among the few works Kafka allowed to be published in his lifetime. Ironically, he read the galley proofs only a few days before his death. Pawel describes the scene:

> On May 11, [his friend Max] Brod came for what he knew would be his last visit, pretending merely to have stopped off on his way to a lecture in Vienna so as not to alarm his friend. Kafka, by then quite unable to eat, was wasting away, dying of starvation [because of throat lesions] and immersed in the galley proofs of "A Hunger Artist." Fate lacked the subtle touch of Kafka's art.

> The effort drained him. "Kafka's physical condition at this point," Klopstock [a medical student] later wrote, "and the whole situation of his literally starving to death, were truly ghastly. Reading the proofs must have been not only a tremendous emotional strain but also a shattering kind of spiritual encounter with his former self, and when he had finished, the tears kept flowing for a long time. It was the first time I ever saw him overtly expressing his emotions this way. Kafka had always shown an almost superhuman self-control."

As a parable, "A Hunger Artist" may be interpreted in as many ways as there are reader's finding words to describe their response to the text. Kafka created in his fiction a metaphorical language akin to music, touching emotions at a level beyond the denotations of the words he used to dramatize his imaginary characters' situations. The title is significant: "*A* Hunger Artist" not "*The* Hunger Artist." There are many kinds of hungers, and many kinds of artists expressing different needs for substance. Students may define the "hunger" as a desire for religious certainty and the "fasting" as the stubborn abstention from a faith without God. Or the key to the parable may lie in the Hunger Artist's statement at the end of the story: "I have to fast. I can't help it.... Because I couldn't find the food I liked. If I had found it, believe me, I should have made no fuss and stuffed myself like you or anyone else." Kafka was tormented by a failure of nourishment — from his faith, his family, his talent, his art.

Questions for Discussion

1. What is a parable? Is "A Hunger Artist" a parable?
2. Is it possible to read Kafka's story literally, as a realistic tale? What gives you the sense that there is more to "A Hunger Artist" than its plot and characters?
3. Is Kafka describing an unimaginable situation? Explain.
4. Gaping spectators, butchers, theatrical managers, circus people — the world of the Hunger Artist is mercenary and materialistic. He is described as a "martyr." A martyr to what?
5. As the Hunger Artist loses his popularity, he joins the circus, and his cage is put on display near the animal cages. What does this symbolize? What does this action foreshadow?
6. Explicate the last paragraph of the story. Analyze the function of the panther and his "noble body."

Topics for Writing

1. Write a parable.
2. "It was not the hunger artist who was cheating, he was working honestly, but the world was cheating him of his reward." Compare and contrast "A Hunger

Artist" and "The Metamorphosis," taking this statement as the theme of both stories.

3. Agree or disagree with this statement by Primo Levi, the Italian author who translated Kafka's *The Trial*:

> Now I love and admire Kafka because he writes in a way that is totally unavailable to me. In my writing, for good or evil, knowingly or not, I've always strived to pass from the darkness into the light. . . . Kafka forges his path in the opposite direction: he endlessly unravels the hallucinations that he draws from incredibly profound layers, and he never filters them. The reader . . . never receives any help in tearing through the veil or circumventing it to go and see what it conceals. Kafka never touches ground, he never condescends to giving you the end of Ariadne's thread.
>
> But this love of mine is ambivalent, close to fear and rejection: it is similar to the emotion we feel for someone dear who suffers and asks us for help we cannot give. . . . His suffering is genuine and continuous, it assails you and does not let you go.

Suggested Readings

Levi, Primo. "Translating Kafka," *In The Mirror Maker*. By Levi. New York: Schocken, 1989.

Pawel, Ernst. *The Nightmare of Reason: A Life of Franz Kafka*. New York: Farrar, 1984.

FRANZ KAFKA

The Metamorphosis (p. 741)

This story admits the broadest range of explications — biographical, psychoanalytical, religious, philosophical. Here is one way it might be read: As the sole supporter of his family after the collapse of his father's business, Gregor Samsa has selflessly devoted himself to serving others. Bringing home "good round coin which he could lay on the table for his amazed and happy family" has given him great satisfaction, and his only ambition has been to send his sister, "who loved music, unlike himself," to study at the Conservatorium. After his metamorphosis, Gregor can no longer justify his existence by serving others. Instead, he must come to terms with himself *as* himself, an alien being whose own nature and needs are perhaps only by a degree more strange to Gregor than those of the human Gregor Samsa would have been, if somehow he had confronted them rather than deferring to the version of himself projected by the supposed needs of his family.

Kafka simultaneously traces Gregor's painful growth to self-willed individuality and the family's liberation from dependence upon him, for the relationship of dependence and exploitation has been crippling to both parties. Gregor learns what food he likes, stakes his sticky claim to the sexually suggestive picture of the woman with the fur muff (which may represent an objectification of his libido), and, no longer "considerate," at last *comes* out, intruding his obscene existence upon the world out of a purely self-assertive desire to enjoy his sister's music and to be united with its beauty. With this act Gregor has become fully himself; his death soon after simply releases him from the misery of his existence.

It is also a final release of the family from dependence and from the shame and incompetence that it entails. As an insect, Gregor becomes quite obviously the embarrassment to the family that they allowed him to be when he was human. Step by step they discover their ability to support themselves — taking jobs, coping with what is now merely the troublesome burden of Gregor, and learning finally the necessity of escaping from the prison that his solicitousness has placed them in. Gregor's battle with his father strangely transmutes the Oedipal conflict. It is triggered by Gregor's becoming a being for whom there is no longer room in the family, just as if he were a youth growing to sexual maturity, but the result is that the father, who has previously been reduced to a state of supine inertia by Gregor's diligent exertions, returns to claim his full manhood as husband and paterfamilias.

Emerging from their apartment, "which Gregor had selected," the family members grow into an independent purposiveness that Gregor himself is never able to attain. The story may be said to end with a second metamorphosis, focused in the image of Grete stretching her young body — almost like a butterfly newly emerged from her cocoon. Gregor, left behind like the caterpillar whose demise releases her, is denied all but a premonitory glimpse of the sexual and reproductive fulfillment for which his sister seems destined.

Questions for Discussion

1. Describe the effect of Kafka's matter-of-fact assertion of the bizarre incident with which the story begins. Are you very interested in how it came to pass? How does Kafka keep that from becoming an issue in the story?
2. What are Gregor's concerns in section I? To what degree do they differ from what would matter to him if he had *not* been transformed into an insect?
3. When Gregor is trying to get out of bed, he considers calling for help but then dismisses the idea. Why?
4. What seems most important to the members of Gregor's family as he lies in bed? his health?
5. Describe the reaction of Gregor's parents to their first view of the metamorphosed Gregor. What circumstances in ordinary life might elicit a similar response?
6. Discuss the view from Gregor's window.
7. Trace Gregor's adaptation to his new body. In what ways do the satisfactions of his life as an insect differ from the satisfactions of his life as a traveling salesman?
8. When Gregor's father pushes him back into his room at the end of section I, Kafka calls it "literally a deliverance." Comment on the possible implications of that description.
9. Describe Grete's treatment of Gregor in section II. Is Gregor ill?
10. What are Gregor's hopes for the future? Is there anything wrong with those hopes?
11. For a time, Gregor is ashamed of his condition and tries to hide from everyone. In what way might this be called a step forward for him?

12. Discuss the conflicting feelings Gregor has about the furniture being taken out of his room. Why does he try to save the picture? What might Kafka's intention be in stressing that it is on this occasion that Grete calls Gregor by his name for the first time since his metamorphosis?
13. "Gregor's broken loose." What does Gregor's father do? Why? Explain the situation that has developed by the end of section II.
14. How does the charwoman relate to Gregor? Why is she the one who presides over his "funeral"?
15. Compare the role of the lodgers in the family with that of Gregor. Have they supplanted him? Why does Gregor's father send them away in the morning?
16. Why does Gregor, who previously did not like music, feel so attracted to his sister's playing? What change has taken place in his attitude toward himself? What might Kafka mean by "the unknown nourishment he craved"?
17. Comment on Grete's use of the neuter pronoun "it" to refer to Gregor.
18. What is the mood of the final passages of the story?

Topics for Writing

CRITICAL ESSAYS

1. How Kafka gains the reader's "willing suspension of disbelief."
2. Gregor Samsa's metamorphosis — a triumph of the self.
3. Kafka's "The Metamorphosis" as a study of sublimated incest.
4. Tolstoy's "The Death of Ivan Ilych" and Kafka's "The Metamorphosis": two studies of dying.

RELATED SUBJECT

1. Consider Kafka's use of apparently symbolic images whose complete meaning seems impossible to state in abstract terms — the apples, the fur muff, or the hospital beyond the window, for example. Write a vignette in which symbolic objects play a role without becoming counters in a paraphrasable allegory. Some examples of symbols: a candle, a cup, the sea, broken glass, ants.

Related Commentary from Part Two

John Updike, Kafka and "The Metamorphosis," p. 1527.

Suggested Readings

Greenberg, Martin. "Kafka's 'Metamorphosis' and Modern Spirituality." *Tri-Quarterly* 6 (1966): 5–20.

Kafka, Franz. *The Metamorphosis*. Trans. and ed. Stanley Corngold. New York: Bantam, 1972. (Contains notes, documents, and ten critical essays.)

Moss, Leonard. "A Key to the Door Image in 'The Metamorphosis.'" *Modern Fiction Studies* 17 (1971): 37–42.

Nabokov, Vladimir. *Lectures on Literature*. New York: Harcourt, 1980. 250–83.

Taylor, Alexander. "The Waking: The Theme of Kafka's 'Metamorphosis.'" *Studies in Short Fiction* 2 (1965): 337–42.

Wolkenfeld, Suzanne. "Christian Symbolism in Kafka's 'The Metamorphosis.' " *Studies in Short Fiction* 10 (1973): 205–07.

JAMAICA KINCAID

Girl (p. 779)

Kincaid's one-paragraph story is a dialogue between a mother and a daughter, consisting mostly of the mother's litany of advice about how to act in a ladylike manner. Students might enjoy reading it aloud. The West Indian prose rhythms are subtly beautiful, and the humor of the mother's advice is revealed in the audible reading process for anyone who has missed it by scanning too quickly. The conflict between the girl and her mother is evident in the mother's fears that her daughter will grow up to be a slut. Everything the mother says is twisted in light of that fear. The daughter wonders, "*But what if the baker won't let me feel the bread?*" And the mother replies, "You mean to say that after all you are really going to be the kind of woman who the baker won't let near the bread?" The following speech rhythm is reminiscent of James Joyce's interior monologues. In fact, we are not amiss to ask whether the mother is actually speaking to her daughter in the story, or whether the daughter has internalized her mother's voice and written it down for us to read to the accompaniment of our own laughter.

Questions for Discussion

1. What are the major subjects in this litany of advice? What kind of a life do they describe?
2. The title of the story is "Girl," yet the girl seems to have only two lines of her own, one a protest and the other a question. Why might the author have decided to call the story "Girl" rather than "Mother" or "Woman" or "Advice" or "Memory"?
3. Identify and discuss Kincaid's use of humor in "Girl." What contribution does it make to the story?
4. What is the effect of fairly precise household rules alternating with comments such as "on Sundays try to walk like a lady and not like the slut you are so bent on becoming." String together the lines that admonish the potential slut. What do we think of the mother? What connection is there between the subjects the mother is speaking of and the idea of a slut? Why does it keep popping up from the most innocuous of items? What does this refrain make us think of the daughter? Is the slut refrain a joke or is the author making a suggestion about the construction of self?
5. Some of the advice seems like it could never have been spoken, but only inferred: "this is how you smile to someone you don't like too much; this is how you smile to someone you don't like at all; this is how you smile to someone you like completely." Throughout the whole piece, do you think the mother is speaking to her daughter? What other possibilities could underlie the story's composition?

6. On page 780 the kind of advice changes: "this is how to make a good medicine to throw away a child before it even becomes a child," says the mother. Surely she's not speaking to a young girl here. In the final line, the mother calls her a "woman," the only direct address in the story; earlier the listener has been addressed as a potential slut and been told she's "not a boy." What's the difference between the advice that precedes and follows the reference to aborting a child? Which is more concrete? More abstract? Why does the advice change because of the listener's age? What kinds of knowledge is her mother able to offer?

Topics for Writing

CRITICAL ESSAY

1. The use of humor to indicate conflict in "Girl."

RELATED SUBJECTS

1. Expand the story through the use of descriptive prose. Is the result more or less effective than Kincaid's original?
2. Write a short story in which you use only dialogue.

Suggested Reading

Kincaid, Jamaica. Interview. *New York Times Book Review* 7 Apr. 1985: 6+.

MILAN KUNDERA

The Hitchhiking Game (p. 782)

The unnamed young man and woman whose frightening adventure Kundera describes emerge from a vague backdrop as sharply defined personalities, but Kundera reserves his most detailed artifice for the purpose of making credible the process that calls the reality of these personalities into question. Because he carefully documents each evolving stage of the hitchhiking game as it is experienced by both characters, Kundera is able to convince the reader not only that this assault of fiction upon real life is motivated, plausible, and even likely, but also that it reveals an important truth applicable to us all.

Setting out on a long-awaited vacation from their burdensome and confining jobs the lovers are inclined toward experimentation and play. Each is also inclined, it turns out, to take a vacation from certain self-imposed and mutually imposed constraints on their relationship. The girl is cut off from full sensual awareness by being shy. Her ambition that her relationship with the young man should be *complete* ironically limits it: "The more she tried to give him everything, the more she denied him something: the very thing that a light and superficial love or a flirtation gives to a person." The young man likes the jealousy that arises from her worry on this score just as he likes the girl's shyness: "In the girl sitting beside him he valued precisely what, until now, he had met with least in women: purity." But by definition this relationship is thus limited for him by the lack of what he has found *instead* of purity in the women he has known before, and "he worshipped rather than loved her."

The hitchhiking game offers a way to break free from these constraints, and its result is to engage the two in a relationship antithetical to what has gone before. The young man puts the girl on a pedestal, all right, but in order to humiliate her rather than to worship her, and the perfect harmony of their bodies as they enjoy intercourse beyond "the forbidden boundary" comes at the expense of the unity of body and soul that they have previously known. Even near the beginning both participants have occasion to see that the game is getting out of hand, but each is so fascinated with the sensation of freedom inherent in acting out an alien role that neither is able to stop its progress.

In pretending to be someone other than themselves, the two not only find the freedom to turn off from the narrow road of their prescribed destiny but they also lose touch with what they have thought themselves to be. The young woman *vanishes* behind a little bush to emerge as a hitchhiker, and later, after *disappearing* with a wiggle behind a screen from the view of the man who propositions her in French, she seems to the young man to be crossing a "horrifying boundary" that changes the nature of the self just "as water ceases to be water beyond the boiling point."

At the end the meaning of their experience becomes clear in the recognition that the assertion of identity, "I am me," is a "pitiful tautology." The substitution of any nontautological content for "me" plunges one into a frightening indeterminacy that carries with it a power of decision more burdensome than the illusory confinement it supplants. As a result of having indulged in the freedom of playing their game, these lovers must now say, "I am a man who has demeaned and humiliated his lover," and "I am a woman who has acted like a whore and enjoyed it."

Questions for Discussion

1. What purposes are served by the opening conversation about running out of gas?
2. Evaluate the young man's attitude toward the girl's shyness and his delight in making her blush.
3. What conflicts about her relationship with the young man trouble the girl?
4. Explain the implications of the paradox that the girl gets "the greatest enjoyment from the presence of the man she loved" when she is alone.
5. Why do you think the girl starts the hitchhiking game?
6. One of the first results of the game is that the lovers get angry at each other. Why do they keep playing? Does their anger contribute to the continuation of the game?
7. What kinds of freedom does the game bring to each player?
8. At what stage does the game begin to get out of control? Or has it ever been in the control of either participant? Explain.
9. Define the change of atmosphere that takes place at the beginning of section VI.

10. When does the girl fully enter into her role? What does that involve? What purposes does it serve for her? Answer the same questions about the young man.
11. Explain the insight about the girl that the young man reaches in section VII. Does she reach a similar conclusion at any stage?
12. "There's no escape from a game." Is that true? Explain by reference to the story and in general.
13. What is the effect of the young man's forgetting that he is playing a game? Why does he do so?
14. Explain the last sentence of section XI.
15. Why is "I am me" a "pitiful tautology"?
16. How does what takes place in this story differ from organized theatrics? from daily role playing?
17. Why does the concluding line of the story sound like a sentence to punishment rather than the declaration of a holiday?

Topics for Writing

CRITICAL ESSAYS

1. The first paragraph of "The Hitchhiking Game" as a microcosm.
2. Kundera's story as a philosophical parable.
3. What the lovers in "The Hitchhiking Game" gain and what they lose.
4. Kundera's use of stock imagery in "The Hitchhiking Game" (for example, the road, the woods, the dark, dirty, and wandering city).

EXERCISE FOR READING

1. With a fellow student, act out the scenes of sections III, V, VII, and IX. Record your sensations and your awareness of the doubly fictitious persona with which you are conversing. How would you feel about acting out the rest of the story?

RELATED SUBJECT

1. Write a sketch in which you portray yourself pretending to be someone very different. Perhaps you are habitually polite and deferential to waiters in restaurants. Imagine yourself behaving in an outrageously assertive manner. Or perhaps you are smooth and confident with members of the opposite sex. Describe an encounter in which you are tongue-tied and embarrassed. Follow your incident through to a conclusion that embodies the insight into your personality that writing it suggests.

Suggested Reading

Carlisle, Olga. "A Talk with Milan Kundera." *New York Times Magazine* May 19, 1985.
Lodge, David. "Milan Kundera and the Idea of the Author in Modern Criticism." *Critical Quarterly* Spring/Summer 1984.

D. H. LAWRENCE

Odour of Chrysanthemums (p. 797)

Because of its unusual vocabulary and emotional complexity, this can be a difficult story for many students to understand. Before they read it, their attention should be directed to the first paragraph of the headnote, which suggests an approach. Elizabeth Bates, the protagonist, is bitter because she feels trapped in her marriage. She is caught between her attempt to relate to her husband and her struggle to break free from her marital bondage. Her husband drinks away most of the meager wages he earns at the coal mine, leaving her to tend the children in a dark, squalid cottage she calls a "dirty hole, rats and all." She is fiercely protective of their two children —daughter, Annie, and young son, John. There is another baby on the way. Consumed with anger toward her husband, Elizabeth channels her love and tenderness toward her children. She feels herself "absolutely necessary for them. They were her business."

Recognizing the pattern of Lawrence's use of symbolism in the story may be one of the best ways to approach it. In the opening paragraph, Elizabeth's emotional situation is prefigured in the image of the nameless woman forced back into the hedge by the oncoming train. The female-male opposition in the story is symbolized here: marriage and home (the hedge) versus the mine and the pub (the train). A little later on, Lawrence has Elizabeth comment explicitly on the symbolism implied in the title of the story. When her young daughter is charmed to see her mother wearing the chrysanthemums— "You've got a flower in your apron" (pregnancy = flowering), Elizabeth tells her that she's speaking nonsense. To the mother, the flowers are not beautiful anymore. Most emphatically she does not treasure them as a hardy symbol of fertility in her otherwise bleak existence. To her, they are a symbol of death: "It was chrysanthemums when I married him and chrysanthemums when you were born, and the first time they ever brought him home drunk, he'd got brown chrysanthemums in his button-hole."

Ironically, near the end of the story, when Elizabeth lays out her dead husband on the parlor floor, she smells "a cold, deathly smell of chrysanthemums in the room." One of the miners coming in with the stretcher knocks the vase of flowers to the floor, and she mops up the spilled water. In this action she is a servant of death, "her ultimate master" at the end of the story.

For most of the story, however, her master is her husband. The word "master" is the common name for husband among the village wives, but Elizabeth has refused to submit to her destiny. The line between female and male is clearly drawn in her world, where the sight of twelve children living at home on a miner's salary is not uncommon. But Elizabeth feels herself apart from the other housewives and miners. She judges everyone she comes in contact with, except herself. Then, as she begins to wash the naked body of her dead husband, she feels herself "countermanded. She saw him, how utterly inviolable he lay in himself. She had nothing to do with him. She could not accept it."

The final scene of "Odour of Chrysanthemums," the description of the mother and the wife laying out the body of the dead man, is one of the most unforgettable moments in Lawrence's fiction. The physicality of the dead man is unmistakable, and it affects the two women differently. Now Elizabeth fully accepts the reality of her individuality, her separate existence in the world. Before, she felt herself apart as an emotional defense against her disappointment with her marriage. Now she knows "the utter isolation of the human soul." The husband she hated existed only in her mind. With his death, she is free to ask, "Who am I? What have I been doing? ... What wrong have I done? ... There lies the reality, this man." The story ends with her horrified by the distance between them. Yet she is at peace.

Questions for Discussion

1. "Odour of Chrysanthemums" is set in the kind of mining village Lawrence grew up in. The first four paragraphs "pan in" on the social world of the story, establishing a relationship among the industrial landscape, wild nature, and human beings. Read the opening carefully, noting the diction of the passage, and try to state Lawrence's vision of the relationship among these elements.

2. Note how Elizabeth Bates appears on the scene merely as "a woman." How does the author go on to establish a closer relationship to her? What is she like when we first meet her? Describe the world she inhabits.

3. When Elizabeth sets out to find Walter, she notes "with faint disapproval the general untidiness" of the Rigleys. Consider the use of dialect in this passage. Who uses it? Can you determine Elizabeth's relationship to her neighbors and her class position? Might it be connected to her general satisfaction with her marriage?

4. In section I the family awaits Walter Bates's return from the mines — and yet his presence seems to haunt the family. What influence does even his absence exert on his wife and children?

5. Elizabeth's mother-in-law arrives, and the two women discuss Walter. How does Lawrence subtly and comically establish their relationship to each other and to Walter?

6. Miners stripped down to work underground; half-naked, white Walter is strangely beautiful as he is brought home. Her husband's body is a revelation to Elizabeth: "And she knew what a stranger he was to her." Try to explain the epiphany Elizabeth undergoes; what does she now understand about her marriage?

7. Lawrence said of literary symbols, "You can't give a symbol a meaning anymore than you can give a cat a 'meaning.' Symbols are organic units of consciousness with a life of their own, and you can never explain them away because their value is dynamic, emotional, belonging to the sense-consciousness of the body and soul, and not simply mental. An allegorical image has a *meaning*" (from an essay that appears in *Dragon of Apocalypse: Selected Literary Criticism*, ed. Anthony Beal (New York: Viking, 1966). Trace the meaning that chrysanthemums take on in each stage of this story. Is it possible to give them a "full" meaning? According to Lawrence, are the flowers symbolic or allegorical?

8. Finally, given the portrait of the social world in the story and the portrayal of this unhappy marriage, how might the two be related? Is Lawrence explicit about the relationship or might you like to argue with him about the causes of feeling in it?

Topics for Writing

CRITICAL ESSAYS

1. Light and dark imagery in "Odour of Chrysanthemums."
2. The use of sound and silence in "Odour of Chrysanthemums."
3. The isolation and alienation of marriage in Lawrence's "Odour of Chrysanthemums" and Mason's "Shiloh."

EXERCISE FOR READING

1. One of the difficulties in understanding "Odour of Chrysanthemums" is its vocabulary. Consult a good dictionary to discover the meanings of words such as "gorse," "coppice," "hips," "spinney," "cleaved," "whimsey," "reedy," "pit-pond" "alders," "tarred," "pit-bank," "headstocks," and "colliery." How does this increase your understanding of Lawrence's story?

Related Commentaries from Part Two

Ford Madox Ford, Review of Lawrence's "Odour of Chrysanthemums," p. 1441.
D. H. Lawrence, The Lust of Hate in Poe's "The Cask of Amontillado," p. 1469.

Suggested Readings

Clayton, J. J. "D. H. Lawrence: Psychic Wholeness through Rebirth." *Massachusetts Review* 25 (1984): 200–21.
Kalnins, M. "D. H. Lawrence's 'Odour of Chrysanthemums': The Three Endings." *Studies in Short Fiction* 13 (1976): 471–79.
Rose, S. "Physical Trauma in D. H. Lawrence's Short Fiction." *Contemporary Literature* 16 (1975): 73–83.
Sager, Keith. *D. H. Lawrence: Life into Art.* Athens: U of Georgia P, 1985.
Schneider, Daniel J. *D. H. Lawrence, The Artist as Psychologist.* Lawrence: UP of Kansas, 1984.
Shaw, M. "Lawrence and Feminism." *Critical Quarterly* 25 (1983): 23–27.
Widmer, Kingsley. *The Art of Perversity: D. H Lawrence's Shorter Fictions.* Seattle: U of Washington P, 1962. 25–26.

D. H. LAWRENCE

The Rocking-Horse Winner (p. 813)

Lawrence's masterful technical control wins the reader's assent to the fantastic premise on which the story is built; without that assent, the thematic statement the story propounds would lack cogency. Rather than confronting us boldly with his improbable donnée, as Kafka does in "The Metamorphosis," Lawrence edges up to it. The whispering voices in the house that drive Paul to his furious rocking begin as a thought in the mother's mind and then become a figure of speech that crystallizes imperceptibly into a literal fact — or rather, into an auditory hallucination heard by the children that expresses their perception of their mother's unquenchable need for funds. Paul's ability to pick a winner by riding his rocking horse to where he is lucky requires even more circumspect handling. Like the family members, we learn about it after the fact, putting together bits of information to explain a set of peculiar but at first not at all implausible circumstances — Paul's claim, "Well, I got there!", his familiarity with race horses, Bassett's reluctance "to give him away" to Oscar, Paul's giving Oscar a tip on a long shot that comes in a winner, and only then, with Oscar's skepticism always preempting that of the reader, the revelation of how much he has won. It is not until the very end that we, with his astonished mother, actually witness Paul in the act of receiving revelation — just as he slips beyond the world of everyday probability for good and into the uncharted supernatural realm from whence his "luck" seems to emanate.

Although no explanation, supernatural or otherwise, is necessary to account for good fortune at the race track, Lawrence persuades the reader that Paul's success is caused by his exertions and therefore has a moral meaning. In Paul's household the lack of love is perceived as a lack of money and the lack of money is attributed to a lack of luck. Since luck is by definition something that happens *to* one, to blame one's troubles on luck is to deny responsibility for them and to abandon any effort to overcome them. As the event makes clear, Paul's mother will never be satisfied, no matter how much money falls her way, because no amount of money can fill the emptiness left by the absence of love. The "hard little place" in her heart at the beginning of the story has expanded until, at the end, she feels that her whole heart has "turned actually into a stone." Paul sets out by the force of will to redefine luck as something one can acquire. He places belief before evidence and asserts, "I'm a lucky person. . . . God told me," and then makes good on his promise by riding his rocking horse to where luck comes from. " 'It's as if he had it from heaven,' " Bassett says, "in a secret, religious voice."

In his single-minded devotion to winning money for his mother at the racetrack by riding his rocking horse (which W. D. Snodgrass has likened to masturbation as Lawrence understood it), Paul diverts his spiritual and emotional forces to material aims, and Lawrence symbolically represents the effect of this *materialization* in the process of petrification by which the mother's heart and Paul's blue eyes, which have throughout the story served as an emblem of his obsession, turn to stone. At the end Oscar states the case with epigrammatic precision: Hester's son has been transformed into eighty-odd thousand pounds — a tidy sum, but of course it will not be enough.

Questions for Discussion

1. How is Paul's mother portrayed at the outset? Does Lawrence suggest that she is blameworthy? Why or why not?
2. Explain the family's "grinding sense of the shortage of money." Why do the voices get even louder when some money becomes available? What would it take to still the voices?
3. Discuss the implications of Paul's confusing *luck* with *lucre*. How accurate is his mother's definition of luck? What would constitute true good luck for him?
4. Explain Paul's claim to be lucky. In what sense is he justified? In what sense is he very unlucky?

5. What function do Oscar and Bassett play in the story, beyond providing Paul with practical access to the racetrack and the lawyer?
6. "Bassett was serious as a church." Is this a humorous line? Does It suggest anything beyond the comic?
7. What is the effect on the reader of the episode in which Oscar takes Paul to the track and Paul's horse Daffodil wins the race?
8. Explain the mother's response to her birthday gift. What is its effect on Paul? Why?
9. Before the Derby, Paul does not "know" for several races. Can this dry spell be explained? What brings it to an end?
10. Analyze Paul's last words in the story. What does he mean by *"get there"*? Where, in fact, does he go? Is *absolute* certainty possible? How? Why is Paul so proud to proclaim that he is lucky to his mother? Finally, comment on her reaction.
11. Evaluate Oscar's remarks, which end the story. Was Paul a "poor devil"? In what senses?

Topics for Writing

CRITICAL ESSAYS

1. The handling of the supernatural in Lawrence's "The Rocking-Horse Winner."
2. The religious theme of "The Rocking-Horse Winner."
3. Luck, will, and faith in "The Rocking-Horse Winner."
4. Realistic elements and the social theme of Lawrence's supernatural tale.
5. Luck, lucre, and love in "The Rocking-Horse Winner."

RELATED SUBJECT

1. Look up a newspaper story about some unexplained phenomenon, ghost, or poltergeist, and work it into a narrative whose meaning is finally not dependent on an interest in the supernatural.

Related Commentaries from Part Two

Janice H. Harris, A Psychosocial Explication of Lawrence's "The Rocking-Horse Winner," p. 1454.
D. H. Lawrence, The Lust of Hate in Poe's "The Cask of Amontillado," p. 1469.

Suggested Readings

San Juan, E., Jr. "Theme versus Imitation: D. H. Lawrence's 'The Rocking-Horse Winner,'" *D. H. Lawrence Review* 3 (1970): 136–40.
Snodgrass, W. D. "A Rocking Horse: The Symbol, the Pattern, the Way to Live." *D. H. Lawrence: A Collection of Critical Essays.* Ed. Mark Spilka. *Twentieth Century Views*. Englewood Cliffs, NJ: Prentice, 1963. Originally published in *Hudson Review* 11 (1958).
Widmer, Kingsley. *The Art of Perversity: D. H. Lawrence's Shorter Fictions*. Seattle: U of Washington P, 1962. 92–95, 213.

DAVID LEAVITT

Territory (p. 825)

Leavitt's sensitive study of the relationship between a dedicated mother and her homosexual son may cause discomfort for some students, but a dispassionate examination of what happens in the story should suffice to show that Neil and Barbara's experience is simply a special case of what everyone must go through. Leavitt unflinchingly confronts certain realities of homosexuality that we customarily obscure with the stereotypes of hostile homophobic humor — the dominating and all-forbearing mother, dogs, debasement, drag queens, promiscuous encounters, bathhouses, and the rest. Although several episodes may make the reader smile, nowhere are we invited to hold ourselves superior to the characters by laughing away their anguish. Instead, we must acknowledge that their pain is real and understand its sources and resolution.

Leavitt surveys Barbara's mothering and Neil's sexual development in a series of flashbacks, but the question the story seeks to answer is not why Neil is homosexual — his sexual orientation is *discovered*, not created — but what must happen for him to finish growing up. For a time, Neil feels awkward and guilty — the embarrassed adolescent — bringing home his lover, Wayne, to "this place of his childhood, of his earliest shame, . . . this household of mothers and dogs." If guilt, like dog urine, goes with the territory for Neil, however, it is not for lack of open acceptance from his mother. Indeed, Barbara, who regards mothers' work as typically "futile, tiresome, and unrewarding effort," has made a point not only of accepting but of actively supporting Neil's "alternative life style," whatever her revulsion or disappointment. "She had been there for him every day," setting up her card table full of helpful pamphlets outside the bathhouses, cheering on the Gay Pride parade, and, perhaps most notably, responding warmly when he first came out: "she hugged him from behind, wrapped him in the childhood smells of perfume and brownies, and whispered, 'It's O.K., honey.' "

That she is "quintessentially a mother," however, invites Neil to linger too long as a child in her embrace. Children must eventually become adults, and parents must let them go. Already Neil observes some changes in his mother since he has been away in New York: she has "grown thinner, more rigid, harder to hug." He is astonished when Wayne calls her "Barbara," and later he delights in thinking about her life before she became his mother. Still, unwilling as yet to acknowledge contrary inclinations, both mother and son, out of love, guilt, habit, and misguided duty, seek to prolong their umbilical link. Barbara welcomes Wayne to her home; Neil strives to bracket the two parts of his life by embracing them simultaneously in the movie theater.

It is an adolescent gesture, however, and Barbara finally realizes that a limit has been reached. Wrapping her arms not around Neil but around herself, she turns away from him: "I guess I'm just an old woman with too much on her mind and not enough to do. . . . Don't worry." Neil, too, finally, lets her go: "I'm not thinking about my mother now." We leave him as no longer a child or an adolescent but a *man*, united in a lasting relationship with Wayne, who represents his adult family.

Questions for Discussion

1. In the opening section, Neil watches his mother through a window that superimposes his reflection on her face. Later, by the pool, he reenacts her inching flight from the sun as he moves his towel to stay out of the shade. What purpose might Leavitt have had for stressing these bits of parallel geometry?

2. Comment on Barbara's various political activities. Why does she feel her causes are "fit only for mothers to keep up"?

3. Neil has no success attracting the interest of the gardener. Why does he try to? What might be the implications of his failure?

4. Discuss the role of the dogs — Abigail, Lucille, Fern, and Rasputin — in the story.

5. Characterize Neil's feelings about Wayne's visit before he arrives. Have you experienced similar feelings when introducing a friend to your parents? Specify the reasons for such discomfort.

6. Why does Neil regret that he is homosexual? Characterize his mother's reaction to the news. Is that the way you would like your parents to react to something you knew would be shocking and disappointing?

7. Barbara immediately joins "the Coalition of Parents of Lesbians and Gays." Why? In your opinion, is it a constructive step?

8. Why do you suppose Leavitt goes out of his way to describe the view from the Dumbarton Bridge and to remark that "only ten miles north, a whole city has been built on gunk dredged up from the bay"?

9. When his mother introduces herself to Wayne as "Barbara," "Neil forgets that she is his mother." Why? How does he feel during the ensuing dinner?

10. Why do Wayne and Neil need to hold hands in front of Barbara? Later, why don't they answer her from in the bushes?

11. Leavitt connects the episode about Luis and the Gay Pride parade with this transition: "Once before, Neil and his mother had stared at each other in the glare of bright lights." What else connects the two incidents? Beginning with Barbara's reactions, how do they differ?

12. Carmen Bologna is proud of her drag queen son, "and," says Barbara, "speaking as a mother, let me tell you, you have to be brave to feel such pride." Analyze this remark. What might it mean to Neil? What might it imply about Barbara's feelings?

13. When Abigail urinates on Wayne, Barbara makes the first of two statements of the story's title line: "It goes with the territory." What does she mean? Why is Neil so amused?

14. When Barbara complains to Neil about "these — shenanigans," Neil feels guilt, sorrow, anger, and eventually pride. Explain the sequence. Do you think Barbara really doesn't mind Neil's having a lover?

15. What does Neil learn from studying his mother's list of things to do for Tuesday?

16. After Neil has put one arm around Wayne and one arm around Barbara at the theater, Barbara says, "I know what you were doing." What was he doing? Explain what happens in the ensuing conversation.

17. Discuss the implications of the phrase "two men" in the last line of the story.

Topics for Writing

CRITICAL ESSAYS

1. Gesture, posture, and significant actions in "Territory."
2. Mother-son relationships in Leavitt's "Territory" and Updike's "Flight."
3. Leavitt's use of flashbacks in "Territory."

EXERCISE FOR READING

1. What happens in the story? On a second reading, read only the sections that are written in the present tense. Then summarize the action that takes place in them, identifying the principal conflict, the turning point, and the resolution.

RELATED SUBJECT

1. Write a vignette about an incident in which the best thing you could have done for someone you cared about was to let go and get away. What feelings did you have when you recognized that? How did you behave?

Related Commentary from Part Two

David Leavitt, The Way I Live Now, p. 1470.

Suggested Readings

"The New Lost Generation." *Esquire* 103 (1985): 85–88.
"New Voices and Old Values." *New York Times Book Review* 12 May 1985: 1+.

Ursula K. Le Guin

The Ones Who Walk Away from Omelas (p. 843)

The tone of Le Guin's story deserves special mention, because it supports the humane wisdom of her theme. Rational, unhurried, calm, and composed, her words flow in long paragraphs like the deep bed of a river. She subtitles her story "Variations on a theme by William James." Read her explanation of the source of her story in Part Two (p. 1472), where she quotes two paragraphs by James, the American philosopher and experimental psychologist (1842–1910) and older brother of the writer Henry James. Students will recognize that Le Guin's tone is similar to James's in his philosophical discourse, which she so admires.

The tone of Le Guin's story is animated by her choice of narrator. Simultaneously certain and uncertain, she is both assured and tentative in her description of the happy, peace-loving community. (Remember *Omelas* means "O-peace," as well as Salem, Oregon, spelled backward.) Le Guin is too modest in her assertion of writing about "fortune cookie ideas." She possesses great authority in her definitions: "Happiness is based on a just discrimination of what is necessary, what is neither necessary nor destructive, and what is destructive." Perhaps students need to discuss this philosophical point to make sure they understand it. Major themes of the story — that ideals are the probable causes of future experience, and that what you touch, touches you — are based on this definition of happiness. The ones who walk away from Omelas have used it in formulating their decision to leave the utopian community.

Le Guin is also wise in matters of human psychology. She purposely leaves the details of the good life in Omelas vague, so that readers can imagine their own utopias, complete with as many or as few drugs and as much or as little sex as they are comfortable with. She also knows that her readers will find her vision of the good life more believable after her description of the tormented child on whom everything depends. For human beings, the ideal becomes real only with the introduction of pain and loss, "the terrible justice of reality." The destination of those who leave Omelas is less imaginable than the city of near-perfection. The ones who leave are unwilling to be bound by the terrible laws of this "utopia"; they must create their own futures. Le Guin's fantasy isn't escapist literature. It's as real and inescapable as life itself.

Questions for Discussion

1. What is the tone of this story?
2. What is the point of view in the story? Who is the narrator? Briefly discuss the dual attitudes of the narrator.
3. How accurate is Le Guin's contention that "happiness is based on a just discrimination of what is necessary, what is neither necessary nor destructive, and what is destructive"? How central is this idea to the themes of the story?
4. What type of society is Omelas? Did you find the narrator's description substantive or vague? Discuss possible reasons the author constructed the story in this manner.
5. What role does the tormented child play in the story? How does it affect the citizens of Omelas?
6. Why do some citizens desert Omelas? What is the place that is "even less imaginable to most of us than the city of happiness"?
7. What is the source of conflict in the story? Who is the protagonist? the antagonist?
8. Discuss the major themes of the story.
9. How would you characterize Le Guin's narrative style? Do you feel her use of the short question is effective? Why?
10. What is your reaction to the story?

Topics for Writing

CRITICAL ESSAYS

1. The societies and philosophies in Omelas and in the small town in Jackson's "The Lottery."
2. The idea of the utopian society in "The Ones Who Walk Away from Omelas."

Related Commentary from Part Two

Ursula K. Le Guin, The Scapegoat in Omelas, p. 1472.

Suggested Readings

Cogell, E. C. "Setting as Analogue to Characterization in Ursula Le Guin." *Extrapolation* 18 (1977): 131–41.

Manlove, C. N. "Conservatism in the Fantasy of Le Guin." *Extrapolation* 21 (1980): 287–97.

Moylan, T. "Beyond Negation: The Critical Utopias of Ursula K. Le Guin and Samuel R. Delany." *Extrapolation* 21 (1980): 236–53.

Wood, S. "Discovering Worlds: The Fiction of Ursula K. Le Guin." *Voices for the Future: Essays on Major Science Fiction Writers.* Ed. J. D. Clareson. Bowling Green: Bowling Green U Popular P, 1976–79. 2: 154–79.

DORIS LESSING

To Room 19 (p. 850)

Lessing traces Susan's long slide into suicide in an ample, undramatic narrative that reflects Susan's personality and explores in their full complexity the reasons for her despair. If one factor is more significant than any other, it is the one Lessing announces at the start: "The Rawlings' marriage was grounded in intelligence." Matthew and Susan are known for "their moderation, their humour, and their abstinence from painful experience." Abstaining effectively from painful experience necessitates abstaining from all experience. Just as Susan does not "feel strongly about" her advertisements, she does not become fully engaged with anything else in her life. The establishment of a marriage and a family that depends on her is not *her*, and it has no purpose to which it is committed. Looking for a focal point, Susan fixes on her husband and "their love for each other," but that love is so reasonable, so well chosen, so painless, that it leaves them feeling "dry, flat." Matthew's affair and Susan's tolerant, intelligent reaction to it devalue their love further without replacing it with anything. "Nothing is important," she feels. The marriage and the house and the children, to which she has given everything she has — her soul — come to seem merely a hiatus in her life. "In another decade, she would turn herself back into being a woman with a life of her own."

"The essential Susan," she supposes, will have been "in abeyance, as if she were in cold storage," for twenty years, but when she is free to reemerge after the twins start school, Susan is surprised to find that there is only an emptiness that needs to be filled, an aimlessness that needs to be kept "occupied." Since she has already alienated herself from the things she has to do to fill up time, the intermittent demands placed on her by the children and the household now seem imprisoning. After trying several unsuccessful strategies to find an intelligent way to be alone, Susan finally turns her old life over to Sophie and retreats to Room 19 of Fred's Hotel.

There she can get in touch with the "dark creative trance" or "dark fructifying dream" in which, if anywhere, the seeds of her new being may ripen and sprout. But when Matthew tracks her down and insists upon a reasonable discussion of the situation, Susan, to hide her last shred of privacy from his intrusions, invents a reasonable explanation. The fiction of Michael Plant, however, proves too exhausting to sustain, and she, for once animated by a clear purpose, has no recourse but to seek the repose of death.

Questions for Discussion

1. Explain the phrase "abstinence from painful experience" as a way of characterizing the lives of Matthew and Susan before their marriage.
2. How important are their careers to Matthew and Susan?
3. Matthew and Susan are good at avoiding mistakes. Is it a mistake to do so?
4. Discuss the way Matthew and Susan handle Matthew's first infidelity. Explain what it would mean for Susan truly to forgive him.
5. Why does "Susan feel (though luckily not for longer than a few seconds at a time) as if life had become a desert"?
6. Comment on the idea that "above all, intelligence forbids tears."
7. Why does Susan compare herself to a root that has been in cold storage?
8. Discuss Susan's reaction to the children's all going to school. What might have prevented her from having such difficulties?
9. If Susan's enemy is "emptiness," why does having the children and others call on her fill her with resentment? Why does she need to be alone?
10. Why does Susan feel imprisoned when given a room of her own?
11. Comment on Susan's vision of the devil. Assuming he is a hallucination, what needs or fears of Susan's may he be expressing? Why does he never reappear? What changes in Susan's behavior after his appearance?
12. Why does Susan want to hire an au pair girl? What is the result of Sophie's arrival? Consider the passage where Susan looks in through the kitchen window. What room does Sophie sleep in?
13. Explain what Susan derives from her hours in Room 19. Is she getting away from her "roles" and in touch with herself, or is she sinking away from herself into nothingness? What effect do her hours in Room 19 have on the rest of her life?
14. Comment on the images of the snail and the moth, which Lessing uses in describing Susan's feelings when she goes back to Room 19 after learning that Matthew has discovered it.
15. Why does Matthew, as Susan realizes, hope that she is having an affair? Why does she try to accommodate him by inventing Michael Plant? Explain her recoil from Matthew's suggestion that they make a foursome.
16. At what point does Susan decide to commit suicide? Evaluate her decision. Given her circumstances, is it an intelligent one?
17. Does it matter if we call Susan insane? Where should the blame for her death be laid? on Matthew? on Susan herself? on society, or her social position? Could Susan's death have been avoided, or was it in the cards from the beginning?

Topics for Writing

CRITICAL ESSAYS

1. The imagery of dryness, moisture, and vegetation in Lessing's story.
2. Lessing's analytic style in "To Room 19."
3. "To Room 19" — social criticism, psychological fiction, or horror story?
4. The concept of enclosure in Lessing's "To Room 19" and Gilman's "The Yellow Wallpaper."

EXERCISE FOR READING

1. Try to state the theme of Lessing's story as a piece of social criticism and as a piece of moral philosophy. How well do these themes reflect the story's impact on the reader?

Suggested Reading

Pruitt, Virginia. "The Crucial Balance: A Theme in Lessing's Short Fiction." *Studies in Short Fiction* 18 (1981): 281–85.

CLARICE LISPECTOR

The Chicken (p. 876)

The critic Giovanni Pontiero tells us that "encounters with the animal world" are frequent in Lispector's stories. The animals "are drawn with exceptional vigor and precision, and define the vital links with primitive life. Her animals, symbolizing brute existence, embody all that is obvious and sentient in a reality that is primordial." Because the chicken cannot form judgments about her existence, she is able to participate in unpremeditated experience, so she shows "a greater participation in what is real."

Lispector's affinity with the existential philosophy of Jean-Paul Sartre and Albert Camus led her to create stories that explore the sudden manifestation of the absurd in everyday life. According to Pontiero, Lispector's perceptions dramatize states of existence in which the mechanical nature of life is revealed, time is recognized as a destructive force (leading to certain death), and characters are placed in an alien world, revealing "a sense of inexorable isolation from other beings. . . . Everything is dispensable."

Certainly a flying chicken seeking to evade the frying pan on a Sunday afternoon is absurd, within or without the context of existential philosophy. But the atmosphere of the story is charged with peril: this is no ordinary tale of a protected barnyard or a nurturing kitchen. This chicken has an active consciousness. We are privileged to enter into its ruminations after successful flight.

Feminists might compare the chicken with her masculine counterpart, who would crow with pride in having led the father of the family such a merry chase across the Brazilian rooftops. But this chicken does all right for herself. She does better than a cockcrow: she lays an egg, and thus performs double magic. In addition to flying, she creates a new life, further extending her own.

Questions for Discussion

1. How does Lispector arouse our compassion for the chicken?
2. How does she keep sentimentality out of the narrative?
3. What is absurd about the story?

Topics for Writing

1. Write a humorous story in which a pet or domestic animal suddenly reveals a spirit of independence.
2. Compare Lispector's "The Chicken" with Malamud's "The Jewbird."

Suggested Reading

Pontiero, Giovanni. Introduction. *Family Ties*. By Clarice Lispector. Austin: U of Texas P, 1987.

BERNARD MALAMUD

The Jewbird (p. 880)

A remarkable story of anti-Semitism, "The Jewbird" is an example of the literary genre of magical realism, like García Márquez's "A Very Old Man with Enormous Wings." Schwartz is a talking bird with a human personality, more humane in his relations with the family than Cohen, the father who bullies his wife, Edie, and son, Maurie, into doing what he wants. Malamud's perspective on the characters is compassionate (Cohen's mother is dying, after all, so no wonder he's on edge), but he reserves his full sympathy for Schwartz, the black crow who is the epitome of the Wandering Jew: homeless, hungry, and harried. As the Jewbird says, "I'm running. I'm flying but I'm also running."

The human characters in this story are drawn boldly. Cohen is the typical working-class father, belligerent and aggressive, insisting on his authority over his wife and son. Edie is the kind, dutiful wife, a clever shopper who fits herring for the bird into the family budget and gets her evening out at the movies every once in a while. Maurie is the Milquetoast son, shy of violence, slow in school, screechy on the violin. The setting is minimally sketched in, a Lower East Side Manhattan apartment, where the family eats in the kitchen. The plot moves swiftly through the exchange of dialogue between Schwartz and the three human characters. Malamud draws his characters, background, and action like a cartoonist, without subtlety but with clarity, vigor, and strength.

The poignancy of the situation lies in the character of the Jewbird. Anti-Semitism is primitive and crude, and it releases stronger feelings than those normally evoked in a domestic sitcom. Malamud takes pains to establish Schwartz's Jewish background — his name, his habits of prayer, food preferences, and language. There is no mistaking his authenticity. Schwartz speaks the Pidgin English (no bird pun intended) of old European Jews, who express themselves more comfortably in Yiddish. His speech is full of homey metaphors: when the cat stops trying to get him, he tells Edie, "we will both be in Paradise." Malamud's point seems to be that there is a pecking order even among Jews. Edie knows that — and she has the final word in the story.

Questions for Discussion

1. Malamud compresses an enormous amount of information about the Cohen family into the opening paragraph. What do we know about the family by the end of this paragraph? What does a sentence like "The frozen foods salesman was sitting at supper with his wife and young son . . ." tell us about the kind of family this is? And what do you make of the first five sentences of this story? Who's speaking here? Notice how these sentences are all about the same length; what effect does that fact create? How are these ideas — "It's open, you're in. Closed, you're out and that's your fate" — attached to the Cohen family?

2. When Edie asks her husband what he has against the bird, Cohen replies, "Poor bird, my ass. He's a foxy bastard. He thinks he's a Jew. . . . A Jewbird, what a chutzpah. One false move and he's out on his drumsticks." Look at the other passages in this story where Cohen reviles the bird. What does he hate about Schwartz?

3. In the paragraph beginning "But the quarrel," the point of view suddenly shifts. Explain the reason for, and the effect of, this change.

4. Consider the following quotation: "So he ate the herring garnished with cat food, tried hard not to hear the paper bags bursting like fire crackers outside the birdhouse at night, and lived terror-stricken closer to the ceiling than the floor, as the cat, his tail flicking, endlessly watched him." Why do we laugh at this series of tortures, even as we grimace for Schwartz's pain?

5. Consider this exchange between Cohen and Schwartz:

   "For Christ sake, why don't you wash yourself sometimes? Why must you always stink like a dead fish?"

   "Mr. Cohen, if you'll pardon me, if somebody eats garlic he will smell from garlic. I eat herring three times a day. Feed me flowers and I will smell like flowers."

   Compare the form of address and the diction used by each speaker. How would you describe the tone of each speech? What effect does this exchange have on your assessment of each speaker?

6. What does Edie mean when she says "When the cat gets to know you better he won't try to catch you any more"? Schwartz doesn't believe this for a second: "When he stops trying we will both be in Paradise." Why would Edie say what she does, and why does Schwartz reject the idea? Are there some parallels between the cat and Cohen? What are the differences between them?

7. When Cohen finally kills Schwartz, we don't have any access to Schwartz's thoughts. Why might Malamud want to distance us from Schwartz in his final moments? What do we learn from having access to Cohen's mind?
8. Edie and Maurie don't get to say much in this story. Why would Malamud give Edie the last word? Is she correct in her assessment? Why does she speak using Schwartz's dialect?

Topics for Writing

CRITICAL ESSAYS

1. Magical realism in Malamud's "The Jewbird" and García Márquez's "A Very Old Man with Enormous Wings."
2. Malamud's use of irony in the theme of anti-Semitism in "The Jewbird."
3. Diction as a conveyor of theme and setting in "The Jewbird."

EXERCISE FOR READING

1. Study the story and list all the ways Malamud delineates Schwartz's Jewish character. Write a paragraph in which you discuss the importance of this characterization to the story.

Suggested Readings

Bell, P. K. "Heller and Malamud, Then and Now." *Commentary* 67 (1979): 71–75.
Bellman, Samuel I. "Women, Children, and Idiots First: The Transformation Psychology of Bernard Malamud." *Critique* 7 (1965): 131–32.
Benedict, H. "Bernard Malamud: Morals and Surprises." *Antioch Review* 41 (1983): 28–36.
Pinsker, S. "Achievement of Bernard Malamud." *Midwest Quarterly* 10 (1969): 379–89.
Raffel, B. "Bernard Malamud." *Literary Review* 13 (1969–70): 149–55.
Shrubb, P. "About Love and Pity — The Stories of Bernard Malamud." *Quadrant* 9 (1965): 66–71.
Stern, D. "Art of Fiction: Bernard Malamud." *Paris Review* 16 (1975): 41–64.

THOMAS MANN

Disorder and Early Sorrow (p. 889)

According to the critic David Luke, Mann always acknowledged being influenced by the late-nineteenth-century naturalist school of German writers, such as Gerhart Hauptmann; these writers used "the theme of sexual infatuation or enslavement . . . emphasizing man's dependence on his physical nature, in accordance with the doctrinaire deterministic positivism that underlay Naturalist theory."

"Disorder and Early Sorrow" dramatizes a father's perception of his five-year-old daughter's helpless infatuation for a friend of her older brother. The nurse Ann tells the child's father, Professor Abel Cornelius, "It's pretty young for the female instincts to be showing up," and Cornelius is so jealous of his little daughter's emotional response to the young man that he uncharacteristically snaps at the nurse, "Hold your tongue."

This is one of Mann's most popular stories, narrated with great charm and humor, "with malice toward none and gentle irony toward all," in the view of Ignace Feuerlicht. The "disorder" in the title refers to the economic "inflation, the postwar shortages and privations, the way of life of the young generation in Germany, specifically in Munich, around 1922 and 1923. To the professor, his feelings for his daughter Ellie represent order and timelessness among the disorder, lawlessness, and irrelevance of his time."

Ellie experiences the "early sorrow" of the title in her crush on Max. Her sorrow is shared less intensely by her father. But he is a professor of history, whose "heart belongs to the coherent and disciplined historic past." He narrates the story in the present tense, as a way of demarcating his own experience against the web of history he professes to interpret. As stated in the headnote, the story is based on Mann's own experience as a father and husband. He was "excessively precise" in recording his family life, according to Joyce Carol Oates, so the story can also be read as a document that preserves the upper-middle-class life of its place and time. However we read it, "Disorder and Early Sorrow" is one of the most skillful and entertaining examples of "autofiction," fiction based on autobiography, in European literature.

Questions for Discussion

1. How does the description of the dinner (croquettes made of turnip greens and a pudding — "trifle" — concocted out of powder) set the realistic scene of the story as being post–World War I Germany?
2. Who are Ingrid and Bert, Professor and Frau Cornelius, Ellie and Snapper?
3. Why does Xaver have more money than Bert for cigarettes? In the comparison between Xaver and Bert, what is Mann suggesting about the dislocation of social roles after the war?
4. What is the social status of the family? Did professors like Abel Cornelius have a different social status in the Germany of the 1920s from that of professors in the United States of the 1990s?
5. What details does Mann give to convey the atmosphere of a party?
6. How does Mann keep the plot and characters from turning sentimental?
7. Why does Mann keep Frau Cornelius so much in the background of the story?

Topics for Writing

1. Rewrite the story so that it takes place in the United States.
2. Rewrite the story from the point of view of Frau Cornelius, Ingrid, Bert, or Xaver.
3. Compare and contrast Mann's "Disorder and Early Sorrow" and Joyce's "The Dead," which also centers on a party and the unhappy disclosure of a hopeless love affair.

Suggested Readings

Feuerlicht, Ignace. *Thomas Mann*. Boston: Twayne World Authors Series, 1968.
Luke, David. Introduction. *Death in Venice and Other Stories*. By Thomas Mann. New
    York: Bantam, 1988.
Mann, Thomas. *A Sketch of My Life*. New York: Knopf, 1960.

KATHERINE MANSFIELD

Bliss (p. 916)

The life that blooms in Bertha Young presses against the restraints of "idiotic civilization" like a blossom bursting out of its bud case. Through all the incidents leading up to the devastating revelation of the liaison between Harry and Pearl, Mansfield develops Bertha's flowerlike vulnerability. We are attracted by her tolerant and amused appreciation of her husband and guests, the delight she takes in her "absolutely satisfactory house and garden," and her love for Little B. But at the same time we must feel a growing anxiety for this young woman, who herself knows that she is "too happy — too happy!" She is so little in command of her life that she must beg Nanny for a chance to feed her own daughter; her catalog of the wonderful things in her life dwindles off into trivia ("their new cook made the most superb omelettes"); and her husband and "modern, thrilling friends" look to the skeptical eye of the reader more like *poseurs* and hypocrites than the charming and sincere eccentrics Bertha takes them for.

Mansfield defines Bertha's condition and the danger to which it exposes her in the explicit symbol of the pear tree in bloom, to which Bertha likens herself, and in the unsettling glimpse of the cats, a gray one and its black shadow, that creep across the lawn beneath it. On the telephone to Harry, Bertha tries and fails to communicate her state of bliss, but she hopes that her fascinating new "find," Pearl Fulton, with whom she feels a mysterious kinship, will somehow be able to understand. In the moonlight the pear tree resembles the silvery Pearl, just as in the daylight it matched Bertha's green and white apparel, and as the two women gaze at it together, Bertha feels that the ecstatic communion she has desired is taking place. And in a sense it is, for the moment seems to release in Bertha for the first time a passionate sexual desire for her husband that, as she too soon learns, is likewise shared by Pearl.

The reader winces as the long-anticipated blow falls at last, and Eddie Warren intones the line that might end a more cynical version of the story: "'Why Must it Always be Tomato Soup?' It's so *deeply* true, don't you feel? Tomato soup is so *dreadfully* eternal." But Mansfield will not leave it there. As the gray cat Pearl and the black cat Eddie slink off into the night, Bertha returns to the window to find the pear tree, an embodiment of the same energy and beauty that wells up within herself, standing "as lovely as ever and as full of flower and as still."

Questions for Discussion

1. Define the impression of Bertha given by the opening section. What is the source of her bliss?
2. What is the function of the scene in which Bertha feeds Little B? Comment on the way the section ends.
3. What does Bertha try and fail to say to Harry on the telephone?
4. What explains Pearl Fulton's limited frankness?
5. Do you agree that Harry's use of phrases like "liver frozen, my dear girl" or "pure flatulence" is an endearing, almost admirable quality? Why or why not?
6. Comment on the juxtaposition of the cats and the pear tree.
7. Can one be "too happy"? Explain.
8. Evaluate Bertha's summary of her situation. Does she indeed have "everything"?
9. Explain the line "Her petals rushed softly into the hall."
10. What techniques does Mansfield use to characterize the Knights and Eddie Warren? What do you think of these people?
11. Comment on the possible implications of Harry's delayed arrival, followed shortly by that of Pearl Fulton.
12. Why is Bertha eager for Pearl to "give a sign"?
13. What transpires as Bertha and Pearl look at the pear tree?
14. Explain Harry's way of offering a cigarette to Pearl and Bertha's interpretation of it.
15. Why does Bertha feel "that this self of hers was taking leave of them forever" as she bids farewell to her guests?
16. What is the effect of Eddie Warren's quoting a poem about tomato soup while the climax of the story takes place?
17. What *is* going to happen now?

Topics for Writing

CRITICAL ESSAYS

1. Names in "Bliss."
2. The rebirth of Bertha Young.
3. Mansfield's use of light and color in "Bliss."

EXERCISE FOR READING

1. The story is divided by white spaces into a number of sections. On your first reading, stop at each one of these spaces and write a few sentences addressed to Bertha Young. What would you say to her at each of those moments? When you have finished the story, review your previous advice and write one more letter to Bertha in response to her concluding question.

RELATED SUBJECT

1. Study the way Mansfield characterizes Harry, the Knights, Eddie, and Pearl. Then write a character sketch of your own using some of the same techniques and devices.

Related Commentaries from Part Two

Willa Cather, The Stories of Katherine Mansfield, p. 1421.
Katherine Mansfield, Review of Woolf's "Kew Gardens," p. 1478.

KATHERINE MANSFIELD

The Fly (p. 926)

The fly is as much a character in this story as is the flowering pear tree in Mansfield's "Bliss." It is called by several pet names ("the little beggar," "a plucky little devil," "you artful little b[astard]," "the draggled fly"). Its determined efforts to clean itself of the ink on its "small sodden body" are compared to a stone going over and under a scythe and a "minute cat" cleaning its face. This is a totally admirable fly, valiant in its energetic attempts to rid itself of the ink, industrious in its labors, heroic in its persistence to survive despite repeated ink attacks by "the boss."

Despite the realistic descriptions, the fly is also a symbol, of course, as is the pear tree in "Bliss." Young, heroic English soldiers "died like flies" on Flanders Field and other World War I battlegrounds, and the boss's only son was among them. Yet Mansfield isn't writing a sentimental story about the horrors of war. Her focus is the horrors of humankind in times of peace and prosperity. The boss should be merciful, having suffered the loss of his beloved son. Instead, he is as void of wisdom and pity as a small boy torturing flies.

All the characters in "The Fly" are old men. Mr. Woodifield is five years younger than the boss, yet he is made weak by a stroke and his retirement, kept like a baby at home by his wife and daughters. "Old Macey," the office assistant, is gray-haired and subservient, waiting expectantly on the boss "like a dog that expects to be taken for a run." The only "man" in the group is the boss, and he is described as fat and healthy, a lover of whiskey and cigars, electric heaters and massive desks "with legs like twisted treacle" [a molasseslike substance made into candy and baked sweet goods]. He is beginning not to see the photograph of his son in uniform over the table near Mr. Woodifield.

Mansfield's sympathy for the victims of overbearing bullies is seen in this story, as in "Bliss." Her technique, like Chekhov's, is transparent, lulling you into a sense of repose and then, before you know it, submerging you in a scene gone wrong. Her description of the sadistic torture of the fly is a brilliant exposure of the torturer's emotional duplicity; he seems to sympathize with the "plucky little devil," yet compulsively compounds its struggle to the point of the insect's exhaustion and death.

There is no comforting moral at the end of this story. If anything, the boss is more of a bully than before. Mansfield seems to be saying that suffering does not ennoble most people; even if the boss was not consciously thinking of the flies buzzing around the bodies of slain soldiers on Flanders Field, he is out for revenge in whatever fashion he can take it.

Questions for Discussion

1. Why does Mansfield give Mr. Woodifield daughters ("the girls") in this story? Does Mr. Woodifield feel toward his daughters the way the boss felt toward his only son?
2. Why does Mansfield take such pains to describe the comfort of the boss's office?
3. What is the significance of the pot of jam the daughters took home as a souvenir of their trip to Belgium? How does it prepare the reader for the boss's treatment of the fly?
4. Explain the boss's image of his son in his grave in Belgium. Is it more clear than his memory of his son's perfection during the year he worked in the office?
5. The boss feels there is something wrong with him when he decides to get up to look at his son's photograph. What do you think is "wrong" with him? How do his subsequent actions with the fly follow naturally from his state of mind?

Topics for Writing

1. Rewrite the story so that the fly survives the third blot of ink the boss drips on him.
2. Compare and contrast the image of the pear tree in "Bliss" and the fly in this story.

Related Commentary from Part Two

Katherine Mansfield, Review of Woolf's "Kew Gardens," p. 1478.

Suggested Readings

Hanson, Clare. *Short Stories and Short Fictions, 1880–1980.* New York: St. Martin's, 1985.
———. *Katherine Mansfield.* New York: St. Martin's, 1981.

BOBBIE ANN MASON

Shiloh (p. 932)

The trip to Shiloh is supposed to be a second honeymoon for Leroy and Norma Jean Moffitt, a chance for them to start their marriage all over again, as Leroy says, "right back at the beginning." The trouble is, as Norma Jean is quick to point out to her husband, they had already started all over again after his tractor-trailer accident brought him home for good, and "this is how it turned out."

It's a topsy-turvy world in Mason's story. Husbands are hurt so they take up needlepoint; housewives are self-reliant so they study composition at community college when they aren't working at the drugstore. Thirty-four-year-old "girls" like

Norma Jean irrationally turn on their mothers after years of obedience just because their mothers catch them smoking cigarettes. And yet it's a familiar world to readers of fiction by women authors about women's domestic rebellion these past fifteen years: Erica Jong's *Fear of Flying*, Sue Kauffman's *Diary of a Mad Housewife*, and Lisa Alther's *Kinflicks*, for example. Norma Jean might scoff at her husband's suggestion that she has been influenced by the feminist movement — he asks her, "Is this one of those women's lib things?" — but he's no fool. She probably wouldn't have told him she was going to leave him if Betty Friedan hadn't published *The Feminine Mystique* and helped bring a feminist consciousness back to America about the time Norma Jean married her high school sweetheart, Leroy Moffitt.

The old patriarchal consciousness still permeates the story, of course, since this consciousness has a tight hold on the mate and the older fictional characters. Norma Jean is introduced in the first sentence as "Leroy Moffitt's wife, Norma Jean." The story is told in the present tense, making the reader aware of the slow passage of time for the characters caught in a static way of life, as mother Mabel says, "just waiting for time to pass." But Norma Jean feels the need for change. The opening of "Shiloh" is one of the most exhilarating first sentences in contemporary American short fiction. "Leroy Moffitt's wife, Norma Jean, is working on her pectorals." Used to be only boys lifted weights to build up their muscles. Now opportunity beckons even for a thirty-four-year-old married woman who bakes cream-of-mushroom casseroles. She doesn't want to be known as somebody's wife, a hackneyed first name between two commas evoking the more famous "real" name of a departed sex goddess from an era before Betty Friedan.

We don't know much about what she's thinking, this fictional Norma Jean, because Mason has structured the story so that her husband's consciousness and feelings are in the forefront. Through his confusion about what's happening with his wife, the reader senses that probably at this point Norma Jean doesn't know exactly what she wants herself, beyond wanting to break free. On their trip to Shiloh she walks rapidly away from Leroy to stand alone on a bluff by the river. He sees her waving her arms, and he can't tell if she's beckoning him or doing another exercise for her pectorals. One thing they both know is that she won't be needing the dust ruffle his mother-in-law made for their marital bed. If this Wonder Woman has her way, she won't be pushing her jogging shoes under her husband's couch or hiding the dust under his bed one day longer than she has to.

Questions for Discussion

1. After reading the story, look back at the first five paragraphs. What do they say about Norma Jean and Leroy's relationship? Does the rest of the story bear out the opening moment?
2. On the first page we discover that, through building an array of kits, "Leroy has grown to appreciate how things are put together." How does his fascination with building comment on Leroy's marriage? What is the impulse behind building the log cabin? How would you compare Leroy's hobby with Norma Jean's interests?
3. In this passage Mason introduces the background of the Moffitts' marriage: "Perhaps he reminds her too much of the early days of their marriage, before he went on the road. They had a child who died as an infant, years ago. They never speak about their memories of Randy, which have almost faded, but

145

now that Leroy is home all the time, they sometimes feel awkward around each other, and Leroy wonders if one of them should mention the child. He has the feeling that they are waking up out of a dream together — that they must create a new marriage, start afresh. They are lucky they are still married. Leroy has read that for most people losing a child destroys the marriage." The figure of a dead child might be expected to haunt the couple in this story. Does the child control their present actions? We discover later that Randy would be sixteen now, so Leroy has been away from home, basically, for sixteen years. What difference does his sudden presence make to the marriage?

4. "When the first movie ended, the baby was dead. . . . A dead baby feels like a sack of flour." Usually, a subject like the death of infants evokes a particular kind of rhetoric, laden with sentimentality and tragedy. How would you describe these two sentences? Why doesn't the narrator use some euphemisms for death? What effect do these perceptions create? How do these sentences influence your assessment of Leroy's character?

5. Although the title emphasizes the importance of "Shiloh," we don't hear anything about it until page 935, when Mabel Beasley says, "I still think before you get tied down y'all ought to take a little run to Shiloh." What does Shiloh represent for Mabel? What does history itself mean to Leroy and Norma Jean? Can they articulate their shared history? Consider the passage about the baby on pages 938–39.

6. When Norma Jean tells Leroy she's leaving him, he asks her, "Is this one of those women's lib things?" Is this a story about feminism? Consider the point of view; discuss the ideology apparent in the opening line of the story. What do we know about Norma Jean's feelings? Consider how a descriptive sentence such as "She is doing goose steps" gives us some access into her emotional life. How would you describe Mabel Beasley within a feminist framework?

7. How does Leroy's opinion that "nobody knows anything. . . . The answers are always changing" comment on the themes of this story?

8. Leroy concludes that "the real inner workings of a marriage, like most of history, have escaped him." This seems like a poignant realization in the face of Norma Jean's departure. Does Leroy assign blame for the dissolution of his marriage? Does this knowledge imply that he will be able to forge a new, vital marriage with Norma Jean? Is the final paragraph hopeful? What do you make of Leroy's inability to distinguish between Norma Jean's exercise and her signals?

Topics for Writing

CRITICAL ESSAYS

1. In an interview Bobbie Ann Mason had with Lila Havens, she said she's more interested in the male characters in her stories than in the females. How has she selected the details of "Shiloh" to portray Norma Jean's husband, Leroy Moffitt, with compassion?

2. The theme of alienation in Mason's "Shiloh" and Lawrence's "Odour of Chrysanthemums."

EXERCISE FOR READING

1. Reread the story and discuss Mason's use of details to enrich its reality.

Suggested Readings

Reed, J. D. "Postfeminism: Playing for Keeps." *Time* 10 Jan. 1983: 61.

Ryan, Maureen. "Stopping Places: Bobbie Ann Mason's Short Stories." *Women Writers of the Contemporary South.* Ed. Peggy Whitman Prenshaw. Jackson: UP of Mississippi, 1984. 283–94.

Smith, W. "Publisher's Weekly Interviews." *Publisher's Weekly* 30 Aug. 1985: 424–25.

GUY DE MAUPASSANT

The Necklace (p. 945)

"The Necklace" has long been one of the most popular of Maupassant's stories, and one of the most interesting aspects of the story is this popularity, since artistically it is far from his best. The story is little more than an anecdote. Mme. Loisel, a woman from the lower middle class, is deeply dissatisfied with her station in life. As she sits down to dinner with her husband — a "little clerk at the Ministry of Public Instruction" — she thinks of "dainty dinners, of shining silverware, of tapestry which peopled the walls with ancient personages, and with strange birds in the middle of a fairy forest."

Her husband, sensing her unhappiness, gets a ticket for a grand ball, and, when she is miserable at not having a fine dress, he gives her money he has been saving for a gun and a shooting holiday with his friends. When she is still unhappy at not having jewels, he suggests she borrow some from a wealthy friend, Mme. Forestier. Mme. Loisel borrows what she thinks is a diamond necklace, is a great success at the ball, but loses the necklace on the way home.

Too ashamed to tell the friend what has happened, the couple borrow money to buy a diamond necklace like the one that was lost. They return the necklace and slowly repay the loan. After ten years, during which the wife has become "the woman of impoverished households — strong and hard and rough," she accidentally meets Mme. Forestier and learns that she had lent her only a paste copy of a diamond necklace. Mme. Loisel and her husband have destroyed their lives for nothing.

Unlike in his finest stories, Maupassant here stays on the surface of the characters. Mme. Forestier and Mme. Loisel's husband are only faintly sketched; they seem to exist merely to act out roles. The anecdote itself is so implausible that a single question — why didn't Mme. Forestier notice that a different necklace had been returned to her? why did M. Loisel allow his life to be destroyed without a protest? — would bring it to earth. But most readers are willing to suspend their disbelief.

When we place the story in the time it was written, its themes stand out even more sharply. On its most obvious level this is one of the tales of moral instruction that were so widespread in nineteenth-century popular literature. Mme. Loisel's dreams of clothes and jewels represent the sin of vanity, and someone who has such dreams must be punished. The punishment inflicted on the woman and her husband is memorably out of proportion to their sin, the better to serve as a warning to those reading the story for moral instruction.

A second theme, which may be less obvious to the contemporary reader, is that Mme. Loisel has dreamed of moving to a higher social level. French society was rigidly structured, and Mme. Loisel's ambitions represented a threat, however vague, to the story's privileged audience. They would, of course, want to see her punished for this ambition.

These facts help to explain why the story was so widely read when it was written — but for today's readers other factors seem to be at work. For example, to one young student the necklace became the symbol for everything the world of adults represents. Perhaps it is the story's weaknesses — its implausible simplicities, the lack of definition of its minor characters, the trite obviousness of Mme. Loisel's yearning, and the pious cruelty of her punishment — that make it possible for other generations to give "The Necklace" their own interpretation.

Questions for Discussion

1. Do we use anecdotes like "The Necklace" to point out moral lessons today? What other examples of this kind of moral instruction can you think of in popular literature?
2. How did an evening at a ball offer Mme. Loisel a chance to present herself in a new guise?
3. What do we learn from the story about the structure of French society at the time "The Necklace" was written?
4. What symbols for wealth and station could be used in a story like this written for today?

Topics for Writing

CRITICAL ESSAYS

1. The symbolic implications of the necklace.
2. The contrast between the lives of Mme. Loisel and her friend Mme. Forestier.

Related Commentaries from Part Two

Kate Chopin, How I Stumbled upon Maupassant, p. 1430.
Guy de Maupassant, The Writer's Goal, p. 1480.

GUY DE MAUPASSANT

The String (p. 951)

Without its masterful use of the kind of sharp observation Maupassant learned from Flaubert (see headnote in text), "The String" would be a lifeless tale of flat characters in a contrived set of circumstances with a preformulated theme. Maupassant's pictures of the peasants on their way to market or of Maître Hauchecorne groping for the string and then, caught in the act, pretending to be absorbed in something important are painted with such clarity and freshness that we believe what he shows us must be true. Because his vision is convincing, Maupassant's message strikes with the force of revelation.

Maupassant was fascinated with delusions and their effect on behavior. In "The Necklace," for example, a couple destroy their lives trying to accumulate enough money to replace borrowed jewels they believed to be diamonds and had lost, only to learn too late that they were paste. In "The String," Maître Hauchecorne is destroyed when those around him falsely presume his guilt. He cannot clear himself of suspicion, and people's reaction to what they take to be his hypocrisy drives him into a terminal depression.

Students will readily acknowledge that Maître Hauchecorne has been unjustly treated, but the story will make little sense aesthetically until they recognize that the main cause of his trouble lies not in an unfortunate coincidence but rather in his character and that of the society Maupassant portrays. Maître Hauchecorne did not find the wallet, but he would have lied about it if he had, just as he dissembles when he becomes aware that Maître Malandain's eyes are upon him as he picks up the string. Maître Hauchecorne is called from the cozy dinner at the inn to answer his accuser, and thereafter his severance from the community that nourishes and sustains him becomes ever more complete. Ironically, it is by maintaining his innocence at such lengths that he cuts himself off from his fellows, who would be quite happy to admire him for his cleverness if he would acknowledge his deceit.

The reader may wish to register dismay at the society based on cunning, trickery, and suspicion that Maupassant depicts, but those qualities are nonetheless the basis of human interaction in the world of the story. Maître Hauchecorne and Maître Malandain "had once had a quarrel *together*" (my emphasis), and they were "both good haters." By insisting on his innocence, Maître Hauchecorne lies to a deeper extent than to that which he is accused. Further, he represents himself as morally superior to those around him, which Maître Hauchecorne well knows to be untrue, so that he finds himself in the doubly ironic position of being fully aware of his own responsibility for the "unjust" ostracism that is inflicted upon him.

Questions for Discussion

1. Why is Maître Hauchecorne embarrassed to be seen stooping for the string? Should he be?
2. Describe what this sentence contributes to the story: "The peasants looked at cows, went away, came back, perplexed, always in fear of being cheated, not daring to decide, watching the vendor's eye, ever trying to find the trick in the man and the flaw in the beast."

3. Describe the atmosphere at Jourdain's. Why does Maupassant have Maître Hauchecorne called to the mayor's office from here?
4. Why do Maître Hauchecorne's old friends seem to admire him for doing what he denies?
5. To what extent and in what ways does Maupassant seek to engage our sympathy for Maître Hauchecorne? Does Maître Hauchecorne deserve his ironic fate? What does Maupassant seem to think of the characters and society he portrays?
6. Does this story exploit an improbable coincidence to tell a grim joke, or does it offer a valid insight into human nature?

Topics for Writing

CRITICAL ESSAYS

1. The thin line between cynicism and sentimentality: Maupassant's tone in "The String."
2. Local color and universality of theme in the stories of Jewett and Maupassant.
3. The tragedy of Maître Hauchecorne.

RELATED SUBJECT

1. Study the descriptive passage that opens the story, noticing how Maupassant makes us see things in a new way. Then write a similar descriptive sketch of your own, trying to discover something heretofore unnoticed about what you describe.

Related Commentaries from Part Two

Guy de Maupassant, The Writer's Goal, p. 1480.
Kate Chopin, How I Stumbled upon Maupassant, p. 1430.

Suggested Reading

Downs, John A. "Maupassant's 'La Ficelle' and Bazan's 'Billet de Mille.' " *Studies in Philology* 57 (1960): 663–71.

HERMAN MELVILLE

Bartleby, the Scrivener (p. 958)

Many students have trouble reading this story because they cannot accept what they consider the weirdness of Bartleby's character. On first reading, the story seems to yield this interpretation. Shortly after it appeared in the November and December issues of *Putnam's Monthly Magazine* in 1853, for example, Richard Henry

Dana, Sr., wrote to Melville's friend Evert Duyckinck saying that he admired the skill involved in creating the character of Bartleby because "the secret power of such an inefficient and harmless creature over his employer, who all the while has a misgiving of it, shows no common insight." Dana's interpretation will probably also be the way 99 percent of present-day college students will respond to the story, sharing his lack of sympathy for Bartleby.

The question is: Did Melville intend the readers of his story to feel this way? Why did he conclude his tale with the lines "Ah, Bartleby! Ah, humanity!"?

Most sympathetic literary critics see this story as Melville's attempt to dramatize the complex question of an individual's obligation to society. Like the dead letters that Bartleby burned in his previous job after they were no longer needed, his life ends when he is no longer useful to his employer. What standards should we use to judge someone's worth? How should we view those who no longer accept the world they are offered?

Questions for Discussion

1. How does the narrator's viewpoint affect your feelings toward Bartleby? What details particularly influence you one way or the other?
2. Do your feelings toward Bartleby change when the narrator reveals Bartleby's previous job in the Dead Letter Office?
3. How does Melville's humorous description of the two other clerks in the law office relieve his heavy presentation of the Wall Street setting? How do these minor characters set off each other, the lawyer, and Bartleby?
4. Do you ever feel like saying "I prefer not to" in reply to figures of authority? What do you do when you feel a bit of Bartleby in you?

Topics for Writing

1. Explicate the paragraph beginning "For the first time in my life a feeling of overpowering stinging melancholy seized me." A close reading of this passage may bring you closer to realizing the complexity of Melville's portrayal of the lawyer's relationship to Bartleby.
2. Analyze the conclusion of the story. How can Bartleby's life be compared to a dead letter?
3. This story has an unusually prolonged and discursive exposition before the title character is introduced. Also, Melville doesn't motivate his behavior until the end of the story, after he is dead and the lawyer finds out about his previous job. Breaking the customary rules of starting a short story with a brief exposition and motivating the characters as they are introduced, Melville might be accused of writing a poorly structured tale. Argue for or against this accusation, remembering that the short-story genre was in its infancy when Melville wrote "Bartleby, the Scrivener."
4. Read the excerpt from Melville's review of Hawthorne's *Mosses from an Old Manse* (p. 1482), discussing what Melville calls "the power of blackness" in Hawthorne's tales. Can you find the same "power of blackness" in Melville's description of Bartleby's situation?

Related Commentaries from Part Two

Herman Melville, Blackness in Hawthorne's "Young Goodman Brown," p. 1482.
John Carlos Rowe, A Deconstructive Perspective on Melville's "Bartleby, the Scrivener," p. 1511.

Suggested Readings

Dillingham, W. B. *Melville's Short Fiction, 1853–1856.* Athens: U of Georgia, 1977.
Fogle, R. H. *Melville's Shorter Tales.* Norman: U of Oklahoma P, 1960.
Vincent, H. P., ed. *"Bartleby the Scrivener": Melville Annual for 1965.* Kent: Kent State UP, 1967. Includes Henry Murray's "Bartleby and I," 3–24.

SUSAN MINOT

Lust (p. 987)

This story may be difficult for students to discuss in class, since it describes personal feelings about a subject (sexual intercourse) that they may consider more appropriately discussed with friends of the same sex, or not at all. To overcome their reluctance, you might ask students to write down their thoughts about the story, which could lead into a discussion of how the class as a whole has responded.

Such a questionnaire (not a quiz) could consist of statements from the story that students are asked to "strongly agree ... strongly disagree" with. For example, 1. "The less they [boys] notice you, the more you got them on the brain." 2. "My parents had no idea. Parents never really know what's going on." 3. "If you go out with them, you sort of have to do something." 4. "Teenage years. You know just what you're doing and don't see the things that start to get in the way." 5. "Lots of boys, but never two at the same time." 6. "The more girls a boy has, the better.... For a girl, with each boy, it's as though a petal gets plucked each time." 7. "After the briskness of loving, loving stops."

The narrative form of "Lust" might be another way to approach the story's content. How does Minot present her material? The theme is dramatized episodically, in short paragraphs, bringing about an effect of intense compression. The reader has as brief an encounter with the story of each boyfriend as the narrator appears to have with the boy himself. Leo, Roger, Bruce et al. appear and disappear so rapidly that it's as if the girl is picking the boys like the petals of a daisy. Yet, as she makes clear, she — unlike the boys she dates — is experiencing emotional vulnerability as her dominant feeling. Minot has effectively dramatized the differences in sexual maturity between adolescent males and females. "Post-coital melancholy" pervades her narrative from beginning to end.

Questions for Discussion

1. How do we know that the narrator is a girl?
2. What is your impression of the narrator? How old is she? What is her social background? Does she have a conscience?

3. What direction and guidance does the narrator get from the adults in her life, her parents and the headmaster at her school? Does she want more advice from them about how to live?
4. What is the narrator's primary interest in boys? How is she vulnerable?
5. How does the short, fragmented paragraph structure of "Lust" contribute to its mood and meaning?
6. Characterize the style of Minot's sentences.

Topics for Writing

1. Rewrite "Lust" in the same form, but from a boy's point of view.
2. Continue "Lust" beyond Minot's ending to bring the narrator to an awareness that she wants to try a different approach to relationships with the boys in her life.
3. Analyze the section with the housemother, Mrs. Gunther. What does it contribute to the story?
4. Compare the voice of Updike's adolescent narrator in "A & P" with that of Minot's narrator in "Lust."

YUKIO MISHIMA

Three Million Yen (p. 996)

Mishima is describing a world where everything has a price tag, except the privately shared feeling of the two contentedly married lovers. Even that is encroached upon in the course of the story, when their income is revealed as coming from their performance in sex shows: "There aren't many that go as well together as you two do." This is their lucky night. The old lady who is their manager has booked them into a private home, where wealthy housewives having a special class reunion will pay them "a good stiff price" (the clients "haven't any idea what the market rate is, of course") and tip handsomely as well.

By the end of the night Kiyoko (the wife) and Kenzō (the husband) will make five thousand yen, more than they've ever made before. It will go into their savings account, for they consider themselves too poor to have a child yet.

The horrible truth is that Mishima is not writing a fantasy story. The "real world" that Kiyoko and Kenzō inhabit is more like a dream than everyday reality, but we know that Mishima's vision has its counterpart in people and cities everywhere. Department stores offer seductive merchandise to coax customers out of their money, including toy flying saucer stations painted so skillfully that their metal surfaces seem "indescribably cool, and it was as if all the discomfort of the muggy night would go if a person but gave himself up to that sky." There are "fun" things to do if you have the money, like ride in the little cars through an aquarium, and "fun" things to eat if you can afford them, like tall fruit parfaits heaped with whipped cream and huge sweet crackers (cookies) cunningly baked in the shape of bank notes, so you have the pleasure of literally consuming your money, as well as using it for trade.

What money can't buy is the enjoyment of these — shall we say "degenerate"? — pleasures. You have to be young or healthy as well as rich. Youth, health, and money are still no guarantees of happiness, of course. This is an inner state of contentment which Kenzō and Kiyoko are fortunate to have found in their love for each other and their plans. Here is the central irony of their situation. They are supremely natural lovers while everything around them is grotesquely commercialized, from the giant neon pagoda that is the landmark of their city (instead of the natural Gourd Pond, now filled in for development) to their use of their bodies to simulate the act of love for jaded housewives.

They are also supremely aware of their own physicality (hairy and shaved armpits; her skin clinging to his "like the layers of some intricately folded insect's wing"). Ironically, their enjoyment of their physicality makes them even more susceptible to the temptations of the goods and services in the department store. They are not critical of their environment. They find the garish neon pagoda beautiful, and Mishima doesn't intrude on their innocent enjoyment: "To Kenzō and Kiyoko the pagoda seemed to encompass in all its purity some grand, inaccessible dream of life." It is only when the night ends and Kenzō is exhausted from performing before the "nasty bunch" of housewives that he feels obscurely angry about the way he senses that money and the "inaccessible dream of life" are related. Kiyoko can't clarify his feelings for him, but she can offer an immediate, physically direct course of action to release his frustration. Tear up the last cookie in the shape of a bank note instead of the money, she tells him. He is as always obedient to her wishes, but the cracker is too resilient for him, and in the end he is "unable to break it."

The unusual structure of this story deserves comment. Mishima organizes it in the simplest, most natural way — chronologically through the course of one night. He goes into considerable detail describing the personalities of the lovers and their responses to things in the department store, all static material brought to life by his sympathy for the young couple and his careful observation of physical details, culminating in the scene in the restaurant where the old lady dips her spoon into the cream of her parfait. Then, where the plot should reach its climax — in the action of the sex show after the department store scenes — there is a void. Nothing. No words at all. They begin again only after the show, when the lovers are back in the neighborhood of the department store, near which they apparently live. In its shadows Mishima gives us a brief, bittersweet epilogue to bring home the darkness at the core of what society offers these characters.

Questions for Discussion

1. What theme does Mishima establish in the image of the pagoda, which "seemed to encompass in all its purity some grand, inaccessible dream of life"? What landmark has the pagoda replaced? What is ironic about this in view of traditional Japanese cultural values?

2. How would you describe Kenzō and Kiyoko? What clue does Mishima give that the pair are very aware of their physicality?

3. What is ironic about Kiyoko's statement that she would be embarrassed to live "in a place with so many mirrors" like those they encounter in the market?

4. Briefly summarize Kenzō and Kiyoko's approach to financial and family planning. How is this in line with traditional Japanese values?

5. Summarize Kenzō's philosophy of life.
6. Explain what Mishima means when he states of Kiyoko, "she soaked in her world of things as she might soak in a bath."
7. What is the symbolism of the million-yen crackers? of the amusement park?
8. How does the love and closeness shared by Kenzō and Kiyoko contrast with their surroundings?
9. What motivates the couple to spend their money on idle amusement?
10. How has Mishima structured the story? Where does this organization change, and why is the change significant?
11. Why is Kenzō so frustrated following their performance for the "nasty bunch" of housewives? What happens at the end of the story?
12. What message is Mishima trying to convey in this story? Do you feel he has accomplished his purpose?

Topics for Writing

CRITICAL ESSAYS

1. Two worlds: materialism versus romantic love.
2. Contemporary American society and the Japanese way of life presented in this story.

Suggested Readings

Boardman, Gwenn R. "Greek Hope and Japanese Samurai: Mishima's New Aesthetic" *Critique* 12 (1970): 103–15.
Enright, D. J. "Mishima's Way." *Encounter* 36 (1971): 57–61.
Falk, Ray. "Yukio Mishima." *Saturday Review* 16 May 1959: 29.
Seidensticker, Edward. "Mishima Yukio." *Hudson Review* 24 (1971): 272–82.
Spurling, J. "Death in Hero's Costume: The Meaning of Mishima." *Encounter* 44 (1975): 56+.
Ueda, Makoto. "Mishima Yukio." *Modern Japanese Writers and the Nature of Literature*. By Ueda. Stanford: Stanford UP, 1976. 219–59.

BHARATI MUKHERJEE

Jasmine (p. 1008)

In "Jasmine" Mukherjee presents one of the often-repeated subjects of nine-teenth-century European literature, the poor girl from the country who comes to the city to work as servant for a wealthy family. In Mukherjee's hand, however, the tale takes on a distinctly modern tone. The story is told from the girl's perspective; we see the new city and family through her eyes. In one of the older variations on the theme, we might have the girl's point of view, but in this modern retelling the girl doesn't lose her values, and she retains enough distance and objectivity to keep from being swept away by her new experiences.

Mukherjee first presents an immigrant family who have managed to buy a motel and an "ice cream parlor" in Detroit; then she introduces an academic couple at the University of Michigan in Ann Arbor. In each instance Jasmine looks at the people with a measuring eye, and she is not overly impressed with what she sees.

The author makes it clear at the end of the third paragraph that Jasmine is not an ordinary immigrant, even though as the story opens she is being smuggled into the United States in a delivery van. Jasmine is "Dr. Vassanji's daughter." We gradually learn that she had worked in a bank in Trinidad, that she had been to college for two years, that her father had simply paid to have her brought to the United States, and that her family had been comfortable enough to have servants in Port-au-Prince. She has left Trinidad because, as she thinks to herself, "Trinidad was an island stuck in the middle of nowhere. What kind of place is that for a girl with ambition?"

Since Jasmine isn't like the usual poor servant girl of similar earlier fiction, it isn't surprising that the things that happen to her aren't like the staple events of these stories. Jasmine is part of today's world: she is not particularly concerned about hiding her prejudice against black men, and she moves from one place to another, and one job to another, with little worry about what might happen to her. Even the climactic event — the seduction by the father of the house that was the staple of the older stories — is presented here with little anxiety. It doesn't seem to be anything more than another in the series of learning experiences Jasmine has been having since she came to Detroit.

The reader's fascination with Mukherjee's story comes in large part because of this old theme dressed in modern style, and also the objectivity that lets Jasmine look at white, middle-class Americans with the same bemused detachment she feels toward her own family. Jasmine is a modern woman in a modern world, and Mukherjee has caught all the subtleties of the situation she has found herself in.

Questions for Discussion

1. It is difficult today for someone like Jasmine to enter the United States by legal means. Is she justified in using illegal means to get to Detroit?
2. What is the basis for the prejudice that someone like Jasmine feels toward the black family she enters at the beginning of the story?
3. Is the family that employs Jasmine in Ann Arbor a typical American family? Is it the kind of family you would expect to meet in a university setting?
4. One could say that Mukherjee is using Jasmine to ridicule the woman in the university family with whom Jasmine goes to work. Is there any justification for this idea? Explain.
5. What do you think Jasmine will decide to do now that she has achieved her goal of coming to the United States?

Topics for Writing

CRITICAL ESSAYS

1. The place of the United States in the dreams of people like Jasmine, who live in the so-called Third World.

2. The theme of the servant girl from the country in the city house, and its relevance to today's way of life.
3. The social legacy that colonialism has left in countries like Trinidad.
4. Young people setting out in the world: Mukherjee's Jasmine and Hawthorne's Robin in "My Kinsman, Major Molineux."

ALICE MUNRO

Walker Brothers Cowboy (p. 1017)

"Walker Brothers Cowboy" is set during the Depression, and it is the Depression itself that determines and motivates the lives in Tuppertown Munro describes. The father in the story has lost his fox farm, and the family has been forced to move into an unfriendly neighboring town while the father works as a door-to-door salesman of household items manufactured by a company called Walker Brothers.

It is interesting to compare the literary techniques in R. K. Narayan's "House Opposite" and this story. The focus of Narayan's story is the interaction between the two characters; the specific setting is of little importance. There is nothing in the story to "date" it; it is, in essence, timeless. Munro's story, by contrast, is specifically in a time, and her narrator devotes much of the early part of the story to describing the setting. Details of her mother working on a dress made of the family's old clothes, and the description of the encounter with the tramp reinforce the sense of economic hardship, but some of the strongest details are the names of the shops and the description of neighbors sitting out, "men in shirt-sleeves and undershirts and women in aprons — not people we know but if anybody looks ready to nod and say 'Warm night,' my father will nod too and say something the same."

The events of the story are slight. The narrator and her younger brother go with their father as he sells his products. At one of the houses he visits, someone empties a chamber pot on him from a second-story window. Although he laughs about it in front of his children, the father is obviously disturbed. Then he takes the children off his route to visit a woman he knew and loved when he was younger.

The slight events of the story are conveyed with poignant restraint and affection by the narrator, an adult who represents the incidents of that afternoon through the eyes of her younger self. The author's intent is to fix a life at a moment and in a place, and her story brilliantly succeeds.

Questions for Discussion

1. When did the Depression take place, and what was its effect on the lives of people like the author portrays?
2. Describe some of the details and incidents of the walk the narrator takes with her father that set the story in its time and place.
3. Why does the father describe himself as a "Walker Brothers Cowboy"?
4. Do men like this father still travel the backroads of the United States selling products like Walker Brothers medicines and household supplies? What has happened to this kind of job?

5. What does Munro tell us of the lives of women like the friend the father takes his children to visit?

Topics for Writing

1. Compare a descriptive paragraph in this story with a paragraph like it in Narayan's "House Opposite," and discuss the kinds of details and incidents that each describes.
2. Find another example of writing about the Depression years and compare it with "Walker Brothers Cowboy."
3. Comment on the following passage from the story, which describes the girl's mother and her attitude toward their new life:

> No bathroom with a claw-footed tub and flush toilet is going to comfort her, nor water on tap and sidewalks past the house and milk in bottles, not even the two movie theatres and the Venus Restaurant and Woolworths so marvellous it has live birds singing in its fan-cooled corners and fish as tiny as finger nails, as bright moons, swimming in its green tanks. My mother does not care.

4. The critic Michiko Kakutani writes that Munro's characters "never completely dispose of their pasts. Unlike so many characters in contemporary fiction, they do not assume that they can continually reinvent themselves, that they can always start over tabula rasa. They tend to stay in touch with ex-lovers, distant family members, childhood friends; they acknowledge, however reluctantly, the ways in which their pasts have shaped their futures" (*New York Times*, March 9, 1990, p. C36). How does this comment apply to "Walker Brothers Cowboy"?

V. S. NAIPAUL

B. Wordsworth (p. 1029)

Often readers of the literature of the Third World are reminded that many of these stories were originally part of an oral tradition. "B. Wordsworth," by the Oxford-educated Trinidadian writer V. S. Naipaul, is an interesting example. Although it is a "literary" story, clearly drawn from the writer's imagination and background, it was written to be read aloud. When Naipaul finished with his university studies, he got a job with the BBC's West Indian Radio Service, and the stories that became the book *Miguel Street* were first read on the air. This fact gives "B. Wordsworth" its colloquial flavor and its spoken, rather than written, rhythm.

Naipaul went on to write novels and long essays but none of his later work has quite the flavor of these stories. Perhaps the greatest achievement of a story like "B. Wordsworth" is its sense of innocence. The story is told by a child, and Naipaul allows nothing into it that the child might not have seen or experienced. Often in his later writing Naipaul expresses bitterness and disappointment, but as a child in Miguel Street what he feels is wonder and curiosity.

Many of the people on Miguel Street are obviously poor, but children don't "see" poverty. This is characteristic of much Caribbean writing, which is often set against such a background. Since poverty is everywhere, there is nothing for the writer to do but accept it. It is B. Wordsworth, and not the environment, who is the center of the story.

There are failed poets in every society, just as there are gentle dreamers and people whose lives are without direction or purpose. Naipaul's achievement in this story is to place one of these archetypal figures in a completely new setting and still find the basic humanity that makes him familiar to us all. Naipaul hints at a reason for his character's solitary life when the poet tells his young friend about a boy and girl who were both poets. When she died in childbirth, the boy never wanted to touch their garden or to do anything again. The reason sounds so real for the character the author has created that when the poet tell his young friend before he dies that he only made up the story, we don't really believe him.

The success of this story lies in its quality of oral presentation, the consistency of its point of view, and the common humanity it finds in one of life's castaways. Its warmth and sympathy open readers to a new world, and let them see themselves in this setting.

Questions for Discussion

1. Is the child in the story from a poor family? How would you characterize his family's life?
2. How do we know that this is a story to be read aloud? How would the language of the first paragraph be different if this story were written to be read on the page?
3. Why does the character in the story refer to himself as the "Black Wordsworth," using an English poet's name? Why doesn't he take the name of an American poet or an African poet?
4. Why do you think the poet begins to work on his great poem after he has met the narrator? Do you think he could have finished it even if he hadn't gotten sick?
5. What did the poet mean by his line "The past is deep"?

Topics for Writing

CRITICAL ESSAYS

1. "English" education in the British colonies and its effect on children like the boy in "B. Wordsworth."
2. The child's-eye point of view in "B. Wordsworth."
3. How the life in Miguel Street is different from our life, and how it is similar.

Suggested Readings

Cudjoe, Selwyn. *V. S. Naipaul.* Amherst: U of Mass. P, 1988.
King, Bruce, ed. *West Indian Literature.* Hamden, CT: Archon, 1979.
Naipaul, V. S. *Finding the Center.* New York: Knopf, 1984.
Theroux, Paul. *V. S. Naipaul.* New York: Africana, 1972.

R. K. Narayan

House Opposite (p. 1037)

Encountering the world of Narayan's stories, one might conclude that she had arrived at a place where the clocks have stopped. Narayan comes from a tradition in which time is marked in centuries rather than years, and his stories convey the sense that there will always be time for the tale to resolve its small dilemma. No one, in a Narayan story, is ever late for anything.

"House Opposite" exemplifies this quality. No details "date" the story. There are no telephones, automobiles, radio, or television. There is no news. There is only a man on one side of a street trying to wrestle with the temptations of the flesh, and across the street a prostitute who comes to embody these pleasures for him. The street, and the village that encloses it, is so lightly sketched that it could be anywhere in a broad swath of the world from Egypt to China.

It is just as impossible to "date" the story by the confrontation of the opposite ways of life it presents. Narayan could be describing a would-be saint struggling with temptation in the desert of Galilee before the time of Christ, or a priest in a back street of a Brazilian town a hundred years ago. Without seeming effort, Narayan has simply given us the story in its barest outline.

As brilliant as he is in presenting these timeless situations, Narayan's genius lies in the sympathy with which he creates his characters. He is conscious of the ridiculous side of the hermit's quest for purity, and he describes the hermit's vanity over his deprivations — "Our hermit . . . kept a minute check of his emaciation and felt a peculiar thrill out of such an achievement" — at the same time he convinces us that the hermit's quest is real. He presents naive images of the pleasure that the prostitute gives her customers, describing her as "the human mattress," but he still convinces us that she is, if not innocent, at least not guilty, and this is an important distinction. It is her customers who are corrupt.

Once he has set his story in motion, Narayan seemingly has only to stand aside and let things take their course. The author, however, still looks at his characters with his signature benevolence. He allows the hermit redemption from his sinful thoughts by letting him leave his little room before he loses the state of purity he has achieved. He is as forgiving with the prostitute, in the story's final paragraph, as he describes her crossing the street with gifts, seeking "a saint's blessing." In an instant the hermit is able to see the prostitute as she is, and not through the physical desire that almost overwhelmed him. She is not the softly rounded seductress he had imagined; she is aging, her face is tired, her arms are flabby — and she is a sincere penitent. Without hesitation the hermit blesses her and, to save himself, continues on, leaving the woman and the street behind.

Such sympathy and forgiveness are not common in today's writing. They are at the opposite pole from the punishment a writer like Flannery O'Connor inflicts on her characters in stories such as "Everything That Rises Must Converge." Narayan's refusal to punish his characters is only another aspect of the timelessness of the world he describes. Whatever the outcome of the story he has chosen to tell, all his people will have to go on as part of one another's lives; there will not even be the pressure of time to hurry their encounters.

Questions for Discussion

1. Narayan's story is set in India, where the largest religious group are Hindus. Could "House Opposite" have been set in another country?
2. Describe some of the torments and temptations which the early Christians, including Christ, experienced in the desert.
3. What techniques does the hermit use to keep his thoughts away from the prostitute? Do other religious faiths have similar practices?

Topics for Writing

1. Discuss the meaning of the parable about the harlot and the reformer in the story: "A harlot was sent to heaven when she died, while her detractor, a self-righteous reformer, found himself in hell. It was explained that while the harlot sinned only with her body, her detractor was corrupt mentally, as he was obsessed with the harlot and her activities, and could meditate on nothing else."
2. Discuss the words, phrases, and actions in "House Opposite" that show the author's sympathy for both the prostitute and the hermit.
3. Outline the meaning of the kind of self-denial Narayan describes as it is practiced in other religions.
4. Compare and contrast the hermit in Narayan's "House Opposite" with Félicité in Flaubert's "A Simple Life."
5. Compare and contrast the changes in perception undergone by the hermit in Narayan's "House Opposite" and the narrator of Joyce's "Araby."

GLORIA NAYLOR

Lucielia Louise Turner (p. 1041)

This searing story demonstrates once again that social realism, as a literary genre, still has the power to disturb us, to move us, and finally to convince us. Despite the experimentation with fictional technique in this century, Gloria Naylor creates here an unforgettable scene with the same stylistic idiom that Charles Dickens or Stephen Crane or Theodore Dreiser used to bring their characters vividly to life.

This is not to suggest that Naylor is not a sophisticated stylist, or not technically adept. She doesn't tell her story chronologically; instead, she moves back and forth, from the day of the child's funeral back to the events that led to it, and were, if even circumstantially, its cause. Within each of the sections the narrative is swift and straightforward.

Another writer might have given us a more detached account, but Naylor, with the power that marks the greatest writing in social realism, seems almost to spew out her story, and we are forced to respond to it as best we can. She has left us no defense against what she is telling us.

If we look back in African-American writing for a predecessor to what Naylor has done here, we are led to the stories of Zora Neale Hurston or the novels of Richard Wright. In our own day the novels of Alice Walker force us to confront the same harsh reality. This is a cry of rage, and finally of acceptance.

It could be said that Naylor has presented a negative portrait of the black man in today's urban environment. We meet only two men in the story. One is a street person, an alcoholic who lives for the "crumpled brown paper bag that contained his morning sun," the "cheap red liquid that moved slowly down his throat." The other is the young father of the dead child. The only person willing to talk to him on the day of the child's funeral is the alcoholic, which in itself is an indictment of the young man's role in the tragedy, even if the author doesn't tell us in detail about his irresponsibility and immaturity.

In the larger dimensions of the story, Naylor has presented us with a grim picture of an entire part of society that has lost its ability to withstand the pressures of modern life. Mattie, with the knowledge she has gained over many years in the ghetto, manages to save the life of Ciel, the heroine of the story, but we see little hope that there will be women like Mattie to save all the women like Ciel, who are doomed by a life over which they have so little control.

Questions for Discussion

1. What does the alcoholic in the opening scene mean when he mumbles, "don't want no summons now."
2. What does the author tell us about the relationship between Lucielia and Mattie?
3. What drives Eugene to leave his family the second time?
4. What does the author tell us about Eugene and Lucielia's relationship that would justify Lucielia's response that "you pray silently — very silently — behind veiled eyes that the man will stay"?
5. "She piled a few plastic blocks in front of the child, and on her way out of the room, she glanced around quickly and removed glass ashtrays off the coffee table and put them on a shelf over the stereo." What does this passage tell us about Lucielia?

Topics for Writing

CRITICAL ESSAYS

1. The relationship of men and women in this story and men and women in the stories of other African-American authors, like Zora Neale Hurston or Toni Cade Bambara.
2. The description of the black ghetto male in "Lucielia Louise Turner" and its relation to reality.
3. A comparison of Naylor's Eugene and Baldwin's Sonny in "Sonny's Blues."

Joyce Carol Oates

Where Are You Going, Where Have You Been? (p. 1055)

Pointing to Oates's remark, quoted in the headnote, that she usually writes "about real people in a real society" should help to keep discussion away from premature allegorization or mythologizing, which — for all its eventual value and interest — smothers the story's impact by diverting attention from its realism. Her further observation that she understands Connie to be "struggling heroically to define personal identity in the face of incredible opposition, even in the face of death itself," may suggest how to go about answering the main question the story poses when considered in naturalistic terms: Why does Connie go out to Arnold Friend?

Connie's life as Oates depicts it takes place in two realms. Within her home and family Connie feels condemned and rejected, and she returns the disapproval. Outside these familiar precincts lies a world defined by movies, the drive-in restaurant, and the ever-present popular music. It is *not* the music of Bob Dylan, as Tom Quirk assures us, but the comparatively mindless, sentimental, and romantic music against which in the early 1960s Dylan stood out in such bold contrast. Connie's idea of the world into which, at the age of fifteen, she is beginning to make her first tentative forays is shaped by these songs and occupied by *boys*: boys who can be snubbed with impunity, boys who merge into one undifferentiated and safe blur in her mind, boys who offer hamburgers and "the caresses of love." And that love is "not the way someone like June would suppose but sweet, gentle, the way it was in movies and promised in songs." To these boys Connie presents herself as undifferentiated *girl*, and she is concerned that she look attractive to them.

The world, however, is occupied not only by frank and tentative boys but also by determined and deceitful men, by evil as well as by innocence, by hypocrisy, perversion, and violence — an exponent of all of which Connie attracts in Arnold Friend. Although in the course of their interview Connie sees through his disguise, the impoverishment of her world provides her no way to resist his advances. Her home offers no refuge, her father does not come when she needs him (he has always been essentially absent anyway), and she is unable to manipulate the telephone because of her panic. Meanwhile, Arnold, who presents himself in the guise of a movie hero, a teenage "boy," and her lover, offers to take charge of her. He places his mark upon her and gives her a role to play in a world of his devising. Because she is cut off from her past and has no idea of a future, she is at his mercy in determining what to do in the present. Like her cultural cousin, Vladimir Nabokov's Lolita, sobbing in Humbert's arms, she simply has nowhere else to go. Not only does Arnold show Connie that she is desired, he also provides her a way to be "good": By going with him she will save her undeserving family from getting hurt. Connie does not so much decide to go out to Arnold as she watches an alien being that Arnold has called into existence in her body respond to his desires. The final ironic horror, of course, is that she will be raped and murdered and buried in the desert not as brown-eyed Connie but as the imaginary "sweet little blue-eyed girl" of Arnold's sick imagination.

Oates acknowledges that her inspiration for the story came in part from reading about an actual case, and Tom Quirk has demonstrated at length the degree to which the circumstances of "Where Are You Going, Where Have You Been?"

seem to be derived from an article in *Life* (4 Mar. 1955) by Don Moser entitled (in a reference to some lyrics from a popular song) "The Pied Piper of Tucson." Even some of the most apparently allegorical details, such as Arnold's trouble with his boots, which has been attributed to his having cloven hooves or wolf paws, reflect the facts about Charles Schmid, a wiry gymnast of twenty-three who stuffed things in his boots, wore makeup, and drove around Tucson in a gold car playing the hero to a group of high-school kids until he was arrested for the rape and murder of three young girls. Quirk's argument that Oates followed the magazine article's theme in relating this horror in the "golden west" to the emptiness of "the American dream" points out an important dimension of the story, and his emphasis keeps the real horror of the incident in focus.

Gretchen Schulz and R. J. R. Rockwood are aware of the *Life* article, but they focus instead on another acknowledged source of Oates's inspiration, the folktale. Their discussion of the story's allusions to and affinities with "The Pied Piper of Hamelin," "Cinderella," "Little Red Riding Hood," and other tales suggests why "Where Are You Going, Where Have You Been?" is such a disturbing work. Their article offers detailed interpretations of the psychological crises Connie passes through, based on psychoanalytic interpretations of the meaning and developmental function of the analogous tales. (They use Bruno Bettelheim as their chief authority.) But whereas folktales most often smooth the passage of their readers through Oedipal conflicts and reintegration of the childhood identity into the adult by working through to a happy ending, "Where Are You Going, Where Have You Been?" taps these powerful psychic forces in the reader only to pour them out on the sand.

Questions for Discussion

1. Define Connie's relationships with her mother, sister, and father. What is missing from this family? Why does Connie wish "her mother was dead and she herself was dead and it was all over"?

2. What are Connie's "two sides"? In your opinion, is Connie's case unusual for a girl her age in our society? In what ways is she atypical? What about June?

3. The girls enter the drive-in with "faces pleased and expectant as if they were entering a sacred building," and the popular music in the background seems "like music at a church service." Explore the drive-in religion further. What are its creeds, its mysteries? Is it a true religion? a guide to the good life? Does Connie believe in anything else?

4. Discuss the similarities between Eddie, who rotates on a counter stool and offers "something to eat," and the emblem of the drive-in on its bottle-top roof. What else does Eddie offer? Compare Eddie with Arnold Friend as we first see him at the drive-in.

5. What does Oates accomplish by returning briefly to Connie's relationship with her family before narrating what happens "one Sunday"?

6. Discuss Connie's daydreams, in which "all the boys fell back and dissolved into a single face that was not even a face, but an idea, a feeling, mixed up with the urgent insistent pounding of the music," and in which she associates sunbathing with the "sweet, gentle" lovemaking "in movies and promised in song." What is the source of the sexual desire reflected in these dreams? What is its object?

7. Asbestos was formerly used as a noninflammable insulating material. Trace the images of heat and fire associated with it in the story.
8. Compare Connie's gentle breathing as she listens to the "XYZ Sunday Jamboree" with her breath "jerking back and forth in her lungs" when she tries to use the telephone at the climax of the story.
9. Why does Connie whisper "Christ. Christ" when she hears a car coming up the driveway? Does the effort to see Arnold Friend as a Christ figure find further substantiation in the text? Does it yield any meaningful insights?
10. Where does Connie stand during the first part of her conversation with Arnold? Is Oates's blocking of the scene realistic? symbolic?
11. Describe Arnold's car and clothing. What purpose is served by his transparent disguise? Why does it take Connie so long to penetrate the disguise?
12. Does Arnold have supernatural knowledge about Connie, her family, and her friends? Can his apparent clairvoyance about the barbecue be explained in naturalistic terms?
13. Account for Connie's idea that Arnold "had driven up the driveway all right but had come from nowhere before that and belonged nowhere and that everything about him and even the music that was so familiar to her was only half real." Explain the importance of that idea for understanding what happens to Connie.
14. Why does Connie's kitchen seem "like a place she had never seen before"? How has Arnold succeeded in making Connie feel cut off from her past and unprotected in her home? What is the implication of "the echo of a song from last year" in this context?
15. What is the role of Ellie in Arnold's assault on Connie?
16. Arnold implies that Connie can protect her family from harm by coming with him. How important a factor is this in his winning her over to his will?
17. Examine the passage in which Connie tries to telephone her mother and then collapses in panic and hysteria. Notice its associations with sex and birth. What is taking place in Connie at this moment?
18. Arnold asks rhetorically, "What else is there for a girl like you but to be sweet and pretty and give in?" In what sense is this true?
19. Explain Connie's feeling that she is watching herself go out the door. What has caused this split in her consciousness?

Topics for Writing

CRITICAL ESSAYS

1. Arnold Friend's obvious masquerade, and why it succeeds.
2. Popular music and religion in "Where Are You Going, Where Have You Been?"
3. Oates's "Where Are You Going, Where Have You Been?" and Jackson's "The Lottery" — technique and theme.
4. Arnold Friend and Flannery O'Connor's Misfit.

EXERCISES FOR READING

1. Read the story once while bearing in mind that it is "based on fact" — something very much like this is known to have actually happened. After

finishing the story, write a personal essay giving your reaction. What does this account imply about human nature? About the society reflected in the story?

2. Reread the story with an eye to its allusions to folktales and fairy tales with which you are familiar. Arnold's "coach" has a pumpkin on it; Connie is nearly asleep when he awakens her; he has big teeth; and so forth. What are the tales alluded to about? Is this story a fairy tale, too?

3. Study the allusions to religion in the story. How would Flannery O'Connor have handled this material?

RELATED SUBJECT

1. Select an item from the news that grips your imagination, and ask yourself why it does. Does it have affinities with folktales or myths? Does it suggest disturbing ideas about human nature and society? Write a narrative of the event, perhaps from the point of view of one of the participants, that incorporates these larger implications.

Related Commentary from Part Two

Joyce Carol Oates, The Making of a Writer, p. 1493.

Suggested Readings

Gillis, Christina Marsden. " 'Where Are You Going, Where Have You Been?': Seduction, Space, and a Fictional Mode." *Studies in Short Fiction* 18 (1981): 65–70.

Quirk, Tom. "A Source for 'Where Are You Going, Where Have You Been?' " *Studies in Short Fiction* 18 (1981): 413–19.

Schulz, Gretchen, and R. J. R. Rockwood. "In Fairyland, without a Map: Connie's Exploration Inward in Joyce Carol Oates's 'Where Are You Going, Where Have You Been?' " *Literature and Psychology* 30 (1980): 155–67.

Urbanski, Marie Mitchell Olesen. "Existential Allegory: Joyce Carol Oates's 'Where Are You Going, Where Have You Been?' " *Studies in Short Fiction* 15 (1978): 200–03.

Wegs, Joyce M. " 'Don't You Know Who I Am?': The Grotesque in Oates's 'Where Are You Going, Where Have You Been?' " *Journal of Narrative Technique* 5 (1975): 66–72.

Winslow, Joan D. "The Stranger Within: Two Stories by Oates and Hawthorne." *Studies in Short Fiction* 17 (1980): 263–68.

Tim O'Brien

The Things They Carried (p. 1069)

In "The Things They Carried," O'Brien has found a brilliant solution to one of the most common problems a writer faces: how to find a new way to approach a subject that has been written about many times before. His subject is men at war, a topic that has occupied writers since remotest antiquity. The earliest epic in the European tradition is Homer's account of the siege of Troy, and the earliest griot narratives from the empires of Africa recount battles fought along the banks of the Niger River.

The Vietnam War has been treated in a stream of stories, books, articles, studies, and debates. O'Brien's innovation is to tell us directly not about the soldiers, or about the meaningless war they find themselves in, but about the things they are carrying on their shoulders and in their pockets. This simple device is startling and effective. The things his "grunts" are carrying are one way to identify them, to bring them to life, and the author also tells us about the things they carry under different circumstances.

This use of the small detail to illuminate the whole picture would not be as effective if it were limited to a simple description of what each of the men is carrying. But as he discusses the items — their use, their importance to the assignment the men are carrying out, and the significance of each thing to each man — O'Brien tells us about the war itself, and the soldiers' attitudes toward what they are doing. By presenting each of these objects as a microcosm of the reality of the war, the author makes the experience more comprehensible. He has found a dimension that shows us the soldiers as human beings, and that is the most important task for a writer who wants to make us face this cruel reality again.

Questions for Discussion

1. What is the effect of O'Brien's use of abbreviations and acronyms: R & R, SOP, M & Ms, USO, Psy Ops, KIA?
2. When the author writes, "Afterward they burned Than Khe," what is he telling us about the attitude of the men toward the people in the villages around them?
3. Why is it important to specify the weight of the equipment each man is carrying?
4. Does the language of the soldiers sound "real"? Do the descriptions of the weapons have the feeling of reality?
5. Why does the lieutenant burn the letters he has been carrying?

Topics for Writing

1. Soldiers from both sides are fighting the war, but the author only tells us about the men from one side. Why doesn't he describe the North Vietnamese soldiers?
2. Discuss the attitudes toward the war in the United States as they are reflected in the attitudes of the soldiers in "The Things They Carried."
3. Stories about men at war usually emphasize heroism and heroic acts that are completely absent in this story. What has caused this change in attitude?

FLANNERY O'CONNOR

Everything That Rises Must Converge (p. 1085)

"Everything That Rises Must Converge" is one of O'Connor's most powerful stories. Although they are emotionally linked as closely as Siamese twins, Julian and his mother are in such fundamental disagreement that only death can bring their souls together, since "everything that rises must converge." O'Connor goes to great lengths to spell out the differences between mother and son. They are so extreme that humor is the one thing that makes them bearable to the sensitive reader. Julian asserts that "true culture is in the mind." His mother says, "It's in the heart." He insists that "nobody in the damn bus cares who you are." She replies, "I care who I am." She always looks on the bright side of things. He glories in scenting out impending disasters. He tells himself he isn't dominated by his mother. She knows he's both financially and emotionally dependent on her, and she gets him to do whatever she asks.

Contrasts and opposites rule this unlikely pair, but the world they inhabit is also in a state of opposition to their sense of themselves. Blacks no longer know their place in the back of the bus; mother and son are exiled from the destroyed family mansion; Julian wants to be a writer after his college education, but he's selling typewriters instead. The only constant is his mother's ridiculous hat. It reappears on the head of the black lady sitting with her little son next to Julian and his mother on the bus. This sight amuses his mother, who hasn't lost her sense of humor, her spirit refusing to be worn down by the remarks and behavior of her critical, hostile son. As a character she is partially redeemed (despite her racial bigotry) by her humor and her fundamental generosity. In contrast, Julian is damned by his sense of pride.

O'Connor makes certain of this damnation by subtly shifting the point of view to Julian's mental outlook during his journey on the bus, when he withdraws "into the inner compartment of his mind where he spent most of his time." He will be alone there, feeling smugly superior to his mother, until he realizes that he has lost her, at which time he will be forced to include her in his emotional state by entering "the world of guilt and sorrow."

Students may enjoy discussing the humor in this story, and O'Connor's sublime ear for the ridiculous in her characters' speech. "Everything That Rises Must Converge" also lends itself well to different critical perspectives. Since O'Connor wrote from a Christian orientation, the religious implications of the narrative can be traced: the references to Saint Sebastian, or the Negro mother's threat to her little boy, "Quit yo' foolishness . . . before I knock the living Jesus out of you!" Or O'Connor's quiet comment about "guilt and sorrow" at the end. Students who are budding social historians, psychologists, or feminists can also find abundant material in this story to explore from their orientations.

Questions for Discussion

1. O'Connor writes that Julian's mother's eyes, "sky-blue, were as innocent and untouched by experience as they must have been when she was ten." Again, when she turns her eyes, now a "bruised purple," on Julian, he gets an "uncomfortable sense of her innocence." What are we to make of her innocence? How do we reconcile this attribute with her racism?

2. Julian seems to hate almost everything about his mother. Does she hate anything about her son? Why does he despise her? Why does she love him?

3. The idea of family mansion implies family ties. How do family ties appear in this story? Does the "decayed mansion" mean more to Julian or to his mother? What does it mean to him? to her?

4. What point of view controls "Everything That Rises Must Converge"? At which points in the story do we have the most intimate access to Julian's thoughts?

5. Describe Julian's relationships with people other than his mother. Consider the paragraphs beginning "He began to imagine" and "He imagined his mother." Who would he like to be friends with and why? Does his acknowledgment of his mother's racism imply positive things about Julian's own character?

6. On page 1090 we discover that Julian's mother doesn't think Julian knows "a thing about 'life,' that he hadn't even entered the real world" yet. Does the narrator agree with her? Discuss this sentence and the closing sentence of the story together. What does this imply about the characteristics that belong to "real life"?

7. After his mother's stroke, Julian looks "into a face he had never seen before." What is different about her face now? What metaphor is O'Connor sustaining behind the description of the literal differences brought on by neurological devastation?

8. O'Connor, a devout Catholic, said her stories were meant to be more like parables than true to life. What elements of this story are Christian? Is the preoccupation central to this story available only to Christians?

Topics for Writing

CRITICAL ESSAYS

1. The two mothers and the two sons in the story.
2. The symbolism of the hat at the convergence of two apparent opposites — the two mothers.
3. Pride and the response to charity in Julian and the black mother.
4. The changing social order between the generations of Julian's mother and Julian.
5. The role of irony in "Everything That Rises Must Converge."

Related Commentaries from Part Two

Wayne C. Booth, A Rhetorical Reading of O'Connor's "Everything That Rises Must Converge," p. 1408.

V.S. Pritchett, Flannery O'Connor: Satan Comes to Georgia, p. 1509.

Suggested Readings

Burke, John J. "Convergence of Flannery O'Connor and Chardin." *Renascence* 19 (1966): 41–47, 52.

Esch, Robert M. "O'Connor's 'Everything That Rises Must Converge.' " *Explicator* 27 (1969): Item 58.

Kane, Patricia. "Flannery O'Connor's 'Everything That Rises Must Converge.' " *Critique: Studies in Short Fiction* 8 (1965): 85–91.

McDermott, John V. "Julian's Journey into Hell: Flannery O'Connor's Allegory of Pride." *Mississippi Quarterly* 28 (1975): 171–79.

Maida, Patricia Dinneen. "Convergence in Flannery O'Connor's 'Everything That Rises Must Converge.' " *Studies in Short Fiction* 7 (1970): 549–55.

Martin, W. R. "The Apostate in Flannery O'Connor's 'Everything That Rises Must Converge.' " *American Notes and Queries* 23 (1985): 113–14.

Nisly, P. W. "Prison of the Self: Isolation in Flannery O'Connor's Fiction." *Studies in Short Fiction* 17 (1980): 49–54.

Pyron, V. " 'Strange Country': The Landscape of Flannery O'Connor's Short Stories." *Mississippi Quarterly* 36 (1983): 557–68.

FLANNERY O'CONNOR

A Good Man Is Hard to Find (p. 1097)

O'Connor's comments (included in Part Two, p. 1495) direct attention to the climax of her story and suggest how she intended the central characters to be viewed and what she meant the story to imply. Students may benefit, however, from struggling at first to interpret the text unassisted by authorial explanation. The effort should reveal dimensions of O'Connor's art that might otherwise be overlooked.

The grandmother's reawakening to reality, which leads to her gesture of grace as she reaches out to The Misfit as one of her own children, may be triggered by the violence of the murders going on just offstage and the extremity of her own case, but her conversion has been carefully prepared for. Throughout the story this old woman longs in various ways to go back *home* — to Tennessee, to the days of her youth, to the mansion with the imaginary secret panel, which is as much in heaven as it is down a hilly back road in Georgia. Death is seldom far from her thoughts, though for a long time she does not apprehend its reality. Her initial worries about The Misfit are disingenuous, but encountering him or returning to east Tennessee come to the same thing in the end. On the road, the grandmother dresses up in nice clothes so that "anyone seeing her dead on the highway would know at once that she was a lady," observes a graveyard, and remembers her mansion at a town named Toombsboro. The Misfit and his men approach in a "hearse-like automobile"; the family awaits them in front of the woods that "gaped like a dark open mouth." The grandmother is at odds with present times. She squabbles with the children (whose behavior even the reader may find unusually improper), easily upstages the cabbage-headed, slacks-wearing woman who is their mother, joins Red Sammy in deploring the state of world affairs, and disastrously deludes Bailey by smuggling the cat into the car. But she loves the world as well, in a selfish, childish way. She *will* have the cat along; she admires the scenery (including a picturesque "pickaninny" for whose poverty she is not yet ready to feel compassion); she wishes she had married Mr. E. A. Teagarden, who courted her with watermelon and would have supplied all her worldly needs from the proceeds of his Coca-Cola stock; and she even makes a play for Red Sammy, the only tycoon in sight.

These desires may be misdirected, but just as it takes very little to upset the valise, release the cat, flip the car off the road, and carry the story into an entirely new set of circumstances, so, under the intensifying presence of death, it takes only a moment for the grandmother's selfish love for and alienation from the world to flip over into the selfless love that leads her to open her heart to The Misfit. After all, she at least rationalizes bringing the cat to protect it; she supportively asserts that Red Sammy is "a good man" in face of his own cynicism and despair; and she offers the same praise to The Misfit from the moment she recognizes him. Without a doubt the grandmother's motive in insisting that The Misfit is "a good man" and in urging him to pray is to divert him from his evident intention and so to save her skin. But as the bullets ring out in the background and the grandmother's maternal instincts burst forth in her repeated cries of "Bailey Boy!" she begins to act charitably in spite of herself. She offers The Misfit one of Bailey's shirts, listens to his confession (although she is the one who is about to die), and when he *is* wearing Bailey's shirt, she reaches out to him in his anguish. A good man *is* hard to find; Jesus may have been the only one who was intrinsically good. But when she loves and pities the radically fallen Misfit, the grandmother becomes for the moment a *good woman* through her Christlike action, as The Misfit himself acerbically recognizes.

As O'Connor mentions in her Commentary, The Misfit has evoked widely differing responses from readers and critics, who have associated him with the devil, the modern agnostic existentialist, or "the prophet he was meant to become," in O'Connor's own phrase. Perhaps The Misfit's daddy provides the best way of distinguishing him from the rest of the characters with his remark "It's some that can live their whole life out without asking about it and it's others has to know why it is, and this boy is one of the latters." Unlike O'Connor, whose vision of the world was grounded in *belief*, The Misfit wants to *know*. With Faustian presumption, he seeks to comprehend the divine mysteries in terms of his own intellect and demands a kind of justice in life that he can understand. When he cannot find the answers to his questions, but only the implication of inexplicable guilt (like Original Sin) in the punishment he receives, The Misfit sees the world not as the charming place it has appeared to the grandmother but as a prison whose empty sky resembles the blank walls of his cell in the penitentiary. In his own calculus of guilt, The Misfit feels he has been excessively punished, and he seems to be going about the world committing crimes in order to right the balance. His most perverse principle, "No pleasure but meanness," is sustained surprisingly well by the world O'Connor portrays. (Is *this* the reason for the story's lack of anything or anyone to admire and its unremittingly ironic tone?) But it gives way after he has been touched by the grandmother to his first true prophecy: "It's no real pleasure in life" — no *real* pleasure in *this* life, though true goodness sometimes appears in those made conscious of death.

Questions for Discussion

1. What is the grandmother's reason for bringing up The Misfit at the beginning of the story?
2. Describe "the children's mother." Why does O'Connor make her such a nonentity?
3. What about John Wesley and June Star? What would have been the result had O'Connor characterized them as something other than totally obnoxious?
4. Discuss the grandmother's reasons for her fatal decision to bring Pitty Sing on the trip.

171

5. Why does the grandmother dress so nicely for the trip?
6. Compare the grandmother's response to the scenery and the trip with that of the children. What does O'Connor accomplish by means of this distinction?
7. Just before the stop at The Tower, the grandmother reminisces about her old suitor, Edgar Atkins Teagarden. Specify the connections between the two episodes.
8. What tower might O'Connor have had in mind in choosing the name for Red Sammy's establishment? Why is there a monkey in a chinaberry tree feasting on fleas posted outside The Tower? What do we learn about the world at Red Sammy's?
9. Contrast The Tower with the mansion the grandmother awakens to remember "outside of Toombsboro."
10. What factors cause the accident? Consider its meaning as a consequence of the grandmother's choices and desires.
11. Describe the manner in which The Misfit arrives on the scene. What effect does his appearance have on the reader?
12. The grandmother's response to The Misfit's remark "it would have been better for all of you, lady, if you hadn't of reckernized me," is "You wouldn't shoot a lady, would you?" Evaluate her question.
13. To what extent is the grandmother correct in her praise of The Misfit? In what ways is he a gentleman?
14. Describe the grandmother's reaction to Bailey's departure. Is her response consistent with her previous behavior?
15. Define The Misfit's experience of the world. To what extent can his criminality be blamed on the conditions of his life? Does The Misfit feel any more free outside the penitentiary than in it?
16. How can the logic of The Misfit's position that "the crime don't matter. . . . because sooner or later you're going to forget what it was you done and just be punished for it" be attacked? To what extent does The Misfit's description of himself apply to everyone? Bear in mind that the whole family is being punished with death for no ascertainable crime.
17. Explain how, to The Misfit, "Jesus thown everything off balance."
18. What is the effect of O'Connor's comparing the grandmother to "a parched old turkey hen crying for water"?
19. Does The Misfit do or say anything to deserve the grandmother's gesture of concern?
20. Explain The Misfit's final evaluation of the grandmother: "She would of been a good woman . . . if it had been somebody there to shoot her every minute of her life."
21. Contrast The Misfit's remark "No pleasure but meanness" with his last words in the story.

Topics for Writing

CRITICAL ESSAYS

1. O'Connor's "A Good Man Is Hard to Find" and Tolstoy's "The Death of Ivan Ilych."
2. The function of tone in O'Connor's story.
3. Techniques of characterization in "A Good Man Is Hard to Find."

4. Horror and irony in O'Connor's "A Good Man is Hard to Find" and Bowles's "A Distant Episode."

RELATED SUBJECT

1. Write a parable or short tale designed to illustrate a religious or philosophical truth. Following O'Connor's example, portray your characters ruthlessly as embodiments of what you want them to represent.

Related Commentary from Part Two

Flannery O'Connor, The Element of Suspense in "A Good Man Is Hard to Find," p. 1495.

Suggested Readings

Asals, Frederick. *Flannery O'Connor: The Imagination of Extremity.* Athens: U of Georgia P, 1982. 142–54.
Browning, Preston M., Jr. *Flannery O'Connor.* Crosscurrents/Modern Critiques. Carbondale: Southern Illinois UP, 1974. 54–59.
Feeley, Sister Kathleen. *Flannery O'Connor: Voice of the Peacock.* New Brunswick, NJ: Rutgers UP, 1972.
Orvell, Miles. *Invisible Parade: The Fiction of Flannery O'Connor.* Philadelphia: Temple UP, 1972.

FRANK O'CONNOR

Guests of the Nation (p. 1111)

O'Connor's story draws exceptional power from its concern with a betrayal of the most primitive basis of human society, the host-guest relationship. The English prisoners, billeted with their guards in a cottage so thoroughly rooted in the land that its occupant still bears traces of indigenous paganism, earn the status of guests and come to feel at home. Belcher's contributions to the household chores call attention to the simple satisfactions of the peaceful, cooperative labor that is disrupted by the war, and Hawkins's learning Irish dances implies the underlying brotherhood of men, in contrast to which the scruples of "our lads" who "at that time did not dance foreign dances on principle" seem absurd —and ominous. The futility of Hawkins's debates with Noble on theology calls further into question the reality of the issues that divide the English from the Irish, and his international socialist politics provide a hint that there are issues of at least equal importance that would not polarize the two pairs of men but unite them against a common enemy.

The inhumanity of the conflict that orders Belcher and Hawkins to be executed by their "chums," their brothers, appears clearer for O'Connor's skillful portrayal of the prisoners as distinct from each other, individualized and consistent in their personalities. Further, by opening the story with a plunge into what seems an ongoing state of affairs, O'Connor shows that it is the war that interrupts the natural friendly interaction among the men rather than their fellowship interrupting a "normal" condition of bitter hostility between the English and the Irish. Even Jeremiah Donovan, who eventually brings down the cruel warrant and carries it out, forms part of the circle around the card table and scolds Hawkins for poor play "as if he were one of our own."

Bonaparte, the narrator, embraces the Englishmen as comrades and chafes at his official duties as their guard. With Noble, he imagines that the brigade officers, who also "knew the Englishmen well," will treat them as men rather than as enemies. But when the moment of decision arrives, Noble's resistance only extends to accepting the secondary role of gravedigger, and Bonaparte, though he hopes the prisoners will run away, finds himself powerless to aid them. Belcher and Hawkins are most fully themselves at the moment of their deaths, Hawkins talking on about his larger cause, Belcher finally revealing the fullness of his loving and generous nature. To Bonaparte and Noble the execution conveys a shock of revelation that changes the world for them. As Noble prays with the old woman in the doorway of the cottage — now become a shrine to the communion that took place within it, the only holy place in a world that seems to Noble composed entirely of the grave of his friends — Bonaparte, made profane in the literal etymological sense ("outside the shrine") and figuratively as well by his participation in the killing, feels himself cast out, alone, cut off from all atonement.

Questions for Discussion

1. Describe and explain the pacing of the story. Contrast the movement of sections II and III with that of section IV.
2. What is the effect of the abrupt beginning of the story? Why does O'Connor introduce the characters before specifying that they are prisoners and guards in a war?
3. Why does O'Connor trouble to introduce the message from Mary Brigid O'Connell about her brother's socks?
4. Distinguish between the two Englishmen. Are they more different from the Irishmen or from each other?
5. Explore the significance of the old woman's superstitions about Jupiter Pluvius and "the hidden powers." Compare her interest in religion with that of Noble and Hawkins.
6. Why is Bonaparte so shocked when he learns what may happen to the hostages?
7. What is the relevance to the story of Hawkins's political beliefs? Do we think less of him when he volunteers to become a traitor and join the Irish cause?
8. What is the effect of Belcher's last-minute confidences? of his apparently sincere repetition of the word *chum* throughout his ordeal?
9. Discuss Bonaparte's role in the execution. Is he culpable? Does he feel guilty?
10. Define the symbolic implications of the final scene. Why do Noble and Bonaparte have contrasting visions? Do their visions have anything in common? Why does Bonaparte burst out of the cottage where Noble and the old woman are praying?

Topics for Writing

CRITICAL ESSAYS

1. The meaning of the old woman and her cottage in "Guests of the Nation."
2. O'Connor's "Guests of the Nation" and Babel's "My First Goose" — introductions to war.
3. Executions in O'Connor's "Guests of the Nation" and Borowski's "This Way for the Gas, Ladies and Gentlemen."

EXERCISE FOR READING

1. Summarize the conflict and the action of this story on personal, public (national, historical, political), and eternal (philosophical, religious, mythical) levels. Could these levels be reconciled so the polarities of value would be parallel?

Related Commentaries from Part Two

Frank O'Connor, The Nearest Thing to Lyric Poetry Is the Short Story, p. 1498.
Frank O'Connor, Style and Form in Joyce's "The Dead," p. 1500.

Suggested Readings

Bordewyk, Gordon. "Quest for Meaning: The Stories of Frank O'Connor." *Illinois Quarterly* 41 (1978): 37–47, esp. 38–39.
Prosky, Murray. "The Pattern of Diminishing Certitude in the Stories of Frank O'Connor." *Colby Library Quarterly* 9 (1971): 311–21, esp. 311–14.

TILLIE OLSEN

I Stand Here Ironing (p. 1122)

One way to begin discussing this story is to look at the ending. "I will never total it all," the narrator affirms and then pronounces the summary whose inadequacy she has already proclaimed. The summarizing passage clarifies and organizes the impressions the reader may have gleaned from the preceding monologue. It is so clear that if it stood alone or came first in the story the validity of its interpretation of Emily could hardly be doubted. But since it follows her mother's "tormented" meditations, the summary seems incomplete in its clinical precision and must give way to a final paragraph of comparatively obscure and paradoxical requests focused in the startling but brilliantly adept image of the "dress on the ironing board, helpless before the iron," which links the story's end to its beginning and directs attention to the true central character.

What is mainly missing from the summary is the love and understanding that Emily's mother feels for her daughter as a result of living through the experiences bracketed by the orderly generalizations. Just as much as Emily, her mother has been the victim "of depression, of war, of fear." By virtue of having had to cope with those circumstances, she can respect Emily's response to them. Doing so enables her to counter the suggestion that "she's a youngster who needs help" with "Let her be." A good deal of the help Emily and her mother have received so far has put them in separate prisons — as when Emily was incarcerated at the convalescent home — and cut them off from love. To let Emily alone is at least to allow her some freedom to grow at her own slow pace.

Her mother is tempted to blame herself for the deficiencies in Emily's childhood, since she learned things about being a mother with her second family that she did not know with Emily. But her consideration of a characteristic incident early in the narrative suggests a crucial qualifying factor: When she parked Emily at nursery school at the age of two, she did not know what she was subjecting her daughter to, "except that it would have made no difference if I had known.... It was the only way we could be together, the only way I could hold a job." As much a victim of rigid and unfavorable economic and historic circumstances as her daughter, Emily's mother can speak her concluding line with feeling. In pleading that Emily somehow be made to know "that she is more than this dress on the ironing board, helpless before the iron," Emily's mother asks that her daughter be spared a condition to which she herself has been subjected. But Emily's mother, unlike Whistler's, does not sit for her portrait passively in a rocking chair; she stands there wielding the iron, controlling the very symbol of the circumstances that have not yet flattened her, painting her own self-portrait, and calling for help not in adjusting Emily to the world but in making the world a place in which Emily can thrive.

Questions for Discussion

1. Who is "you" in the first sentence? What is the mother's first response to the request to unlock the mystery of Emily? Does her position change?
2. Does Emily's mother feel guilty about how she has cared for Emily? Why? What factors have affected her dealings with her daughter?
3. Why is the passage in which Emily throws the clock so effective?
4. Discuss the "help" Emily gets at the convalescent home. How does it compare with the help her mother calls for at the end?
5. Emily has suffered from the absence of her father, the exhaustion of her mother, poverty, asthma and other diseases, sibling rivalry, and unpopularity, among other complaints. What is the effect of these hardships on the young woman she has become? What is the effect of her discovery of a talent?
6. What has her mother learned from Emily?
7. Does Emily's mother love her daughter? How can we tell?

Topics for Writing

CRITICAL ESSAYS

1. Like mother, like daughter — Emily's talent and her mother's.
2. The function of the interruptions in "I Stand Here Ironing."
3. "I will never total it all" — the importance of indeterminacy in Olsen's analysis of Emily.

4. The politics of "I Stand Here Ironing."
5. Mothers in Olsen's "I Stand Here Ironing" and Hwang Sun-won's "Conversation in June about Mothers."

RELATED SUBJECT

1. Write a summary statement in general terms about the personality of a sibling, relative, or friend you have known closely for a long time. Put it aside and cast your memory back to three or four specific incidents involving your subject. Narrate them briefly but in specific and concrete terms. Read over your sketches and compare the personality of your subject as it emerges with what you wrote in your generalized summary. Do you still think your summary is accurate? What are its limitations?

Suggested Readings

Frye, Joanne S. " 'I Stand Here Ironing': Motherhood as Experience and Metaphor." *Studies in Short Fiction* 18 (1981): 287–92.
O'Connor, William Van. "The Short Stories of Tillie Olsen." *Studies in Short Fiction* 1 (1963): 21–25, esp. 21–22.

CYNTHIA OZICK

The Shawl (p. 1130)

The yellow Star of David sewn into Rosa's coat identifies the people on the march as Jews whose destination is a Nazi concentration camp. The prosaic details of Ozick's story are horrible. Rosa's inability to save her baby, Magda, when the prison guard throws her against the electric fence is the grim conclusion to a hopeless situation. Ozick's poetic language and skillful pacing of her narrative transform the nightmarish details of her fiction into art.

The title of the story suggests its blend of fact and poetry. "The Shawl" is on the one hand a prosaic linen shawl that Rosa uses to wrap her baby and carry her under her coat during the forced march to the camp. On the other hand, Ozick tells us that "it was a magic shawl." It nourishes Magda after Rosa's breast milk dries up. It hides the baby in the women's barracks in the camp for many months. It smothers Rosa's scream after she sees Magda thrown against the fence. The shawl appears to have a life of its own, drying like Rosa's breasts; yet before drying it nourishes Rosa: "Rosa drank Magda's shawl until it dried." That is, perhaps, until the memory of her baby's death is bearable.

The narrative develops through two conflicts, the Jewish-Aryan conflict dramatized through the camp setting, and the personal conflict between the two sisters, the baby Magda and the fourteen-year-old Stella. The resolution of Stella's jealousy toward the baby — when Stella takes the shawl to cover herself against the cold and Magda totters outside the women's barracks looking for it — precipitates the climax of the story. There is no resolution to the larger Jewish-Aryan conflict, except that Rosa's will endures. She smothers her screams and survives the death of her baby.

The blend of fact and poetry is reinforced by Ozick's use of sound and silence in "The Shawl." Most of the time, the events described are unvoiced, evoking the eerie echo of silence in the black-and-white documentary films shot by the Allies liberating the concentration camps. Many students will have seen these films on TV programs about the Holocaust and will remember the images of the prison barracks, the hundreds of emaciated prisoners, the mounds of skeleton corpses.

Ozick suggests these familiar images by her use of poetic language to describe the malnutrition of her characters in "The Shawl." Stella's knees are "tumors on sticks, her elbows chicken bones." For the baby, death is a kind of deliverance. She makes a noise for the first time since her scream on the road. But the noises of the baby's scream and her cry "Maaaa" are subhuman, like the chicken-bone elbows. They reinforce the terror of the situation, people degraded into subhuman forms. In a way, silence is a relief. Rosa swallows the shawl to smother her howl so the prison guard won't shoot her. Silence is a means of survival in this story. Ironically, the silence of Ozick's words on the printed page is a testimony to the endurance of her people.

Questions for Discussion

1. How does Ozick use details to allude to the plot situation without naming it specifically? What mood does she create by her method of introducing details?
2. What two conflicts are evident throughout the story? How is the shawl central to these oppositions?
3. In what ways is the shawl "magic"? Whom does it nourish? How?
4. Discuss Ozick's use of poetic language to present the images of the story. Give examples of this use.
5. Who is the protagonist of the story? the antagonist? Is there more than one possible answer to these questions? Explain.
6. Sound and silence are integral to the total effect of the story. Discuss.
7. What is the climax of the story? Are any of the conflicts resolved? What is Ozick protesting? What human qualities does the story commemorate?

Topics for Writing

CRITICAL ESSAYS

1. The quality of endurance in O'Brien's "The Things They Carried" and Ozick's "The Shawl."
2. The theme of quiet desperation in Ozick's "The Shawl," Gilman's "The Yellow Wallpaper," and Steinbeck's "The Chrysanthemums."
3. Ozick's use of sensory images and their contribution to the overall story.

RELATED SUBJECT

1. Rewrite the story from the point of view of Stella.

Suggested Readings

"Cynthia Ozick: Lesson of the Master." *In Praise of What Persists.* Ed. Stephen Berg. New York: Harper, 1983. 181–87.

Epstein, J. "Fiction: Cynthia Ozick, Jewish Writer." *Commentary* 77 (1984): 64–69.

Ottenberg, E. "Rich Visions of Cynthia Ozick." *New York Times Magazine* 10 Apr. 1983: 46–47.

Rosenberg, R. "Covenanted to the Law: Cynthia Ozick." *MELUS* 9 (1982): 39–44.

Strandberg, V. "Art of Cynthia Ozick." *Texas Studies in Language and Literature* 25 (1983): 266–312.

GRACE PALEY

A Conversation with My Father (p. 1135)

The story the narrator writes in response to her father's request is so interesting that it is easy to forget for a while that it is only an element within the larger story Paley has to tell. Confronted with the inescapable fact of the father's imminent death, the narrator and her father respond in differing ways because of their differing needs. Both use gallows humor to make the situation less intolerable, as when the father remarks, "It so happens I'm not going out this evening"; but the narrator seeks that refuge much more often, and her father chides her repeatedly for doing so. Things *matter* to a dying man, and it is not surprising that he should prefer the straight line of tragedy — in which failure and defeat are compensated for by a perception of the real value of what has been lost — to the idea of "the open destiny of life," which, by holding out hope of recovery from any disaster, implies that there is nothing indispensable, no absolute loss. A man on his deathbed knows better.

The narrator's first attempt to write a story that suits her father's taste reflects her discomfort with the assignment. Her "unadorned and miserable tale" remains so sketchy that it lacks verisimilitude and conviction, like meaningless statistics on highway deaths or counterinsurgency body counts. Challenged to try again, she partly confirms her father's complaint that "with you, it's all a joke" by writing a brilliantly comic and incontrovertibly realistic version of the story, whose merits even her father has to recognize: "Number One: You have a nice sense of humor." In a few deft strokes, Paley renders an incisive satiric portrait of two contemporary "life-styles," their hypocrisy, and their destructiveness, focused neatly in the competing periodical titles, *Oh! Golden Horse!* (heroin) and *Man Does Live by Bread Alone.* The narrator knows as well as her father how thorough a perversion of true spiritual values is embodied in each of these titles, and she dramatizes her understanding in the destruction of the mother in her story. But she cannot quite "look it in the face," and she ends her tale with one last grim joke: "terrible, face-scarring, time-consuming tears." Her father spies her desperate evasion: "Number Two: I see you can't tell a plain story. So don't waste time." Ironically, the clarity of his disillusioned vision enables the dying man to feel a purer sympathy for the mother in the story than does the narrator herself, although she claims to care so much about her characters that she wants to give them all a second chance. "Poor woman," he says. "Poor girl, born in a time of fools, to live among fools. The end. The end. You were right to put that down. The end." Not necessarily, the narrator argues, and goes on to invent the kind of future for her character that we always imagine for the dying, in the probably misguided effort to ease their anxiety. But her father, as usual, knows better: " 'How long will it be?' he asked. Tragedy! You too. When will you look it in the face?' "

Questions for Discussion

1. Describe the medical condition of the narrator's father. How important is it to understanding his position in the conversation?
2. Explain the phrase "despite my metaphors" in the first paragraph. What other writerly tactics of the narrator does her father ignore?
3. The narrator says she *would* like to tell a story with the kind of plot she has always despised. Analyze her conflict.
4. What is the point of the first version of the story? What is wrong with it as a piece of fiction?
5. When her father asks for details, the narrator comes up with things he calls jokes. Are they? What makes them jokes rather than facts?
6. Why does the narrator's father consider that "it is of great consequence" whether the woman in the story is married? Is he simply old-fashioned?
7. What does the narrator add to her story in the second version? Does the point of the story remain the same? Does her father get the point?
8. The woman in the story "would rather be with the young." Consider that motivation and its results from the point of view of the narrator and of her father.
9. What techniques does Paley use to satirize the woman's son and his girlfriend?
10. Explain the term "time-consuming" at the end of the inset story.
11. The narrator's father makes three separate responses to the story. Account for each of them. Do they cohere?
12. What does the narrator's father mean by the statement he makes in various forms culminating in his final question?

Topics for Writing

CRITICAL ESSAYS

1. Attitudes toward death and life in Paley's "A Conversation with My Father" and Tolstoy's "The Death of Ivan Ilych."
2. "A Conversation with My Father" as a story about writing.
3. Tragedy versus satire in "A Conversation with My Father."

RELATED SUBJECT

1. Write your own version of the narrator's story. Start from her first version and elaborate on it as you choose, without necessarily using the material the narrator includes in her second version and subsequent commentary.

Related Commentary from Part Two

Grace Paley, A Conversation with Ann Charters, p. 1501.

EDGAR ALLAN POE

The Cask of Amontillado (p. 1141)

Poe is the great master of the contrived suspense story, and "The Cask of Amontillado" is a model of narrative compression toward a single effect. Students should understand that Poe had a theory on the short story; its essential points are suggested in his review of Hawthorne's tales in Part Two (p. 1506).

Despite Poe's rational explanation of how a writer should compose a story, his own fiction is directed toward eliciting irrational emotions. Poe's literary style aims at using as many extravagances of character, setting, and plot as he could invent, exploiting the reader's emotional vulnerability to disturbing images of darkness and chaos. The hectic unpredictability of the carnival season, the creepy subterranean wine cellar, and the ancient family crypt with its molding skeletons all challenge us emotionally, and make us want to read further.

In the reading, our own fears become the true subject matter. As in a nightmare, Fortunato finds himself being buried alive, one of the most basic human fears. On a more conscious level, we rely on a social contract to bind us together as a human family, and Montresor's lawlessness plays on our fear that any person can take the law into his or her own hands without being checked by conscience. Poe doesn't have to give us a great number of details about his characters; our imagination draws from the depths of the common human psyche to supply all that we need.

This story is a good example to use in stressing the importance of the students' close reading of a text. It's easy for readers to miss, in the last paragraph, the sentence "My heart grew sick — on account of the dampness of the catacombs." Yet upon this sentence rests the interpretation of Montresor's character: Can we excuse his action on grounds of insanity? Was he insane at the time he buried Fortunato alive, or did he go insane in the half century during which, he tells us, his crime has remained undetected? If the reader has not paid careful attention to that sentence, he or she will have missed an essential detail in understanding the story.

The book *Mysterious New England,* edited by A. N. Stevens (1971), suggests that Poe first heard the anecdote upon which he might have based this story when he was a private in the army in 1827. Supposedly only ten years before, a popular young lieutenant named Robert F. Massie had also been stationed at Fort Independence in Boston Harbor; when Poe was serving there, he saw a gravestone erected to the memory of Lieutenant Massie, who had been unfairly killed in a duel by a bully named Captain Green.

> Feeling against Captain Green ran high for many weeks, and then suddenly he vanished. Years went by without a sign of him, and Green was written off the army records as a deserter.

According to the story that Poe finally gathered together, Captain Green had been so detested by his fellow officers that they decided to take a terrible revenge on him for Massie's death.

Visiting Captain Green one moonless night, they pretended to be friendly and plied him with wine until he was helplessly intoxicated. Then, carrying the captain down to one of the ancient dungeons, the officers forced his body through a tiny opening that led into the subterranean casemate. His captors began to shackle him to the floor, using the heavy iron handcuffs and footcuffs fastened into the stone. Then they sealed the captain up alive inside the windowless casemate, using bricks and mortar that they had hidden close at hand.

Captain Green shrieked in terror and begged for mercy, but his cries fell on deaf ears. The last brick was finally inserted, mortar applied, and the room closed off, the officers believed, forever. Captain Green undoubtedly died a horrible death within a few days.

Questions for Discussion

1. How does Poe motivate the behavior of Montresor? Does the story provide any hints as to the "thousand injuries" he has suffered? Are any hints necessary?
2. Why is the setting of the story appropriate?
3. What does Montresor's treatment of his house servants tell us about his knowledge of human psychology, and how does it prepare us for his treatment of Fortunato?
4. How does Poe increase the elements of suspense as Fortunato is gradually walled into the catacombs?

Topics for Writing

(Remind the class that there is a student paper in "Writing about Short Stories," p. 1566 in the anthology, comparing and contrasting this story with Hawthorne's "Young Goodman Brown.")

1. Montresor doesn't tell his story until a half century after the actual event. Analyze how Poe adapts the flashback technique to affect the reader of "The Cask of Amontillado."
2. Explicate the passage in the story in which Montresor entices Fortunato into the crypt.
3. Compare elements of the macabre in Poe's "The Cask of Amontillado" and Fuentes's "The Doll Queen."

Related Commentaries from Part Two

D. H. Lawrence, The Lust of Hate in Poe's "The Cask of Amontillado," p. 1469.
Edgar Allan Poe, The Importance of the Single Effect in a Prose Tale, p. 1506.

Suggested Readings

Adler, Jacob H. "Are There Flaws in 'The Cask of Amontillado'?" *Notes and Queries* 199 (1954): 32–34.

Carlson, Eric W., ed. *The Recognition of Edgar Allan Poe*. Ann Arbor: U of Michigan P, 1966.

Gargano, J. W. " 'The Cask of Amontillado': A Masquerade of Motive and Identity." *Studies in Short Fiction* 4 (1967): 119–26.

EDGAR ALLAN POE

The Tell-Tale Heart (p. 1146)

"The Tell-Tale Heart" is a story about what has been called "the demonic self" — a person who feels a compulsion to commit a gratuitous act of evil. Poe wrote explicitly about what he calls this "spirit of perverseness" in his story "The Black Cat," published in 1843, two years before "The Tell-Tale Heart":

> Of this spirit [of perverseness] philosophy takes no account. Yet I am not more sure that my soul lives, than I am that perverseness is one of the primitive impulses of the human heart — one of the indivisible primary faculties, or sentiments, which give direction to the character of Man. Who has not, a hundred times, found himself committing a vile or a silly action, for no other reason than because he knows he should *not*? Have we not a perpetual inclination, in the teeth of our best judgment, to violate that which is *Law*, merely because we understand it to be such?

According to the critic Eric W. Carlson, "The Tell-Tale Heart" was one of Poe's favorite stories. In addition to dramatizing the "spirit of perverseness" in his narrative, Poe combines other elements of the gothic tale (the evil eye, the curse), the psychorealistic (the narrator's paranoia), the dramatic (concentrated intensity of tone, gradually heightened series of dramatic events), and the moral (the compulsion to confess).

Questions for Discussion

1. How would you describe the narrator of the story? How does your description compare or contrast with what he would like to have you believe about him?
2. What disease is the narrator referring to in the first paragraph?
3. What caused the narrator to murder the old man? Was his reason valid?
4. What narrative devices does Poe use to heighten the suspense of the tale? Give examples.
5. Poe believed in the existence of the "spirit of perverseness" within every man. How is this revealed in the story?
6. Do you feel the confession at the end of the tale is necessary? Why? What is Poe's purpose in presenting this confession?

Topics for Writing

CRITICAL ESSAYS

1. The significance of the light and dark imagery in "The Tell-Tale Heart."
2. The effect of premeditation in "The Tell-Tale Heart."
3. Use of sight and sound as dramatic devices in "The Tell-Tale Heart."
4. The dichotomy between the narrator's view of himself and our view of him in "The Tell-Tale Heart."
5. Reality versus illusion in "The Tell-Tale Heart."

RELATED SUBJECT

1. Rewrite the story from the point of view of the police officers; from the point of view of the old man.
2. Consider the events that might result from the action of this story, and write a sequel presenting these developments.

Related Commentary from Part Two

Edgar Allan Poe, The Importance of the Single Effect in a Prose Tale, p. 1506.

Suggested Readings

Carlson, Eric W. *Introduction to Poe: A Thematic Reader*. Glenville, IL: Scott, 1967.
Pitcher, E. W. "Physiognomical Meaning of Poe's 'The Tell-Tale Heart.' " *Studies in Short Fiction* 16 (1979): 231–33.
Robinson, E. A. "Poe's 'The Tell-Tale Heart.' " *Nineteenth Century Fiction* 19 (1965): 369–78.
Tucker, B. D. "Tell-Tale Heart and the Evil Eye." *Southern Literary Journal* 13 (1981): 92–98.

KATHERINE ANNE PORTER

Theft (p. 1152)

The narrator of this story begins by describing her reaction when she discovers her purse is missing. The opening paragraph is in the past tense, but it describes the moment after the narrator realizes her loss and tries to re-create the events of the previous evening. Her description in this flashback is lucid, calm, rational. She remembers a series of encounters with friends who accompanied her in the rain from a party back to her apartment. First Camilo, the man who walked her to the subway —and she remembers she had her purse, because she checked inside to see that she had a nickel to pay her fare. Then Roger, who asked her for a dime to pay the cabbie who dropped her off at her apartment. Then Bill, who invited her in for a drink as she climbed the stairs past his door, and asked her to forget about the fifty dollars he owed her. Finally, the narrator thinks about the author of the letter she took out of her purse when she reached her apartment; apparently, he was ending their relationship. She reread his letter before she spread the purse out to dry and finally went to bed.

Next the narrator recalls her actions that morning, when she sat in the bathtub and heard the janitress come in and out of the next room. Still calm, despite her belief that the janitress has stolen the purse, the narrator dresses and drinks coffee, thinking that she should "let it go." Suddenly she feels a "deep almost murderous anger." Confronting the janitress, she gets her purse back, but the exchange is so upsetting that the narrator realizes, "I was right not to be afraid of any thief but myself, who will end by leaving me nothing."

The story suggests different levels of theft, or self-deception. The narrator is always generous with her friends, but she has very little money of her own. She is too easily persuaded to drop her claim on the fifty dollars her neighbor owes her; she doesn't value her own writing enough to insist he pay her for it. She is the epitome of the "nice" girl who lets the men in her life dominate her in various ways. Finally the encounter with the angry janitress, who has even less than she does, makes the narrator see herself as others see her, and she cannot escape the realization that she is no longer a young woman, that she is impecunious, and that she is alone and apparently of little importance to the men whose lives she props up.

Questions for Discussion

1. Why doesn't Porter give the narrator a name?
2. Is the narrator a sympathetic character? What details make you aware of her propensity to depreciate herself and her abilities?
3. What motivates the narrator finally to acknowledge her situation?
4. What details in the story make you realize that it is occurring during the time of the so-called Great Depression in the United States?

Topics for Writing

1. Katherine Mansfield's symbolic technique influenced Porter. With this in mind, analyze the purse as the central symbol in "Theft."
2. Compare and contrast the girl in Minot's "Lust" or the woman in Hemingway's "Hills Like White Elephants" with the narrator of Porter's "Theft."

Suggested Readings

Liberman, M. M. *Katherine Anne Porter's Fiction.* Detroit: Wayne State UP, 1971.
Katherine Anne Porter: A Critical Symposium. Ed. Lodwick Hartley and George Core. Athens: U of Georgia P, 1969.

Leslie Marmon Silko

Yellow Woman (p. 1158)

This story, like Singer's "Gimpel the Fool," is told in the first person and presented episodically in several sections. It takes place over two days, beginning the morning Yellow Woman wakes up beside the river with Silva, the stranger she has spent the night with. The story ends at sundown the next day, when she returns to her family in the Pueblo village.

Like "Gimpel the Fool," "Yellow Woman" is built on different traditions from those in the cultural background of most American students. Both Silko and Singer write fiction that preserves their cultural heritage by re-creating its customs and values in stories that dramatize emotional conflicts of interest to modern readers. Singer's fiction is in the tradition of Yiddish folktales; Silko retells Pueblo Indian myths and legends.

As Yellow Woman narrates the story of her abduction and return to her family, the reader comes to share her mood and her interpretation of what has happened. As a girl she was fascinated by the stories her grandfather told her about Silva, the mysterious kachina spirit who kidnaps married women from the tribe, then returns them after he has kept them as his wives. These stories were probably similar to the imaginary tales passed down in an oral tradition whose origins are lost to contemporary American folklorists. Silko has created their modern equivalent, her version of how they might be reenacted in today's world. The overweight, white Arizona rancher is familiar to us, as is the Jell-O being prepared for supper, and we have no difficulty imagining the gunnysacks full of freshly slaughtered meat bouncing on the back of Yellow Woman's horse.

The dreamlike atmosphere Silko creates in "Yellow Woman" makes such realistic details protrude sharply from the soft-focus narrative. Yellow Woman doesn't think clearly. She seems bewitched by the myths her grandfather told her, and her adventure following the man she calls Silva holds her enthralled. At the end she says, "I thought about Silva, and I felt sad at leaving him; still, there was something strange about him, and I tried to figure it out all the way back home." We are not told what — if anything — she does figure out.

Instead, action takes the place of thought in the story. Yellow Woman looks at the place on the riverbank where she met Silva and tells herself that "he will come back sometime and be waiting again by the river." Action moves so swiftly that we follow Yellow Woman as obediently as she follows her abductor, mesmerized by the audacity of what is happening. There is no menace in Silva, no danger or malice in his rape of Yellow Woman. The bullets in his rifle are for the white rancher who realizes he has been killing other men's cattle, not for Yellow Woman — or for us.

Questions for Discussion

1. Why is Yellow Woman so eager to believe that she and Silva are acting out the stories her grandfather told her?
2. How does Silko structure the opening paragraphs of the story to help the reader suspend disbelief and enter the dreamlike atmosphere of Yellow Woman's perceptions?

3. Why does Silko tell the story through the woman's point of view? Describe the Pueblo Indian woman we know as Yellow Woman. Is she happy at home with her mother, grandmother, husband, and baby? Why is Yellow Woman's father absent from the story?
4. Are there any limitations to Silko's choice to tell the story through Yellow Woman's point of view? Explain.
5. Why doesn't the narrator escape from Silva when she discovers him asleep by the river as the story opens? What makes her decide to return home the next day?

Topics for Writing

1. Tell the story through a third-person omniscient narration.
2. Compare "Yellow Woman" with an Indian folktale about the kachina spirit who kidnapped married women.
3. Compare the way Silko's "Yellow Woman" and Singer's "Gimpel the Fool" use traditional elements of their authors' cultural background to create new stories.
4. Compare Silko's "Yellow Woman" and Oates's "Where Are You Going, Where Have You Been?" as rape narratives.

Suggested Readings

Allen, Paula Gunn. *The Sacred Hoop: Recovering the Feminine in American Indian Traditions.* Boston: Beacon, 1986.

——— ed. *Spider Woman's Granddaughters: Traditional Tales* and *Contemporary Writing by Native American Women.* Boston: Beacon, 1989.

ISAAC BASHEVIS SINGER

Gimpel the Fool (p. 1168)

Gimpel's life as a fool seems to encompass three stages. In the first, he is a boy in school, teased unmercifully by the other students and the townspeople. When he goes to the village rabbi for advice, the rabbi tells him to accept the situation, because it is "better to be a fool all your days than for one hour to be evil. You are not a fool. They are the fools. For he who causes his neighbor to feel shame loses Paradise himself." Comforting spiritual advice, yet a minute later Gimpel is made a fool of by the rabbi's daughter.

In the next stage of Gimpel's life as a fool he is a successful baker, employing an assistant. But his wife, Elka, sleeps with his assistant. Gimpel loves the children she produces, and again the rabbi is no help, advising Gimpel to divorce his unfaithful wife but making him wait nine months when Gimpel changes his mind about divorce. Gimpel weeps when he thinks he has misjudged his wife's behavior: "What's the good of not believing? Today it's your wife you don't believe; tomorrow it's God Himself you won't take stock in."

After his wife's death Gimpel is in despair, since with her dying breath she confessed that she had deceived him. In his anger he urinates into the bread dough, but the spirit of his wife reproaches him: "Because I was false is everything false too?" Gimpel buries the bread he has spoiled, leaves his money with his children, gives up his business, and becomes a wanderer.

The final page of the story is the third stage of Gimpel's life, when — free from his wife and his business — he becomes the wise fool, resigned to his fate. He dreams constantly of his wife, who has become a saint to him. He prays for death and carries his shroud in his beggar's sack: "When the time comes I will go joyfully. Whatever may be there, it will be real, without complication, without ridicule, without deception." In God's heaven, Gimpel tells us, he "cannot be deceived," so he will finally be free from his role as a fool.

Questions for Discussion

1. "Gimpel the Fool" is told by a first-person narrator. What does Singer gain from this point of view? Does it have any limitations?
2. Singer is saying that the world we live in is difficult to understand; we may all be fools if we are "deceived" or taken in by what people tell us. Agree or disagree with this interpretation.
3. In what ways is Gimpel a "holy fool"? What definitions of a fool or foolish characterize him?
4. Who else might be called fools in this story?

Topics for Writing

1. Analyze the details in the story that create the atmosphere of the Jewish villages of Poland before the Second World War.

CRITICAL ESSAYS

1. Persecution in Singer's "Gimpel the Fool" and Jackson's "The Lottery."
2. The theme of "the little man" in Singer's "Gimpel the Fool" and Gogol's "The Overcoat."

Suggested Reading

Alexander, Edward. *Isaac Bashevis Singer*. World Authors Series. Boston: Twayne, 1980.

SUSAN SONTAG

The Way We Live Now (p. 1180)

Most stories by contemporary authors in this anthology are told from a limited-omniscient point of view. Leslie Marmon Silko narrates her story through the perceptions of Yellow Woman; Ann Beattie shows us the misery of a Connecticut weekend as experienced by a wife caught in a loveless marriage in "The Burning House." Isaac Bashevis Singer uses first-person narration in "Gimpel the Fool." Susan Sontag does something very different in "The Way We Live Now." The story chronicles the last months of a man dying of AIDS, but we never learn directly what he sees or feels. Instead, we hear what he is suffering through the comments of his many friends. The end result is a work that deliberately treats its subject the way most people treat AIDS itself — at a distance, through hearsay, with mingled fascination and horror, as something terrible that can only happen to other people.

We never learn the name, occupation, or physical description of the AIDS victim in Sontag's story. Instead, we are told the responses of his friends, like a roll call of potential victims of the virus. These friends — more than twenty-five of them — are also not described, only presented by name as they talk to one another about the sick man. Their names follow one another so rapidly we are not given any explanation of their relationships: Max, Ellen, Greg, Tanya, Orson, Stephen, Frank Jan, Quentin, Paolo, Kate, Aileen, Donny, Ursula, Ira, Hilda, Nora, Wesley, Victor, Xavier, Lewis, Robert, Betsy, Yvonne, Zack, and Clarice. The first-name basis is fitting, since the majority of the people know one another and inhabit the same world. We are never told what city they all live in, but we assume from the way they talk and their large numbers that they live in New York and are part of its cliques of people active in the arts, literature, and cultural journalism.

The first-name basis of the conversations is also aesthetically appropriate, because for the most part the characters are using the telephone. They repeat the latest gossip they have learned from one another; for all their sophistication, they pass along news of the stages of their friend's illness like the voices of tribal drums alerting the inhabitants of villages in Africa. The reader has the same sense of a closely knit community joined by common interests and means of livelihood. Because the community is left unspecified, the setting and the characters become mythologized into "Anyplace" and "Everyone." Sontag's implication is that we are all participants in this human tragedy. AIDS can happen to anyone.

As we read "The Way We Live Now," our rational impulses function despite the lack of specificity about the central character. The short conversational exchanges function as a literary code that we try to unlock. We attempt to trace relationships (Quentin, Lewis, Paolo, and Tanya have all been lovers of the AIDS victim); we categorize important information about lives outside the main story (Max gets AIDS too, as does Hilda's seventy-five-year-old aunt); we highlight generalizations that suggest a broader social and moral significance to this individual tragedy (the age of "debauchery" is over).

Close readers may even be able to interpret the fragments of conversations to gain psychological insights of use in other contexts. For example, Kate tells Aileen that the sick man is "not judging people or wondering about their motives" (when they come to see him in the hospital); rather, "he's just happy to see his friends." By presenting the numbers of people linked to a specific AIDS victim who appears to be well known and highly regarded in his community, Sontag is making an ironic comment about the isolation of all AIDS victims. Her story is an attempt to write about a taboo subject and encourage compassion toward those suffering from the disease.

189

Questions for Discussion

1. The story is developed chronologically, from the news of the patient's illness, through his first hospitalization, to his return home and rehospitalization. How does this progression give coherence to the story?
2. How do the relationships suggested among the twenty-five characters in the story give you a sense of the occupation and lifestyle of the central character?
3. Hilda says that the death of the pianist in Paris "who specialized in twentieth-century Czech and Polish music" is important because "he's such a valuable person . . . and it's such a loss to the culture." Do you think Sontag shares Hilda's opinion? Do you? Why or why not?
4. Agree or disagree with Ursula's idea at the end of the story.

Topics for Writing

1. Write a review of Sontag's nonfiction work *AIDS and Its Metaphors*.
2. Choose any five characters in "The Way We Live Now" and invent backgrounds for them.
3. Rewrite the story from the point of view of the AIDS patient, perhaps in the form of his diary.

Related Commentary from Part Two

David Leavitt, The Way I Live Now, p. 1470

Suggested Reading

Sontag, Susan. *AIDS and Its Metaphors*. New York: Farrar, 1989.

JOHN STEINBECK

The Chrysanthemums (p. 1195)

The instinctive life that Elisa Allen loves as she tends her chrysanthemum plants lies dormant under her fingers. She is good with flowers, like her mother before her. Elisa says, "She could stick anything in the ground and make it grow." But it is December, and Steinbeck tells us it is "a time of quiet and waiting." The Salinas landscape lies peacefully, but Elisa is vaguely unfulfilled. She begins to transplant her little chrysanthemum shoots, working without haste, conscious of her "hard-swept" house and her well-ordered garden, protected with its fence of chicken wire. Everything in her little world is under control. The tension in the scene is in herself, something she vaguely senses but refuses to face: the difference between her little world and the larger one encompassing it. Elisa is strong and mature, at the height of her physical strength. Why should she lie dormant? She has no fit scope for her powers. Steinbeck suggests the contradiction between her strength and her passivity in his description of the landscape: "The yellow stubble fields seemed to be bathed in pale gold sunshine, but there was no sunshine in the valley now in December." Like Hemingway, Steinbeck uses physical and geographical details to suggest the *absence* of positive qualities in his fictional characters. There is no sunshine in the valley, and the chrysanthemum plants aren't flowering, but what is natural in the annual vegetation cycle is out of kilter in Elisa. She experiences the world as a state of frustration.

Steinbeck has written an understated Chekhovian story in which ostensibly nothing much happens. It is a slice of life as Elisa lives it, sheltered and comfortable, yet — in Henry David Thoreau's words — life lived in a state of "quiet desperation."

The two male characters feel none of Elisa's lack of fulfillment. They live in a male world and take their opportunities for granted. Her husband, Henry Allen, is having a fine day. He's sold his thirty head of steer for a good price, and he's celebrating this Saturday night by taking his wife out to dinner and the movies in town. The traveling man is a trifle down on his luck, but it's nothing serious. He's found no customers this day so he lacks the money for his supper, but he knows a mark when he sees one. He flatters Elisa by agreeing with her and handing her a line about chrysanthemums for a lady he knows "down the road a piece." Elisa springs into action, delighted to be needed. Her tender shoots need her too, but she is not sufficiently absorbed by her gardening. The men do the real work of the world in this story. Gardening is a hobby she's proud of, and her husband encourages her to take pride in it, but she needs to feel of use in a larger dimension. Elisa mistakes this need for the freedom she imagines the transient knows on the road. Steinbeck gives her a clue as to the man's real condition in the state of his horse and mule, which she as a good gardener shouldn't have missed: "The horse and donkey drooped like unwatered flowers."

Instead, Elisa is caught up in her romantic fantasy of his nomadic life. Her sexual tension reduces her to a "fawning dog" as she envisions his life, but finally she realizes the man doesn't have the money for his dinner. "She stood up then, very straight, and her face was ashamed." Ashamed for what reason? her lack of sensitivity to his poverty? her sexual excitement? her sense of captivity in a masculine world, where apparently only motherhood would bring opportunities for real work? Elisa brings the man two battered pots to fix and resumes talking, unable to leave him or her fantasy about the freedom she thinks he enjoys. He tells her outright that "it ain't the right kind of a life for a woman." Again she misreads the situation, taking his comment as a challenge. Her response is understandable, since she's never had his opportunity to choose a life on the road. She defends her ability to be his rival at sharpening scissors and banging out dents in pots and pans.

When the man leaves, Elisa is suddenly aware of her loneliness. She scrubs her body as rigorously as she's swept her house, punishing her skin with a pumice stone instead of pampering it with bubble bath. Then she puts on "the dress which was the symbol of her prettiness." An odd choice of words. Without understanding her instinctive rebellion against male expectations, Elisa refuses to be a sex symbol. Again she loses, denying herself pleasure in soft fabrics and beautiful colors. When Henry returns, he is bewildered by her mood and unable to reach her. She sees the chrysanthemums dying on the road, but she still can't face the truth about her sense of the repression and futility of her life. Wine at dinner and the idea of going to see a prize fight briefly bring her closer to the flesh and the instinctive life she has shunned outside her contact with her flowers, but they don't lift her mood. She feels as fragile and undervalued as her chrysanthemums. She begins to cry weakly, "like an old woman," as Henry drives her down the road.

Like Lawrence's heroine in "The Odour of Chrysanthemums," Elisa is frustrated, cut off from the fullness of life by her physical destiny as a woman in a man's world. Does Steinbeck understand the sexual bias that undermines Elisa's sense of herself? He makes Henry as considerate a husband as a woman could wish for — he takes Elisa to the movies instead of going off to the prize fight himself. Like Hemingway, Steinbeck was sensitive to women's frustration, depicting it often in his fiction, even if he didn't look too closely at its probable causes in the society of his time.

Questions for Discussion

1. Based on Steinbeck's description in the first three paragraphs, how would you characterize the initial tone of the story? What do you associate with Steinbeck's image of the valley as "a closed pot"? In what way does this initial description foreshadow the events of the story?
2. What kind of a character is Elisa Allen? What are the physical boundaries of her world? What is Elisa's psychological state at the beginning of the story?
3. Characterize the two men who are part of Elisa's world. In what ways are they similar and different? How does their way of life compare and contrast with the life Elisa leads?
4. What is the role of the chrysanthemums in Elisa's life? What do they symbolize?
5. How does Elisa delude herself about the life of the tinker? What other fantasies does this lead her to indulge in?
6. In what way does the tinker manipulate Elisa to accomplish his goals?
7. When the tinker leaves, a change comes over Elisa. What has she suddenly realized, and what course of action does she adopt?
8. As Elisa, both realistically and symbolically, goes out into the world, has she achieved any resolution of her problem? Why does she end the story "crying weakly — like an old woman"?

Topics for Writing

CRITICAL ESSAYS

1. Steinbeck's use of setting to establish theme in "The Chrysanthemums."
2. The isolation of Elisa Allen.
3. Elisa's illusions about the tinker and his interest in her as contrasted with reality.
4. Male versus female societal and sexual roles in Lawrence's "Odour of Chrysanthemums" and Steinbeck's "The Chrysanthemums."
5. Woman in a man's world: Steinbeck's Elisa, Head's Life and Silko's Yellow Woman.

RELATED SUBJECT

1. Recall a time when you felt threatened and frustrated by events that isolated you. Write a narrative recounting this experience from a third-person point of view.

Suggested Readings

McMahan, Elizabeth. "'The Chrysanthemums': Study of a Woman's Sexuality."
Modern Fiction Studies 14 (1968-69): 453-58.
Marcus, Mordecai. "The Lost Dream of Sex and Children in 'The Chrysanthemums."
Modern Fiction Studies 11 (1965): 54-58.
Miller, William V. "Sexual and Spiritual Ambiguity in 'The Chrysanthemums.'"
Steinbeck Quarterly 5 (1972): 68-75.
Renner, S. "The Real Woman behind the Fence in 'The Chrysanthemums.' " *Modern Fiction Studies* 31 (1985): 305-17.
Sweet, Charles A. "Ms. Elisa Allen and Steinbeck's 'The Chrysanthemums.'" *Modern Fiction Studies* 20 (1974): 210-14.

AMY TAN

Two Kinds (p. 1205)

"Two Kinds," which was first published in the February 1989 issue of *The Atlantic Monthly*, is an excerpt from Amy Tan's best-selling book, *The Joy Luck Club*. It is a skillfully written story that will probably pose no difficulty for most students; plot, characters, setting, and theme are immediately clear. The narrator states what she's "learned" from her experience in her final paragraph: she has come to realize that "Pleading Child" and "Perfectly Contented" are "two halves of the same song."

Looking back to her childhood, the narrator appears to be "perfectly contented" with her memories. Her interpretation of her relationship with her mother is presented in a calm, even self-satisfied way. After her mother's death, she tunes the piano left to her in her parents' apartment. "I played a few bars [of the piano piece by Robert Schumann], surprised at how easily the notes came back to me." The painful memory of her fiasco as a piano student has dissipated. Now she is her own audience, and she is pleased with what she hears. There is no real emotional stress in "Two Kinds"; the girl has had a comfortable life. She has survived her mother and can dispose of her possessions as she likes. She is at peace with her past, fulfilling her mother's prophecy that "you can be best anything."

The mother earned her right to look on the bright side of life by surviving tremendous losses when she left China. Her desire to turn her daughter into a "Chinese Shirley Temple" is understandable but unfortunate, since it places a tremendous psychological burden on the child. A discussion about this story might center on parents' supporting children versus "pushing" them to succeed in tasks beyond their abilities or ambitions.

Still, the narrator doesn't appear to have suffered unduly from her mother's ambitions for her. By her own account she was more than a match for her mother in the contest of wills on the piano bench. After her wretched performance at the recital, the daughter refuses to practice anymore. When her mother shouts, "Only two kinds of daughters. Those who are obedient and those who follow their own mind! Only one kind of daughter can live in this house. Obedient daughter! The girl answers by saying the unspeakable: "I wish I'd never been born! I wish I were dead! Like them [the mother's twin baby girls lost in China]." This ends the conflict but the narrator goes on to tell us that she was unrelenting in victory: "In the years that followed, I failed her many times, each time asserting my will, my right to fall short of expectations. I didn't get straight As. I didn't become class president. I didn't get into Stanford. I dropped out of college." She tells us that only after her mother's death can she begin to see things in perspective, when she is free to create her version of the past.

Since most students in class will be of the age when they are also asserting their will against parents in a struggle to take control of their lives, they will probably sympathize with Tan's narrator and accept her judgments uncritically. Will any reader take the mother's side?

Questions for Discussion

1. Why is the setting of this story important? What do you learn from it about the experience of Asian immigrants in their first years in the United States?
2. What advantages are offered to the child? What disadvantages?
3. How typical is Tan's story of the mother-daughter conflict? Explain.
4. Explain the meaning of the last paragraph of the story.

Topics for Writing

1. Compare and contrast the theme of initiation in Ellison's "Battle Royal" and Tan's "Two Kinds."
2. Analyze the use of dialect in Wright's "The Man Who was Almost a Man" and Tan's "Two Kinds."
3. Compare and contrast the mother in Tan's "Two Kinds" with Olenka, the protagonist of Chekhov's "The Darling."
4. Compare and contrast Tan's "Two Kinds" with Munro's "Walker Brothers Cowboy," in which the narrator does *not* try to justify her actions or feelings for a parent.

JAMES THURBER

The Secret Life of Walter Mitty (p. 1215)

Like a good joke, a successful comic story may be easy to enjoy but hard to explain. Thurber has rendered his hero so convincingly that "Walter Mitty" has long since entered the popular vocabulary as a shorthand term for a certain personality type. The triumph of the story does not come, however, at the expense of the henpecked and bullied daydreamer. Stephen A. Black rightly points out that Mitty's escapism risks a denial of the self in its retreat from reality, but it is important to note that Mitty's fantasy life, despite its dependence on pulp fiction clichés, is just as real on the page as his (equally stereotypical) impatient and condescending wife, the officious policeman, and the insolent parking-lot attendant. Thus the reader may respond with admiration to Mitty's imaginary competence, courage, and grace under pressure.

Throughout the story Thurber uses things from the real environment to trigger Mitty's fantasies, but he also shows that the fantasies can have an impact on his actual life. The phrase "You miserable cur" reminds Mitty of the forgotten puppy biscuit. Near the end, after the sergeant tells "Captain Mitty" that "It's forty kilometers through hell, sir," Mitty has his life in Connecticut in mind when he musingly replies, "After all, . . . what isn't?" In his fantasy, "the box barrage is closing in," but Mitty is just as courageous in standing up to the salvo of questions and criticism launched moments later by his wife, which elicits his vague remark, "Things close in." As he stands against the drugstore wall in the Waterbury rain to face the imaginary firing squad, the reader can agree that he *is* "Walter Mitty the Undefeated" — because his inner life remains, for his banal tormentors, "inscrutable to the last."

Questions for Discussion

1. What is Walter Mitty actually doing in the first paragraph of the story?
2. Explain Mitty's attitude toward his wife. Why does she insist that he wear gloves and overshoes?
3. How familiar is Walter Mitty with medical terminology? What is the purpose for Mitty of his medical fantasy?
4. Do Mitty's fantasies help or hinder him in dealing with reality?
5. Explain Mitty's words "Things close in."
6. Where do you think Walter Mitty gets his ideas of heroism? Is there any sense in which his real life can be called heroic?

Topics for Writing

CRITICAL ESSAYS

1. Walter Mitty's final wish.
2. The romantic and the banal: The basis of Thurber's humor in "The Secret Life of Walter Mitty."

EXERCISE FOR READING

1. Find as many connections as possible between Mitty's actual experiences and his fantasies. How are they related? What do you think will be the consequence, if any, of Mitty's imaginary execution?

Suggested Readings

Black, Stephen A. *James Thurber — His Masquerades: A Critical Study*. The Hague: Mouton, 1970. 15, 18–19, 32, 42–43, 49–50, 54, 56, 119.

Morseburger, Robert E. *James Thurber*. Twayne's United States Authors Series 62. New York: Twayne, 1964. 18–19, 44–48, 123, 151-52.

LEO TOLSTOY

The Death of Ivan Ilych (p. 1220)

No one who comes to "The Death of Ivan Ilych" from a direction other than that of *War and Peace* and *Anna Karenina* is likely to share the opinion of some Tolstoy scholars that it is parable-thin in its evocation of life, providing only a transparent surface of detail through which Tolstoy's allegorical intentions are exposed. The story is studded with brilliantly realistic representations of experiences that the reader encounters with a twinge of sometimes embarrassed recognition — Peter Ivanovich's struggle with the pouffe, for example. But it is nonetheless a product of the period following Tolstoy's religious crisis and a story written by one whose explicit theory of art rested on a utilitarian moral didacticism.

The story's effectiveness depends on Tolstoy's avoiding, until the last possible moment, preaching the sermon that, as the headnote suggests, he eventually means to preach. The opening section places us in the shoes of Peter Ivanovich, causing us to sympathize with the desire to look away from death, at the same time that it subjects that desire to a devastating satiric attack. Then, by returning to a long, chronological survey of Ivan Ilych's life, Tolstoy forces us to do exactly the opposite of what Peter Ivanovich does: to confront death and its meaning in an extended and excruciatingly matter-of-fact account. What we see is not a life, but a death — or a life viewed as death. For Ivan Ilych's life, as he eventually comes to realize, is a slow but accelerating process of dying. The narration, however, decelerates, so that the reader may expect it to be nearly over around section VI, whereas in fact there are six more (albeit shorter) sections to come, containing a series of painful revelations that burst through the screen Ivan Ilych has built up to hide himself from reality.

Tolstoy tortures the reader just as Ivan Ilych is tortured, so that the precept finally advanced by the story arrives as the answer to the reader's fervent need. Ivan Ilych is not a particularly bad man; and — bad or good — all men, as Gerasim remarks, come to the same spot. Tolstoy makes this recognition virtually intolerable by his vivid rendering of Ivan Ilych's suffering. Then he offers a way out by proposing that one simple motion of the soul toward charity can release the sufferer from his mortal anguish. Tolstoy prepares us for this revelation by stressing the relief Ivan Ilych finds in the kindness of Gerasim, whose health, strength, and repose are bound up with his simple acceptance of sickness and death as necessary parts of life. Some critics have claimed that Tolstoy's art fails to encompass the illumination Ivan Ilych receives at the end, which rests on doctrines extrinsic to the text; but at least it can be said that he avoids sentimental piety by providing for an ironic interpretation when he caps Ivan Ilych's triumphant assertion "Death is finished. ... It is no more!" with the paradoxical conclusion "He drew in a breath, stopped in the midst of a sigh, stretched out, and died."

The preoccupations and activities of Ivan Ilych and his peers during Ilych's lifetime in the society portrayed by Tolstoy contrast sharply with those of the unselfish peasant Gerasim. They are directed to no constructive end, serving only to gratify the ego with a sense of power and to hide the fear of death under a surface awareness of pleasure and propriety. Ivan Ilych is never more content than when manipulating the inert objects which are so plentiful in the story — as when decorating his new house — and he does his best to relate to people as he relates to things, insulating himself from true human contact. After he has received his death blow from the quite inert knob of a window frame, however, Ivan Ilych experiences a similar dehumanizing treatment by the doctors, his wife, and his friends, none of whom can bear to face the implications of his evident mortality. As his sickness steadily reduces him to a state of infantile dependency, Ilych comes to recognize first his own powerlessness and then the error in his strategy of living. Finally, as the coffin-womb he has built for himself falls away and he is reborn into the light of spiritual understanding, he sees the fundamental truth he has worked so hard to deny: the feelings of others are as real as his own. At this moment, moved by pity for his wife and son, he at last finds something worthwhile to do; and, in doing it, he attains the sense of ease and "rightness" that has previously eluded him. That the single positive act of Ivan Ilych's life is to die may be seen as either a grim irony or an exciting revelation, depending on the perspective from which the reader views it. But either way the conclusion of the story embodies the kernel of Tolstoy's social theme. As Edward Wasiolek puts it, "Death for Tolstoy now, as the supremely shared experience, is the model of all solidarity, and only the profound consciousness of its significance can bring one to the communion of true brotherhood."

Questions for Discussion

1. How does the authorial voice qualify our view of Ivan Ilych's survivors' reactions to his death in section I?
2. Evaluate Peter Ivanovich's view of Ivan Ilych's son when he meets him near the end of section I.
3. Comment on the implications of Ivan Ilych's hanging a medallion bearing the motto *respice finem* (consider your end) on his watch chain.
4. What is wrong with Ivan Ilych's marriage? with his work? with his ambitions?
5. By examining the authorial comments in sections III and IV, define the attitude toward Ivan Ilych that Tolstoy asks the reader to share. Does this attitude change?
6. Consider the opening sentence of section VI. Is this section a low point in the story? If so, what kind of rise ensues?
7. Why does Ivan Ilych find relief in having his legs supported by Gerasim?
8. What is the effect of the shift to the present tense about one-third of the way through section VIII?
9. In section IX, Ivan Ilych complains to God in language similar to that of Job. Compare and contrast their plights.
10. What is the meaning of Ivan Ilych's reversion to childhood shortly before his death?
11. How might Ivan Ilych's dream of the black sack be interpreted?

Topics for Writing

CRITICAL ESSAYS

1. The opening section as a story in itself, but one fully understood only after reading sections II–XII.
2. Bridge as an epitome of the life Ivan Ilych and his friends try to live.
3. Tolstoy's use of symbolic, descriptive details in "The Death of Ivan Ilych."

EXERCISE FOR READING

1. Stop after reading section I and write a paragraph or two on the theme and tone of the story as you understand them so far. After reading the rest of the story, write a paragraph evaluating your original response. This exercise could serve as preparation for the first topic under Critical Essays.

RELATED SUBJECTS

1. Using "The Death of Ivan Ilych" as the basis of your knowledge of society, write a manifesto calling for revolution or reform.
2. Write a sermon, using the demise of Ivan Ilych Golovin as your occasion.

Related Commentary from Part Two

Leo Tolstoy, Chekhov's Intent in "The Darling," p. 1520.

Suggested Readings

Christian, R. F. *Tolstoy: A Critical Introduction.* Cambridge: Cambridge UP, 1969. 236–38.

Greenwood, E. B. *Tolstoy: The Comprehensive Vision.* New York: St. Martin's, 1975. 118–23.

Simmons, Ernest J. *Introduction to Tolstoy's Writings.* Chicago: U of Chicago P, 1968. Esp. 148–50.

Wasiolek, Edward. *Tolstoy's Major Fiction.* Chicago: U of Chicago P, 1978. Esp. 165–79.

Amos Tutuola

The Palm-Wine Drinkard's First Journey (p. 1266)

It is helpful to compare the Nigerian Amos Tutuola's story with the Trinidadian V. S. Naipaul's "B. Wordsworth." Both are oral narratives, but each comes out of its own creative concept, illustrating some of the range that is possible with this narrative technique. Naipaul's story was written to be read aloud, and it is kept brilliantly within the point of view of the narrator. Tutuola's story, by contrast, comes directly from an oral tradition. It was meant to be told in a small village. It is almost by accident that it was written at all; Tutuola has said that he began putting his stories down on paper because he was bored with the empty hours on his job as a messenger.

One of the difficulties a Third World writer faces is that his own language often does not have a literary tradition in the European sense. None of the areas of Africa south of the Sahara Desert, in fact, developed a written language. The lore and history of each culture is carried by the storytellers, the griot poets, and the family elders. For writers who come from a background like Tutuola's, the act of writing in a European language already sets their work outside their own tradition, and if they present it in the form of a European narrative, as many Third World writers do, they have taken their work still another step away from their own cultures. This process has been described as a kind of "double exile."

Tutuola's writing gives us a glimpse into a different culture, and a different way of describing experience. To Tutuola's fellow Nigerians, the story would seem as familiar as a grandmother's bedtime story: to Westerners it seems richly fanciful and exotic. It is just these qualities, for those of us who are outside the author's culture, that make his books so valuable, although Tutuola's own spontaneity and humor bring the writing vividly to life.

The narrator's favorite drink is a staple alcoholic beverage along much of the West African coast. Palm trees are tapped, and their watery sap is collected in dried gourds. The author has exercised considerable poetic license, though, not only in describing the quantity of palm wine the drinkard absorbs every day but in having the tapster bringing him wine from the tree the day it has been tapped. In fact the sap must ferment in the heat for a few days before it develops a frothy head and is ready to drink. The wine is sold at rickety roadside stands, and often a village will prepare for an important dance or festival by making a large supply of palm wine days in advance.

Questions for Discussion

1. Tutuola is a Nigerian of the Yoruba tribe. Research Yoruba culture and come to class prepared to discuss the Yoruba in relation to other Nigerian cultures, such as the Ibo (of which Chinua Achebe is a member).
2. How do we know that this story comes from an oral tradition? Identify its "oral" qualities.
3. What does the language of the story convey about the colonial policies of the British, who occupied Nigeria for more than fifty years?
4. What does the story tell us about the myths and legends of the Yoruba tribe? Have they survived the religious and cultural pressures of first the Moslem teachers and then the Christian missionaries?

Topics for Writing

1. Imagine how the narrative would change if it were European literary style. Either describe the changes or retell the narrative in a more "Western" style.
2. Discuss the importance of oral tradition in a culture without a written language.
3. Discuss whether an oral tradition exists in European culture.
4. Compare the elements of Achebe's "Dead Men's Path" with those of Tutuola's "The Palm-Wine Drinkard's First Journey."
5. The idea of "double exile" and its meaning for Third World writers.
6. Compare the journeys of other characters — the narrator of Joyce's "Araby," Phoenix Jackson of Welty's "A Worn Path," or Robin of Hawthorne's "My Kinsman, Major Molineux"—with the journey of Tutuola's Palm-Wine Drinkard.

Related Commentary from Part Two

Chinua Achebe, Work and Play in Tutuola's *The Palm-Wine Drinkard*, p. 1385.

Suggested Readings

Collins, Harold R. *Amos Tutuola*. Boston: Twayne, 1969.
Lindfors, Bernth. *Critical Perspectives on Amos Tutuola*. Washington, DC: Three Continents, 1975.

JOHN UPDIKE

A & P *(p. 1273)*

Although Updike was a precociously successful writer who spent his apprenticeship living in New York City and writing for *The New Yorker* magazine, much of the strength of his writing stems from his ability to take the reader back to the atmosphere of the small town where he grew up. "A & P" showcases this ability. This story about a nineteen-year-old at a checkout counter in an A & P supermarket skillfully sustains the point of view of a teenage boy from a small-town working-class family.

The incident the story describes is slight. What gives "A & P" its substance is the voice of the narrator. He is obviously what the author thinks of as an ordinary teenager, impatient with old people, not interested in his job, and deeply aroused by girls. The longest descriptive passage — almost a third of the story itself — dwells on the body of one of the girls; as the story's slight action unfolds, the bodies of that girl and one of her friends are mentioned several times again. The narrator's adolescent desire and adoration are amusingly played off his clumsy bravado and the idiom of sexist stereotypes he is trying to master. "You never know for sure how girls' minds work (do you really think it's a mind in there or just a little buzz like a bee in a glass jar?)." His view of adult women is no less callow: "We're right in the middle of town, and the women generally put on a shirt or shorts or something before they get out of the car into the street. And anyway these are usually women with six children and varicose veins mapping their legs and nobody, including them, could care less."

It is probably true that when the story was written, in the late 1950s, its attitudes were not considered unusual. Today we have to ask ourselves whether the deplorable sexism is redeemed by the artfulness of the story, the technique Updike brings to constructing his narrator's voice.

Questions for Discussion

1. What does the language of the story tell us about the narrator's social background?
2. Are there any details in the story that place it in a specific part of the United States, or could it be happening anywhere within a few miles of a beach? Explain.

3. Is the boy's discomfort with older people limited to women, or is he also uncomfortable with men? Is there anyone in the store he *is* comfortable with? Explain.
4. Compare this story with Munro's "Walker Brothers Cowboy." How do the descriptive details in the two stories establish a specific time and place?
5. Do you think Updike shares the narrator's attitudes?

Topics for Writing

CRITICAL ESSAYS

1. The strengths and limitations of the first-person narrative in "A & P."
2. "Acting like a man": Updike's bag boy in "A & P," Wright's, Dave in "The Man Who Was Almost a Man," and Wolff's characters in "Hunters in the Snow."
3. Adolescent narrators in Updike's "A & P" and Joyce's "Araby."

Related Commentary from Part Two

John Updike, Kafka and "The Metamorphosis," p. 1527.

JOHN UPDIKE

Flight (p. 1278)

Allen Dow's problem is to find a way to mount a meaningful rebellion against a family and a community that expect him to leave, encourage him to leave, and thereby co-opt his departure. Because everyone recognizes that his unusual talents exceed the scope provided by Olinger, his most obnoxiously conceited behavior is accepted ("the privileges of being extraordinary"), while his efforts to pursue the normal social activities of adolescence ("the pleasures of being ordinary") are frowned upon. Allen feels "simultaneously flattered and rejected."

The ambiguity of his position is focused in his relationship with his mother, whose desire for him to "fly" springs from her own disappointment. When her father moved to Olinger from the farm, she was torn from her childhood home but compensated by the widening horizons made possible by prosperity. Since the Great Depression, however, she has found herself imprisoned in a home that is not her own, in a town where she feels unwelcome. By casting Allen in the role of the phoenix, "destined to reverse and redeem" the family misfortunes, she effectively forbids his escape, just as her father forbade her going to New York. In his peculiar fantasy it is Allen, not his mother, who is represented as the earthworm surrounded and held down by the "huge root."

Youth finds a way, however, and Allen's emergence takes the ironic form of a relationship with Molly Bingaman, the personification of all the comfortable limitations of Olinger that are forbidden him by his special status as outsider, bird of passage, man of destiny. His mother's recognition of the threat his interest in Molly poses to her desires is immediate, but Molly provides Allen with a base for an identity apart from the burden of expectations heaped on him by everyone, a "negative space" into which he can grow. Molly's passivity is her most attractive quality, evident even in her climactic coming out to him, and although Allen never brings himself to tell her so, his love for her is real. When he gives her up as the down payment on his freedom from the "black mass of suffering" that flows from his grandfather to his mother and threatens to overwhelm him, too, his mother both wins him back from Olinger and loses him for herself. The "typical melodrama" of her farewell may be in character, but it admirably expresses the difficulty for both parent and child of letting go.

Questions for Discussion

1. Point out some of the "microscopic accuracies" (see the headnote) that make this story convincing.
2. Comment on Allen Dow's habit of speaking of himself in the third person. Why does he do so? On what occasion does he explicitly *not* do so? Why?
3. What does the view of Olinger from atop Shale Hill mean to Allen's mother? What is the effect of her remark on Allen? Consider the implications of the town's name.
4. Summarize the history of the Baer family. Is it true that "each generation of parents commits atrocities against their children"? Why?
5. Explain the implications of Allen's examining the snapshot of his mother "on the stained carpet of an ill-lit old house in the evening years of the thirties and in the dark of the warring forties."
6. Discuss Allen's feelings about his grandmother and the asparagus patch.
7. How important is Allen's father to the story? Why do you think Updike stresses his device of committing imaginary suicide with a cap pistol in his classroom?
8. Allen realizes that his mother fights with her father "because *she could not bear to leave him alone.*" Explain the implications of this insight for Allen himself. How does it relate to Allen's mother's ambition for him to be "the phoenix"?
9. Comment on Updike's choice of the words "mounting" and "slumping" in his account of the debate team's departure.
10. Why does Allen become interested in Molly Bingaman? How important are the circumstances under which they become acquainted? Exactly what is she able to provide for Allen, for example, on the train ride home?
11. How is it that Allen's mother can diagnose his relationship with Molly so readily? Analyze her remark "Don't go with little women, Allen. It puts you too close to the ground."
12. Why does *nobody* want Allen to go with Molly Bingaman? What benefit accrues as a result?
13. What does his involvement with Molly reveal to Allen about his mother?
14. Why does Updike set the stage for the final scene by discussing the radio? What other music is heard in this scene? What do the two strains mean to Allen and his mother?
15. Why does Allen say he'll give up Molly? Why does his mother say "with typical melodrama, 'Goodbye, Allen' "?

Topics for Writing

CRITICAL ESSAYS

1. Updike's "Flight" and Olsen's "I Stand Here Ironing."
2. Updike's techniques of characterization in "Flight."
3. Replication of the central conflict as a mode of developing theme in "Flight."

RELATED SUBJECTS

1. Interview people about their parents' shortcomings. If possible, interview your own parents or other members of your family. Write an essay in which you explore Updike's speculation that "each generation of parents commits atrocities against their children which by God's decree remain invisible to the rest of the world."
2. Does any of the material from your interviews suggest itself as the basis of a story? Try to write one. Follow Updike's example by focusing your theme in a single image, such as *flight*.
3. Study Updike's one-paragraph character sketches. Pick one to imitate, and sketch a character based on a person or people familiar to you.

Related Commentaries from Part Two

John Updike, Franz Kafka and "The Metamorphosis," p. 1527.
John Updike, Writing about Adolescence in "Flight." p. 1525.

Suggested Readings

Detweiler, Robert. *John Updike*. Twayne's United States Authors Series 214. New York: Twayne, 1972. 75–76.
Lyons, E. "John Updike: The Beginning and the End." *Critique* 14.2 (1972): 44–59.
Samuels, C. T. "Art of Fiction: John Updike." *Paris Review* 12 (1968): 84–117.
Seib, P. "Lovely Way through Life: An Interview with John Updike." *Southwest Review* 66 (1981): 341–50.

Luisa Valenzuela

I'm Your Horse in the Night (p. 1292)

This short story is told through first-person narration. It is arranged in three brief sections, each shorter than the one before. The character of the female narrator is only suggested, and she seems the stock heroine of revolutionary dramas. Her lover, Beto, and the police are also conventional figures. Their lack of individuality adds to the story's dreamlike atmosphere. As the narrator says at the conclusion, the only physical evidence remaining from the night she and Beto spent together is the Gal Costa record and a half-empty cachaca bottle. The rest is memories and fantasy scenarios of prison or revolutionary struggle.

The story forcefully communicates the instability of private lives in a Latin American country caught up in political chaos. The justice or injustice of the revolutionary cause is not an issue; it is assumed to be just, because it has prompted the brutal police attempts to suppress it. We hear the voice on the telephone (a police spy pretending to be a friend) suggest that Beto was thrown alive out of a helicopter. Later, when the police come to the narrator's apartment and tear it apart looking for evidence that Beto has been there, she expects them to torture her: "Go ahead, burn me with your cigarettes, kick me all you wish, threaten, go ahead, stick a mouse in me so it'll eat my insides out."

The narrator herself doesn't speculate about economic or political injustice. She thinks in personal and mythic terms. She hears the song on the record Beto brings from Brazil as "a saint's song. Someone who's in a trance says she's the horse of the spirit who's riding her." Beto corrects what he considers a naive interpretation: "If you're my horse in the night it's because I ride you, like this, see?" He insists that she face facts and has little patience with her spiritual interests. But the narrator's interpretation is also correct. She is the physical incarnation of the spirit of love that Beto needs as much as he needs the economic and political justice he is fighting for. He proves this by jeopardizing his life to visit her. She, in turn, proves her worthiness by going to prison because of her loyalty to him. Her bravery consists of her elevating the memory of her lover over what "really happened": "If by some wild chance there's a Gal Costa record and a half-empty bottle of cachaca in my house, I hope they'll forgive me: I will them out of existence."

Questions for Discussion

1. How does Valenzuela establish the political context for her story?
2. How old is the narrator? How long has she had a relationship with Beto? What does he mean when he says, "We'll make it someday, Chiquita."
3. What does Valenzuela achieve by organizing her story in three parts?
4. Where is the narrator at the end of the story?

Topics for Writing

1. Compare and contrast Valenzuela's story with Babel's "My First Goose" or Hwang's "Conversation in June about Mothers."
2. Compare the suppression of reality ["I will them out of existence"] in Valenzuela's "I'm Your Horse in the Night" and Lispector's "The Chicken."
3. Compare Valenzuela's narrator with another fictional woman beleaguered by a lover or love — Gilman's narrator in "The Yellow Wallpaper," for example.

ALICE WALKER

Roselily (p. 1296)

This is the story of a black woman, Roselily, on her wedding day. Contrary to what we might expect, however, the tone is not joyful, but tense and apprehensive.

Roselily is full of doubts, about herself and the man who will soon be her husband. Her motivation to marry this man is not love of him as an individual. In fact, she admits "she does not even know if she loves him." What she does love are some of his qualities and properties, "his sobriety," "his pride," "his blackness," "his gray car," "his understanding of her *condition*," and, most important, his ability to "free her" from her current life. And what of his love for her? Roselily is realistic enough to know that he loves her, but again, she admits, he does not love her because of who she is. She acknowledges that "he will make [an effort] to redo her into what he truly wants." We are left with a picture of a woman trying to escape her past by marrying a man who will "free her" to "be respectable and respected and free" and a man marrying out of an apparent desire to reform.

"Roselily" has as its seminal concept the number *two*. It presents two opposite individuals at a crucial moment in their lives. Yet, as they symbolically fuse their lives into a single relationship, each brings very different experiences and backgrounds to the marriage. Roselily knows only the southern, small town, country way of life, complete with its provincial religious beliefs and its sense of connectedness with family and community. Her husband is "against this." A northerner from Chicago, his ways are city ways, his religious beliefs are alien and restrictive. Rather than a feeling of community, he knows independence and anonymity.

Roselily wants freedom: "She wants to live for once. But doesn't know quite what that means. Wonders if she has ever done it. If she ever will." She spends the entire ceremony rationalizing that this marriage is the right thing to do, despite the fact that she "feels shut away from" this man. By the last paragraph she is finally able to formulate her feelings: "She feels ignorant, *wrong*, backward." By then, however, it is too late. The ceremony is complete, and "her husband's hand is like the clasp of an iron gate."

The structural framework for "Roselily" is the Christian marriage ceremony. It provides form as well as forward movement for a story that is essentially a stream-of-consciousness remembrance and narrative of the lead character, Roselily, from a third person point of view. Contrast is the subject of the story. Conflict is the theme.

The title, "Roselily," does more than introduce the heroine. It also foreshadows the scope of the story. The rose becomes a lily. By means of the marriage vows, Roselily changes from a woman who is passionate, natural, and, in the eyes of society, impure and immoral to one who is resurrected and reborn, but passionless and dead. For a price, she gains respectability. Now she must decide whether or not the cost is equal to the value. The conflict has not been resolved; it has only been postponed.

Questions for Discussion

1. Walker uses the marriage service to break up Roselily's reflections. What does this particular structure emphasize? What effect does it create?
2. Roselily's first passage opens with her dreaming of "dragging herself across the world. A small girl in her mother's white robe and veil, knee raised waist high through a bowl of quicksand soup." What subjects in these sentences persist throughout this story? Describe the qualities of this girl that reflect Roselily's own representation of herself in this story. Is she helpless, vulnerable, childish, struggling, or playacting?

3. Why does Roselily spend so much time thinking about her fourth child's father? Do we know as much about the man she is marrying as we do about her ex-lover? What do Roselily's reflections on his character tell us about hers?

4. What does Roselily's fourth child, the one she gave to his father, represent? What kind of a connection does she feel to the child? Can she imagine his future?

5. Part of Roselily's reflections are devoted to wondering "what one does with memories in a brand-new life." What alternatives are open to her? Can she just shut her memories away, or break them off and start again? Consider the question of memory and the burden of the past against her sudden dream of having no children. Roselily's own mother is dead, yet Roselily still feels a connection to her. What are the "ghosts" that Roselily believes in?

6. Much of this story depends on oppositions. "Her husband's hand," Roselily thinks, "is like the clasp of an iron gate." What are the positive and negative qualities of an iron gate? Roselily thinks of "ropes, chains, handcuffs, his religion." What other images does she associate with this man she is marrying? He's going to "free her." How do you reconcile the images of bondage and freedom? Consider the diction in this passage: "A romantic hush. Proposal. Promises. A new life! Respectable, reclaimed, renewed. Free! In robe and veil." Yet suddenly, Walker presents "a rat trapped, concerned, scurrying to and fro in her head, peering through the windows of her eyes." What is the difference in the language in both examples? Is one kind of diction stronger than the other? Why?

7. What do you infer about Roselily's feelings from these sentences: "The rest she does not hear. She feels a kiss, passionate, rousing, within the general pandemonium. Cars drive up blowing their horns. Firecrackers go off. Dogs come from under the house and begin to yelp and bark." Look first at the syntax of these sentences. Why do you think they are all short and unconnected to one another? What effect does that create? What is the subject of each sentence? Why might Roselily only be able to receive certain kinds of impressions?

8. How do you interpret the final paragraph of this story? Does this paragraph control your understanding of the story retrospectively? How did you weigh the oppositions until this paragraph? Were Roselily's hopes and fears in equilibrium? Which words carry the heaviest burden of meaning for you? Would the paragraph — and your judgment — be very different without them?

Topics for Writing

CRITICAL ESSAYS

1. Roselily's culture and environment and those of her husband-to-be.
2. The concept of marriage in Walker's "Roselily" and Lawrence's "Odour of Chrysanthemums."
3. The disparity between Roselily's dreams and situation.
4. The point of view in "Roselily."

RELATED SUBJECT

1. Think back in your own life to a time when your thoughts received stimulation from an outside event but were not totally controlled by that event. Try to re-create your thought patterns and structure them into an interesting narrative account.

Suggested Readings

Bell, Roseann P., Bettye J. Parker, and Beverly Guy-Sheftall, eds. *Sturdy Black Bridges: Visions of Black Women in Literature*. New York: Anchor, 1979.

Cooke, Michael. *Afro-American Literature in the Twentieth Century: The Achievement of Intimacy*. New Haven: Yale UP, 1984.

Davis, T. M. "Alice Walker's Celebration of Self in Southern Generations." *Women Writers of the Contemporary South*. Ed. Peggy Whitman Prenshaw. Jackson: UP of Mississippi, 1984. 83–94.

Erickson, P. "Cast Out Alone/To Heal/and Re-create/Ourselves: Family Based Identity in the Work of Alice Walker." *College Language Association Journal* 23 (1979): 71–94.

Evans, Mari, ed. *Black Women Writers (1950–1980): A Critical Evaluation*. New York: Anchor, 1984. 453–95.

Stade, G. "Womanist Fiction and Male Characters." *Partisan Review* 52 (1985): 265–70.

FAY WELDON

Weekend (p. 1301)

Weldon's sympathy for the put-upon wife, Martha, is the strongest emotional statement in this story. Martha herself is allowed to comment less directly on her emotional life. Weldon ends "Weekend" by interpreting Martha's instinctive, unvoiced response to her daughter Jenny's news that she has started menstruating in the statement "Her daughter Jenny: wife, mother, friend." The sorority of nurturing women is evoked here, a closer relationship than any between Martha and the men in her life.

"Weekend" is one of the strongest feminist stories in this anthology. The male students in the class may be too young to consider whether they have overworked their wives, but they might be reminded of the countless services they expected their mothers to provide for them. Other students may attack Weldon's portrayal. Martha may be seen as overbearing, overmanipulative, or even stupid in her lack of defenses. She could have insisted that store-bought fish and chips would be a happy meal out for the family on Saturdays, and that three cooked meals a day at the cottage aren't in the spirit of weekend fun for the entire family.

Inevitably the question arises: why doesn't Martha stand up to her husband? He doesn't do anything except blow up the embers in the fireplace and drive the family to the country (which he probably wouldn't do if Martha hadn't had her license suspended). We are given a clue in Weldon's references to Martha's "paranoid" mother, who made her childhood cold and emotionally sterile. So Martha chose to have her three children, and her role as their primary caretaker, and her lowly position as the chief cook and bottle washer for her demanding ménage. Martha is starved for love. She has little self-respect, and her years as Martin's wife have undermined any feelings of accomplishment she may have had before marriage.

This story might be taught with Doris Lessing's "To Room Nineteen" and Ann Beattie's "The Burning House."

Questions for Discussion

1. Which character in the story is most sympathetic? Why?
2. Could you blame Martha's difficulties managing her schedule on the fact that she is a working mother? Explain.
3. Why is the difference between the cars Martin and Martha drive so significant?
4. Is Weldon's story a realistic description of a marriage in trouble? Explain.
5. What is the role of humor in the story?
6. How does Weldon arouse our dislike for Martin and his friends?

Topics for Writing

1. Compare Weldon's "Weekend" with Thurber's "The Secret Life of Walter Mitty," another humorous story about a sadist-masochist marriage partnership.
2. Analyze "Weekend" from the perspective of a feminist critic, a Marxist critic, a deconstructivist critic.

EUDORA WELTY

Why I Live at the P.O. (p. 1314)

This story may be troublesome to some readers, especially if they have been sensitized to racial issues in short fiction through a discussion of Achebe's criticism of Conrad's "Heart of Darkness." The word "nigger" used as a racial slur occurs three times in Welty's story. The narrator who uses the word is clearly an uneducated bigot, but her contempt for people of color living in her community is underscored by her assumption that they are fit only for the lowest kind of work. Here are the passages concerned:

> So I merely slammed the door behind me and went down and made some green-tomato pickle. Somebody had to do it. Of course Mama had turned both the niggers loose; she always said no earthly power could hold one anyway on the Fourth of July, so she wouldn't even try. It

turned out that Jaypan fell in the lake and came within a very narrow limit of drowning.

> There was a nigger girl going along on a little wagon right in front. "Nigger girl," I says, "come help me haul these things down the hill, I'm going to live in the post office." Took her nine trips in her express wagon. Uncle Rondo came out on the porch and threw her a nickel.

In both cases, African-Americans are assumed to be stupid workhorses, barely tolerated as human beings and undeserving of respect. In the first instance the two house servants are "turned loose" (like animals?) on the Fourth of July, but they are so immature and irresponsible that they go wild on their chance to celebrate Independence Day (irony?); they get drunk, and one of them, Jaypan, nearly drowns. In the second case, African-Americans are presumed to be so stupid that a black child won't mind stopping her play with a wagon to help move a white woman; the child will also be satisfied being paid a pittance for working so hard. Welty is writing a humorous story, of course, told from the point of view of a Mississippi cracker, but humor doesn't negate the racism, any more than Marlowe's naiveté condones his judgments about Africans in "Heart of Darkness." Racist jokes aren't any more tolerable because they are meant to be "funny."

Insensitive literary critics discussing "Why I Live at the P.O." usually comment on "the exasperation and frustration, loneliness and near-madness" of the narrator, trapped in a provincial Mississippi town. Or they view her as "a solid and practical person struggling to keep her self-possession and balance in the midst of a childish, neurotic, and bizarre family." In Welty's commentary on the story, she stresses the normalcy of characters like Sister (the narrator) and her family in the South. Thrown against one another with limited social resources, they bicker and feud but usually reconcile their differences, because family solidarity is important to them. At the end of the story we learn that Sister's outburst has been provoked after five days of living by herself in the post office; Welty has said that once the character's anger has cooled, she'd move back home. She writes, "I was trying to show how, in these tiny little places such as where they come from, the only entertainment people have is dramatizing the family situation, which they do fully knowing what they are doing. They're having a good time. They're not caught up; it's not pathological. It's a Southern kind of exaggeration."

Questions for Discussion

1. Can we equate Sister's voice with Welty's opinions? Explain.
2. Does the humor in the story soften or increase the tension between the members of the family? Why or why not?
3. Why do the two sisters fight so much?

Topics for Writing

1. Retell the story through the eyes of the house servant Jaypan or the little girl with the express wagon.
2. Compare Mississippi small towns as backgrounds for Welty's "Why I Live at the P.O." and Faulkner's "A Rose for Emily."

Related Commentaries from Part Two

Eudora Welty, Plot and Character in Chekhov's "The Darling," p. 1534.
Eudora Welty, The Sense of Place in Faulkner's "Spotted Horses," p. 1536.

EUDORA WELTY

A Worn Path (p. 1324)

Try not to force the Christian or mythological schemes of allegory the story supports until you encourage students to savor the beauty of the literal narration. Phoenix Jackson is an embodiment of love, faith, sacrifice, charity, self-renunciation, and triumph over death in herself, quite apart from the typological implications of her name or the allusions to the stations of the cross in her journey. Phoenix transcends her merely archetypal significance just as she transcends the stereotype of old black mammies on which she is built. Welty accomplishes this act of creation by entering fully into the consciousness of her character. There she discovers the little child that still lives within the old woman and causes her to dream of chocolate cake, dance with a scarecrow, and delight in a Christmas toy. Phoenix is right when she says, "I wasn't as old as I thought," but she does not merit the condescension of the hunter's exclamation, "I know you old colored people! Wouldn't miss going to town to see Santa Claus!" Even in her greatest discomfort, lying in the weeds, losing her memory, getting her shoes tied, "stealing" a nickel, or taking one as a handout, Phoenix retains her invincible dignity, an essential component of the single glimpse we receive of her triumphant homeward march, bearing aloft the bright symbol of life she has retrieved through her exertions.

In her comments on the story (included in Part Two, p. 1531), Welty implies that the meaning of Phoenix's journey is that of any human exertion carried out in good faith despite the uncertainty of the outcome: "The path is the thing that matters." In keeping with this theme, Welty repeatedly shows Phoenix asserting life in the face of death. Her name itself, taken from the mythical bird that periodically immolates itself and rises reborn from its ashes, embodies the idea. (She even makes a noise like "a solitary little bird" in the first paragraph.) Phoenix makes her journey at the time of the death and rebirth of the year; her own skin color is like the sun bursting through darkness; she overcomes discouragement as she tops the hill; she extricates herself from a thorn bush (of which much may be made in a Christian allegorical interpretation); she passes "big dead trees" and a buzzard; she traverses a field of dead corn; she sees a "ghost" that turns out to be a dancing scarecrow; she is overcome by a "black dog" but rescued by a death-dealing hunter whose gun she faces down and whom she beats out of a shiny nickel; and she emerges from a deathlike trance in the doctor's office to return with the medicine her grandson needs to stay alive. Phoenix's strength lies in the purpose of her journey, and her spirit is contagious. The hunter, the woman who ties her shoes, and the doctor's attendant all perform acts of charity toward her, and lest the reader overlook the one word that lies at the heart of Welty's vision, the nurse says "Charity" while "making a check mark in a book."

Questions for Discussion

1. Notice Phoenix's identification with "a solitary little bird." What other birds does she encounter on her journey? Explain their implications.
2. What techniques does Welty use to suggest the laboriousness of Phoenix's trip?
3. Before she crosses the creek, Phoenix says, "Now comes the trial." Does she pass it? How? To what extent is this event a microcosm of the whole story? Are there other microcosmic episodes?
4. What effect do Phoenix's sequential reactions to the scarecrow, the abandoned cabins, and the spring have on the reader's view of her?
5. What is your opinion of the hunter? What conclusion might be drawn from the fact that even though he kills birds and patronizes Phoenix, he helps her in a way he does not know?
6. Interpret the passage that begins with Phoenix bending for the nickel and ends with her parting from the hunter.
7. Describe Natchez as Phoenix perceives it. Is it a worthy culmination for her journey?
8. In her comments reprinted in Part Two (p. 1531), Welty remarks that Phoenix's victory comes when she sees the doctor's diploma "nailed up on the wall." In what sense is this moment the climax of the story? What is different about the ensuing action from the action that leads up to this moment? Are there any similarities?
9. How does Phoenix describe her grandson? What is Welty's reason for using these terms?
10. Explain the irony in the way the nurse records Phoenix's visit.

Topics for Writing

CRITICAL ESSAYS

1. Why readers want to think that Phoenix Jackson's grandson is dead.
2. Phoenix and the other birds in "A Worn Path."

EXERCISE FOR READING

1. After your first reading of "A Worn Path," write a paragraph giving your opinion of Phoenix Jackson. Then study some symbolic interpretations of the story (such as those by Ardelino, Isaacs, and Keys, cited in Suggested Readings). Reread the story and write another assessment of the central character. Does she bear up under the freight of symbolic meaning the critics ask her to carry? Does her relation to these archetypes help to account for your original response?

RELATED SUBJECT

1. Read Welty's account of how she came to write "A Worn Path" (Part Two, p. 1531). Following her example, write an account of what you imagine to be the day's experience of someone you catch a glimpse of who strikes your fancy. Use the intimate interior third person limited-omniscient point of view that Welty employs for Phoenix Jackson.

Related Commentaries from Part Two

Eudora Welty, Is Phoenix Jackson's Grandson Really Dead? p. 1531.
Eudora Welty, Plot and Character in Chekhov's "The Darling," p. 1534.
Eudora Welty, The Sense of Place in Faulkner's "Spotted Horses," p. 1536.

Suggested Readings

Ardelino, Frank. "Life out of Death: Ancient Myth and Ritual in Welty's 'A Worn Path.'" *Notes on Mississippi Writers* 9 (1976): 1–9.

Isaacs, Neil D. "Life for Phoenix." *Sewanee Review* 71 (1963): 75–81.

Keys, Marilynn. "'A Worn Path': The Way of Dispossession." *Studies in Short Fiction* 16 (1979): 354–56.

Phillips, Robert L., Jr. "A Structural Approach to Myth in the Fiction of Eudora Welty." *Eudora Welty: Critical Essays.* Ed. Peggy Whitman Prenshaw. Jackson: UP of Mississippi, 1979. 56–67, esp. 60.

EDITH WHARTON

Roman Fever (p. 1332)

Nearly every detail of this seemingly meandering narration that leads up to the final sequence of three dramatic revelations has a function in preparing for the climax. Wharton knits better than Grace Ansley, and her story does not fully unravel until the last words are spoken. When the secret is finally out, the reader experiences a flash of ironic insight that Wharton has been preparing from the beginning through her masterful delineation of the characters and their situation.

Face to face with "the great accumulated wreckage of passion and splendor" that spreads before them, and deserted in their advancing age by the pair of daughters who are now their sole concerns, the two widows may evoke the reader's condescending pity. They seem as small and pale as the images of one another each sees, in Wharton's metaphor, "through the wrong end of her little telescope." But as the two characters become differentiated, Alida Slade takes on depth and coloration. As the story of her flashy but parasitic life and of the jealousy and guilty resentment she has harbored toward her friend gradually emerges, the reader can no longer pity her but can hardly admire her either. Her revelation that it was she, not Delphin Slade, who wrote the letter inviting Grace to a tryst in the Colosseum may be unexpected, but it follows perfectly from her character as Wharton has established it. Its blow to Mrs. Ansley is severe, and it seems the more cruel to the reader, who has no reason as yet to revise the original estimate of her as merely pitiable. Mrs. Ansley staggers, but to the reader's surprise and gratification she gradually recovers herself. Impelled by the shock for once to assert herself, she caps Mrs. Slade's revelation with an even more dramatic one of her own.

Grace Ansley's reticence, and the quietness of her life in contrast to Alida Slade's, expresses neither emotional pallor nor weakness of character. She had the spunk to take what she wanted from Delphin Slade twenty-five years before, and she has been content with her memory ever since, not needing, as Alida Slade would have (and indeed *has*) needed, to get reassurance by parading her conquest in public. Thus, it is Mrs. Ansley who manifests greater independence and vitality. Mrs. Slade, by contrast, has been conventional and dependent. Widowhood is such an uncomfortable lot for her because she can no longer shine with the reflected brilliance of her husband. Barbara may be unlike Horace Ansley because Delphin Slade was really her father, but her differences from Jenny derive from the fact that Grace Ansley, not Alida Slade, is her mother.

Wharton has constructed her plot with a precision O. Henry would have admired, but she has based it less on contrivances of circumstance than on an understanding of her characters. By placing them in a setting that spans millennia — from ancient Rome to the airplane — she implies the universality of the passions, triumphs, and defeats that make up the lives of even these New York society ladies, whose wealth and status do not protect them from the human condition after all.

Questions for Discussion

1. What do Barbara and Jenny think of their mothers? How accurate is their estimate?
2. Why does Grace Ansley place an "undefinable stress" on "me" and "I" in replying to Alida Slade's questions about her reaction to their view of the Roman ruins?
3. Why does Alida Slade consider Grace and Horace Ansley "two nullities"?
4. Compare and contrast the two ladies' responses to widowhood and advancing age. Who takes them harder? Why?
5. Alida Slade remembers "that Mrs. Horace Ansley, twenty-five years ago, had been exquisitely lovely." Explain the importance of this fact to Mrs. Slade, to Mrs. Ansley, and to the structure of the plot.
6. What is "Roman fever" — literally and figuratively?
7. Why has Alida Slade "always gone on hating" Grace Ansley?
8. What reaction does Alida Slade seem to have expected from Grace Ansley in response to her confession that she forged the letter? Why?
9. Alida Slade remarks, "Well, girls are ferocious sometimes" What about ladies?
10. Near the end of the story, why does Grace Ansley pity Alida Slade? Why does Mrs. Slade at first reject that pity?
11. Comment on the meaning of the way the ladies walk off stage.

Topics for Writing

CRITICAL ESSAYS

1. The importance of setting in "Roman Fever."
2. Wharton's manipulation of point of view in "Roman Fever."
3. "Roman Fever" and Wharton's principles of the short story as stated in the excerpt from her book *The Writing of Fiction* (included in Part Two, p. 1539).

EXERCISE FOR READING

1. On your first reading of the story, mark passages whose significance is not entirely clear — such as Grace Ansley's peculiar intonations when acknowledging her memory of a former visit to Rome. After reading the story to the end, return to the marked passages and write explanations of them.

RELATED SUBJECTS

1. Which of the two ladies is more guilty of reprehensible behavior? Consider arguments on both sides, or organize a debate.
2. Write a story of your own about a secret that comes out or a misunderstanding that is resolved. Try to make both the perpetuation of the error or deception and the emergence of the truth dependent on character rather than circumstance.

Related Commentary from Part Two

Edith Wharton, Every Subject Must Contain within Itself Its Own Dimensions, p. 1539.

TOBIAS WOLFF

Hunters in the Snow (p. 1344)

Wolff has said that the writer must have "the willingness to say that unspeakable thing which everyone else in the house is too coy, or too frightened, or too polite to say." His "Hunters in the Snow" is a striking example of what he means. By the power of his writing, Wolff forces us to experience every disturbing moment of this story.

In another comment on his work, Wolff has suggested that no subject for a story is too outlandish actually to have happened: "No lesson is to obvious, no sentiment too coarse, no plot too intricate or tidy or preposterous to actually happen. And it all, as we say in creative writing classes, 'works.' "

The events of "Hunters in the Snow" are progressively extreme and outlandish, but there is no doubt that the story "works." The author has presented a situation that is ominous and disturbing, but from the beginning of the story, when the truck coming to pick up one of the men almost runs him down, the author forces us to deal with characters who match the mood of his narrative. One of the men has nearly psychotic potential for violence, another is about to abandon his wife and children for a fifteen-year-old baby-sitter, and the third is a glutton who lies to his friends about the reasons for his obesity. At first unsettling, the story grows more alarming as we watch the three armed men simmer together in the freezing truck.

The story could almost be a moral fable, in which rage, lust, and gluttony play off one another. "If you have men like this," Wolff seems to be telling us, "this is what they will do to each other." By implication, this is also what they will do to us. The details of the story keep it from being a moral fable — the specificity of the description of the day of hunting, the places the hunt takes the three men, and the people they encounter. It is the cruelty and violence that are generalized, and that gives the story its moral resonance. It is almost as though Wolff were saying that this is what men in America are like today. Perhaps this is, in part, what he means by writing that the writer says the things the rest of us are "too coy, or too frightened, or too polite to say."

Questions for Discussion

1. When do we realize that there is something wrong about the characters in the story?
2. How does Wolff catch the feeling of the snowy day? Give some examples.
3. How does Wolff give us a sense of his characters? Give some examples.
4. Wolff seems to be making a specific comment about men who like to hunt. Do you feel this is part of his intention? Why or why not?
5. What is there about the story that makes it specifically American?
6. Wolff doesn't seem to accuse the two men left in the truck of what has happened to their companion. Do you think he feels they are innocent? Explain.

Topics for Writing

1. Compare the men in Wolff's "Hunters in the Snow" with those in O'Brien's "The Things They Carried."
2. Compare the attitudes toward women in Wolff's "Hunters in the Snow" with those of the central character in Updike's "A & P."
3. Discuss the attitudes toward guns and hunting in Wolff's "Hunters in the Snow" and Wright's "The Man Who Was Almost a Man."

VIRGINIA WOOLF

Kew Gardens (p. 1358)

This sketch might puzzle some students, since its point of view (clearly dictated by Woolf) seems so unusual. No particular person is having his or her story told. Rather, Woolf seems to be telling the story of a snail in a plot of flowers in Kew Gardens. "Cosmic" rather than "omniscient" might be the best word to describe Woolf's perspective, which blends blue sky and green earth so closely as to exclude the people strolling the garden paths between the two elements.

Woolf's story is experimental, and her concentration as she attempts to record "the essential life" of the creatures in the garden is almost palpable. According to the critic Susan Dick, in 1919 Woolf learned from studying Chekhov that "inconclusive stories are legitimate." Dick goes on to say that the narrator in a typical story by Woolf functions "as a perceptive observer of the external scene. . . . [or] the narrator dramatizes from within the minds of the characters, their perceptions of themselves and their world." In "Kew Gardens," Woolf moves seamlessly in and out of her characters' minds, recording their thoughts and feelings more substantially than the actual words they exchange.

The thoughts and words of the first couple, a married pair with two children, shape the reader's expectations for the rest of the story. Simon, the husband, thinks of Lily, an earlier love, to whom he'd proposed marriage in Kew Gardens when he was young. He remembers the shoe she wore, "with the square silver buckle at the toe," which symbolized her attractiveness and her lack of interest in his proposal. His wife, Eleanor, when he asks her if she ever thinks of the past, answers him bluntly, perhaps jealous that he is thinking of the beautiful Lily. Eleanor's memory of past love in Kew Gardens is the kiss given to her by "an old grey-haired woman with a wart on her nose, the mother of all my kisses all my life." We hear no more of this old woman (Eleanor's art teacher?), and we are not told why the kiss was so unsettling that Eleanor's "hand shook all the afternoon so that I couldn't paint." The married couple leave with their children, as much strangers to us as when they appeared.

The snail is the next character, and his conflict is a physical problem: how should he get around a dead leaf? This shift to the nonhuman prepares the reader for Woolf's shift to a cosmic view. The couples on the garden paths are reduced to colors as she lets the descriptive elements of the scene dissolve "like drops of water in the yellow and green atmosphere." The heat of the summer afternoon overcomes everything, reducing the "gross and heavy bodies" to a drowsy torpidity, but their voices continue as a manifestation of their spiritual essence, "as if they were flames lolling from the thick waxen bodies of candles." The silence is found to be composed of pure sound, the sound of buses, people, and the petals of flowers, whose colors seem to Woolf to be heard in the air.

Questions for Discussion

1. How does Woolf organize her sketch so that her description seems continuous and coherent?
2. Describe the people in the scene. What other living elements in the garden are treated as characters?
3. What is Woolf's tone? To which social class does she belong? Comment on her treatment of the two "elderly women of the lower middle class." How are they described? What can you tell about Woolf's attitude toward them from the words they exchange?
4. What is Woolf's attitude toward romantic love? old age? Do these two elements serve as the extremes of dramatic human conflicts in her sketch? Explain.

Topics for Writing

1. Rewrite "Kew Gardens" as it might be the following afternoon, when it's raining.
2. Analyze Woolf's range of vocabulary in this sketch. How does she suggest a poetic atmosphere in her descriptions of the garden and its inhabitants and visitors?

Related Commentary from Part Two

Katherine Mansfield, Review of Woolf's "Kew Gardens," p. 1478.

Suggested Reading

Baldwin, Dean. *Virginia Woolf: A Study of the Short Fiction.* Boston: Twayne, 1986.

RICHARD WRIGHT

The Man Who Was Almost a Man (p. 1364)

Dave Saunders dislikes being laughed at, and his discomfort at becoming an object of amusement for accidentally shooting old Jenny, the mule, precipitates his final step into manhood. Although the anecdote around which Wright builds the story is comical enough, the reader probably should accede to Dave's wish to be taken seriously, for the fate that lies ahead of this young man as he rolls toward his unknown destination atop a boxcar with nothing in his pocket but an unloaded gun is likely to be grim.

At the same time, however, Dave's self-esteem and independence deserve respect. At the beginning of the story he dissociates himself from the field hands and fixes on his ambition to declare his manhood by owning a gun. Throughout the story the idea that *boys* do not have guns recurs, and Dave not only wants a gun but also chafes at being call "boy" by his parents and at being treated as a child. Just before he goes out to master the gun and hop a freight, Dave grumbles, "They treat me like a mule, n then they beat me." His resolution to escape his inferior status will involve not only leaving home but taking potshots at the facade of white society just as he wants to shoot at "Jim Hawkins' big white house" in order "t let im know Dave Saunders is a man." The question Wright leaves hanging for the reader as his story trails off into ellipses is whether Dave has killed the mule in himself or whether he himself, like Jenny, may become the victim of his own wild shots.

Questions for Discussion

1. Explain the pun in the last sentence of the first paragraph.
2. Define our first impression of Dave. What reasons do we have to admire him? to laugh at him? to pity him?
3. What does it take to be a man in the world of the story? Is a gun enough? How does one get a gun?
4. What is ironic about the way Dave gets the money to buy his gun?
5. How is Dave treated by his father? Why does Ma say of the gun, "It be fer Pa?"
6. With the gun under his pillow, Dave feels "a sense of power. Could kill a man with a gun like this. Kill anybody, black or white." What does Dave still have to learn before he can be called a man? How does the story bring it home to him?

7. Explain what happens the first time Dave fires the gun. What does he do differently the next time?
8. Why does Wright describe the death of the mule in such detail?
9. Explain why being laughed at is so painful for Dave. What might enable him to join in and laugh at himself?
10. Comment on the possible implications of Dave's remark "They treat me like a mule, n then they beat me," both within the story and in a broader social and historical context. Does Dave's killing the mule have a symbolic significance?
11. Where might Dave be headed as he hops the Illinois Central? What might he find at the end of his journey?
12. Why is the title not "The Boy Who Was Almost a Man"?

Topics for Writing

CRITICAL ESSAYS

1. The tone of Wright's story.
2. "The Man Who Was Almost a Man" and Wright's social themes. (See the story's headnote.)

RELATED SUBJECT

1. Write a sequel to Wright's story, another episode in the life of Dave Saunders — something that happens on the train ride or when he arrives in New Orleans or Chicago or wherever. Try to sustain and develop as many themes and motives already present in Wright's story as you can, but make the material your own by imagining what you think happens, not necessarily what you guess Wright would have written. Decide whether to adopt Wright's style and point of view or employ a different mode of narration. Remember that the story is set during the Great Depression.

Suggested Readings

Felgar, Robert. *Richard Wright.* Twayne's United States Authors Series 386. Boston: Hall, 1980. 156.

Margolis, Edward. *The Art of Richard Wright.* Crosscurrents/Modern Critiques. Carbondale: Southern Illinois UP, 1969. 75–76.

CHRONOLOGICAL LISTING OF WRITERS AND THEIR STORIES

Nathaniel Hawthorne (1804–1864)
My Kinsman, Major Molineux (1832)
Young Goodman Brown (1835)

Edgar Allan Poe (1809–1849)
The Tell-Tale Heart (1843)
The Cask of Amontillado (1846)

Nikolai Gogol (1809–1852)
The Overcoat (1840)

Herman Melville (1819–1891)
Bartleby, the Scrivener (1853)

Gustave Flaubert (1821–1880)
A Simple Heart (1877)

Leo Tolstoy (1828–1910)
The Death of Ivan Ilych (1886)

Ambrose Bierce (1842–1914?)
An Occurrence at Owl Creek Bridge (1891)

Henry James (1843–1916)
The Beast in the Jungle (1903)

Sarah Orne Jewett (1849–1909)
A White Heron (1886)

Guy de Maupassant (1850–1893)
The Necklace (1884)
The String (1884)

Kate Chopin (1851–1904)
Regret (1894)
The Story of an Hour (1894)

Mary E. Wilkins Freeman (1852–1930)
The Revolt of "Mother" (1891)

Joseph Conrad (1857–1924)
Heart of Darkness (1902)

Anton Chekhov (1860–1904)
The Darling (1899)
The Lady with the Pet Dog (1899)

Charlotte Perkins Gilman (1860–1935)
The Yellow Wallpaper (1892)

Edith Wharton (1862–1937)
Roman Fever (1936)

Stephen Crane (1871–1900)
The Open Boat (1897)

Willa Cather (1873–1947)
Paul's Case (1905)

Colette (1873–1954)
The Hollow Nut (1925)

Thomas Mann (1875–1955)
Disorder and Early Sorrow (1925)

Sherwood Anderson (1876–1941)
Hands (1919)
Death in the Woods (1933)

Virginia Woolf (1882–1941)
Kew Gardens (1919)

James Joyce (1882–1941)
Araby (1916)
The Dead (1916)

Franz Kafka (1883–1924)
The Metamorphosis (1915)
A Hunger Artist (1924)

Isak Dinesen (1885–1962)
The Blue Jar (1942)
The Blue Stones (1942)

D. H. Lawrence (1885–1930)
Odour of Chrysanthemums (1909)
The Rocking-Horse Winner (1926)

Katherine Mansfield (1888–1923)
Bliss (1920)
The Fly (1922)

Katherine Anne Porter (1890–1980)
Theft (1935)

Isaac Babel (1894–1939?)
My First Goose (1925)

James Thurber (1894–1961)
The Secret Life of Walter Mitty (1942)

F. Scott Fitzgerald (1896–1940)
Babylon Revisited (1935)

William Faulkner (1897–1962)
A Rose for Emily (1931)
Spotted Horses (1931)

Ernest Hemingway (1898–1961)
Hills Like White Elephants (1938)

Jorge Luis Borges (1899–1986)
The Garden of Forking Paths (1941)

Zora Neale Hurston (1901–1960)
Spunk (1927)

John Steinbeck (1902–1968)
The Chrysanthemums (1938)

Frank O'Connor (1903–1966)
Guests of the Nation (1931)

Isaac Bashevis Singer (1904–)
Gimpel the Fool (1953)

R. K. Narayan (1906–)
House Opposite (1985)

Richard Wright (1908–1960)
The Man Who Was Almost a Man (1961)

Eudora Welty (1909–)
Why I Live at the P.O. (1941)
A Worn Path (1941)

Paul Bowles (1910–)
A Distant Episode (1948)

John Cheever (1912–1982)
The Swimmer (1964)

Tillie Olsen (1913–)
I Stand Here Ironing (1961)

Julio Cortázar (1914–1984)
Blow-Up (1956)

Ralph Ellison (1914–)
Battle Royal (1952)

Bernard Malamud (1914–1986)
The Jewbird (1963)

Hwang Sun-won (1915–)
Conversation in June about Mothers (1976)

Heinrich Böll (1917–1985)
Like A Bad Dream (1966)

Doris Lessing (1919–)
To Room 19 (1963)

Shirley Jackson (1919–1965)
The Lottery (1948)

Amos Tutuola (1920–)
The Palm-Wine Drinkard's First Journey (1952)

Tadeusz Borowski (1922–1951)
This Way for the Gas, Ladies and Gentlemen (1948)

Grace Paley (1922–)
A Conversation with My Father (1974)

Italo Calvino (1923–1985)
The Distance of the Moon (1965)

Nadine Gordimer (1923–)
Town and Country Lovers (1980)

James Baldwin (1924–1987)
Sonny's Blues (1957)

Clarice Lispector (1925–1977)
The Chicken (1960)

Yukio Mishima (1925–1970)
Three Million Yen (1966)

Flannery O'Connor (1925–1964)
A Good Man Is Hard to Find (1955)
Everything That Rises Must Converge (1965)

Alice Adams (1926–)
The Oasis (1985)

Yussef Idriss (1927–)
A House of Flesh (1971)

Carlos Fuentes (1928–)
The Doll Queen (1964)

Gabriel García Márquez (1928–)
A Very Old Man with Enormous Wings (1955)

Cynthia Ozick (1928–)
The Shawl (1980)

Milan Kundera (1929–)
The Hitchhiking Game (1969)

Ursula K. Le Guin (1929–)
The Ones Who Walk Away from Omelas (1976)

Chinua Achebe (1930–)
Dead Men's Path (1953)

John Barth (1930–)
Lost in the Funhouse (1968)

Donald Barthelme (1931–1989)
The School (1974)

Alice Munro (1931–)
Walker Brothers Cowboy (1968)

Robert Coover (1932–)
   The Gingerbread House (1969)

V. S. Naipaul (1932–)
   B. Wordsworth (1959)

John Updike (1932–)
   A & P (1961)
   Flight (1962)

Susan Sontag (1933–)
   The Way We Live Now (1986)

Fay Weldon (1933–)
   Weekend (1978)

Woody Allen (1935–)
   The Kugelmass Episode (1977)

Andre Dubus (1936)
   The Curse (1988)

Bessie Head (1937–1986)
   Life (1977)

Raymond Carver (1938–1989)
   What We Talk About When We Talk About Love (1981)

Joyce Carol Oates (1938–)
   Where Are You Going, Where Have You Been? (1970)

Luisa Valenzuela (1938–)
   I'm Your Horse in the Night (1982)

Toni Cade Bambara (1939–)
   The Hammer Man (1966)

Margaret Atwood (1939–)
   Happy Endings (1983)

Angela Carter (1940–)
   The Werewolf (1979)

Bharati Mukherjee (1940–)
   Jasmine (1988)

Bobbie Ann Mason (1942–)
   Shiloh (1982)

Alice Walker (1944–)
   Roselily (1973)

Tobias Wolff (1945–)
   Hunters in the Snow (1980)

Tim O'Brien (1946–)
   The Things They Carried (1986)

Ann Beattie (1947–)
    The Burning House (1979)

T. Coraghessan Boyle (1948–)
    The Overcoat II (1982)

Leslie Marmon Silko (1948–)
    Yellow Woman (1974)

Jamaica Kincaid (1949–)
    Girl (1984)

Gloria Naylor (1950–)
    Lucielia Louise Turner (1982)

Amy Hempel (1951–)
    Daylight Come (1990)

Amy Tan (1952–)
    Two Kinds (1989)

Louise Erdrich (1954–)
    The Red Convertible (1984)

Susan Minot (1956–)
    Lust (1984)

David Leavitt (1961–)
    Territory (1984)

THEMATIC INDEX

Story Pairs

1. Carter, *The Werewolf* (p. 206) and Coover, *The Gingerbread House* (p. 351) [Contemporary retellings of fairytales]
2. Gogol, *The Overcoat* (p. 542) and Boyle, *The Overcoat II* (p. 174) [A masterpiece of short fiction and a contemporary revision of it]
3. Gordimer, *Town and Country Lovers* (p. 567) [Two stories — *Town Lovers* and *Country Lovers*—About love in South Africa unter apartheid]

4. Lawrence, *Odour of Chrysanthemums* (p. 797) and Steinbeck, *The Chrysanthemums* (p. 1195) [Stories about the role of women as reflected in the institution of marriage]
5. Crane, *The Open Boat* (p. 374) and *The Sinking of the Commodore* (p. 1431) [A short story masterpiece and the newspaper narrative upon which it is based]

On Writing

Atwood, *Hapy Endings*, 47
Barth, *Lost in the Funhouse*, 89
Barthelme, *The School*, 107
Borges, *The Garden of Forking Paths*, 140
Cortázar, *Blow-Up*, 362
García Márquez, *A Very Old Man with Enormous Wings*, 521

Melville, *Bartleby, the Scrivener*, 958
Naipaul, *B. Wordsworth*, 1029
Paley, *A Conversation with My Father*, 1135
Sontag, *The Way We Live Now*, 1180

Fantasy and the Supernatural

Achebe, *Dead Men's Path*, 10
Barth, *Lost in the Funhouse*, 89
Calvino, *The Distance of the Moon*, 196
Carter, *The Werewolf*, 206
Cheever, *The Swimmer*, 238
Coover, *The Gingerbread House*, 351
Cortázar, *Blow-Up*, 362
Dinesen, *The Blue Jar*, 394
Dinesen, *The Blue Stones*, 396
García Márquez, *A Very Old Man with Enormous Wings*, 521
Gilman, *The Yellow Wallpaper*, 528
Gogol, *The Overcoat*, 542
Hawthorne, *Young Goodman Brown*, 598

Hurston, *Spunk*, 628
Jackson, *The Lottery*, 644
Kafka, *The Metamorphosis*, 741
Kafka, *A Hunger Artist*, 734
Lawrence, *The Rocking-Horse Winner*, 813
Le Guin, *The Ones Who Walk Away from Omelas*, 843
Lispector, *The Chicken*, 876
Silko, *Yellow Woman*, 1158
Singer, *Gimpel the Fool*, 1168
Thurber, *The Secret Life of Walter Mitty*, 1215
Tutuola, *The Palm-Wine Drinkard's First Journey*, 1266

Childhood

Adolescence and Initiation

Identity and Renewal

Love, Marriage, and Infidelity

Parents and Children

War and Revolution

Looking At the Wall

SHORT STORIES ON FILM AND VIDEO

Babylon Revisited (F. Scott
   Fitzgerald)
Movie Title: *The Last Time I Saw
   Paris*
116 min., color, 1954
Cast: Elizabeth Taylor, Van
   Johnson, Donna Reed, Eva
   Gabor
Directed by Richard Brooks
Distributed by: Films, Inc.

Bartleby, the Scrivener (Herman
   Melville)
Movie title: *Bartleby*
28 min., color, 1969
Distributed by: Encyclopaedia
   Britannica

Movie title: *Bartleby*
29 min., b&w, 1965
Videotape from the American Short
   Stories Classics Series
Distributed by: Michigan Media

The Cask of Amontillado (Edgar
   Allan Poe)
19 min., color, 1979
Directed by Bernard Wilets
Distributed by: BFA Educational
   Media

29 min., b&w, 1965
Videotape from the American Short
   Stories Classics Series
Distributed by: Michigan Media

15 min., b&w, 1955
Cast: Monty Woolley
Distributed by: Audio Brandon

The Dead (James Joyce)
82 min., color, 1988
Cast: Anjelica Huston, Donal
   McCann, Helena Carroll,
   Cathleen Delany
Directed by: John Huston
Distributed by: Vestron Video, Inc.

The Death of Ivan Ilych (Leo
   Tolstoy)
29 min., color, 1978
Part of the Begin with Goodbye
   Series
Distributed by: Mass Media
   Ministries

Heart of Darkness (Joseph Conrad)
Movie title: *Apocalypse Now*
153 min., color, 1979
Cast: Martin Sheen, Marlon Brando
Directed by Francis Ford Coppola
Distributed by: Paramount Home
   Video

The Lady with the Pet Dog (Anton
   Chekhov)
Movie title: *The Lady with the Dog*
86 min., b&w, 1960
In Russian with English subtitles
Cast: Iya Savvina, Alexei Batalov,
   Alla Chostakova
Directed by Joseph Heifitz
Distributed by: Audio Brandon

The Lottery (Shirley Jackson)
18 min., color, 1969
Distributed by: Encyclopaedia
   Britannica

The Man Who Was Almost a Man
   (Richard Wright)
Movie title: *Almos' a Man*
39 min., color, 1977
Available on film or videotape
Cast: Levar Burton
Directed by Stan Lathan
Distributed by: Perspective Films

An Occurrence at Owl Creek Bridge (Ambrose Bierce)
27 min., b&w, 1962
Cast: Roger Jacquet, Anne Cornaly, Anker Larsen
Directed by Robert Enrico
Winner at Cannes and American Film Festivals
Distributed by: Films, Inc.

30 min., b&w, 1964
Same as 1962 version, with prologue for its showing as an episode of *The Twilight Zone*
Distributed by: Classic Film Museum, Inc.
McGraw-Hill Films
Northwest Film Study Center
Viewfinders, Inc.

The Open Boat (Stephen Crane)
29 min., b & w, 1965
Distributed by: Michigan Media

Paul's Case (Willa Cather)
55 min., color, 1980
Available on film or videotape
Distributed by: Perspective Films

The Rocking-Horse Winner (D. H. Lawrence)
30 min., color, 1977
Cast: Kenneth More
Adapted by Julian Bond
Directed by Peter Modak
Distributed by: Learning Corp. of America

91 min., b&w, 1950
Cast: John Mills, Valerie Hobson
Directed by Anthony Pelessier
Distributed by: Films, Inc.
Budget Films

A Rose for Emily (William Faulkner)
27 min., color, 1983
Distributed by: Pyramid Film and Video

The Secret Life of Walter Mitty (James Thurber)
110 min., color, 1947
Cast: Danny Kaye, Virginia Mayo
Directed by Norman Z. MacLeod
Distributed by: Arcus Films
Audio-Brandon
ROA Films
Twyman Films, Inc.
Westcoast Films

The Swimmer (John Cheever)
94 min., color, 1968
Cast: Burt Lancaster, Janet Landgard
Directed by Frank Perry

The Tell-Tale Heart (Edgar Allan Poe)
26 min.
Cast: Alex Corde, Sam Jaffe
Distributed by: Churchill Films

Where Are You Going, Where Have You Been? (Joyce Caol Oates)
Movie title: *Smooth Talk*
92 min., color, 1985
Cast: Laura Dern, Treat Williams
Directed by Joyce Chopra
Distributed by: Vestron Video, Inc.

A White Heron (Sarah Orne Jewett)
26 min., color, 1978
Distributed by: Learning Corp. of America

The Yellow Wallpaper (Charlotte Perkins Gilman)
15 min., color, 1978
Produced by: International Institute of Television
Distributed by: Indiana University

Young Goodman Brown (Nathaniel Hawthorne)
30 min., color, 1973
Directed by Donald Fox
Distributed by: Pyramid Film and Video

Directory of Film Distributors

Arcus Films
1225 Broadway
New York, NY 10001

Audio Brandon
45 MacQuesten Parkway S.
Mt. Vernon, NY 10550

BFA Educational Media
2211 Michigan Ave.
Santa Monica, CA 90404

Budget Films
4590 Santa Monica Blvd.
Los Angeles, CA 90029

Churchill Films
662 Oral Roberts Blvd.
Los Angeles, CA 90060

Classic Film Museum, Inc.
4 Union Sq.
Dover-Foxcroft, ME 04426

Encyclopaedia Britannica Educational
Corp.
425 North Michigan Ave.
Chicago, IL 60611

Films, Inc.
Film and Tape Division
733 Greenbay Rd.
Wilmette, IL 60091

Indiana University
Audio Visual Center
Bloomington, IN 47405

Kit Parker Films
P.O. Box 227
Carmel Valley, CA 93924

Learning Corp. of America
1350 Avenue of the Americas
New York, NY 10019

Mass Media Ministries
2116 N. Charles St.
Baltimore, MD 21218

McGraw-Hill Films
1221 Avenue of the Americas
New York, NY 10020

Michigan Media
University of Michigan
400 Fourth St.
Ann Arbor, MI 48109

Paramount Home Video
5555 Melrose Ave.
Hollywood, CA 90038

Perspective Films
65 East South Water St.
Chicago, IL 60601

Phoenix Films
470 Park Ave. S.
New York, NY 10016

Pyramid Film and Video
P. O. Box 1048
Santa Monica, CA 90406

ROA Films
1696 N. Astor St.
Milwaukee, WI 53202

SL Film Productions, Inc.
P. O. Box 41108
Los Angeles, CA 90041

Twyman Films, Inc.
329 Salem Ave.
Dayton, OH 45401

Vestron Video, Inc.
P.O. Box 4000
Stamford, CT 06907

Westcoast Films
25 Lusk St.
San Francisco, CA 94107